Revolt in the Palace

Adventures of a Jump Space Accountant

Book 7

Andrew Moriarty

Andrew Moriarty

ISBN: 978-1-956556-22-3

This is a work of fiction.

Other names, characters, businesses, places, events and incidents are either the products of the author's imagination or used in a fictitious manner. Any resemblance to actual persons, living or dead, or actual events is purely coincidental.

Special thanks to my dedicated team of beta readers – Alex, Bryan, Catherine B, Christopher G, Dave M#1, Dave W, Dave M#2, Djuro D, Greg D, Haydn H, Jolayne W, Keith C, Kent P, Michael G, Michael R, Peter B, Scott, Skip C, Susan G, Tigui R, Vince, and to my editor Samantha Pico.

CHAPTER 1

"I do wish we could have shot him." Admiral Edmunds flexed his pine fishing pole up and down. "Mad dogs should be put down. Not rewarded with a plum job."

Dashi, sitting next to him on the wooden dock, flipped his own pole. "Would you consider sailing alone in the World Ocean for weeks at an end as a reward?"

"Wouldn't have to listen to whining subordinates, so yes."

A ship banged against the next pier. A single crew member carried boxes of food trays down the gangplanks and loaded them onto the small sailboat.

"Have you even been in a small boat for weeks on end?"

"I've been in cutters on patrol for several weeks in my younger days."

"Was that an enjoyable experience?"

"We'd go on three-week patrols in the rings, visiting stations, checking ships for safety violations, maintaining beacons, that sort of thing. It wasn't too bad."

Dashi and the admiral sat on the older wooden pier at Point 37, TGI's main operational base, at the end of the monorail line.

"I've lost my bait again. Checking ships for safety violations? What safety violations? How did you check? Surely, you weren't trying to enforce Imperial codes."

"We'd hail some freighter on the long-haul routes. The crew would be as bored as we were. They were coasting, so we'd burn fuel to come alongside, lock on, and we'd do an inspection of the fusion plants, thrusters, drives, and navigational instruments."

3

"Fusion plants never break, and even if they did, you couldn't fix them." Dashi hauled his line up hand over hand, a fishing pole without a reel. Since the thin line was vegetable-based polymer, the tight bending circle of a traditional reel would have broken it. He coiled it with his hands until the bare hook arrived. "Same with old-Empire electronics. What's the point of an inspection?"

"It was a good way to meet girls. Those Francais Free Trader women were bored and always willing to talk, and you could usually count on meeting up with them later at a station somewhere."

"You surprise me, Admiral," Dashi said. "You don't like the Free Traders, or the Francais, male or female."

"Married one. Nadine is one-quarter Francais."

"Explains her temper."

"Yup. That came from her mother. I'm always the soul of reason, of course."

Dashi skewered a chunk of rabbit meat with his hook. "This is the third bait in a row that I've lost. What am I doing wrong?"

"Nothing." Edmunds checked the time. "The tide has turned. The current is running out now. We're not going to catch anything in this part of the tidal cycle—the water's moving too fast, and the few fish that are in the water don't want to hang out and munch on some strange food. They're heading out into the bay to chow down on all that tasty algae. Wait till the tide turns when they sail back in over the waterfall. Then they'll eat."

"Why are we here, then? If there's no chance of catching anything?"

"It's a glorious day to go fishing. It's the fishing that's important, not the catching."

The lone sailor on the adjacent pier finished stowing his boxes. Upon flipping the rope, he was free and floating down the river, joining a small fleet of dawdling fishing boats. The river, or more properly estuary, created an east-west aligned lake where it entered the World Ocean. The

Dragon, the fourth major planet in the Sigma Draconis System, created huge tides on its planet-sized moon of Delta. The current switched directions twice a day as the tides swapped. A rocky squeeze canyon forced passing traffic to wait till the churning waters shoved the ocean back. Once the outbound current won over the inbound tide, the sailing fleet could sail past the rocky shore, but only for a short while. Like most rivers' valleys on Delta, the bottom dropped sharply over rock ridges. When the river and ocean were reasonably level, sailing was the preferred means of exit. Once the ocean tides receded too far, the stepped bottom became a series of lakes separated by steeper and higher waterfalls. Ships could only safely move between these lakes when the tide suppressed the waterfalls.

A horn blasted from a shore station, and the circling fleet lined up and washed out to the ocean. The lone sailor from before hauled a dirty gray sail up and took his place near the end of the line.

"He's cutting it fine. Again," Edmunds said. "I should put a squad on the dock to surveil him, catch him out."

"Roi? As long as he's untied, he meets the requirements of his exile. He is allowed to come in for supplies, as you recall." Along with a group of Militia officers, most now deceased, the sailor, Roi, had previously revolted against the Delta Governing Council. Admiral Edmund's current position as head of the Militia and member of the Imperial Council was the result of his bloody suppression of that rebellion. Dashi's current position as head of said council was the result of him being the Emperor presumptive of the known galaxy—or at least the tiny part that was the Delta System. The remaining Imperial computer in the Agriculture building confirmed his lineage. Instead of shooting Roi, the most senior of the rebel Militia officers alive, along with the remaining rebels captured under arms, he'd arranged for Roi to be exiled to a life of sailing the World Ocean. Charting unknown areas, searching for harbors, food resources, and suchlike.

"Funny how he organizes his return so that he's stuck here for a full tide cycle," Edmunds said.

Dashi flipped his rod and coughed. "My bait has been taken. Again. Enough of this. I will never make a fisherman." He hauled his line up. "I am done fishing for the day, Admiral. And Roi has sailed from the dock, which is sufficient. I have no complaints with his work. He's located an astonishing number of algae patches offshore, and his suggestions for using rowed boats to tow nets and haul them has been, as you would say, 'outstanding'."

"I'm not saying he isn't a competent sailor and that he isn't helping us produce more food. I'm saying I hate his rebel guts and want to shoot him. I don't need another reason."

"Well, please, 'cool your jets,' as you Militia people would say. We need all the diversification of effort we can get now." Dashi braced himself against a nearby bollard and hauled himself to his feet. He needed a stout cane leaning nearby to stand upright. After levering himself, he took a moment to regain his breath and wipe the sweat from his brow. "We're still on a knife edge for resources here."

"Should have killed more people during the revolt."

"I surely tried, Edmunds. I surely tried." Dashi threw his fishing line in a bucket and tottered down the dock.

Admiral Edmunds raised his eyebrows and chased after him. "I forget how ruthless you are sometimes."

Dashi grinned up at Edmunds, white teeth contrasting brown skin and a bald head. "That is part of my success. As is your 'plain talking soldier' mode, which you adopt when talking to your troops, to distinguish yourself from the putrescent political types. Which reminds me, you haven't filed for election to the Imperial Senate."

"Don't you think we're being a bit presumptuous calling three dozen politicians from a small moon an Imperial Senate?"

"An Empire requires a Senate, so we shall have one. And having my advisers come from an elected Senate gives the semblance of democracy."

"Hooray for semblance. What if I don't want to be in your Senate?"

"I need a Militia representative. Perhaps your young Ms. Shutt—sorry, Major Shutt—can serve as a representative."

"She's got the Militia's best interests at heart for sure. But she's not senatorial material."

"I disagree. I told her to file to run in the election."

"Filed to run? Against me?"

"Senators are elected at large. As such, she's not running against you but in tandem. She's popular with a certain class of the general population, the ones that want strong government. And your Militia troops like her as well."

"That would be another voice in the Senate to support mine. But she should have discussed it with me."

Dashi stumbled to the end of the dock and sank onto a bench. The short walk down the dock had made him pant. He fumbled into his pockets, producing a pill bottle and shook one out, which he dry swallowed. "I'm sure she felt that the pressure of other matters was occupying you."

"You need to go easy on those pills, Dashi," Edmunds said.

"Concerned for my health?"

"Concerned for mine. If you die, I'll probably become Emperor and then every two-bit assassin will be after me."

"You're that sure that you would be chosen?"

"Who else has the stature to run things?"

The dock shook. A sliver gleam flashed along the sky, and TGI's orbital lifting body slid overhead, wobbled slightly, then splashed down onto the lake. Alert boats on the water churned alongside, tied on towlines, and commenced dragging the steaming shuttle to its custom-built dock. Like the other piers, floating wooden docks connected to a higher deck by a ramp. The changing tide rolled the ramp up and down, allowing loading at any water height. The top of the dock fronted on the side of the monorail station. When the tug's engines churned, pushing the lifting body to its slot, flatcars silently rolled into the station.

Passengers disembarked from the first two cars. Automated lifters pushed empty containers and replaced them with ones filled with processed algae and seaweed. These would be shipped to automated factories and turned into food trays, the production of which was the reason for the founding of the colony.

"I'll give it to your boy, Jose. He knows how to set up efficient schedules. He makes the trains run on time. Like they used to in the old Empire, I guess."

"We're the old Empire now," Dashi said. "The Empire, the way things were. The abandonment is official. The Empire's gone. Something may arise in its place, but whatever it is, it will be different. Stature in the old way of doing things doesn't matter as much as it used to."

"Is one of your disciples going to take over? Your young Jake Stewart, wherever he is now on that stupid voyage of exploration you rammed through? Or your Mr. Jose, your inside man?"

"Mr. Jose is a tribune now, which is an official position. But it wouldn't have to be Mr. Jose or Mr. Stewart who take over. Perhaps one of your Militia people."

"The senior ones are all dead."

Crews transferred industrial parts machined in orbit onto the train—basic electronic parts—and selected special metal alloys. The belt abounded in metals and solar power and orbiting fusion-plant powered stations ran the machines. Even water was present in the belt in quantity. Boxes of food trays and some specialized planetary products replaced them in the lifter. Heavy lift shuttles in Landing kept the orbital factories fed, but this lifter didn't require the colossal mass-driver-powered launches the city-based ships did. TGI guarded their flexibility jealously.

"Which is why you sleep at night," Dashi said.

"Which is why I sleep at night."

"What about your Ms. Shutt—she's a contender. Perhaps she could become Emperor?"

"Someday, perhaps. Too junior right now."

"The Free Traders might put forth a candidate. Ms. Marianne. Legate Marianne I should say."

"I trust her only slightly more than I trust that Roi fellow. Since our ride is here, we should get along." Edmunds pointed at the train. "Loading passengers now." Edmunds held out his hand. Dashi grasped it, and Edmunds helped heave him upright, and they walked along the shore to the waiting train.

"Dashi, you've convinced me."

"Convinced you of what, Admiral."

"To run for Senate. I'll file the papers today. I'll join Shutt and a few other loyal Militia people, and I'll get myself voted onto your council again. We'll keep you honest and keep this rock of a moon running along."

"The Empire appreciates your dedication. You do understand that the council is purely an advisory body, as is the Senate? The Emperor still rules."

"I understand completely, Dashi, and I'm the last one to argue with tradition. I'm very fond of tradition. One in particular, one you may have forgotten."

"Which one is that?"

"You can't name an heir without the Senate approving it. I looked it up. If you want to promote one of your minions to Emperor after you die, you'll need to convince the Senate to support it."

"I was aware of that. But I don't think it will be a problem."

"You might be surprised. And one other thing, Dashi."

"Yes?"

"If you die without having an officially appointed heir, the Senate will vote on your successor."

Dashi grasped the door of the train, sucked in a big breath, and pulled himself up the step. The admiral crossed his arms. Dashi's sweating form clambered onto the train and stumbled into the next compartment, taking the seat reserved for him. He waved off the hovering train crew and slumped in his seat.

Edmunds hopped on board and sat across from him. "Injuries still bothering you?"

Dashi nodded. "Quite a bit. Never get blown up, it's even more uncomfortable than it sounds. And it turns out a spleen is more important than I initially thought."

"Well, that's what those pain pills are for. Have another. Take one." Edmunds smiled. "In fact, we're all friends here. Take two."

CHAPTER 2

"Do you have to smoke here?" Jose asked.

Sergeant Russell held his pack of cigarettes in his hand. "Where should I smoke?"

"It's a disgusting habit. Pollutes the air."

The two stood at the entrance to the shuttle unloading dock, not far from the mass driver and its associated power station. Smears of soot from a firebomb thrown during the recent unpleasantness marred the white concrete of the control building. Dull metal of the original power conductors interspersed with the gleaming copper of new replacements. Less than a hundred meters from the shuttle unloading dock, the mast of a sunken fishing boat protruded from the water. The street leading to the dock had been swept clean, piles of charred wood shoved to the side and not removed.

Jose glared at Russell, then cursed and rubbed his eyes. Wind from the mountains carried grit and dust from destroyed buildings at the edge of town.

Russell hid a grin and pocketed his cigarette. "Well, we wouldn't want polluted air, would we?" He glanced over his shoulder to make sure Chaudhari, the Kims, and his whole squad waited down the road out of earshot.

A remaining surface-to-orbit shuttle crested over the mountains to the west of Landing and lined up for a water landing. They waited in silence as it drifted lower, then splashed down in a cascade of steam and spray.

"Easy shot from here," Russell said.

"Did you lose another set of missiles?"

"Don't know. Not my day to watch them."

"Whose day is it?"

"Don't know."

"A lot you don't know."

"That's why I'm a sergeant, and you're Mr. Tribune."

"Just Tribune."

"Sorry, that's why I'm a sergeant, and you're a just—Tribune."

"Are you mocking me, Sergeant?"

"Oh, no, sir. Never that."

Jose rubbed his eyes. "Why are you here, Sergeant?"

"Admiral is going up top, sir. And you? Out sightseeing?"

A nearby door swung fully out, then banged into the wall behind. A dark-haired woman in a major's uniform marched out.

Jose clasped his hands. "I don't answer to you, Sergeant."

Major Shutt stopped next to them. "Who don't you answer to, Tribune Jose?"

"Not you, that's for sure," Jose said. "What are you doing here, Major?"

"To coin a phrase, I don't answer to you, Tribune." Shutt pocketed a comm she had been carrying. "But to be polite, I'm here to see the admiral off. Along with Sergeant Russell and his squad. The admiral is going to inspect the orbital stations. Are you going to return the politeness and tell me why you're here?"

"Emperor Dashi asked me to greet Ms. Marianne."

"Dashi asked you to do that, did he?" Shutt grinned. "Couldn't you just roll over in bed and kiss her goodbye?"

Russell made a smothered chortle, then pursed his lips as Jose glared at him.

"She is arriving from orbit right now. She's on that shuttle."

"And Dashi's not going to meet her."

"The Emperor has many demands on his time."

"Like taking another nap, given his recent attendance at council meetings."

Jose bit his lip but didn't reply.

Russell pointed. "Good pilot, that."

The shuttle pilot had timed their landing perfectly, the waiting tug wasn't needed as the shuttle drifted to a stop near the dock. Magnetic grapples fired, and the shuttle docked itself.

"Militia trained, must be," Shutt said.

"Or any corporation, or the Free Traders," Jose said. "The Militia doesn't have a monopoly on competency."

"Really? Because when we're flying our shuttles, they work, unlike a lot of things here in Landing."

"How good would your flying be if your crew was blowing things up or setting them on fire?"

"We keep those type of people out of our crews."

"Perhaps we'll keep those type of people out of Landing," Jose said.

A gangplank clanked onto the dock, and passengers trooped out of the shuttle, passing those waiting to ascend. Marianne's brightly colored skin suit adorned with patches stood out over the bland corporate skin suits or the monochrome gray of the Militia. She stopped to talk to a group of Militia near the back of the line, shook hands with one, and disappeared inside the shuttle control building. The waiting passengers climbed on board. The hatch slammed shut, and the loitering tug towed the shuttle across the bay to the nearby mass driver launchers.

"Your admiral is gone. You can go now," Jose said.

Shutt laughed. "I'll go when I'm ready. Thank you, Tribune. And anyway, the admiral has deputized me to replace him at the council meeting. Will Dashi be attending today?"

"As I said, Emperor Dashi has many demands on his time. I will be speaking for him today."

"How truly good." The control room access door slammed open again. "Oh, look, here's your girlfriend."

Marianne sauntered across to them. She tilted her head up and gave Jose a kiss. "Cheri. Thank you for meeting me."

"Do I get a kiss, too?" Shutt asked.

Marianne nodded at Shutt's uniform. "That uniform makes you look fat."

"That's all? I was worried it made me look like I was sleeping with a councilor for political gain."

Marianne beamed. "It's so good to be working with the Militia again, isn't it, Cheri. They are so . . . focused. But on the wrong things. We have a meeting, do we not? If we are walking, we should go. I do not want to be late."

Jose waved at a car down the road. "I've got Dashi's car."

"Daddy let you borrow the car? That's so nice," Shutt said. "Maybe later you can borrow his big-boy pants."

"There's that focus again," Marianne said. "Enjoy the rest of your day, Major. It's been a pleasure talking to you, but we've got important people to see."

Shutt coughed loudly into her fist.

Jose grimaced. "Mar—Legate, the admiral has deputized Major Shutt. She will be representing him at the council meeting."

"Is that so?"

Shutt smiled. "So, it is. It is so. So-so. So, since we're going to the same meeting, perhaps I can ride with you. Unless the two of you need some privacy?"

"It is only a ten-minute ride," Marianne said.

"That would be five minutes too long, from what I hear," Shutt said.

Russell smothered another chortle. Jose rounded on him. "Something funny, Sergeant?"

"No, sir. Just full of the joy of serving the Empire."

Marianne grabbed Jose's arm. "We should go. Come along, Major. We will find you a room." She and Jose walked to the car.

Russell snapped to attention and saluted Shutt. "Orders, ma'am?"

"Serve the Empire. Patrol the city. Meet me at Militia

HQ this afternoon one hour after lunch." She returned the salute, then marched after the happy couple.

Russell stood easy. Chaudhari came up from the waiting squad to stand beside him.

"Orders?"

Russell put his hand on his revolver. "Serve the Empire. Patrol the city."

"What's that mean?"

"Find people breaking the law and rough them up."

Shutt paused at the door of the ground car. "Sergeant?" she yelled.

"Ma'am?"

"No shooting anyone. Understood?"

"Ma'am."

She climbed into the car.

"That's no fun." Russell put his hand in his pocket.

The window on the ground car rolled down. "Sergeant?"

"Ma'am?"

"No smoking, either." The window rolled up.

Russell removed his hand from his pocket and cursed.

"Well"—Chaudhari shrugged—"even less fun."

"Gimme your shock stick," Russell said.

"Shock stick? What for?"

"Patrol, but no shootings and no smoking." Russell scowled. "But nothing about giving out a savage beating or two."

***

Jose winced as the university professor's voice echoed from the walls of the council room. The council room— formerly the Imperial Department of Agriculture's main hall—had horrid acoustics, and the speaker's flat delivery didn't help with comprehension. Imperial agricultural departments didn't need giant stone-floored two-story-tall meeting rooms. Either the original builder had been a fanatical ballroom-dancing advocate, or it had belonged to

15

a high wire circus act that brought their own floor mats.

"What is he saying?" Marianne whispered to Jose.

"He's talking about the abandonment."

"And?"

"He's against it." The speaker sat and Jose led the room in a round of polite applause. Then he stood and surveyed the crowd. Except it wasn't a crowd. It consisted of him, Marianne, Shutt, a representative from the university, a frowning, unaligned corp member, and an old man slumped in the corner. The old man didn't appear to be anyone's aide, and Jose assumed he was a random guy who had come in for a nap. Jose counted eight spectators in the gallery. A uniformed Militia private and a Free Trader with the Legio Sigma Draconis shoulder patch guarded the door. Both were armed and didn't speak to each other.

Fires, the civil war, burnings, shootings, weather, food shortages, and apathy had destroyed interest in the public council meetings after the excitement of Dashi's ascension to the throne. With more and more people granting their proxies to either the Militia, TGI, or the Free Traders, attendance had dropped to almost zero.

Jose stood and thanked the speaker for their report on the abandonment. The university had a single vote, meaningless in the context of the maneuvering going on, but no sense messing with tradition. Not without a good reason.

The university people left. They clearly understood their single vote counted not at all.

Jose gave his report on the planetary projects he was involved in. After ten minutes, with no questions, Marianne delivered the Free Traders issues and responses, and Shutt finished with the Militia's update. Jose asked for any other business. The unaligned rep at the end of the table shook his head.

"The council will now go into private session to discuss sensitive matters. Guards, please clear the room."

The eight spectators in the gallery filed down the internal stairs and out the main door. The Free Trader/Militia guards hustled upstairs to double-check nobody remained, then locked the doors. The old man didn't respond to a shake or to a slap, so the Militia guard threw him over his shoulder and carried him out.

The slap woke the unaligned corp representative out of his stupor. He realized he was the last one there, muttered something and skittered out the door. The Militia guard half saluted as he carried the snoring old man outside. The Free Trader gave Marianne a cheerful wave, called her 'Cheri' and sauntered out, pulling the door shut behind him.

"Well, that's an hour of our lives that we'll never get back," Shutt said.

"It's important that the public know what we're doing," Jose said.

"You mean what Dashi is doing."

"We represent the people's wishes to Dashi."

"Which he can completely ignore, as long as the Militia, the Traders, and the Corps come to an agreement."

"Very cynical."

"I prefer the term experienced."

Marianne coughed. "There is too much dust in here."

Shutt ran a finger along the table and held it up. It was black with dust. "Who's responsible for cleaning?"

"Not the Free Traders," Marianne said.

Jose shook his head. "Not TGI."

Shutt rubbed the dust off her fingers. "Not it, either. Of course, if we held this meeting at Militia HQ, we wouldn't allow this sort of squalor."

"Could have it on my ship," Marianne said. "We clean there."

"Then the spectators can't come," Shutt said.

"All eight of them?"

"It's a public meeting. The public can come, hear what's proposed to Dashi and his reaction. Then, when it doesn't happen, they know who to blame."

"Enough bickering," Jose said. "We're in private session here. Is there anything that you want to propose?"

Shutt waved at the comm in the center of the table. The red recording light was lit. "How private, exactly."

"All Imperial meetings are recorded, you know that."

"Right. Well, Mr. Jose." Shutt smiled. "I sent you a list of minor concerns before the meeting. Some small pay arrears, shortages, things like that. I was expecting a response."

"I'll look at them and get back to you, after the meeting."

"That's what you said about the last communication I sent you, a month ago."

"And did I get back to you?"

"Yes. You said you're working on them."

"There you go."

"Are you still working on them?"

"Yes."

Shutt nodded. "I see. Nothing more from me. Legate Marianne?"

Marianne shook her head and glanced at Jose.

"Then we're almost done here," Jose said. "One more thing, you know that Dashi has announced that we will be having elections for the Imperial Senate shortly. Just a reminder, Major, that your admiral must register here in person if he wants to run. He cannot apply remotely."

"I'll tell him that," Shutt said. "I'm running myself."

"You?" Marianne said. "Whatever for?"

"I think I will represent a certain segment of the population."

"Your admiral will run and, no doubt, win a seat. Why bother?"

"He's not my admiral. He's our admiral. And I believe the Militia requires more representation in this Senate than just him."

"Who would be foolish enough to vote for you?"

"We'll see, won't we?"

"But you do make a good point. Perhaps I will run for this Senate as well. Jose, Cheri, what sort of powers will this Senate have."

"Welllllll . . . ." Jose looked at the two women. "It's advisory. But they choose the Emperor's successor if he dies without issue. And they have to ratify his choice of heir."

"And," Shutt said, "They can't be dismissed by the Emperor, like certain council members I could name. Once elected, they stay in the Senate till the next election. Only the Senate can fire its own members. And there's the question of taxes."

"Taxes?" Marianne asked.

"The Senate can raise and spend money, independent of the Emperor. Isn't that right, Tribune Jose?"

Jose nodded.

"And they can spend the taxes as they wish. Interesting isn't it, Legate?"

"It is. I must go file these papers, perhaps."

"Indeed." Shutt grinned. "Tribune Jose, if there's nothing else, perhaps we could close the meeting."

Jose spoke the formal closing words. They all pledged loyalty to the Emperor and the Empire, and the meeting broke. Shutt wished them cordial, obviously fake best wishes and marched out of the room.

"Even crossing the room, she marches," Marianne said.

"They march all the time," Jose said. "It must become a habit."

"She's plotting something."

"Just her?"

"Why Cheri, don't you trust me?"

Jose tilted his head. "Truthfully. Nope. Not for a moment. Not even a little bit."

Marianne laughed, pinched his cheek, and stood. "I knew you were smart. I like that in a man. I'm off to the tailor."

"The tailor?"

"Of course. I have to put in my order for Senator's robes." Marianne grinned. "I need to beat the rush."

CHAPTER 3

"It's true that there has been no organized resistance since the coup," Rajput, formerly VP of security for TGI, said. He sat in Jose's office on TGI main, reporting on recent developments on the corporate stations. Jose had taken the shuttle back to the station two days after the last council meeting. "But that's because we're crewed mostly by TGI people, and they love you for keeping them from dying. And the Free Traders are pretty happy with you, too."

"Because I also kept them from dying." Jose twirled a pen in his hands. "The only people who hate me are the Militia because so many of them died in our civil war."

"You did everything you said you would. Not your fault if it didn't work."

"They don't care." Jose twirled the pen again.

"Planning on stabbing somebody?" Rajput said. "A knife would be better."

"Sorry." Jose dropped the pen. "Nervous habit."

"According to my checklists, we're doing everything we can to help feed people."

"Is anybody still starving?"

Rajput shrugged. "Don't think so. No way to tell."

"You put too much trust in your checklists."

Rajput typed on his comm. "I like checklists. They comfort me. Now, on to the production checklist."

"Everything is a checklist with you."

"Follow the checklist. You never go wrong."

"What if people die?"

"Not my fault, I—"

"Followed the checklist, I get it. What if something

21

new comes up."

"I make a new checklist."

"Do you have a checklist for making new checklists?"

Rajput swapped screens and showed Jose his comm. "Of course."

Jose shook his head. "Stupid of me to ask." He picked up the pen again.

"Where'd you get that pen, anyway?"

"Dashi gave it to me. It's old, he says it was used to sign Imperial edicts in the past. I keep playing with it when I'm nervous."

"Given how much of our operations you're running now, anything that makes you nervous makes me nervous. What's going on?"

"Nothing special. Our replacement program isn't going as fast as it could. Especially the wood." Jose had spearheaded a program to replace dwindling old-Empire resources with locally grown and capable technology. Some, like extra wooden fishing boats to increase the catch of fish and algae had been popular and successful. Others, like wood fires in housing dirtside to compensate for electrical shortages had been neither.

"Who wants to stay in a house full of stinking smoke?"

"Whoever doesn't want to freeze to death," Jose said.

"You need to sell it better," Rajput said. "Everyone thinks that you're hanging out in luxury up here, rather than staying on the surface and dealing with the shortages."

"This isn't luxurious." Jose waved. "I live in a metal box."

"A metal box with heat, light, electricity, and good comms."

"We eat from trays." Jose tapped his display and a view of a cargo lock appeared on the screen next to his desk.

"Most of the surface people do, or so I've been told. I don't know much about the surface. Never been."

Jose stopped typing. "You've never been to the

surface?"

"Well, not in years. Born dirtside. My dad got a job with TGI—came up here when I started school. I was five. Been in orbit ever since."

"Didn't you join the Militia?"

"Conscripted here in orbit. I did a year in the Militia as an engine room scut level-zero, hated it, quit as soon as I could, and I've been in TGI security ever since. Almost twenty years now. Twenty glorious years!" Rajput laughed. "That was sarcasm, in case you didn't get it."

"I got it," Jose said.

"Wasn't as bad as it could be. Steady work, steady promotion. Until this revolt thing, I'd never been shot at. Not shot back at anyway. Shot at a few people."

"TGI has been good to you."

"But I never got this."

"What this? An office? You have an office, a big one, bigger than mine. I've seen it."

"Yes, it's bigger. I've got the arms locker in there— storage for fifty revolvers and a hundred shock sticks takes space. But I don't have wooden furniture, wooden doors, or fabric chairs." Rajput tapped his finger on Jose's polished desktop. "This desk costs more than everything I own. At least up here it does."

Jose ran his finger along the smooth top. "I got it when I became Dashi's assistant. He suggested it."

"Of course he did. You were acting for him so often he needed you to appear important, not just be important. You had to wow over the others. And you didn't disagree, did you?"

"It matches, well, it matches—"

"All the other expensive stuff here. The wooden chairs. Cushions. The wall paneling. This is the nicest office on the station, other than Dashi's. Certainly, the most expensively furnished."

Jose surveyed his office. "It's where I work."

"Because everybody comes to see you now, rather than

you going to see them."

"The nicest on the station? That can't be true."

"You even have a carpet."

"It's a rug, not a carpet." Jose stamped the dark blue fabric. "It really ties the room together."

"I'm sure the admiral and the Militia people think that's a fine thing. Sets them at ease while you cut their pay."

"I don't care what the Militia thinks, or the admiral. They put us in this mess. They can help pay for it."

"Cutting their pay won't make them friends."

"They're not my friends. They're obstacles to the rational running of this system. And like most obstacles, once they're removed, things work better."

"Going to do some removals?"

"Maybe. One admiral less might make things better."

"Or perhaps one Major less?"

Jose fingered his pen again. "I'll do what needs to be done."

Rajput ran his hand along the desktop again, but remained silent.

Jose pulled up more data on the screen. "Well, regardless, we're not here to discuss my furniture. I have a task for you. Here's a listing of all the ships in the system, as near as I can organize. Look at these numbers."

Jose brought up displays of freighters, cutters, Free Trader ships, shuttles, and mining barges, with a detailed breakdown by tonnage, cost, speed, range, and weaponry.

"Okay."

"Okay? Just okay."

"That's how many ships in the system, fine. I get it. So what."

"Look again." Jose paged through again, highlighting certain numbers. Rajput shook his head. Jose sorted the lists again and displayed a chart.

"Still not getting it." Rajput tapped his comm. "Spell it out for me."

"The Militia has the bulk of the armed ships in this

system. The Free Traders have a respectable number, enough that you wouldn't want to mess with them. There're a number of unaligned factions that have a few, but for our size we are woefully under resourced in the strike area."

"Woefully under resourced?"

"We have ships to move things. We have ownership of, or control of, plenty of stations, processing plants, foundries, that sort of thing. What we don't have is a solid strike force of cutters."

"Do we need a strike force?"

"It would be helpful."

"What do we do about that."

"I want you to come up with a plan to steal some," Jose said. "Think you can make a checklist for that?"

***

Shutt attended Admiral Edmunds at their daily meeting in the main briefing room. His return had been delayed two days when his cutter broke down while he was inspecting a far-orbit station. She'd become his de facto senior aide after most of the Militia officer corps had joined the Empire Rising revolt and been killed in battle. Or, frequently, killed by their own crews after unsuccessful battles. The majority of the Free Trader crews who had served in the Militia had resigned or walked away. They'd returned to their families and ships. Officers and enlisted related to corporations had tended to drift back to their companies, crewing corporate ships, or working in key roles on stations. Thus, promotion for remaining, reliable, and even mildly loyal, troops had been swift.

Competence was no longer much of an issue.

"Dirtside, we have enough ground troops to police Landing," Shutt said. "Keep Militia HQ secure, guard the Agriculture building—I mean the Imperial Council chambers. Keep units near the fusion plant, shuttle docks, the main monorail station."

"In conjunction with the Free Traders, and TGI and their security forces, of course." The admiral picked up a poker and stirred the fire. Unlike most of the old-Empire buildings in town, Militia headquarters had rooms with actual fireplaces and vents to allow smoke out. One of her jobs had been to arrange the delivery of truck loads of applewood billets. It burned bright, giving the headquarters rooms a woodsy scent. It also melded with dark wooden panels, wall hangings, and replica old military weapons, resembling a study of some pre-Empire general on old Earth. All that was missing were expensive looking dogs sleeping on the rug by the fire.

"In conjunction with them, yes." Shutt fired up some numbers on the screen at the end of the dark wood table. Bloodred drapes that normally hid the displays opened. A list of military units appeared on the screens. "Plus some other minor corporations and a small breakaway Free Trader group. The little units don't matter. With the forces we have, we can take either of the bigger opponents on the surface in a stand-up battle. If we had a surprise, we could take them both."

"We're not going to start another war." the admiral dropped the poker. "The last one didn't go so well. What about the rest of the surface?"

"All corporate of one type or another. TGI has a big chunk out west with some big plants, including the rest of their lift and on-ground production capability. Everywhere else has reverted to corporate control. Whoever runs the local plants at each monorail stop runs the local security. And the eastern monorail is still damaged. We can't get over that busted bridge. Most of the far east plants have been evacuated or mothballed, except for those who could get good or resources in and out by sailing ship."

"We need some of those ocean sailing ships," Edmunds said.

"We'll get 'em. We're trying at least. I've got a half dozen sailing back and forth under Militia crews, and we're building more next to the shuttle dock."

"When did you learn about sailing ships?"

"That Roi guy has been super helpful. And some of the Empire Rising people had sailing experience, and they had contacts with the professional sailors on the surface."

"I had them all shot, didn't I?"

"Some of the more . . . useful ones were offered a deal—help us with our new wet-navy, and we won't kill you. Keep helping and we'll keep not killing you. We've even kept the station on south continent up, staffed with some former Empire Rising types and regular troopers."

"I don't remember ordering that," Edmunds said.

"You didn't. Not exactly," Shutt said. "But you were pretty busy for a while there, and there were a lot of things going on, so I showed some initiative to get things moving."

"Offering pardons?"

"They're not pardoned, completely. Think of it as more work-release."

Edmunds glared at her.

"You can't think of everything, sir. I saw something needed doing and I did it. I wouldn't be much use to you if I didn't show my initiative, right?"

"No."

"Besides." Shutt grinned. "It worked. I find it's easier to get forgiveness than permission."

"Don't do it again."

"Okay."

Edmunds raised his eyebrows. "That's it? Okay?"

"Yes, sir. Understood, sir. Don't do that again, sir."

"Better tell me the rest."

Shutt diagrammed their remaining problems. A lot of the space-based Militia were dead and a number of ships destroyed. The remaining ships weren't in the greatest shape. Ships outnumbered competent crews, so some were mothballed by docking them at stations and having just a caretaker crew on them. Or no crew at all.

"And there is the subject of pay," Shutt said.

"What about it?"

"We're short. TGI and the others haven't been sending money like they used to. We need them to pay their bills."

"You mean taxes, and I'll deal with it. I'll speak to Dashi."

Shutt killed her comm screen. "Maybe, sir, maybe talk to Jose instead."

"Jose works for Dashi. He'll do what Dashi says."

"He will, eventually," Shutt said. "But Jose handles all of the day-to-day stuff now. And Jose is aware of the issue already. He's the one who is holding things up. Might be better to approach him directly."

"Dashi will come down on him if he doesn't do what he's told."

"Sir." Shutt bit her lip. "Sir, everybody loves Dashi. The Emperor, that is. Heck, I love him. He's a great unifying presence, and he seems to be the only one who has a plan to get us out of this mess and keep things from getting worse. But have you looked at him recently?"

"I saw him in person a few days ago. He looked fine."

"Still on his cane?"

"Yes."

"Sleepy? Quiet?"

"Dashi, I mean the Emperor, has always been the quiet type."

"He fell asleep in a council meeting the other day. You were up touring the stations. He nodded off."

"So, you woke him up."

"It's not the first time, sir. He's disengaged these days."

"He gives Jose instructions, I'm sure."

"Jose kept going, dealing with things like he was in charge. When Dashi woke up, he looked dazed. Jose shoved some documents in front of him, got thumbprints, and moved on. I'm not sure Dashi knew what he was signing. He takes pain pills, you know."

"I know," Edmunds said. "But it's not relevant. I can

talk Dashi around."

"But can you talk Jose around?"

"What's that supposed to mean?"

"Nothing, sir. Just pointing out that Dashi listens to you because you're his friend, and you've known him for years. Jose isn't your friend. He's something else."

"Is Jose my enemy? Want to get rid of him?"

"Is that an order, sir?"

Edmunds and Shutt sat in silence for a long time, then Edmunds flicked the screen display off. "I'll speak to Dashi later about the pay arrears. That will be all for today, Major."

"Sir." Shutt stood, collected her comms and a few papers, and marched to the door. Edmunds steepled his hands the way Dashi often did when he was thinking. Shutt reached the door, turned, executed a perfect salute, then exited, closing the door behind her.

Edmunds tapped his fingers on the desk. Shutt hadn't exited like a subordinate who had made her boss angry. She didn't seem upset, or worried, or angry.

Cocky. She seemed cocky.

CHAPTER 4

The air lock door clattered open, and the three captains stepped across. "Why do we have to come to her," the senior one, Captain LaFerme, said. "We are all equal on the council."

Captain Lalond unscrewed his helmet and held it in his hand. "On the Free Traders council, we are all equal. But she is now Lay-gate Marianne, by Imperial decree, and we are grubby merchants transporting hunks of metal and dirty water."

"Without my dirty water, no fuel for her ships. Or yours for that matter." Captain Mathieu slapped his gloves into their straps and examined the walls. "That girl does like pink."

"And paintings." LaFerme pointed at a drawing on the bulkhead. "Is that a dog? Or a tomato?"

"If you have to ask—" Mathieu rapped the hatch and called out. "Hallo? We are here. Nous sommes ici."

"Down here, Captains," a voice called from the hab module, down the ladder. "Come on down."

The three captains removed helmets and gloves, loosened vacuum collars and cuffs, then pulled themselves down the ladder from the air lock. The ship engines were ticking over—just enough acceleration to provide a down toward the stern of the ship. Dropped items would come to rest eventually, spilled liquids would pool on surfaces rather than float. Enough gravity to soothe the stomach and make clean-ups simpler.

Falling into the lounge, Mathieu flipped over and landed feet first, catching with his boot magnets. A uniformed crewman was setting a table on the far side of the compartment. Metal cutlery, cups, and plates littered the table, next to a large jug. The smell of warm bread filled the lounge.

"Ms. Marianne will be up in a moment. She is on the comm," their crewman waiter said.

"Having important conversations with the Emperor, no doubt." LaFerme sat. "Too busy for us."

Mathieu hefted a jug on the table, unscrewed the cap, and sniffed. "Plenty of time to finish her wine, then. Everyone?"

The other two captains seated themselves, collected a metal cup and extended it to be filled. The waiter, fussing with the oven, extended his own. Mathieu filled that as well.

"Sante!" Mathieu drank his down in one swallow and refilled his glass. Lalond took a mouthful, swirled it, swallowed, and nodded.

LaFerme took a sip, grimaced, and sat hers down. "I am unhappy with the way resources have been allocated recently. I have been giving too much in the way of spare parts and fuel and not receiving sufficient in return."

Mathieu drank. "Then take your ship off and do your own trading. We're a cooperative, not a coercion. If you don't like the deal, go and make your own. I, for one, am happy that we're getting at least some supplies from those corporate couchons. We got nothing before, at least now we get something."

"If you spent less time in your cups and more running your ship, you'd understand."

Mathieu dropped his cup and placed both hands on the table. "I do understand. I understand that it is my ship, not yours, and I don't need your advice. We made a deal, and if you don't want to follow the deal, then don't. But stop whining at me. It turns the wine sour."

Lalond laughed. "Even if it's sour, I'm sure you will drink it. But this wine is not sour, it's not bad. Better than she usually serves."

"She feels guilty making us wait," LaFerme said. "While she has secret discussions with those Empire people. Discussions concerning the Free Traders. We should be part of those talks."

Marianne pulled herself up from the cabins below. "Bonjour. Sorry to make you all wait. Part of what?"

"Who were you talking to?" LaFerme asked. "What were you talking about? Why were we not invited."

Marianne slopped a half glass of wine and drank it down. "A fine vintage." She refilled her glass. "I better get my share before Captain Mathieu drinks it all. What is your opinion, Captains? Is it a good wine?"

"We did not come here to talk wine," LaFerme said. "We are concerned about your secret discussion with the Empire and your recent activities on the council. I remind you we are the senior members of the Free Traders council."

Mathieu sipped his wine and sloshed it inside his mouth. "Very smooth. Not much acid. I like it. Thank you, Captain Marianne. This is a good vintage."

Marianne clinked his cup. "You are welcome."

LaFerme slammed his cup down. "Why do you not answer my questions? We are captains, not children to be trifled with."

Lalond stirred. "Who were you talking to, ma petite? You should not be having private conversations like this. Not private to the council."

"Uncle, you have no right to know my private communications."

"If they are related to the council, then yes. That was our agreement."

"If you are so interested." Marianne shrugged. "I was speaking to my lover. We were planning our next meeting. I promised to lick him all over the—"

LaFerme choked. "We don't need to know that."

"I disagree," Mathieu poured more wine. "Let me top up, then you can continue. Licking. Were you going to pour something on him first? This excellent wine, perhaps?"

Marianne laughed. LaFerme scowled. Lalond shook his head. "We don't need to know your personal issues, we need to know issues of interest to the Free Trader's council."

Mathieu grinned. "Not me. I am fascinated by this licking."

Lalond ignored him. "By your lover, I assume you mean Tribune Jose?"

"Yes."

"Leaving out the details of your . . . personal activities. What is behind this proposed Senate election?"

Marianne sipped her own wine. "It is Dashi's idea. He wants to make things more formal. And more like the Empire. The more we follow the old-Empire rules, the more stable and secure he believes his government will be."

"Now it's his government, is it?" LaFerme said.

Lalond grunted. "We need rules. We need some sort of government. Dashi will do, as long as we can continue our traditional ways. But you must keep us informed of what is being discussed and allow us to have our input."

"Uncle," Marianne said, "the last time I allowed your input you and the council argued for four days deciding where you would stockpile spare parts. The planetary council, the Imperial Council, they cannot wait that long for every decision. I am your representative. I need to be able to make decisions regarding our position."

"That is not our way," LaFerme said. "Not our traditions."

"Our traditions are fine for running a single ship," Marianne said. "But not for helping govern a planetary system. I must have more authority. I must speak with the authority of the council."

"Never," LaFerme said.

"We will discuss this," Lalond said.

Mathieu extended his glass. "Could I have more wine?"

The debate went on for some time. The captains were not stupid, but they were suspicious. Having closer organization between different factions was necessary if they were to survive the next few years. The revolt had thrown their problems into sharp relief. They could not continue on the way they had since the abandonment. The Empire was not coming back. The problem, as Lalond pointed out, was what would replace it. Marianne had pushed for the new council, with her as their representative.

"I have arranged with Jose—"

"Your lover."

"Yes."

"Perhaps you would not be so enamored of him if he were not so powerful. Power and wealth is attractive."

"Should I tell Aunt Helene that is why you married her? Was it her beauty and sparkling conversation, or was it her one-quarter share in the family starship?"

"Impudent child," Lalond said. But he smiled.

"One-quarter of a starship seems like a good reason to court somebody." Mathieu belched. "And a case or two of this wine. What do we get, Cheri?"

"Get?"

"If we agree to this election thing, or at least not cause a fuss. What do we get?"

"Get? From me. Nothing."

"Then you do not get my agreement. If you want something from me, you must give the guild something of value."

"The guild is getting my services as a representative free of charge. That should be sufficient."

"Pshaaw." Captain LaFerme spit her wine into her cup. "Enough of this. You are our representative on the council. You represent us. You will do as we tell you to."

"Don't do that," Mathieu said. "That's a waste of good wine."

Marianne refilled her glass. "Or else what?"

"What?"

"I'm on the council, appointed by Dashi. You can't remove me." Marianne raised her glass and took a deep swallow.

"We can. I will take your place on the council."

Mathieu laughed. Lalond smiled. Marianne snorted as she giggled. "Tabernac. Pardon, Captain Mathieu, that was an accident. You have no chance of taking my place on the council."

"I can represent the Free Traders as well as you."

"First, I have a good history. As the corporate people say, 'my numbers are good.' Our people stayed out of the fighting. Mostly. The family guilds were able to continue operating. The only ones who were of any risk were the youngsters who volunteered for the legion."

"Another silly idea," LaFerme said. "Sending Traders out to fight and die for these maudit corporations."

"They are maudit, agreed. But joining a legion is much more fun for a twenty-two-year-old space hand, who has only a lifetime of working for his aunt, cleaning the ship, and loading cargo, patching his suit alone at night, never getting a promotion."

"We do not do others' dirty work."

"Only our own. The youngsters can see the decline in this system better than you. You have a ship. You have had a full life. For them, who knows what will happen. Your beloved Empire has been gone forever, never to return. For them, they can shine a cargo lock every day. Or they can join the legion. They get a weapon, some training, and a uniform. They go to the planet and fight the hated Militia, or the greedy corporations. Smuggle weapons or supplies or other fighters. Action. Excitement."

"Sounds like fun," Mathieu said. "I might join myself. Will there be wine?"

Marianne held up her glass. "Of course. And pretty girls. Or rich, handsome corporate executives with fine beards."

"Do the youngsters believe they will meet these bearded corporate boyfriends?" Lalond asked.

"Why not? As you are fond of reminding me, I found one."

"This legion, these silly youngsters. This is not the way the Free Traders do things," LaFerme said. "We look to our own problems, not get involved in others."

"The others' problems have found us, whether we want them or not, and these silly youngsters helped save Dashi and the city. They fought the Militia and the other corporations, and they won. They are proud of what they have accomplished. And I—" Marianne swallowed the last of her glass. "I am their leader. I, Marianne, Legate in the Imperial government, leader of the Legio X, Sigma Draconis, shipmaster, delegate to the council and soon-to-be Imperial senator."

Mathieu clapped loudly.

"Shut up, you drunken fool," LaFerme hissed.

"I may be a drunk, but I am not an idiot. This smells like success, and I am always on the successful side. You have convinced me. Vive la revolution, I say. And Vive Senator Marianne. You have my support. More wine, please." Mathieu waved his glass.

LaFerme glared. "I will not—"

"You will," Lalond said. "Remember, you alone are not the Traders' Council, either. We share that responsibility. And I, too, think shipmaster Marianne has been successful in representing and protecting us. If she has gained much more for herself, then good for her. Will you continue to support us?"

"I will not forget where I came from."

"Good. As long as you remind your friend Jose and your other friend Dashi of that. Bien. So, we continue to support you on the council and help make you a senator. What do we get?"

"Part of a station. All of it if we are careful."

"TGI—Dashi, the Emperor, whoever. Your Mr. Jose. They are offering us a station?"

"They are not." Marianne smiled. "But they are busy with this election, their council, killing a few stray Militia people, and organizing trade in the system. Which organization they require our help and our legion of troops. While they are distracted, I believe we may find a few things . . . unattended . . . that we may acquire for our own. We need another repair yard, one with good Downport shuttle connections, with space for storage and, perhaps, a small foundry. One of the corps that sided with the Militia was nearly destroyed. TGI is taking over their people and assets, but they do not have a full accounting, and they will be slow. If we were to . . . occupy one station before TGI arrived, it would not be worth it to remove us."

Mathieu held up his glass in salute. "You are a true Free Trader. I always told your father you were the smartest in the family."

"My father told me you said that about cousin Gerald."

Mathieu bit his lip, then swallowed his wine. "The smartest girl, then. Salut."

Minor Free Trader business took up the remaining time and a willingness to provide 'support', meaning armed crews to take over the stations. After finishing the jug, the three captains retreated to their respective ships. Marianne sat at the table and opened another jug of wine.

The waiter cleaned up. "So, cousin, we will have our own station, oui?"

"We will, Henri. We are allies of the Imperial Council, and our side won. The current station owners are out of favor and are in no position to object to a joint operation."

"We will run it jointly with them?"

"That is what we will tell them." Marianne squirmed on the chair, then pulled a pink revolver she had hidden in her pocket.

"You always carry that?"

Marianne flipped open the cylinder and checked the bullets. "Better to have it and not need it, then need it and not have it. Like while acquiring this station."

"Huh. What does Mr. Jose say to this?"

"He does not know. I have not told him. Yet."

"Do you think he'll allow you to take over a station for our own use?"

"He is reasonable. I'll explain it to him in a way he understands. Afterwards."

Henri shrugged. "You want him to give up an entire station. Well, bring wine. Do that licking thing you were talking about first. And cousin?"

"Oui?"

Henri pointed. "Keep that revolver handy. You know. Just in case."

CHAPTER 5

Shutt was reading in her office when Sergeant Russell arrived. He walked into her office, closed the door, and sat in her chair.

"Lousy military courtesy, Sergeant."

"No, ma'am," Russell agreed. He pulled out a pack of cigarettes. "Can I smoke?"

"Nope."

"Okay." Russell put the cigarettes back in his pocket. "You got somebody needs shooting?"

"Not right now, no."

"You really know how to ruin a guy's day, Clarisse."

"It's going to get worse, Scott. I need you to take your squad and run herd on a bunch of troops picking up a factory load of equipment."

"We're breaking into a factory to steal some equipment? Outstanding."

"Not breaking in, no."

"You've got an inside person? We sneak in there in the middle of the night, load up, and go."

"Middle of the day."

"Clarisse"—Scott rubbed his face—"middle of the day is not the best time to steal things."

"We bought them. They're paid for. You just have to pick them up."

"Pick them up? No stealing? This day keeps getting worse and worse."

"Sorry to disappoint you."

"I'm in the Militia, I'm used to it. Is that a book? A real book?"

"Yep." Shutt held up a novel. "Jose gave it to me. He

says it's original old Empire."

"If that's true, you could buy a cutter with what that's worth."

"I think we're coming to a time when a cutter will be worth a lot more than a book, no matter how old."

"Even so. What's it called?"

"The Prince. By some guy called Niki something."

"What's it about?"

"Power."

"Power? What's he saying about power?"

"He's in favor of it."

"So am I. Sounds like a smart guy. Anything else?"

"He says it's better to be feared than loved."

"I could have told you that. In fact, I did tell you that, I'm pretty sure."

"You tell me a lot of things. You do gabble on."

"A lot of those things got you where you are now. I hear you're running for senator."

"Will you vote for me?"

"Maybe. What's in it for me?"

"A steady job. Reasonable economic prospects."

"Boring."

"How about this." Shutt flipped through the book and read it out. "Whoever believes that great advancement and new benefits make me forget old injuries is mistaken."

"Meaning?"

"Any old injuries you want to take some action on?"

Russell nodded. "I can think of a few."

"We need this factory moved and set back up. We're too dependent on TGI and some others for basics. This will give us our own food supply and some basic metalworking shops. We can fix weapons."

"Can we make bullets? I like making bullets."

"I didn't ask, directly. But there are some machines there that could be modified." Shutt leaned back on her desk. "You look like the type of guy who can make bullets for revolvers."

"It's a hobby of mine," Russell said. "I make 'em in small quantities for fun."

"Think you could make 'em in quantity?"

"I can try. If you give me the right equipment, sure."

"I'm not sure if this is exactly the right equipment. I couldn't really ask. But I think it's close. It's a start. Take your squad out east, get the equipment we need. There're workers there who will load a water ship, and you'll supervise. Take the ship back."

"Another ship. Outstanding."

"And there might be some rebels out there that need to be dealt with."

"By rebels you mean rebel Militia?"

"They're not political rebels. They are more of the 'we're really hungry. Somebody burned our factory housing down, so we ran away, and we attack people to get food' and things like that."

"And by dealt with you mean kill them all and leave their bodies to rot in the woods."

"Must you always want to kill everyone?"

"It simplifies my day. If I can't kill them . . ."

"If they shoot at you, shoot back. Capture them if you can."

"Then they'll be killed?"

"They'll be brought back into town and put on some work project. It's not really their fault that their houses were burnt down."

"It's their fault if they shoot at me."

"I'll leave that part of things to your discretion. I know I can count on your good judgment."

"It's pretty early in the day for you to be drinking, isn't it? Because the only way that you would say that is—"

"I'm as surprised as you," Shutt said. "But you have a depth of competence hidden behind a veneer of laziness and cynicism. The admiral and the Militia didn't recognize that, thus your current rank and miserable attitude. I'm making use of that."

"My competence or my misery?"

"Both. I need competent, miserable people to support me."

"You mean the Militia needs competent people?"

"That's what I meant, sure."

Russell sat in silence, thinking hard. "What do I do with these bullets when I'm done?"

"Make a list of those old injuries and bring them to me. Dismissed."

Russell stood. "I'll do that. But Clarisse?"

"What?"

"It's going to be a long list."

***

Russell called his squad together. "We're going on a trip. Get yourself ready for some marching. Collect weapons, get your paperwork filled out, and meet back here in two hours. Make sure you're carrying at least four days of rations."

"Where are we going, Sergeant?" Kim One asked.

"Am I a travel agent? Shut up. Everyone, get moving."

Russell's squad scattered to various places in the headquarters. Russell spent two hours sitting in an empty headquarters office, filling out mind-numbing forms. The forms allowed squads out on independent command. After certifying his troops who had assigned addresses for receipt of parcels, he approved their wills on file. One of the Kims had decided to donate her money to the local animal shelter in the event of her death. He considered doing that for himself when Kim One stuck her head in the door.

"They won't give us four days of rations, Sergeant."

"They will if you ask."

"Already asked, Sergeant."

Russell glared at Kim One. "Ask again."

"Asked three times, Sergeant. Chaudhari asked, too. They told him no as well."

"Chaudhari?" Scott yelled. No answer. He marched out into the hall and yelled into the foyer.

A hand touched his shoulder and he spun and drew his revolver.

Chaudhari regarded the revolver. "Shooting practice today, Sergeant?"

Russell holstered the revolver. "Don't do that."

"You don't like to be touched?"

"Don't sneak up on me. Don't startle me."

"But it's okay to touch you, then?"

"Shut up. Why won't they give us rations?"

"Oh, they'll give us rations."

"Then get them."

"Well, they won't give them to us as we are."

"As we are? They want us to become somebody else? Fine, tell them I'm a tall blonde woman with large breasts."

"Backpacks."

"You call them backpacks? That's a weird slang term, but whatever suits you. Tell them I'm a blond with large backpacks."

"Two backpacks?"

"That's right."

"They won't give us rations unless we have . . ." Chaudhari counted the squad members in view. "Twelve backpacks."

"They want me to be a twelve-breasted woman? That's sick."

"Backpacks. Not a slang term for breasts. Actual backpacks, things that you put stuff in. We need something to carry the rations in. They won't give us rations unless we produce backpacks to put them in."

"So, get the backpacks, then get the rations."

"There's a hitch."

"What kind of hitch."

Chaudhari smiled. "You're going to love this part."

43

The equipment issue station was a ten-minute walk from Militia headquarters. In the opposite direction from the food plant where the rations were stored, of course. The fires, troop movements, thievery, loss, general destruction, and administrative cussedness had split issuing departments all across the town.

"Explain again," Sergeant Russell said, gritting his teeth, "why you can't give my squad new backpacks."

"I told you before, Sergeant," the clerk said, "regulations."

The clerk smirked a tiny smirk at Russell. The smirk was the only part of him that was tiny. His belly hung over his belt, neck swelling at his Militia skin suit collar, and his jowls hung so far down he might as well have had face handles. If he'd been a pig for sale in a supermarket, you'd have had to invite all the neighbors to dinner to handle the load.

"I understand regulations. I believe in regulations. I follow regulations. And regulations say that if we have a valid mission plan signed by an officer, you have to give us food."

"Yes, Sergeant, that's correct. But we have to see what type of carrying apparatus you'll be using, so we can determine what type of rations to issue you."

"Carrying apparatus?"

Chaudhari leaned in. "Fancy name for what type of backpack they issue us."

"What types are there?"

The clerk typed on his desk computer. "Well, there is NX-400-2312-4C/D—carrying apparatus, tactical, standard, day trips for the use of and then NJ-340-777/C-231 carrying apparatus, local operations, extended, for the use of, then 8732133-4, carrying apparatus, strategic operations, dismounted ground combat, extra."

Russell pivoted the desk computer display and glared at the screen. "Those names don't mean anything to me."

"Not my problem, Sergeant," the clerk said. "I issue

what I'm told. But you need to tell me which one."

"Those IDs aren't the same pattern. They don't even have the same number of digits."

"Well, one of them was part of the original Imperial numbering scheme of the original system, the other was when we migrated versions, oh, seventeen years ago, part of the new plan for rationalizing supply storage, and the other is a temporary number issued as part of the emergency acquisition during the budget shortfall—"

"Never mind."

Chaudhari leaned in again. "Small, medium, and large?"

"Yeah, give us the largest one."

"Can't do that. We have to have an accounting of the rations, before we issue their carrying items. We need to see the rations first."

"The rations people told us they can't give us the rations till we have something to carry them in. They need to see the carriers."

The clerk shrugged. "That's the rules. Will there be anything else, Sergeant?"

Russell leaned on the counter. His face turned red, and his breath started to come in gasps. He death-stared the clerk.

"Scott," Chaudhari whispered. "Don't kill him. He's not worth it."

"Nobody will know. The squad won't talk."

"Somebody will miss him. They might not care about him, but they'll surely complain if a bunch of carrying apparatuses, tactical, tabbo feces, for the conveyance of, are missing."

Kim One coughed behind them. "Sergeant?"

"Not now, Kim One," Chaudhari said. "Not now."

"I used to work in supply. I might have a solution."

All faces turned to Kim One. "Well?" Russell asked.

"There're other types of carrying apparatus listed in the supply database. There's one that doesn't have the requirement to demonstrate the loaded items."

"Talk Standard."

Kim pointed. "This one here—MU-1100-L, carrying apparatus, mobile, can be issued in place of any carrying apparatus, and it's not necessary to demonstrate a load requirement. Says so right in the database."

Russell held out his hand. "Gimme." He read the database entry that Kim's comm showed him. "Huh. Good job Kim One."

"Thank you, Sergeant."

Russell rounded on the clerk. "Give us those MU-1100-L's, then. One for each of us. Twelve of them."

"I can't give you those . . ."

"It says here you can. That's the regulations. Now, you don't want me to report you for disobeying regulations."

"I don't think you want—"

"Listen buddy, the regulations say you have to issue them if we have the right paperwork, and the paperwork is clear. You either give us those, or I'm going to tie you up and haul you back to see the admiral and point out you were disobeying orders. Right now, the admiral doesn't have a lot of patience for people not obeying his orders. The last ones he caught doing that were shot, shoved out an air lock, or sent on ships for years. Or all three at once. What do you think he'll do to you?"

The clerk shrugged again. "If that's what you want, you can have them, but you have to come out back."

The squad marched down the street two by two. Russell leading, Chaudhari in the back. Kim One marched next to Russell.

"I'm very sorry, Sergeant," she said.

"I hate you."

"It seemed like a good idea."

"I really hate you."

"I was just trying to help."

"Still hate you. Double hate you. Everybody, halt," Russell yelled. The column stopped. "I need a cigarette." A nose stuck over Russell's shoulder, and a giant tongue slurped across his face. "Stop that, you stupid animal."

The squad stood in the street, grasping halters. As ordered, the clerk had issued them a dozen MU-1100-L, carrying apparatus, mobile. Or, to give them another name, a dozen mules.

Kim patted her mule's head. "I'm going to call mine Sweet Pea." Sweet Pea leaned over and slurped Russell's head again. "I think she likes you, Sergeant."

The clerk at the monorail station didn't blink an eye. "Let's see—space for a dozen evil-smelling, undisciplined, cantankerous, stubborn beasts of such low intelligence they're fit only for simple tasks. That's car thirteen. And a dozen mules. That's car 14."

"Funny," Russell said. "See me laughing. Ha-ha."

"Jovial lot, you Militia."

"We need transportation to this factory place, GG-22."

"We can drop you just short of the river, at the bridge. That's as far as the monorail goes now, after the war. You'll have to walk from there, or ride. It's about eight hours to your factory."

"Will there be enough space?"

"Only if you can promise you won't crap on the floor."

"They're mules."

"I wasn't talking about the mules."

Russell thumbed the paperwork and ordered the squad on board. Two members had grown up at rural stations with knowledge of how to care for animals, and the boxcars for the mules were functional. The number of animals moving between stations had increased recently, and monorail cars had been outfitted to handle them.

Russell had the former farm hands show him how to tie and settle his animal, then went to sit in the next car. Chaudhari was waiting for him.

"I hate my life," Russell said. "And you and the squad and the officers and Shutt and the council and the entire world."

"That's not news. When have you ever liked the squad or the officers or Shutt?"

Russell pondered. "Some days I haven't totally hated them. Well, not for the entire day."

"We'll look for progress, then. Guess what I got?"

"An unspeakable disease from your girlfriend?"

"You're getting my girlfriend and your mother confused. I've got a mortar."

"I'm sorry to hear—wait, a mortar? Like in the vids. Shells, tubes, that sort of thing?"

"Fifty rounds of explosive shells."

"What are we going to do with a mortar?"

"Blow things up."

"What things?"

"I don't know." Chaudhari pointed. "How about that. We could blow that up."

"That's a garden storage yard. Those are wheelbarrows."

"They could be rebel wheelbarrows. Sounds like something needs blowing up."

"Not yet. Do you know how to make this thing work?"

"No idea whatsoever."

"How are we going to carry all this stuff?"

"We've got mules! Nature's truck. Each one can carry like a hundred fifty pounds. As long as we give 'em water and something green to eat, we're good."

"And we're going to march along a river. Hmm. How about food for us?"

"Kim One pulled the regs on them again. The rules said they had to see how big our 'carrying apparatus' was before issuing 'sufficient rations to fill it' so she insisted they load a dozen of the mules completely with rations. We've got tons of food."

"You mean lots of food?"

"I mean thousands of kilograms of food. Actual tons. Food that we don't have to carry."

"Huh. And a mortar."

"And fifty shells. And spare ammo and a sextant."

"What's a sextant?"

"Some nautical thing that will help us navigate the 'trackless wastes of the desert.'"

"There's no desert up north. It's all forest and plains and farms."

"We'll find a desert."

"Why are you so excited?"

"Fifty mortar shells." Chaudhari grinned. "Think of the fun!"

CHAPTER 6

"Will this take much longer?" Rajput crowded over the burglar. "Jose will be on my back if we don't get inside."

"Keep your shirt on, chief." The burglar poked at the door locking pad. "These Model Seven-Bravo locks are a tabbo's butt to break into."

"I should have been a locksmith." Rajput had searched the corporate records for people arrested for burglary. He found three. One was killed in the recent fighting. One had taken a sabbatical at a northern monastery, and the third had been in custody for selling stolen skin suit parts he claimed had "fallen off a shuttle." An administrative transfer, a few threats, a set of screwdrivers, and a few hours later he and the skin suit thief stood next to the magnetic door panel on the air lock leading to a mothballed Militia cutter. "It didn't seem that hard, but I never got around to it after my injury."

"It's not for everybody."

"You're supposed to be an expert burglar."

"I am. I'm the Mike Angelo of burglars."

"Mike Angelo?"

"That painter guy. He did ceilings."

"You mean Michelangelo?"

"Yeah, him. The painter dude. That's what I meant. It's just these Seven-Bravos are in a real class of their own."

"We're behind schedule. You said you could break any lock in sixty seconds. That's what I put on the checklist."

"Any five bravo. Or five delta. Or even a Six-Alpha, now that's a lock. Those Six-Alphas, see—"

"Imperial Anus. I don't care what the freaking model number is. Why haven't you cracked it?"

"Seven-Bravos have the extra metal strap across the control unit so that you can't get inside it."

"If you can't get inside it, how will we open it?"

"Like I said, keep your shirt on chief. First, I push this here screwdriver . . ." The burglar slid a needle nosed screwdriver under the outer case of the door lock mechanism. "Under here, and I apply gentle pressure."

"Don't break it, for Empire's sake. We don't want anybody knowing that we're here and stole it."

"Keep your shirt on, I just need to push a bit—"

"It's been ten minutes. We're supposed to be inside and starting the engines up by now."

The burglar stepped back and fiddled with his tools. "Just a minute longer."

Rajput grabbed the burglar's shoulder. "Hurry it up, you leprous insect. You're acting like a complete moron, and my boss will think I'm one, too."

"Subtlety takes time. An artist like myself—"

Rajput shoved him back to the lock. "Less artist talk, more artist prying. Get it open."

"Young people today, no respect for artistic endeavor. But you're in a hurry, I get it. I slide the screwdriver in here, and apply gentle pressure—"

CRACK. The faceplate of the lock mechanism snapped apart, and pieces flew across the air lock. The largest smacked Rajput's face. "Imperial Anus. You incompetent toad."

"Oops. Sorry. Little too much pressure."

"You're an idiot and a horrible burglar."

"These things happen, chief."

"I could have smashed the lock off myself, you moron."

"I don't have to take that from you." The burglar dropped his tools. "I'm an artist. I don't deserve this level of abuse."

"Fine." Rajput waved his finger in the burglar's face. "Then I'll put you back in jail, where I found you, and you can rot there forever for all I care."

The burglar blinked, then bent down. "Then again, as a professional, I can ignore uncouth babbling and make my art, even if the people watching don't understand or appreciate what I'm doing."

"Get this sorted out."

"Sure boss. You know you're bleeding?"

Rajput rubbed his face and examined his red hand. "That was the master burglar's doing. I should have found a better burglar."

"I'm a good burglar."

"Maybe we should have found somebody who wasn't in jail instead?"

The burglar stood. "Ha. Ta-da!"

"Well?"

"I cross this wire and that wire, then push here and voila!" He pinched the wires together and a shower of sparks blew past them.

The lock remained closed.

"Emperor's hairy ankles. What is going on?" Rajput yelled.

"That's what I want to know." A new voice came from behind them. A uniformed Militia guard had appeared from the hall. "What are you doing with this ship lock?"

Rajput shuffled his feet. The burglar stood.

"Well?" The guard put his hand on his shock stick. "What are you doing here?"

"Mr . . ." Rajput shut his mouth. Jose had told him on no account was he to be identified. "I'm Mr. Rajput."

"Pleased to meet you, Mr. Rajput. What are you doing."

"We want to get in this lock."

"I see that. What's the problem?"

"Well," Rajput said, "We've had discussions with the council."

"The council?"

"Yes. They've authorized us to check into the situation

and determine the optimal way to modify the scheduling parameters, and, uh, we need to evaluate the situational nexus of fueling options."

"Situational fueling nexus? What in the Emperor's wrist bones does that mean?"

"Well, it's the nexus."

"Nexus?"

"Of fueling situations. As the council directed."

The Militia guard unsnapped the cover over his shock stick. "You better start making sense. I don't want to hear about any nexus. What's going on here?"

"The council directed—"

"I don't care about the council. What are the two of you doing?" The guard yanked out his shock stick and held it in his hand.

The burglar held up his hands. "The thing is, chief, we can't get the lock open."

"You can't get the lock open?"

The burglar pointed at Rajput. "I'm trying to open the lock for this guy. He's got some razzmatazz paperwork to check something or other. It's all legit."

"That's all you need? Get in the ship?"

"That's it, chief."

"Sure," Rajput said. "That would be nice. If it's not, you know, too much trouble."

"Why didn't you say so?"

"We did."

"No," the guard said, "You didn't. You talked about nexusing and councils and all that. Nothing about opening the lock. You need to get into this ship?"

"Yes, we have a—"

The guard held up his hand. "I don't care what you have. These ships are mothballed, nothing in them worth stealing. What's the problem getting in?"

"The lock," the burglar said. "They're a Bravo-7."

"Oh yeah, those model B7's, they're a pain."

"Exactly. Complete—"

"Complete pieces of junk. They break all the time. Cheapest ones on the market. That's why the Militia bought them. The codes always jammed up. They erase themselves all the time. I'll bet the code that Militia HQ gave you doesn't work, does it?"

Rajput coughed. "Why, yes. Our um . . . codes aren't working on this lock."

"I told Militia HQ once. I told them a thousand times these pieces of crap are always breaking." The guard waved them away. "Make room."

The two stepped away. The guard holstered his shock stick and bent down. "Yup, B7 piece of crap." He used his fingers to space measure along the wall, away from the lock plate. "You need to find where the solenoid is. Measure six fingers to the left." He counted, put a finger on the wall. "There." He stepped back and slammed a fist onto the wall. The mechanism clicked, and the lock light turned green. "See? Such a worthless piece of crap. Lucky it's easy to break into."

Rajput glared at the burglar.

The burglar smiled. "There you go, chief, we're in."

The lock clicked, and the access light flashed red.

"Or not," Rajput said.

"But you know how to get in now." The guard adjusted his belt. "Six fingers and then a kick. You guys never were in the Militia, were you?"

"A long time ago," Rajput said. "Years ago. Things change."

"They do."

"So, we bang the door there six fingers away?"

"Yep. Of course, if it's reset itself, you use the factory access code."

"The factory access code?"

"Boy, it's been a long time since you were in, huh, if you don't know the code."

"I'm an old man," Rajput said. He glowered at the burglar. "Feeling older by the minute."

"Well." The guard leaned in. "I didn't realize you hadn't tried the code—I figured you already tried it, and the lock was still stuck." He punched the buttons. One. Two. Three. Four. The lock clicked, and the light flashed green again. "There you go. Use that. Good luck with your paperwork thing. I gotta go."

The guard walked down the corridor and waved off their thanks. Rajput typed the default code in several times, locking and unlocking the door. He waited till the light turned green for the third time before swinging the hatch open. Then he crossed his arms and glared at the burglar.

"Yup. Those Bravo-7's," the burglar said. "A real special case. Let's get inside. I can help with the other locks!"

Rajput glared at him.

"Can't I?"

***

Their breath fogged the air as they cleared the internal air lock.

Rajput shivered. "Cold in here."

"Thanks for the update, chief," the burglar said. "I should have brought mittens."

"Can't stand getting your hands cold?"

"Can't work on frozen steel with bare hands. Need to keep my hands warm. And I need some way to keep my tools warm."

Rajput offered precise suggestions on where to place his tools to keep them warm and volunteered to assist in the storage.

"That's pretty mean, chief."

"Ow. Ow." Rajput yanked his hands back from the hatch locking wheel. "That hurts. Touching the hatch. All my skin is on it."

"Told you."

Rajput ducked his hands under his armpits. "We need to get forward to get on the bridge. You're the burglar.

Open it."

"Didn't bring any gloves, chief."

"And I didn't ask if you had any. Get a towel or something."

"I don't—"

"Don't want to go back to jail because if we leave this ship without getting it started, we're going right back to your cell and leaving you there until the Empire comes back. How about that?"

The burglar cursed under his breath and tried to grip the locking wheel with his arms. No go. Rajput sucked his bleeding finger and took the burglar's screwdriver and managed to force the hasp on a locker. The door swung open—the locker was empty. They took screwdrivers and forced the other lockers open. They were all empty, except for one that had rags on the bottom.

"Ripped socks or something," Rajput said. "But it will keep your hands from freezing while turning the lock."

"Good idea, Chief," the burglar said.

Rajput nodded at him.

The burglar tapped his chest. "You mean you want me . . . ?"

Rajput nodded again. The burglar grimaced, stuffed his hands into the dirty socks, and stepped to the lock.

"Always the little guy gets the shaft while the fat cats are standing jawing." The burglar pushed the wheel. It grated open, caught, grated again, then shrieked as it spun open.

"You were arrested once for stealing sweet nutritional growth supplements from a pediatric medical clinic, weren't you?" Rajput asked.

"Yeah, so?"

"Meaning you literally stole candy from babies. Stop complaining about fat cats. Pull the locking bar."

The burglar transferred his sock clad hands and yanked the bar, and the lock swung open. A cloud of mist formed in the corridor ahead of them.

"That's new," Rajput said.

"Air in there must have been dry and cold. We're bringing station air into the ship. Warmer. Wetter. I figure they must have dehumidified it or something."

They stepped over the hatch, coaming and deeper into the ship. Rajput's teeth chattered. "So much work to preserve the ship. You think they would have kept the heat on."

"Heat needs electricity." The burglar rewrapped the socks over his hands. "Electricity costs money and needs fuel, even with a fusion plant. You can use it for something else. Air just sits there—it doesn't need power, or heat. Vacuum is bad for lots of things. Cold doesn't bother electronics so much."

Rajput stared at him.

"What? I can't know something about ships? I did my tour in the Militia, just like everyone else."

"You mean just like everyone else who got caught breaking and entering and did a tour rather than go to jail."

"Well, yeah, chief. That's what I meant. But I spent some time on ships. And speaking of, that's not good." He pointed to the wall, covered in white hoarfrost.

"Frost? You're worried about frost?"

"I'm worried about water freezing onto the electronics. We should close that door behind us, keep the humidity out." The burglar swung the door shut behind them.

"That'll keep the equipment safe?"

"Nope. Sorry, Chief, but we're water vapor factories, all of us."

"Then let's be quick." Rajput waved the fog away and headed for the cockpit.

The cockpit door was not locked, but the board was. Jose had anticipated this and provided them with a series of standard unlock codes. They turned on the breakers at the ship's main electrical panel and checked that the breakers on the station side were enabled. The main board started up. Both were shivering now, and Rajput had to borrow the dirty socks to type in his override codes. The third one worked.

"There you go chief, we're in."

"Yes, yes, we are." Rajput grinned, which made his teeth chatter more. "Where's the heating controls?"

"I think I found 'em. Turning them to max right now."

A warning blinked from the panel. They were still drawing station power.

"Even have a startup checklist here."

"Here too," the burglar said. "Handy dandy list of items. Doesn't look too hard. First, the engineer brings the fusion drive up from standby, gets ship power turned on, then we disconnect from the station power, pull the cables, unhook the chains, then when the pilot is ready to go, he drops the mag links and maneuvers us away. Where is the pilot?"

"What?" Rajput asked.

"Pilot, chief. Need a pilot and an engineer. Standard practice when stealing a ship—bring your own pilot and engineer, to get it out of the way. I mean." The burglar's eyes widened. "I mean that's what I've heard, of course. I've never actually done anything like that myself. No stealing a ship, ever. But since you are inspecting this ship, or nexusing. Whatever. You need a pilot and an engineer. Where are they?"

"I didn't . . ." Rajput stared at the board. "I've never been in a cutter before. Not for years. I don't suppose you . . . ?"

The burglar shook his head. "I'm strictly an inside guy. Not a pilot?"

Rajput shook his head.

"Not an engineer?"

Rajput shook his head again.

The burglar exhaled and watched a cloud of water vapor blow away like an ice-cold smoke ring. "Say chief."

"Yes?"

"This is your first burglary, isn't it?"

CHAPTER 7

"Last stop. Anyone going east from here walks," the speaker boomed. The monorail had traveled all night and slid to a stop at first light.

Chaudhari nudged Sergeant Russell awake. "Time to go."

"Where are we?"

"Middle of nowhere."

"And we're getting out. Why?"

"No power on the line past this bridge. We need to get the troops moving."

"Fine, we'll get out and cross this bridge." Russell hauled himself to his feet and marched back to the luggage—now cattle, really, mule car.

A clerk appeared at the front of the car. "Who's the ringmaster of this circus?"

"Sergeant Russell at your service," Russell said. "We're going to GG-33. Down the line."

"Gotta walk from here, sorry. No power past the bridge. Rebels blew it up. Blew up the electrical conduits, not the bridge. You can cross on foot, but the train can't."

Russell untied his mule from the post in the car. "What happened to those rebels do you know?"

"Didn't follow. Heard some of them died in the fighting later."

"Any of them still here?"

"Why?"

"We need the height of the bridge surveyed."

"The height surveyed? How you do that."

"Tie a rope to them, toss them over the railing, see how long the rope is when they hit bottom. Want to volunteer?"

"You first, show me how it's done. Can you get your people and your mules off the train now?"

"It'll take a while. They're pretty cantankerous. I have to whip them, beat them up, sometimes I set one on fire."

"On fire, you mean you burn them?"

"A little bit."

"What an Imperial anus you are. Hitting defenseless animals. Make you feel like a big man, does it? You probably have a tiny—"

"Animals? What animals?"

"The mules."

"Mules?"

"You said you whip 'em, beat 'em, and set 'em on fire?"

"Ohhhh." Russell slapped the man on the shoulder. "I get it. Don't worry about that. I don't do that."

"You don't beat 'em and set 'em on fire?"

"Oh, I do." Russell laughed. "But not the mules, that's all. That's what I do to the troops."

"Sweet Pea doesn't want to go, Sergeant," Kim One said.

"Don't treat that beast like a person," Russell yanked on the bridle of his mule. But even his anger and strength couldn't budge his animal. Stubborn as a mule was a phrase for a reason. "Move it you daft beast. We need to get across the bridge." The Militia had disembarked under the clerk's direction from the cargo car. Their place had been taken by a pile of crates, sitting by the side of the track. The clerk had an inventory—the last of the outbound shipments from the factory. Russell had considered seizing them before loading, but didn't have enough info on conditions yet.

"It's hard for them, Sergeant. The temporary bridge is made for people, not mules. That walkway is too narrow, and it's a grid, not a flat plate. Hurts their paws."

"They don't have paws. They have hooves or hoofs or

something like that."

"Either way, Sweet Pea says she doesn't want to cross the bridge. They want to go around, she says. Take the other bridge farther up the river."

"She says? What, did that stupid animal send you a comm? Or login to the satellites and send an email?"

Kim One stroked Sweet Pea's chin. "There, there, little one. Pay no attention to the mean old man. You don't have to go over the bridge."

"We have to cross the bridge."

"We have to cross the river, Sergeant. We don't have to cross it right here." Kim One pointed upriver. "We cut inland so we're not right at the edge of the continent, go past that hill-thingy over there, and we head into that forest up there. The river ravine won't be as steep way up there—you can see spots where it's right at ground level. The map says there is a bridge and a camp up there. We can cross there."

Russell shaded his hands. "That's miles out of our way. We'll be hiking all day to get there."

"You say 'March or die' all the time, Sergeant. You always said marching is good for us. You said it builds character."

"I did not say that."

Kim One, fumbled with her comm, then played a recording. A cursing Russell was demanding his troops march faster. "See, Sergeant? You like it when we march."

"You record my orders?"

"Some of them, Sergeant. Your more memorable ones."

"What makes them memorable?"

"Your expressions, Sergeant. They're very . . . inspiring. Like 'March or die.' Or just die-die-die."

"I'm glad you pay such close attention."

"Besides, Sergeant, we don't have to follow the monorail. We can hike cross-country, and crossing upriver makes it shorter. Look at the map."

She displayed her comm's mapping software, and Russell examined her proposed route. It was shorter.

Russell glared at the hill. "It would be good to get used to these mules. There's water at the river, and a day or two marching with them would be worthwhile."

"Besides, Sweet Pea is carrying all that water and food, as are the others. We'll only have to walk. We don't need to carry much."

"Alright Kim, you've convinced me. We march."

Sweet Pea pooped a pile of green grassy poop right in front of them.

Russell waved in front of his nose. "Or die from the smell. Let's go."

They left the rail line behind them and marched parallel to the river. The river wound down a canyon, too deep to cross at this point, but they stayed close to it. Midday, they crossed a feeder stream. Animals drank their fill, as did the troops, after dumping chlorine tablets into their water bottles. Bromine and Iodine based disinfectants were not common on Delta, and they were expensive to manufacture, so the troops used chlorine tablets to kill microorganism. Pre-made tablets dissolved one part-per million, knocking out any bad bugs

The terrain was all trees, the soil too poor for farming. Delta grew its food on the wider river bottom lands. Luckily, there were plenty, as the northern mountains shed continuous streams of meltwater, replenished every two months by Delta's several-week-long winter.

Kim One's mule, Sweet Pea, was relaxed, tractable, and appeared to understand exactly what was wanted of her. She went wherever Kim One wanted her to, and the other mules fell into line behind her. Kim spent the whole time on the march talking softly to her mule. She described the terrain, the water, where they were going, and the foibles and characteristics of her squad mates. Russell worried that she might be going nuts, or turning part mule herself. Or that he might. The flow of conversation was mesmerizing. A couple of times, he caught Sweet Pea turning to the person Kim was commenting on, like she knew the people's names.

They called a halt at a second stream and let the animals drink again. Chaudhari sauntered up till he was standing next to Russell.

"Enjoying your walk, Sergeant?"

"No."

"It's a beautiful day."

"No."

"No what?"

"No whatever you're going to ask. We're going to march up to where we can cross this stupid river, cross it, march down, and get to this factory. Whatever you want, we're not doing it."

"You seem frustrated."

"Head of the class, you are."

"Bet a good fight would make you feel better."

"And where in the middle of a giant pine forest can I find a good fight? I could punch these mangy animals, but I'll admit they're pretty tough. They'd probably punch back."

"Mules aren't mangy. That's dogs."

"Whatever. What do you want?"

"To take two squad members, sneak behind these trees, and capture the guy hidden on the top of that hill there, watching us through binoculars. Or possibly a telescope."

Russell dug through his pockets. He knew he didn't have any cigarettes, but it gave him time to think. "You saw the glint of the glass?"

"Twice."

"Know exactly where he is?"

"Yes, I can sneak off to the left there, circle up the hill, and be behind him in ten minutes."

"He'll see you coming."

"Not if you lose your temper."

The screaming started up five minutes later.

Kim One slapped Skippy's face. "Stop grabbing my butt!"

Skippy rubbed her face. "I didn't touch your butt."

"Liar. You grabbed it."

"I'm not interested in your butt. I don't like women's butts."

"Why'd you grab it then?"

"I didn't, and even if I was interested, I wouldn't be interested in as skinny and bony a butt as yours."

"Skinny? You think it's skinny?"

"And bony. Very bony."

Kim stopped slapping and switched to punching and wrestling. Which evolved into a snarling, yanking fight on the ground. They rolled over in the dirt, thumping into Sweet Pea, who regarded them for a second, then continued to eat grass.

Russell gave them a few minutes of fake hair pulling and biting, then stepped in. He had the grinning squad members separate the two women. Using his sergeant's voice, he dressed the two of them down. He commented on their behavior, their habits, their clothing. He didn't sound happy. After dressing them down personally for five minutes, he still hadn't seen Chaudhari come back, so he changed tactics.

"It's not only the two of you I blame. No, the whole Militia has gone to the dogs. Used to be a professional, organized force you could be proud of. Now it's two levels above pond scum, diseased pond scum that's too scummy scum for making into food, or not even good enough for food packaging, not even good enough to make into paint thinner to thin paint that's going to be used to paint the stinking bottom of a machine that's slated to be junked and made into recycled machine parts, not even good enough to thin the paint that's going to paint the trash bin that holds the parts that were too scummy to be recycled—"

Nothing yet from Chaudhari. He kept going for a few minutes more on the paint thinner topic, and still, no notice. He switched topics again.

"In fact, it's not the Militia, or the government, or the corps, it's the whole stinking lot of the educational institute—"

The university, schools, and teachers were good for another ten minutes of screaming. Now he was worried. Even for him, screaming in rage for over twenty minutes took a lot of effort.

"And really, I trace it all back to my seventh-grade geology teacher, Mr. Drossong, he, and all the others whose classes I just sat in. I read comic books all day, right there in class, rather than listening to him. I fell asleep in the lectures because they were so boring I kept talking back in class. I told him he should be driving a bread truck. Now, I won't apologize for that. We need bread, bread has to be delivered. And if there's bread, there're bread trucks. And those trucks need drivers and geology needs to be taught and comic book reading isn't enough to drive a bread truck. They should have teachers who do that especially, not teaching bread readings, I mean. Emperor's finger bones. That's it I'm done."

Russell inhaled. "I'm done. I need a cigarette."

Clapping came from the woods behind him. Chaudhari stood there with his two squad members. They dangled a redheaded young boy between them.

"How long have you been there?"

Chaudhari grinned. "A long time. Fifteen minutes, at least. Kim, what's the total elapsed time?"

Kim One checked a timer on her comm. "Thirty-nine minutes."

"No repetition?"

"None that we heard. Didn't repeat himself once." Kim One held up her comm unit. "We can check the recording."

Russell glared at Chaudhari. "What are you two talking about?"

"Congratulations Sergeant Russell. You successfully complained, without stopping, for thirty-nine minutes."

"I don't believe you. Even I can't whine that long."

Kim One held up her comm. "Timer says otherwise, Sergeant."

"Shut up." Russell looked at the redheaded child. "Who's this?"

"This." Chaudhari pointed. "This is Rene. He'll be your rebel bandit for today. Rene, say hello to the nice sergeant."

The redheaded kid rolled his eyes. "He's not nice. He complained for like an hour."

"Only thirty-nine minutes. That's why I called him nice."

"Whatever. Do you have food?"

"Lots," Russell said. "Want some?"

"Yes, please. May I join your gang?"

"We're not a gang."

"You have guns, and you use them to get food from people. That's a gang."

"We're not a gang."

Chaudhari shrugged. "By his definition, we kinda are. Sergeant, Rene will show us where his bandit people are and help us sneak up on them and capture them."

Russell crossed his arms. "He will, will he. When did he say this?"

"We had a chat, him and I, while we were listening to your rant."

"It wasn't a rant."

"Kinda was. Raise hands who thinks it was a rant." Chaudhari made eye contact with the squad. They all raised their hands. "Rant it is."

Russell grimaced. "Fine. Kid, you'll tell us where your friends are, how to get there."

"They're not my friends. I hate them. I haven't eaten in

two days. They only feed me every other day."

"If they only feed you every two days, then why join up?"

"It was a step up. At the plant, we only ate every three days."

"Well, I do like young people with some ambition. You'll show us where they are, how to capture them?"

"Sure."

"What type of weapons do they have?"

"Half dozen revolvers. A shotgun."

"Anything else?"

"Nope."

Chaudhari rubbed his hands. "We can use the mortar!"

"No, we can't."

"Gotta keep 'em from retreating."

"Retreat where? Kid, where will they go if we fight them?"

"My name is Rene."

"I know that. I also don't care. How will your friends fight? Where will they go?"

"Nowhere far. They sneak down to the factory, steal food at night. They try not to fight much."

"Why not?"

"Too hungry. I'm not the only one got fed every other day."

"Why didn't the factory feed you?"

"I wasn't part of the corp. My parents were Free Traders who had worked at the plant."

"Where are they now?"

"Dead. Killed in the fighting in the city."

"Sorry to hear that."

"You didn't kill them."

Russell shut up. He might have. He got directions to the bandit camp, a few miles away, a list of weapons, numbers, everything he wanted. "Right, get ready to move out. Keep red boy tied up till we get there. You understand it will go badly with you if things aren't as you say?"

"Can I eat first so I don't die hungry?"

The squad moved out. Chaudhari came up next to Russell, leading his mule. "I thought you liked geology?"

"I did. I do. It's interesting."

"And Mr. Drossong? Was he that bad?"

"My favorite teacher. Dedicated, hardworking, knowledgeable. A credit to the profession."

"But you told him to drive a bread truck?"

"Bread needs to be delivered. And I hate everybody. Any thoughts on this attack?"

"Use the mortars."

"We don't need mortars to capture starving rebels."

"We might."

"No."

"You can't rule it out."

"I'll evaluate the situation when we get there and give you my decision."

"Thanks." Chaudhari rubbed his hands. "Oh boy. Boom. Boom." He grinned. "Boom."

CHAPTER 8

"There's nothing in this ship," the burglar said, digging through the cabinets.

"Nothing worth stealing, I know." Rajput settled into the lounge's chairs. "Which is why it wasn't locked up, and the code worked and we can steal it."

"Not what I mean."

The intercom cracked. "Ready to drop up in the control room, buddy."

Rajput pushed the intercom button. "Thank you. Carry on. And it's Vice President Rajput, please."

"Sure thing, Mr. Vice President Rajput. Want to come up and assist in undocking? You can bring those checklists of yours that you like so much, the ones you showed us."

"No, I'm sure a crew as competent as yours can handle this simple task. We'll intervene if it becomes necessary."

"Intervene? How you going to do that from the lounge, Mr. Vice President Rajput."

"We'll discuss it later. Undock and take us out."

"You did promise to provide us with a destination, Mr. Vice President Rajput."

"After we're undocked." Rajput killed the connection.

The burglar opened another cabinet. "You should have stolen the ship with a special team, not go into the local spacers market and pick up a scratch crew."

"At least that tug company had crew to hire." After their failed first burglary, Rajput had scurried back to cargo docks, chased down the local spacers, and found the crew of a tug who sent three people to help them move the nearly stolen ship for a fee. A substantial fee.

"That's why you're the executive and wear the nice

suit." The burglar opened another cabinet. "Hey, food trays, finally."

"You could stand to upgrade your wardrobe." Rajput unrolled his left sleeve and rerolled it. In an unconscious imitation of Jose, Rajput had replaced his TGI corporate coveralls with a dark business suit. Trouble was, the suit was too large and flopped over his mandatory skin suit. He'd had to roll up the sleeves and pant legs, and they wouldn't stay up—every ten minutes he was fixing them again.

"What's wrong with my wardrobe? Ow. Cold." The burglar tossed the food tray from hand to hand, then pushed it into the microwave and fussed with the buttons. "You said to make sure I didn't look like a TGI employee."

"But I didn't say to look like a rim refugee. Torn shirt and shorts?"

"I wear coveralls to work, and I don't have much of a budget for other clothes."

"You could have found something not so stained."

"Give me a raise to buy some new clothes, then."

"Maybe if this theft is successful."

"You work for that Mr. Jose guy, right?"

"Who told you that?"

"This microwave isn't working." The burglar hammered the buttons. "Cold trays for us. Everybody knows Mr. Jose. He's very impressive. The way he took on the Militia and handled those Free Traders. Smart guy. He should have done this himself."

"He's an executive now. A real one. He doesn't have time for this—he's keeping an eye on the Militia."

"Those Imperial dirt bags." The burglar produced a spoon from his pocket and hammered at his tray. "They deserve what they get. Hope he shoots them all."

"You do?"

"Sure. Things were nice and easy till that stupid Militia coup-thing. Now half of what we had before is burned or blown up. It's harder to get anything, and I heard we all would have starved to death if Mr. Jose and Mr. Dashi hadn't gotten things fixed."

"It's more complicated than that." Rajput said, "But he does win a lot. You like him?"

"Dashi and his people—Jose and Stewart, the other one. They're on our side. They want something done, something stolen. I don't ask too many questions. They're smarter than me." He hit the microwave. "And I'm just a burglar."

"Will there be any food?"

The burglar slammed his tray. "It's frozen solid. Can't even pry it out. I'll get some basic. Add 'nonfrozen food' to your checklists."

Rajput brought up his checklist on his comm. "I'll do that. We'll know the next time I steal a ship."

"You really going to put that on your checklist?"

Rajput tapped, then sighed. "I like checklists. Checklists help me relax. Keep me organized. Let me know when I'm finished."

"That's boring."

"So? It's why I'm an executive now because I follow checklists."

All the power died. Lights went out, fans stopped, engines died, anything electric failed.

The burglar's voice came out of the dark. "Is a total power failure on your list?"

"Not completely out of fuel," the intercom voice said. "But not enough to run the main engines."

"We were in the dark here," Rajput said. "No lights at all."

"Took a while to switch over. Didn't you turn on your helmet lights?"

Rajput unclicked the intercom and waved to the burglar. The burglar picked up his helmet and examined it. A tap on one side and a spotlight spun out, illuminating the entire compartment. "That's cool. Forgot that was there. Haven't had a helmet on in so long."

Rajput clicked the intercom back on. "You could have told us we didn't have enough fuel."

"Enough for what? You didn't give us a destination, remember?"

"You could have said that we didn't have any fuel at all."

"We do have fuel. Enough to run life support for weeks after we cut the main engines out of the system. We're fine for now."

The burglar was playing with his helmet—spotlight on, spotlight off, spotlight on, spotlight off. Rajput screwed his eyes shut and cut the intercom. "Stop that."

"The light?"

"Yes, the light. Stop playing with your suit. Eat a tray or something."

"They're frozen—"

"Then pry them off or freeze your lips. Stop flashing me with that light." Rajput pushed the intercom button. "Fine for now? Are you planning on sitting here for a few weeks?"

"We get paid either way. So, yeah, sitting around isn't that bad. I've had worse gigs."

Rajput ground his teeth. "We need to get to a TGI station. Transfer-five is the closest."

"That's where you want to go? Transfer-five?"

"Yes."

"That wasn't so hard, was it?"

"Just tell me how we get there."

"Well, we could be there in two hours, if we had fuel."

"Yes. How can we get fuel?"

"At the station we could have got it pumped on, now that we've dropped and are drifting, we can either get a tug to refuel us, or have the tug tow us back in—"

"Which is faster?"

"Stand by."

The burglar pried a piece of frozen mush from his tray and chewed it. "Don't you mean which is cheaper?"

"We need to get out of here before the Militia notices us stealing a ship."

"Tugs are expensive, even I know that."

"Thanks for reminding me."

"Tug companies as well. Surprised that there's a commercial company working out of a Militia station. Can't be much work here."

"And you base that on your extensive tug experience?"

"Well, you know, when I was younger, thought of being a tug pilot. Till the injury—"

"I don't need to hear that right now." The intercom flashed at Rajput. "What?"

"Fuel requirements on the way to your comm. As well as a recommendation for a tug company to deliver the fuel and get us started. And a truly awesome billing charge, plus extra for immediate dispatch, plus—"

"Just send me the bottom line."

"Sending." He paused. "Should be there. Will you authorize the charges, Mr. Vice President Rajput?"

Rajput compressed his lips as he read the amount. "Call them. Do it."

"On their way."

Rajput hammered the intercom off. "Dead Emperor's rotting toenails." He raved for two minutes, spitting curses.

The burglar grabbed the comm and examined the amount. "Wow. That's a lot."

Rajput continued to curse.

"You know, when I was younger—"

"Yes. Yes, I know." Rajput yelled. "When you were younger, you often thought of being a food tray, or a fork until the accident. And you thought maybe that there was a better way. But you didn't tell anybody till afterwards because you were a food tray or a hatch cover. And you always wanted to be a hatch cover, but you couldn't because of the accident. Shut up about your accident. Look, I'm sick. Sick of your after-the-fact complaining and second guessing. All you do is sit there and bad talk every idea I have. So, shut up. Just shut up. Try to do something useful for a change rather than just telling me what you would have done. Got it? Got it?"

The burglar blinked, pried another piece of frozen mush from his tray and chewed on it.

"Well?" Rajput asked.

The burglar swallowed, then gulped some air. "Sure boss, whatever you say."

"No more doom talking, no more complaining, no more stupid comments."

"Got it."

"Good. Now, do you have anything useful to say? Remember, these tug people are coming here whether we want them to or not."

"I'm sure they'll do a good job boss."

"They better."

"And the price—well, it's an emergency. And TGI—I know you work for TGI—has plenty of money, right?"

"Right."

"So, we'll get there with the ship, a new cutter, like you wanted, right?"

"Exactly."

"So, it's all good, really."

"Very good, right?"

The burglar nodded, then chewed for a long time. Rajput watched him in silence. "Well?"

"What boss?"

"What else?"

"Does there have to be something else?"

"With you, there always is."

"Well, this getting the cutter and the fuel and all that. It's done, so that's what you wanted, right?"

"Yes."

"But this was supposed to be a secret, wasn't it?"

"Yes."

"So, you see, boss." the burglar swallowed the last of the frozen mush. "Did you see who owns the tug company coming for us?"

Rajput knew he was in trouble when Jose met them at the air lock.

"Rajput. You're here . . . and you brought . . . friends."

The burglar waved. "Hello Mr. Jose."

"You're the burglar."

"We brought you a ship."

"The shell of a ship," Jose said. Four figures in dark blue skin suits and matching coveralls exited the ship behind them. "Hello."

"Mr. Jose?"

"Yes, are you Mr . . . . Sigmunds?"

"Second Lieutenant Sigmunds, actually." Sigmunds pulled a handful of patches from his thigh pocket and snapped them onto his coveralls. "We don't wear the rank tags when we're doing our civilian work."

Rajput's mouth dropped open. "You're Militia?"

"Militia reserve technically."

"But I hired a civilian company . . ."

"You sure did—and at a great price, I might say. We're going to get a big bonus for this trip, right, boys and girls?" The three other crew members with Sigmunds cheered. One of the women clapped. All busied themselves placing their own patches."

"You're all military?"

"Militia reserve I told you. One weekend a month for training, a few weeks a year. Rest of the time we have regular jobs."

"But, but—"

Jose crossed his arms. "How is it that on-duty Militia personnel are crewing civilian ships?"

"What makes you think we're on duty?"

Jose pointed at the coveralls, now revealed to be standard Militia issue. "You appear to be donning uniforms. Uniforms can only be worn on duty."

"We're not on duty." One of the women twisted her long hair into a bun and settled it on her head. "Not yet. We're getting ready to be on duty."

"On duty where?"

"The transport cutter is docking here in a couple hours. We're going to be the relief crew. Part of it anyway."

"The Militia transport cutter?"

"Sure." The woman fussed with her hair some more, then settled a soft cap on her head. "The station-to-station courier, carries personnel, packages, you know, crew reporting to new duty stations, dead head crew, high-value parts that need to be expedited, that sort of thing. How do I look?"

"Outstanding." Sigmunds settled his own cap. "Tribune Jose, here's your ship. Your man Rajput here already authorized payment, so we'll expect that in the normal course of events. I have to say, I appreciate your honesty in all of this."

"Our honesty?"

"Well, once we found out this was a personal project, not a corporate thing, we expected that you would want a discount. But when we called Major Shutt, the admiral's assistant, she said that someone of your integrity wouldn't stand for it and that we should charge you the full mill rate, no discounts."

"You called Major Shutt?"

"Yep. Your folks here didn't seem to have much paperwork, so we double-checked with headquarters. She was surprised when we called her, but she looked it up and said it had all been authorized to transfer a surplus cutter to you for your operations. Sent us the details and everything."

"I see," Jose said. "But how did you know that I was involved."

All four pointed at the burglar. "He told us."

Jose glared at the burglar.

The burglar grinned. "Just talking boss."

"Indeed," Jose said. "Well, you have a ship to catch. You wouldn't want to be late."

Sigmunds saluted Jose, the full formal cross-chest salute. "The Empire."

"The Empire," Jose agreed.

The burglar saluted back. Sigmunds slapped him on the shoulder. "You in the service, buddy?"

"No."

"Only serving members in uniform salute. Otherwise, it looks stupid."

"I was going to be in the Militia," the burglar said. "I was thinking of joining, but after my accident—"

"No time, sorry. Crew-237—let's get moving." The four Militia trooped off.

The burglar watched them go. "I could have—"

"Please be quiet," Jose said.

"But—"

"Don't talk." Jose looked at the lock. "We have a Militia cutter."

"Yes, sir," Rajput said.

"But with no fuel?"

"The tug brought us this way."

"Anything else?"

"The entire heating system is shot. Circuits are disrupted, and they scavenged all of the heaters from the ship."

"I see. Other life support?"

"Minimal. The pumps are . . ."

"Missing. Stripped. Removed."

Rajput nodded. "Right."

"In fact"—Jose tapped through the screens by the lock. All showed red—"in fact, it appears that every spare part on this ship has been removed. The whole ship had been cannibalized for repairs, which is why it wasn't secured by

Militia Service Police. They didn't care if anyone stole it or not because it was so worthless."

"We thought the ship itself would be worth something."

"I wanted a cutter that I could use to train crew, practice weapons, make some sort of impact. Instead, I've got a hulk that is missing most of its components, can't move under its own power and isn't even livable."

"Sorry, sir. I'll do better next time." Rajput typed on his comm.

"What"—Jose lowered his voice—"what are you doing?"

"Updating my checklists, sir."

"Your checklists?"

"Yes, sir. My ship stealing checklists. Steps to take. I'm adding take an inventory of what's missing."

"You think you should stop in the middle of a theft and take inventory?"

"Well—"

"Where does that step go? Between 'see if we freeze to death' and 'plan to starve to death from no food'?"

"Um. I put it after checking for old socks or sweaters in the lockers."

"Old clothes? Socks?"

The burglar spoke up. "See Mr. Jose, we can hunt around the ship to find discarded clothes, then use them to cover our hands, and that way, if the ship is frozen, we won't have to freeze."

"Or you could just bring gloves," Jose said. "Which you should have for your suits regardless."

"That's a great idea," the burglar said. "Isn't that a great idea, Rajput? That's why he's the boss. Great idea."

Rajput gritted his teeth but kept quiet.

"I've got a hulk of a spaceship that I paid a fortune for," Jose said. "Crewed by the most incompetent thieves anyone has ever employed, and the Militia and Major Shutt know all about this, so any possibility of deception is gone.

How could this day possibly get worse?"

A figure stuck her head through the entrance door. "Oh, good, you're here. Which one of you is Mr. Jose."

Jose raised his hands. "Can I help you?"

"Yep. Gotta sign here for docking fees, power connections, security, trash, suchlike. Did you negotiate a contract beforehand."

"We did not."

"Gonna be day rates then. Expensive." The clerk shoved the comm at Jose. "Taking up a complete class-D air lock. Very, very expensive."

CHAPTER 9

"Sweet Pea is worried about this, Sergeant," Kim One said. "She thinks we can't trust those people."

"Donkeys cannot talk." Sergeant Russell ducked under a tree branch. He and Kim One slid through the forest to the rebel camp. Closely spaced trees made them leave the donkeys behind.

"It's more of a mystic connection, Sergeant."

"Wonderful. Psychic Donkeys."

"She's a mule, Sergeant, not a donkey."

"Course she is."

"And she isn't psychic. She can't predict the future or read your mind."

"Too bad. Then she'd know that every time I see her I think steaks, rare, with potatoes."

"You won't eat Sweet Pea, Sergeant! She's my friend!"

"I might."

"I'll stop you!"

"How?"

Kim One pushed a branch aside. "I'll find a way."

"I'd like to see that."

SNAP. Kim released the branch, and it smacked Russell in the face. He cursed, flipped bark and leaves out of his ear, and shoved through.

Then froze. Kim One had her gun out. It wasn't pointing at him, but it was in her hand. And her face was red, and her eyes glittered.

Russell eyed the gun, then her face. Her eyes narrowed.

Russell considered. On the one hand, he was twice her mass, an experienced fighter—and of a mean disposition. She was tiny and skinny, even for a woman. If he got that gun in his hand, he'd be fine.

On the other, she and Kim Two, unsuccessful at quieting a prisoner, had tied him up and kicked him repeatedly in the balls until he shut up. After that, she stormed an orbital station, followed him to the southern continent with an escaped Militia officer, and attacked Empire Rising rebel group members. He wouldn't be the first Militia person she'd shot.

And, he remembered, her arrival in his squad had been a bit irregular. A transfer without a lot of details—he might not be the first sergeant she'd shot, either.

"Put that gun away."

"Are you going to hurt Sweet Pea?"

Russell shook his head. "I was only kidding. I'm tired, angry, and frustrated. Sorry. I won't hurt your friend."

"Promise?"

"I promise."

"Okay." She holstered her revolver and marched on.

Russell followed behind her. "That's it? I could be lying."

"You never lie. If you promise not to shoot her, you won't."

"I never lie?"

"Never. The squad all know it. We think it's weird."

"Huh. I'm too honorable to lie?"

"We all think you're too lazy to make stuff up."

Russell nodded. "That works. I am lazy. But I'm still tired, angry, and frustrated."

"Me too, Sergeant. This march-or-die thing is hard."

"It is. I want to shoot somebody."

"Me, too."

"Well, if these rebel types give us any backtalk, I'll let you shoot one of them."

"Thank you, Sergeant."

"You know, Kim One, I'm glad you volunteered for this."

"Me too, Sergeant. Sweet Pea said I should."

"I'm glad Sweet Pea did that."

"And Chaudhari said I should keep an eye on you."

"Keep an eye on me?"

"Remind you of all the things that he told you to do."

"What things?"

"Corporal Chaudhari said he talked to you and made all sorts of suggestions about how to conduct negotiations and have people surrender without violence."

"He did?"

"Do you remember them?"

"Not all of them. I should have written them down."

They stumbled through another thicket and emerged into a clearing. Russell wiped leaf crud from his eyes to see where they'd arrived. Which turned out to be right next to twenty armed rebels, sitting around a fire. By the piles of plates, they'd been eating. By the guns in their hands they had heard Russell and Kim.

"Hello," Russell said, raising his hands. "We're the Militia. Surrender or die."

The man in front pointed a shotgun at Russell's face. "What?"

Russell kept his hands up. "I said if you surrender now we won't kill you."

The man in front kept the shotgun pointed at them. "There's only two of you."

"There's only two of us here right now. Lots more behind us. Your choice. You're all going to die if you don't let us go."

"That makes no sense. Even if you have somebody with you, we'd kill you before they could rescue you."

Russell looked at Kim One, who also had her hands up. "Did I mess this up?"

"You were supposed to try negotiation."

"Right." Russell turned to the man. "Let's negotiate."

"Negotiation was supposed to come first," Kim One said.

"Got the order wrong. I should have written that

down. Look, sorry, we're from the Empire, the Militia, the government, ummmm . . . do you want some food?"

The crowd behind stirred at the mention of food. The camp was in good repair, with houses and a warehouse. But the people were all skinny, and the warehouse was empty.

The lead man lowered his gun. "We want some food. Maybe we'll trade your corpses for food."

Kim One dropped her arms. "What is this place? You have houses and storage—and did you build that bridge?"

The river narrowed here, and somebody had constructed the sturdy wooden truss bridge across it. It was wide enough to take four persons abreast, had a parapet, railings, and reinforced piers. It was scuffed and covered with dirt, and some of the truss pieces were obvious replacements.

"Imperial Boy Scout Camp. There's an old road that goes up into the mountains. It was for lumber originally. Then it was abandoned, but the scouts built the bridge to let them hike up the road and these shelters to stay in while they were camping. In the winter."

"People camp voluntarily?" Russell asked. "In the woods? In the winter?"

"Sure. Takes all kinds."

"It does." Russell dropped his arms as well. "We caught your kid. That's how we snuck up on you. We know you don't like the people at this GG-33 place. I don't care. We don't, either. Want to join up with us?"

"With you? But we're rebels?"

Russell shrugged. "Against who? Not me. Long as you don't rebel against me, you're citizens. We're going to march down to that station, help load up a factory and ship it out on boats or ships—those water things."

"Then what happens to the factory?"

"Beats me. Close down, I guess. Nothing for you to raid for food after that, that's for sure. Why don't you come with us? We'll feed you, you help load things up, be on our side if there's any unpleasantness with the station people, and we'll take care of you. Food, and we'll take you with us on the ships when we leave."

"I've never been on a ship," shotgun man said.

Russell took off his hat and rubbed his hair. "You'll hate it. You get sick, you puke, you feel like you're dying, you slither around in your own vomit, sleep in it, and feel like you're going to die."

"And when you leave the dock," Kim One said. "It gets even worse."

The man uncocked his shotgun. "We're not rebels. We're just hungry, and things at that factory aren't so good. They'll probably want to leave with you."

"Outstanding. Now I have to evacuate an entire town."

Kim laughed. "You joined the Militia for challenges, Sergeant."

Russell made a lewd gesture with his hands. "I got your challenge right here. Do we have a deal?"

"We can keep our guns?"

"Keep your guns and anything you can carry from here. Show us the quickest way to this factory. Help us load up. Anybody shoots at us, you shoot back—you're with us. Help us load some ships. We'll feed you the whole time, get you a spot on the ships, take you to Landing, discharge you there. Once we're in Landing, you're on your own, but I will put in a good word with the Militia recruiting people if you're so inclined, but no promises. I don't have any control on that."

The shotgun man's crew were nodding. "We agree! We're with you!" His people cheered and chanted "Food! Food!"

Russell turned to Kim. "How about that?"

"Sergeant, they're going to—"

The bandit crew danced and pointed guns up in the air. "Food! Food!"

"Don't do that."

BANG. The bandits shot in the air.

"Emperor's kneecaps," Russell said. "Why'd you have to do that?"

Kim One cursed and dropped flat, hands over her head.

"Do what?" shotgun man asked.

"Shoot up like that." Russell dropped to his knees, then lay full length on the ground, cupping his hands over his head. "I left instructions on what my people were supposed to do if they heard shooting. All of you might want to get down."

"Why?"

A mortar round whistled down from above, impacted one of the huts, and blew splintered wood across the clearing as it exploded.

"To try to stay alive."

***

Marianne checked her holster as she left the ship. Satisfied, she gestured to everyone to start walking.

"Do you expect fighting, shipmaster?" the young woman next to her said.

Marianne checked the cylinders—all loaded. "Not precisely. But I do expect there to be some . . . noise. So, the more willing we are to look tough, the less likely we are to act tough."

"Act tough?" Sikar scrunched up her brow. She was a third cousin of Marianne, foisted on her by Captain LaFerme. Taller than her, dark haired, and serious, with a disapproving facial expression, she looked like she mistrusted everyone she met. Somebody you wanted to grab by the hair and slap some sense into.

Marianne had asked the council for an aide. Captain LaFerme had provided this youngster.

Captain Mathieu had sent more wine.

"It is better to threaten violence, than to do it."

"Why?"

"Because it takes less effort to threaten, and you can

always back down or modify a threat if you get what you want, if need be. More efficient that way. If you start with violence, you have nowhere else to go."

"What if they don't believe you will get violent?" Sikar asked.

Marianne stopped her. She snagged Sikar's ear and pulled it close. Sikar squawked, so Marianne yanked tighter.

"Do I look like somebody who keeps my promises to you?"

"Yes, shipmaster."

Marianne shoved Sikar away. "And so will I to them. D'accord?"

"D'accord."

Marianne marched on. One of her crew stepped up beside Marianne. "But why don't you expect violence, shipmaster?"

Marianne waved behind her. Two full over strength crews marched behind her. Twenty-five Traders—most in the uniform of the Imperial Legion—Legio X Sigma Draconis. "We have two ships' worth of crews, all armed, looking competent and angry. We will assume control of this station."

"But won't they fight for it?"

"Fight for what? It's not theirs to start with. It belonged to some corporation whose leaders got themselves killed or arrested during the rebellion. They work here. Maybe some are stockholders, but not many. It's not like they're all one family. This is a job for them. They can find another."

"What if they do fight?"

"Then, we fight back. Quickly, aggressively, and we win."

"Won't your boyfriend be upset if you do that?"

Marianne grinned. "My boyfriend?"

"Tribune Jose. Everybody says he's your boyfriend."

"We are good friends. He will do many things for me.

87

I'm not sure he will give me an entire station."

"Even if you ask nicely?"

"Even if I ask very, very nicely. Getting him to give me a station, is a stretch. But you know what they say. It's easier to get forgiveness than permission."

"What?" Sikar said. "That's, that's not right."

"Are you related to Captain LaFerme?"

"Yes. How do you know?"

Marianne snorted. "I can see the resemblance. I will call you Chip. An expression in Standard. Chip off the old block. Means the same as something else. You remind everybody of Captain LaFerme."

"I volunteered to be here," Sikar said. "When Captain LaFerme offered, I took it right away. I fight for the honor of the Free Traders."

"Is that so?" Marianne nodded. "Honor?"

Sikar grinned. "And some fun and excitement."

"The Free Trader's honor. And fun and excitement. Well." Marianne smiled. "Perhaps there is hope for you yet."

Marianne rounded the corner of the corridor and entered an office labeled 'Station main office.'

A dozen workers were sitting at desks, typing, reading, drinking coffee, or gossiping. They all stopped and gaped as more than twenty Free Traders crowded in.

"Who is in charge here?" Marianne called.

An elderly man in dusty coveralls stood at the back. "For my sins, I am. I'm Administrator Lee Higgers. You folks off those two Free Traders that just docked?"

"We are. I am Legate Marianne. We have been appointed by the council to take over control of this station, to coordinate the shipments of goods received, items produced, and take control of the shipyard and the mine here."

"Shipyard? You mean the four repair trusses?"

"Those are the ones, yes."

"Not the biggest repair docks in the system."

"They fit smaller cargo ships, don't they?"

"Small cargo ships," Higgers said. "But I guess that's what you Free Traders have, small cargo ships."

"We will shortly be upgrading them to dock more ships."

"Plenty of room to dock ships," Higgers said. "Getting staff or parts to work on them is another thing."

"You have printers here and a nickel mine, do you not?"

"Sure. Great mine. Lots of variety, but not much quantity, if you know what I mean. We produce a little of everything. Mostly nickel, but also iron, some chromium, and cobalt, all sorts of stuff. Not great amounts, though. I thought we were going to be shut down."

"Variety is more important to us—to the council, then the actual quantity."

"Uh-huh. To the council. Got it. Should I be contacting the council to ask about this?"

Marianne crossed her arms. "I'm telling you that it is this way. Do you recognize me?"

"You're that war leader—the legion lady."

"Legio X Sigma Draconis."

"Sure. The council is still going to pay us. We need to eat, you know."

"Of course, of course. You will continue at your current salary, perhaps a small bonus."

"Uh-huh."

"Are any of you shareholders?"

"Everyone on the station," Higgers said. "All of us."

"Everyone?" Marianne's eyes widened. "All of you."

"Sure. I've got ten shares, Sashi there"—he pointed—"has, what five?"

The woman at the desk next to the door held up seven fingers. "Inherited my Mom and Dad's when they died."

"The rest have one or two. Most of us have something. Why are you asking about shares."

"No reason."

"We don't get much out of them. It's a big corporation, and we're a small station. But they count for something."

"We can work something out."

"Of course. Well, what does this appointed control mean, in practice?"

"Your people stay at your jobs. Continue what you are doing. We will assign our people to work with them. To learn your jobs. How many people work here?"

"About a third, maybe half on a good day," Higgers said. Everyone laughed.

"We will see if we can change that," Marianne said. She smiled at the office crew. "One way, or another."

CHAPTER 10

"You have to admit," Chaudhari said. "It was great shooting."

"You're an idiot and I hate you." Russell adjusted the bandage on his head, then pulled the bridle off his mule. "Let's go, SPD."

"That's a stupid name for a mule. And it was great shooting. We took that bridge out with one shot!"

"Kim One named her mule after something she liked, so I named mine after something I like." Russell scanned the trail ahead. They were finally on the eastern side of the river, following along the banks. Scanning their maps, they looked for a creek to climb up to the interior tablelands and cut across the peninsula and down into GG-33. "Pass the word that it's steep here, no more than one mule at a time climbing down."

"And one person?"

"Any person who wants to roll down the hill and crash into the river, be my guest. Just don't hurt the mules. I've got more people than mules right now."

Chaudhari gave instructions to the rest of the squad, and they waited on the ridge as Russell climbed down behind SPD. The mule wasn't as surefooted as he expected, and eventually, he just threw the bridle over the pack and jogged down behind it. When they reached the bottom, the mule detoured to the river and drank. Russell followed, patted its haunches and waited as the rest of the squad arrived behind him. In line behind them, the fourteen bandits who had decided to come with them climbed down. Out of twenty, he had sent two ahead as scouts. Two had disappeared the third night, and two had gotten in a fight, the details of which still escaped him. One knifed his friend in full view of twenty people, then threatened a squad member, who shot him dead at Russell's direction. After that, none of the new members even exchanged harsh words.

Nobody was to kill anybody without his explicit order.

Chaudhari arrived. "We're making good progress. Should be in town in two days."

"We'd have been there two weeks ago if you hadn't blown up that stupid bridge."

"With my first shot, too! I still say it was great shooting!"

"Were you aiming for the bridge?"

"Nope. Aiming to your left. But we adjusted. We were on target by the third round."

Russell pointed at his bandage. He'd been hit by shrapnel from the third mortar round. "Was I your target?"

"Scott, you told us that you would hide in the woods and observe, and if you were attacked, you'd fire three shots in a row, and we were to shell the town to cover your escape. You weren't supposed to be in the middle of them."

"You could have checked."

"You could have called on the radio."

Russell grimaced. "Should have. Got a little caught up in the action."

"All's well that ends well."

"We'll be two weeks late getting to that factory. I've got two troopers injured—one of which is me—and twenty, well, sixteen extra mouths to feed."

"You'll sort it out."

"I don't really do this. I kill people and break things."

"No, you don't," Chaudhari said.

"What? I do. That's the Militia's job."

Chaudhari waved the other mules to the river, where they could drink. The soldier-farmer types had shown them all how to let the animals drink and hobble them loosely so they could eat. They split into groups, pitching tents, digging a latrine, collecting water, and a dozen other camp tasks. "Not anymore. Maybe before. Why did you let me play with that mortar?"

"Because I'm an idiot with a death wish?"

"Because you didn't know how to use a mortar."

"Should I?"

"The Militia isn't about fighting, or it wasn't. We were firefighters, technicians, laborers, police, that sort of thing. Remember that antiair missile that Roi tried to shoot the shuttle down with?"

Russell did remember the rogue Empire Rising officers attempt to blow up a shipment of critical spare parts. "I stopped him, remember? A lot of good it did me."

"Right. Well, neither of us had ever touched one of those missiles. We'd only seen videos. Same with that mortar. If that supply clerk hadn't misread my orders, we wouldn't have got this. I doubt there're a half dozen of these on the planet, and we've got probably twenty percent of the planetary ammunition. And we'll never see another of Roi's missiles again."

"We might, but I get your point. What does it have to do with us?"

"Things are changing. Before the abandonment we were like a discount police force and a way for discharged Imperial officers to hang with friends and drink beer and talk about old times. Now, who knows? We've done more strange things in the last while than ever before. Boarded stations, fought on them. Marched in the woods."

"Rebuilt bridges that incompetent subordinates blew up."

"Conscripted civilians who were bandits into the Militia. Managed a mule train of supplies."

"Learned how to sew my own scalp back on after shrapnel from same incompetent subordinates nearly blew my head off."

"Yeah, I'm kind of sorry about that. Look, all I'm saying is that things are changing. Why'd Shutt give you this job?"

"Because I'm mean and angry?"

"Because you're flexible. When she gives you a mission, you accomplish it, whatever it takes. Even if you have to learn new skills, like sewing your own scalp back on. Think about that. It's not like it was before."

"What do you mean?"

"Everything is different now. The Empire Rising people wanted things to go back to the way they were. No chance of that. Everything is different now. This is your time. Make the most of it."

"I'm not doing anything except what I'm ordered to."

"All I'm saying is that the troops and I will support you, whatever you want. You're not just a mean angry guy. You're an intelligent, thoughtful, flexible mean angry guy."

One of the bandits came to speak to them. He took one look at Russell's glowering face and turned around and walked away.

Russell scratched his chin. "But I like being mean and angry."

A day later, they were climbing down from the hills above the factory, GG-33. The original highly detailed satellite survey of Delta was old—almost a thousand years old, but mountains don't move that often. The creek they were following had migrated north, but overlaying recent orbital pictures onto the mapping software meant that they were never lost.

The path down from the hills to the coast was obvious. Wild bison used it to access the creek and its water and to move up and down the mountain as the weather changed.

"Beautiful flowers, Sergeant," Kim One said, at the front with Sweet Pea leading the way.

"I hate flowers," Russell said automatically. He sniffed the meadow. "Strike my last. Those flowers are pretty. And smell good." Waist-high dark green bushes with bright red blossoms littered the hillside. Between them, fields of grass glittered with yellow blooms. Every dozen feet, bluish white blooms adorned scrub trees. Clusters of two-foot-high stalks covered with hundreds of tiny red blooms swayed in the wind.

"I've never seen anything like this," Russell said.

"I grew up in a stop like this on the monorail line. The flowers bloom every six weeks. It's always fun to be out here." Kim stumbled and grasped Sweet Pea's shoulder to hold herself up.

"I told you that you weren't ready to march yet."

"I'm fine, Sergeant. It was only the one piece of shrapnel."

"If you want, I'll let you beat on Chaudhari for blowing you up."

"He was doing his best, Sergeant. And you told him to do it. Shouldn't I beat on you for ordering it?"

"Shut up," Russell said. But he smiled when he said it.

Their trail zigzagged across the meadow. It was too steep to go straight down, so they were switchbacking down the four hundred meters to the plain below. GG-33 and its buildings were visible in the far distance, near the ocean. Delta's settlements were where a river crossed into the World Ocean. River bottoms were where the flatlands lay. Water was necessary for the crops, and the ocean provided fish and algae. Most settlements had been overpopulated before the recent rebellion, but the fights between the Empire Rising, corporate security troops, Free Trader Legions, and various Militia factions had thinned things out. But with the damage to transportation infrastructure, getting food to people was still a problem. Supplies and spare parts to the factories was an increasing issue.

"Can we eat these plants?"

"Nope. But we can cut down trees for lumber. And if the factory is working, we can feed everybody. Everything else is the problem. Parts, supplies, clothes, and machines, that all comes from Landing. On the monorail. I guess now it will come by boat."

"Easy place to defend," Russell said. "If we put competent troops up by the bridge and at that river."

"Unless they landed by shuttle," Kim One said.

"There's a limited number of shuttles on this moon," Russell said. "And if they land here, we don't have a mass driver, so they can't launch again. Big waste of a shuttle to land here. That lifting body thing could do it, but only if the tide was right, and it only carries a hundred people, maybe less. Interesting."

"What's interesting, Sergeant?" Kim asked.

"Never mind. I see the scouts up ahead. Let's find out what they have to say."

"What do you mean, nobody there?" Russell asked the scout.

"All gone. The housing is cleared out, the factory's empty. Company store is cleared out, too. Most everything is gone. Stuff too heavy to carry is still there."

"They can't have just left . . ."

"They did."

"How many were there living there? When you were here."

"Couple hundred, maybe a thousand in its heyday—but that was years ago. Lots of people left after the monorail got bust. Specialists and the like—technicians, those types who fixed the machines. They traveled a lot, and without the monorail . . ."

Russell queried the second scout and got the same story. They had walked past the town down to the water. There weren't any water ships there, either.

"There were supposed to be ships."

"Two weeks ago, there were supposed to be ships." Chaudhari said. "Bet they came and left."

"Shutt said she's sending ships."

"Her ships, or did she hire them because if she hired them, they might have taken a better offer to take all those people back, all at once, with a bunch of equipment."

"But why now?"

"You said Shutt had arranged to buy up the factory—maybe they didn't want to work for the Militia, maybe they didn't think the place was going to be viable, maybe they thought we would shut things down, and they'd be left here to starve. A couple ships show up, take a few hundred passengers, the rest hike up along the coast to the monorail bridge. We wouldn't see them."

"Our way was shorter."

"Only if our bridge was working. Which it wasn't."

Russell glared at the scout. "Did your comm work?"

"Don't have one." The man shrugged. "Never needed it. Lived in the housing. Worked at the plant. My friends were all in town. Didn't need a comm."

"Where did your friends go?"

"My friends left months ago, after the first disruption. I was stupid to stay. They fired me. No work. I didn't have any money to get on the monorail and no family in Landing, either. So, I hung around here—they let me stay for free, but no food unless I worked. Some of us tried to go hunting out in the bush."

"And?"

"It's a lot harder in reality than in the vids. Winter came. Deetter and his boys froze to death—legs froze solid when they fell in the river, and we couldn't thaw them out fast enough. Buried them, came back to town. By then they were eighty percent closed. They didn't want me around causing trouble. I got run out at gunpoint. Me and the others snuck back in, stole some revolvers and food. Ran up to the woods. We've stayed there ever since, sneaking into town when we needed food. They can't guard all the warehouses, so after a while they left 'em open."

"How much food is left there?"

"Lots," the scout said. "Years. Remember, till the power went out, this was a major processing plant. Carrots, onions, algae, super-potatoes. There are fields and fields of them. The automated harvesters and planters mostly still work. They're solar. But I don't know how to do maintenance."

"This group of us." Russell waved. "Enough food for all of us there?"

"All like thirty of us? Sure. Enough for years and years. Even with what they loaded on the ships."

Russell yanked his mule. "Right. Everyone mount up. We're moving into town. We'll get shelter and we can eat there. I'll contact Shutt and get instructions."

"And ask her to send a ship to come pick us up."

"Sure. That. That, too." Russell nodded. "If that's what you really want."

CHAPTER 11

"So, how many do you think work here now, Legate?" Higgers climbed to the bottom of the stairs and turned spinward on the outer ring. "A half or a third?" Noisy crowds of people surged past them as the shift changed. He waved and called greetings to people.

"This is not to be made light of," Marianne said. "Important repairs are being held up. How far to the metal shop? I'm lost. Perhaps describe our route for us. Or the entire station."

"Three groups of spinning rings here. Alpha, Beta, Gamma, connected via a hub and cross-connects. Each group has an outer, a middle, and an inner ring. We're in ring Alpha, the bottom," Higgers said. "And the outer corridor, number one. So, ring Alpha-1. Alpha-1 is mixed residential and offices—anything where people spent lots of time and need gravity."

"Metal shops need gravity."

"Not as much. People like to eat, sleep, poop, and spill drinks on the floor the way nature intended. When they're working, they can adapt." Higgers pointed along the corridor. "Past where it disappears, we'll go back up the stairs to Alpha-2, the next ring coreward on the alpha stack. Then we take a cross connection through Beta-2, then antispinward to the metal shop. The level-2 rings— Alpha-2, Beta-2, Gamma-2, contain the repair and working shop. Beta-3, the outermost middle ring is where the cargo locks and docking trusses are."

"Where are the containers loaded?"

"Small ships chained off on a truss on Gamma-3 use their own air locks to move suited passengers down into centrally located air locks or hand carried small cargo in. Ships moving full containers don't even approach the station, they hover near a container park a kilometer away—the loose containers are netted or cabled together and orbiting separately from the station. There, they discharge full containers from their chain locks or collect new ones."

"We know how containers work, and how they are discharged," Marianne said. "We're Free Traders, we've been doing this for years."

"Yeah, but I'll bet you never came onto the station, did you? You dropped and picked up containers at the yards, probably refueled there, and you never spent any time moving around the station."

"I spent a great deal of time moving around the station," Marianne said. "In my younger days. Going from bar to bar. And avoiding old boyfriends."

"Why avoid old boyfriends?" Sikar asked.

"Because I had new boyfriends," Marianne said. "What about the other rings?"

Higgers frowned. "We've had issues there. Larger ships, like the drop-ship passenger carriers, maneuver to chain directly onto the last ring, number three. They maneuvered so that they docked in parallel with the ring. That way, as they took on the station's spin they both shared a common down and passengers could board easily. Of course, that made expanding the station difficult—since the 'side' of the ring was occupied by docking bays. No more rings on that side."

"Indeed." Marianne shoved past a group of chatting workers."

"We should make these work faster." Sikar made a fist. "Captain Mathieu would beat me if I didn't work hard enough."

"Capital punishment, always an excellent way to motivate technical workers," Higgers said. "Perhaps cut off their right arm?"

Higgers stopped at an air lock door. The light showed red, so he peered through the hatch. "Then threaten to cut off the other one too if they don't speed up?"

"Exactly." Sikar nodded.

"Suse," Higgers said into his comm. "Air lock twenty-two is acting up again. I've got a red, but nobody in it. Can you confirm the other side is aired? No hurry. We'll wait till you talk to them."

"We are in a hurry."

"To cut off arms? And I'm curious how you think a worker with one arm will work faster than a worker with two. Of course, you could go through with your threat of cutting off both arms, which will bring working efficiency to zero for that department."

Sikar huffed. "We would never allow an air lock to malfunction like this on one of our ships."

"How often do you use your air locks?" Higgers asked.

"How often? Every docking."

"Maybe once a week, you dock, everyone goes out to the station for their business, you lock up. They come back at end of shift, you stay a few days. Maybe do that for a few days. A duty cycle on an air lock is, what, one hundred thousand openings? You might do a hundred in a week, so that's a thousand weeks—twenty years, or longer. This air lock opens a hundred times a shift, every shift. Do the math."

"Even so, with regular maintenance—"

"We can't just grease it, kiddo. The hatch has warped, so it doesn't seal. To fix it, we'll have to either jam in some new seals, if they're even available, or grind one side down and build the other side up."

"It doesn't take long to replace a seal," Marianne said. "Not even a day."

"If you have a seal big enough." Higgers's comm beeped. "Confirmed? Thank you." Higgers popped a panel and pulled an override lever, then spun the hatch locking wheel open. The red light remained.

"What about these people?" Marianne pointed behind. A line was forming.

"More the merrier." Higgers waved them in. The group crowded in until the lock was filled shoulder to shoulder. "Have a lock on any of your ships that can fit thirty people, Trader?"

Sikar leaned back from a sweating bearded man. "Why even have a lock here?" There's no vacuum on either side."

"Not now. But a blowout somewhere, and you'll be happy to be able to segment sections of this station off. Even your tiny ships have an air lock to the bridge and one to engineering, in case something happens."

"Our ships are not tiny!"

Higgers grinned. "I did time on cutters when I was in the Militia. I thought those were tiny, and in terms of hab space, they're bigger than a lot of your ships. Free Traders are small. That's why the corps leave you alone." The last person in pulled the door behind them shut, and the light flashed green. Higgers spun the far hatch locking wheel open, stepped out, and waved everyone past. Marianne and Sikar stood there waiting while he conversed with the control center. He swung the hatch cover open and closed several times, checking, crossing some wires, and talking to control.

"Well, Trader Marianne, your first executive decision. Or shipmaster. You know, how about we call you Stationmaster—since the council put you in charge and all."

"Call me what you like. What's the problem?"

"Lock remote sensing isn't working. I can put it on local control here for now, disable the remote access, and the lights will report properly. Crews can move back and forth, and the doors will report properly. No greens unless both doors are shut."

"That sounds reasonable," Marianne said. "Why don't you do that."

"Well." Higgers cocked his head. "If I put them in local control, the main board in control won't know the status of the doors—whether they're opened or closed. And if they don't know the status, they can't remotely lock them, either. So, if there is a blowout, they'll have to send somebody down."

"No, keep full remote access," Marianne said.

"Which is broken, so the only way anybody will get through is to call up like I did and have the station override. And hope they turn the remote control back on after." Higgers stepped back as the lock door swung open, and another group of workers surged through. "We'll have to put up a sign or something."

"Call a repair crew," Marianne said.

"Our repair crews are fully occupied right now. I'll send you a list. You tell me which project to take them off of."

"Surely, this is higher priority than regular repairs."

"I agree. But you have to tell me which regular repair it's higher priority for."

"That's your job to decide."

"No problem. I can pick somebody." Higgers tapped through his comm. "I assume it's not any of the crews working on your ships you want reassigned. I'll pick another. Of course, while they're working on the lock, we'll have to shut off traffic through it."

A group of four station people in skin suits, carrying a small ship drive nozzle waddled by. They put it down while the leader spun the hatch open. Once the door was clear, they chambered in hauling the nozzle between them, then slammed the door shut.

Higgers pointed. "Metal shop is that way. Any parts need refurbishing, grinding, anything like that has to go there. By the way, there's only one other lock that takes us to this truss, and it's only two people. It wouldn't take that part. They'd have to haul it outside. Which takes ten times as long, of course."

"Which means that taking this lock out of service to be repaired, will make this truss nearly useless," Marianne said.

"Got it in one," Higgers said. "Of course, Legate, if you want to authorize pass-through on the lock . . ."

Marianne grimaced. Pass through meant both doors were latched open. Easy to transit, death if there was a blowout. "We will not be doing that. Suggestions?"

"The crew will be here in a few minutes. Right now, the lock is on local control. They can do a quick assessment. Maybe they'll find something I missed. Either way, they'll have proper tools and some parts, so they can give a good estimate for repairs."

"We'll wait for them," Marianne said.

The lock door banged open again, and a stream of delivery workers marched through with boxes and carts of food.

"Sure. That way, you can make your decision right away. On the spot leadership. This will make people feel good about the Free Traders taking over."

Marianne glared at him. "What's your guess as to what they say?"

"Not sure. But probably that the lock needs to be fully refurbed. If we put it in local control, it can be used and not fixed. If we shut it down to fix the remote circuits, we might as well fix a bunch of other stuff at the same time. That's what I think they'll say."

"But you don't know," Sikar said. "And you're just a maudit administrator. An administrative type. The corporate people we are always complaining about."

Marianne glared at Sikar, but Higgers laughed. "I don't know what maudit means, but it's probably not complementary. And yes, my job is administrative. I make these decisions every day. But I'll tell you two, I'm really, really glad that you're here and in charge now. You can figure these things out. I'm tired of it. I'm sure you ship-captain types will do a better job. I'm just an administrator.

What do I know?"

Higgers checked his comm. The repair team reported they were five minutes out, so he suggested waiting.

"You seem sure of the repair diagnostic they will give," Marianne said.

"Pretty sure, yeah."

"How long have you been in charge of this station?"

"Six years. My wife wanted to be closer to her grandkids, so here we are."

"What did you do before then?"

"Chief engineer on a big transport," Higgers said. "In charge of all the ship's maintenance. I came up through the ranks. I was trained as an electronics specialist."

Marianne raised her eyebrows. That was a technical job, and the classes were difficult to qualify for. Even Sikar looked impressed.

The air lock panel crackled, the display died, and a small wisp of smoke rose from the control panel.

"Oops," Higgers said. "Looks like the local control unit shorted out as well." He grinned at Marianne. "What should we do about that, Stationmaster?"

***

"We have no radios, no power, and no people," Russell said, walking around the empty factory's manager's office.

"Not exactly." Chaudhari pointed out the window. "We've got our squad, the sixteen others we brought with us—the rebels, bandits—whatever you want to call them. And they think there are a few more hiding in the woods trying to make a go for it."

"But no radios?"

"We don't have no radios. We have no long-range radios. Our comms work. We can talk to each other, line of sight, that sort of thing. But this is all space gear. Remember, no boosters."

"No, I don't remember. Boosters?" Russell looked out the office window. The bay opened up below the bluff.

Mud-brown beaches lined each shore, clouds rolled in from the ocean. Occasional shafts of sunlight made the bright blue water dazzle the eyes.

"In space, we talk to the ship or the station. Here, we use the office comms, which are hardwired to the network, or boosters to let our comms join the network."

"Why aren't they working?"

"As a radio-repair agent, I make a good Militia Corporal. How in the Emperor's name should I know?"

"Anybody on the squad . . ."

"Already asked. Come with me." Chaudhari led Russell out of the office and into the yard in front of the factory. He pointed at a communication tower. "That one is working, but Skippy thinks the repeaters between here and Landing are down. Probably no power, since that issue at the bridge. That's his best guess. How do you like being a farmer?"

"How'd you like having a mule shoved up your—"

"Understood. I did an inventory of equipment, if you're interested."

Russell pointed at a garage full of four-wheeled vehicles with cutting tools on the front. "Those harvester things work?"

"Sure do. Solar. They charge up during the day, and they don't run at night."

"So, solarize the plant."

"What does that even mean?"

"I don't know. It sounds managerial. Is there anything here that works?"

"More food than we can eat in a thousand years, even after they stripped the warehouses, whoever they were. Leaving, and the water and sewage system is great, for us. It's all gravity fed, the pipes run into the hills and down to the ocean. It uses ultraviolet light to clean the water, and before you ask, that's solar as well, with batteries."

A shaft of sunlight lit up the courtyard, lighting the hills above, and illuminating the bright splash of wildflowers.

"I gotta admit, it's pretty here." Russell said. "And we've got somewhere to live. And we've got all these machines . . ."

"Which makes food. Which isn't an in-demand commodity right now."

"We need to find a commodity that's in demand."

"Like what?"

"Like ammunition. I used to make my own revolver ammunition as a hobby. I've looked at some of these machines. Metal presses. Lathes. Tool and die type of stuff. With a little work, we could make cartridges."

"Don't cartridges need gunpowder? Or something like that."

"Yes. But with the right precursors, we can make that. It's like cooking—you have the right ingredients, the right recipe—you just need a big bowl and a spoon."

"Where do you get these precursors?"

"Might find some in a mortar shell, for starters. We could modify some machines, take a few mortar shells apart, use them as primers. Primers have to be high quality. Use them to set off a larger amount of gunpowder. And regular gunpowder is easy to make. Shutt's interested in her own supply of ammunition. Think we could trade for that?"

"Yes. But if anything goes—any parts or anything, we could have problems."

"We've got one of those printer things."

"And a limited supply of metal powder to make new things, and they took all the plastic and suchlike. We're on the edge."

"Why would whoever was here before take all that stuff?"

"Sell it, probably. Somebody will buy it."

Russell walked across the courtyard and into a warehouse. Metal boxes of food trays stacked up to the ceiling. "Plenty of food. What about drugs and medical supplies."

"Only what we brought with us. And I don't remember anybody being a doctor."

"Outstanding." Russell led the way back into the office. "I'm in charge of a decrepit factory."

"Pretty nice decrepit factory, though. Why'd everybody leave?"

"All that other stuff you mentioned. Medical, parts. This factory does one thing—makes food, and with the monorail down, the food was too expensive or hard to get to, or easier to get from somewhere else. I'll bet they were having problems even before the monorail shut down."

"Well, I guess we hang out till Shutt comes to get us."

"Maybe." Russell reached his office, sat, and spun his chair in a circle.

"Having fun spinning?"

"Helps me think. How far do our direct comms reach—line of sight and all that?"

"No idea."

"Send a half dozen of the troops out. March somebody along the monorail till we lose contact, have 'em come back. Same with up that trail to that bridge. Take good notes. And no backtalk."

Chaudhari bowed. "Okay, Sergeant, whatever you say Sergeant. You are like a god, Sergeant. I would never question you, no matter how stupid your ideas sound."

"Glad we've got that out of the way. After that test, do it again. Only this time send somebody up that mountain back there. In fact, send the mountain people up first."

"It's not a mountain. It's a hill. Only a couple thousand feet."

"Whatever. Get somebody up there with a radio, some binoculars. Listening, watching post. Watch for ships, try to get readings off the satellites. We should be able to get comm off one of the satellites, right?"

"Not if we don't have the right radios."

"And see if they can get eyeballs on that bridge that we crossed and on the monorail. What's east of us here?"

"Don't know."

"Find out. Have one of the crew hike that way."

"The squad is only so big . . ."

"Use some of the locals we found and try to find those others they say are missing."

"Okay, what next?"

"Even if the ships that Shutt sent, came, and went, she won't forget us. She's not like that. She'll send another. Or send somebody to walk along the monorail."

Shutt did both. A week later, Russell had two of the troops up at a listening post above them on the hill. With a tent and lots of food, one did binocular sweeps and the rest chopped wood or napped or had sexual congress with squirrels. Russell didn't care as long as they kept watch day and night. They had an excellent view of the wooden bridge up in the hills, and the bridge where the monorail ended. Two other troopers with a mule hiked up to the monorail terminus, and were rewarded when a train pulled in with sealed message chips from Shutt that she'd been sending every trip for the last four days. After the crew hand carried them back to Russell, he decoded them, then called a meeting. He had a total of forty-three people, including himself, in the cafeteria of the factory.

"First," Russell said. "Welcome to our new friends."

Another dozen refugees, or perhaps vagrants, had joined them, attracted by the promise of free food and a place to stay. They all sat together in a corner, Not to be together, but to be apart from the rest. "I hope you are all getting lots to eat. We have plenty. Eat it up."

The whole crowd cheered.

"First notice, Major Shutt is sending a sailing ship out. It should dock in a couple of days or so. Perhaps longer, something to do with the winds. She didn't have a good idea of what was going on out here, so she's let me improvise. My regular Militia will be staying here for now while we get a few things sorted out. Any of you other folks want to head back to Landing? We'll cram you on board and have you head back. I'm sending Chaudhari back with the ship to talk to the Major, so the ship is going anyway. You're all welcome to head back to Landing."

"If we'd wanted to be in Landing, we would have left with the others," one of the newcomers yelled from the back."

"Noted," Russell said. "But why do I care?"

"What if I don't want to go back to Landing? What if I wanted to stay here?"

"This is now a Militia facility," Russell said. "Only Militia or Militia authorized can stay."

"You're kicking us out, like the last corporate people?"

"Nope. You can stay. But if you stay, you join the Militia. Regular or auxiliary, which do you want?"

"What's the difference?"

"Regular are for fighting. Auxiliary we teach you to fight, but you only work on that one day a week. Rest of the time, you do a civilian type job."

"Sounds like a corporation."

"Corporations can fire you. I can't. You don't break the rules. I have to put up with your crap forever. Even if I hate you. Ask Kim One and Kim Two. They've been with me forever, and I hate them both."

Kim One stood. "You don't always hate us, Sergeant."

"Not every day. Not all day. Not all day, every day."

"You don't hate us for part of the day? Wow." Kim One turned to the crowd. "That's a big deal coming from Sergeant Russell."

The crowd laughed.

The same man called. "So, if we want to stay, we work for you."

"Yup. And I'm easy to get along with and a great boss."

The crowd laughed even longer this time.

"Okay, I'm not impossible to get along with. Not all the time. But yeah, you work for me. You do soldier things one day a week, the other days you do a civilian job. We need as much of this factory as we can keep running, to keep running."

The talker from before stood. "I can do that. I was a mechanic. But we need tools, and parts, and supplies—lubricants, things like that. They came from other plants, and they were expensive. The only thing we had to trade before was food, and that's a problem now with the monorail being down."

"I've got plans for other things to trade. I need to talk with Shutt. Can you make a list of what we'd need, to run this place for a year?"

"Sure," the man said. "It's in the computer. Print out what they bought in the last year. That's a good start."

"If you're going to stay here, that's your first job. How many of you want to go back to Landing on the ship?"

Nobody raised their hand. "How many want to work for me?" All the newcomers raised their hand. The current squad did not. "None of you Militia want to work for me?"

"Doesn't matter what we want," Chaudhari said. "We work for you regardless."

"Excellent point. Glad you have accepted your servitude. Right, we'll set it all up. Ship will be here in a week-ish. The rest of you can stay. Anybody who joins up can stay as long as they want. Unless I get a valid order from Shutt ordering us out of here, we'll be here for the duration. Dismissed to duties."

The crowed thinned out, and Chaudhari wandered up.

"I thought Shutt already ordered you back?"

"I said a valid order. She doesn't know what I found out here, so the order isn't valid. Let's go see the mules."

"That's not the way it works."

"It is now." Russell led the way outside and down to the field where the mules grazed. SPD saw Russell coming and trotted over. Russell rubbed his ears and gave him the carrot he had secreted in his pocket.

"You're getting pretty attached to that mule."

"SPD and I understand each other."

"Have you told the others what it means?"

"None of their business. Kim One called hers after something she liked. I'm calling mine after something I like. You good with talking to Shutt?"

"I'm willing to see Shutt with your proposal, but what if she's unhappy."

"I can put up with her unhappiness."

"Because you'll be five hundred kilometers away. I'll be right there. What if she has me shot?"

"She's not as mean as me. She won't shoot you."

"Maybe she's learning."

"Well, we'll find out." Russell rubbed SPD's ears again, and the mule brayed a happy bray. "You don't want to go? I can go?"

"No, you're right. It shouldn't be you. I'll be fine. I hope."

"Good. Thanks for doing this."

"Things are so screwed up these days, who knows. Scott, are you sure about this?"

"Why wouldn't I be?"

"Some people might call it treason."

"It isn't because everybody knows treason doesn't prosper."

"True."

"Because if it does, none dare call it treason." Russell grinned. "Here's to prospering, then!"

CHAPTER 12

"I'll be happy to crush their arms for them if they want," Marianne said. "Does it have to be so loud."

Higgers shook his head. "They don't want their arms cut off. And anyway, it's more likely they'd have their hands or wrists crushed. The machines—"

"Give me a hammer, and I'll do it for them."

"Up to you. How are you going to choose."

BLAART. Marianne covered her ears with her hands. She and Higgers were on a tour to introduce the 'council appointed administrator' to her new workers. The repair shop, and the metal shop, was the heart of the station's space capabilities. Shippers, like metal foundries or even mines, filled entire containers of refined goods locally and shipped them to the transshipment point.

"I'll bet you've never been in a repair shop on a station. Or even unloaded break bulk on a station."

"I will admit this is true. We always docked at the container truss, or went direct to the container farm." The large container truss had three cranes sitting at equal distances around the ring. On this station, they were on the Beta ring. Those cranes resembled giant gripping claws. With three degrees of motion, they could pivot out and snatch a container off a docked ship. Assuming the ship released the chains, they could drag it into a container-sized lock and into the station, where workers could break bulk. The Free Traders stayed on their ship and watched their cameras.

"It's dangerous. We should stop them. Look there." Marianne pointed at a metal press. "That woman has her entire hand inside that press. If something happens, and she powers on, she'll crush her hands. She's even taped the switch down. Merde, they've all done that."

To their left, four 3D printers—two metal, one plastic, and one mixed—ground out parts, controlled by a computer station near the back. They hummed between the other punches. On their right were traditional metalworking tools for parts needing a touch up—grinders, welders, drill presses, punches, and a stamping press.

The stamper had two buttons on the front, widely separated and well away from the press. Both buttons had to be depressed to make the stamper fire.

But the woman operating it had taped a button down. Rather than clamping the metal down for each push, she held it and slapped the other power button with her free hand.

"Arret. Stop. Stop." Marianne waved in front of the operator. "That is dangerous. You'll hurt yourself."

The operator stopped and glared at Marianne. "What do you want?"

"You need to—"

"Are you ninety-five?"

"Ninety-five? I'm not that old."

"I don't care how old you are. Are you ninety-five?"

"Ninety-five what? I'm the administrator—"

"Administrator? One of our corporate overlords, then. I only talk to ninety-five."

"What's a ninety—"

The wham of the press drowned her voice. Marianne retreated and leaned into Higgers ear. "What is she saying?"

"Couldn't hear the conversation, sorry."

"They're all acting unsafe. That one, too." Marianne stepped up to the man at the drill press—another two-power-button unit with one taped off. This time she waited till he finished drilling a hole and waved at him.

He turned off the press. "What?"

"Why do you have one button taped closed?"

"Makes it easier to work. Faster."

"But it's dangerous."

"Are you ninety-five?"

"I'm not—what is this ninety-five?"

The drill press operator shrugged, and the bam bam bam of the drill started up. Marianne frowned at Higgers. He waved her over and walked up to the man controlling the 3-D printers.

"Hey, Higgers. How's bloodsucking going?" the 3D man asked in a pause in the noise.

"Great fun. How's the working man doing?"

"Being exploited every day. Who's your pretty friend?"

"This is Marianne, the new administrator. Marianne, this is Helmut. Helmut"—Higgers pointed at the operator—"is single, in case you were wondering. And even if you weren't because he'd tell you regardless. Which explains why he still is. Single, that is."

Helmut smiled at Marianne. "It's true. Just myself. What's a pretty girl like you doing in here?"

"What's a ninety-five?" Marianne asked.

"I gather you're not, if you are asking."

"I have no idea what it is."

"That's their union local number. They're local ninety-five of the Delta union of mechanics, metalworkers, piper fitters and postal workers."

"Postal workers?"

"Not a lot of Imperial post left going through the system, so they had to merge. This is a big union shop. Only union workers allowed here. Except me."

"Why do they keep asking me that?"

"They don't like anybody who isn't union. Like me, or you."

"But I'm just talking to them."

"Guess they don't want to talk to you."

"But they don't know what I'm going to say."

Helmut opened his mouth, but the whine of the

grinder drowned him out. Marianne covered her ears till it stopped. "Can we talk outside?"

Helmut shook his head. "Sorry, can't leave the machines during working hours."

"But they're automatic—busy printing things, they don't have to be watched."

"I'm not watching, I'm guarding," Helmut said.

"Guarding? From whom?"

Helmut waved toward the other workers.

Marianne furrowed her brow. "You're keeping them from getting hurt on your printers?"

Helmut laughed. "You're a funny one. Are you for real? Higgers, is she for real?"

"Ms. Marianne is the new council appointed administrator of our station."

"Council appointed? Isn't that the tabbo's knees. Run a station before, have you, Ms. Marianne?"

"I have captained a starship. A station should not be much different."

Helmut laughed louder. "Boy, are you in for a surprise. Ever dealt with a union before?"

"We have no unions on Free Trader ships."

"Oh boy." Helmut grinned. "I'm going to get some popcorn. This will be awesome."

"It surely will," Higgers said.

Marianne pointed at the workers with the taped buttons. "You need to stop these unsafe practices."

Helmut shook his head. "Not my job."

"If you're not going to, then I will." Marianne waved at the operators in the room. She yelled, cursed, pointed, and jumped up and down. The workers all stopped what they were doing to stare, except the female press operator, who ignored her for another twenty seconds until Marianne pushed her face five inches in front of the woman. Even then, she took her time setting the metal brace she was working on aside.

"I am Legate Marianne."

The female press operator folded her hands. "So?"

"I have been appointed administrator of this station by the council."

"So?"

"You are operating in an unsafe manner."

"We're operating according to standard protocols, and we're following union guidance."

"You all must stop taping down the extra power button. It is there for safety reasons."

"You want us to what?"

"Stop taping down the other button. Use both hands to operate the power switch."

"Use both hands?" The woman operator smiled and turned to her buddies. She winked at them. "Use both hands! She wants us to use both hands."

One of the men raised his hand. "Hey, administrator lady?"

"Yes?"

"You want us to use both hands."

"I just said that. It is a requirement."

"You mean you are Changing Our Working Conditions?"

You could hear the capital letters in his voice.

"Well—"

"No, no, no," the drill press operator said.

"Not allowed," the grinder said.

"Wildcat! Wildcat! Wildcat!" the other presser said. The other workers took up the call, downed tools, and marched out of the shop."

Marianne's mouth gaped as the workers left. She turned to Higgers. "What is going on?"

"Wildcat! Wildcat! Wildcat!" chorused the workers outside the shop. The volume increased as others took up the call.

Higgers shook his head. "You just caused a general strike, Administrator Legate Marianne. All the workers in the station will stop working for the next three shifts."

"But why? I don't understand."

"You can't change contract terms without a negotiation. That includes all working conditions."

"But I was trying to keep them safe."

"They disagree," Higgers said.

"Can you go talk to them?"

"Nope. Not my job. Not anymore. It's you now. And even if I did, I'd have to wait till they voted in a negotiating committee, and that will take a day. And they still wouldn't talk to me. They want the senior executives to speak to, which means you."

"But, but . . ." Marianne stopped talking. "What do we do now?"

"Lock up here, make sure they can't get back in."

"Lock up, why?"

"Keep them from sabotaging the equipment."

"But it's their equipment."

"Nope. They just work on it. It's the company's equipment. Yours, sort of. And if they break it, they don't have to work, but still get paid."

"Merde." Marianne said. "Jose didn't say anything about this."

"Jose? Tribune Jose? Dashi's number two guy?"

"That's him."

"I like him. He seems levelheaded," Helmut said. "He was going to come here, talk to everybody. Discuss our ongoing labor problems. That would have been interesting. Probably won't now, I guess, since you're in charge."

"He never said anything about strikes," Marianne said. "Does this happen often?"

"Fifteen times last year," Higgers said. "We're the worst performing station in the system. Unhappiest unions. Worst on-time delivery. Highest cost. Worst place to work, and all the workers know it. That's why they're so bitter, the ones that work here. Everybody who could, left, and the people left know they're stuck here. Never get another job this good."

"Merde."

Higgers slapped her shoulder. "But I'm sure you'll fix it. I'm really glad you're in charge now."

CHAPTER 13

"Finally, we note, haaaagur—" the university delegate exploded in a fit of coughing. Dust blew down from the second-floor gallery through the upper windows. She put an arm to her mouth and coughed again. The fall dust storms had arrived.

Jose poured a glass of water from the pitcher in the middle of the council table and slid it down to the delegate. The delegate nodded thanks, but didn't drink yet.

"One of you guards get up there and close those windows, please," Jose said from the head of the council chamber.

Two guards covered the door. The Free Trader guard wore blue coveralls over a standard skin suit. The coveralls sported bright red patches of ship names, yellow rank insignia, and blue departmental badges, six pockets, including two thigh and two side pockets, a zippered breast pocket for a comm, and a slender arm pocket for comm chips or credit chips. She slouched against the wall, tapping the shock stick in her hand on her thigh.

The Militia guard didn't have a skin suit on, but did have shined boots, pressed dark green pants with shined belt, dark green tunic, light-green shirt, and soft green cap. His revolver sat in a shined holster on his right hip, balanced on his left hip by shined ammo pouches. He stood at parade rest, hands clasped behind his back.

"Excuse me, could you get up to the second floor and close the windows? One of you, please."

The Free Trader Legion guard laughed. Marianne hid a small grin by staring down at the table.

The Militia guard tilted his head to see Shutt's face and

raised an eyebrow.

"It's all right Senz." Shutt nodded. "Please."

Senz saluted and marched up the stairs.

Marianne lifted her head, caught the Legionnaire's eye, and jerked her head to the stairs. The Legionnaire hoisted herself upright and scurried to follow Senz. The council sat in silence through the noise of windows slamming shut. Senz returned to his post by the door and nodded at Marianne. The Legionnaire returned and slumped against the other wall.

The university delegate watched the byplay, then pushed the glass of water away and coughed her way through the rest of her report before sitting. Jose read the standard reports into the record, saying he was acting on behalf of Dashi, who was back in bed. Shutt indicated that the admiral was 'absent on unavoidable administrative duties.'" Marianne read a short note from the Free Traders council expressing confidence in her representation and thanking her for her efforts on their behalf and exhorting the council to take her issues 'most seriously.'

Both Jose and Shutt snickered when she read that.

The university person sneezed into her hand and swept her gaze across the table. After checking each principal's carefully controlled expressions, she stood and asked to be excused, citing important ongoing experiments, then scuttled out.

"Let's go into private session." Marianne reached for the recording comm in the center.

"Yes, let's," Shutt said.

The two guards stood and each grasped their door, preparatory to hauling it closed.

"Stop with those doors," Jose said.

The guards halted and looked back at the council. Shutt jerked her head, and Marianne waved at them to continue.

"I said stop," Jose said. "We're not done yet."

Marianne scowled. "We need to speak privately."

"We will," Jose said. "When I say so. We're not

finished with the public portion of the meeting yet."

"I have important points—"

"And I'm the council chair, and I'm not finished yet."

Marianne leaned forward. "Who are you to say—"

"This is the Emperor's council, not yours."

"You're not the Emperor."

"I'm the Emperor's appointee."

Shutt chortled. "Lover's spat? Did somebody wake up on the wrong side of the bed."

Marianne glared at her. "You are a coarse and rude person."

"Sure am." Shutt leaned forward. "Want a further demonstration of my coarseness."

"Ladies," Jose said.

"Not now, Cheri."

"Yes, now. This is a formal meeting. Stop this sniping. Bring yourself to order while I finish my announcement, and KEEP THOSE DOORS OPEN." Jose was yelling at the end. "This is the Delta council chamber, not a Militia Barracks or a Free Trader trading hall. Those doors stay open till I say so."

"Technically, the Imperial agriculture building—"

"Shut up, Major, you're out of order. Admiral's representative or not."

Marianne put her hand on Jose's arm. "Cheri, you're so forceful when you act like that."

Jose glanced down at the hand, then up at Marianne. His eyes narrowed. Marianne withdrew her hand.

"Somebody is sleeping alone tonight," Shutt muttered.

"What was that, Major?"

"Tribune, I said what's keeping your announcements? We're waiting."

"Details of the vote for senator. I want it read into the record." Jose gave a thorough briefing about the upcoming Senate elections, requirements, availability, paperwork. The two women slouched through his presentation until the last two points made them sit up.

Marianne frowned. "A week? We never agreed to move the date up by a week."

"We don't have to. Dashi does. And he says that we need to get the Senate and a new council in place quickly. That gives us faster elections. Nominations close in two weeks, and the vote will be one week after that."

"That's not a long time to campaign," Shutt said. "I'm not sure that I agree."

"All of us know there won't be much of a campaign. We're simply appointing people to represent different factions. And nobody cares if you agree, Shutt, this is an advisory council to the Emperor. He can take your advice or not."

"Thank you for that correction, Tribune Jose." Shutt grinned a cheery smile. "I'll keep that in mind with the rest of the advice I offer." The grin stayed on her mouth, but her eyes didn't match.

"These changes require discussion," Marianne said. "I would like to understand the reasons."

"This is what Dashi wants, so we'll have to deal with it."

"Nevertheless, I would like to ask him some questions about the timing of this."

"Well, he's not here, so that will be difficult."

"Perhaps he can make himself available for discussion."

"Dashi does not work for you."

A new voice rang out from the doorway. "He does not work for one person, but for all the people of Delta." The council stood. A stooped figure, leaning on a cane appeared through the dust. "The Emperor-designate is here. Ask away, Ms. Marianne."

***

Sergeant Russell marched up to the dock with Kim One. The squad had been at the factory for almost ten days after receiving the comm chip from Shutt when the hilltop listening post signaled an incoming ship.

"I know this ship." Russell put his binoculars up. "And I know that captain. That's Balthazar." He and his squad had kidnapped and boatnapped Balthazar when fleeing from the Militia, since the Militia thought them criminal rebels. Major Shutt had saved them from that and enlisted them in a plot to save the planet. Doing so would locate the last rebel officers and foil their mission to shoot down a shuttle full of vital parts. In return for her rehabilitating them, Russell had toed her line ever since. He had to because she was the only thing keeping the Free Traders from tossing him out an air lock, as they objected to his involvement in the failed coup.

"One of the brothers? I liked him. You'll like him, too, Sweet Pea." Kim stroked her mule's neck. "He's a good sailor."

"You sound completely bonkers when you talk to that mule."

"I don't care. You sound completely bonkers half the time when you talk to the squad, Sergeant."

"Are you saying I'm as crazy as you are?"

"Could be that the squad is as dumb as the mules, too."

Russell lowered his binoculars. "Good point. Maybe I'll test that theory by putting Sweet Pea in charge next time I'm gone."

"Sweet Pea would be an excellent squad leader, Sergeant. She keeps herself clean by washing in the river, eats regularly, follows orders, and doesn't like strangers."

"An ideal trooper, then," Russell said. "Help me with the lines."

One of Balthazar's brothers—either Steph or Mel—sailed the ship up parallel to the makeshift pier, the other dousing the sails. Bal stood in the bow and tossed a rope at Russell.

Russell caught the thrown rope, walked backward, and looped it around a protruding wooden post. The boat's momentum kept it moving past him. But as it took the slack in on the line, the helmsman swung the boat left and into the pier as the rope caught. It pulled taut and thrummed as it stretched tight, and the boat thumped against the pier. Bal tossed another rope at Kim One, who also whipped it tight around a pillar. Bal hopped down with a third rope in his hand, hustled forward, and pulled the bow tight to the dock. The boat sagged into the dock, held tight by three lines. Bal bustled around adjusting things before turning to the two Militia.

"Sergeant Russell. Good to see you again."

"Wish I could say the same, Bal, you pirate. What are you here to steal from me this time."

Bal slapped Russell's shoulder. "What have you got worth stealing? I'll take it. Hello Kim sweetie." Bal and Kim exchanged hugs.

Sweetie? Russell thought. What did I miss before?

Bal pointed at Sweet Pea. "Who is this beast?"

"This is my friend, Sweet Pea," Kim said. "Sergeant Russell is going to put her in charge of the squad when he's away."

"Sounds like one of his better ideas."

"You think a mule can do a better job than Chaudhari?" Russell asked. "Or any of the rest of the troops?"

"I've met your troops. So, yes. And the mule will probably leave my boat cleaner than your troops did."

"Mules defecate every hour," Russell said.

"Like I said, cleaner." Bal examined the ramshackle pier that he was tied to. "I've been to sturdier docks."

"You don't like it. Tie up somewhere else."

"You're as welcoming as I remember. We're here for at least the turn of the tide. We'll bottom out shortly, and we need to be tied to something so we don't tip over."

"What happened to your old boat? The catamaran?"

"Some idiot blew a hole in the bottom and half sunk it." That had been Russell and Nadine while they were stopping the Militia's own leader, Roi, from shooting down the shuttle. "It went in as salvage, and the council

125

gave me this to work with in compensation."

"Bigger." Russell rapped the hull. "Metal—and higher as well. More storage?"

"Lot's more." Bal rapped the hull as well. "Sturdier, full keel but flat enough for grounding, metal rudder for protection against damage, and because it's a monohull, it points higher."

"Blah Blah blah. Nautical speak. Blah blah." Russell said.

"It's what we have now. I'm supposed to collect up to thirty people and a bunch of factory equipment and take them back to Landing. I was supposed to do that last time, but the people waiting here convinced me to load them up and take them away. Said it would be the humane thing to do. And you know what a humanitarian I am."

"They paid better than Shutt, didn't they?"

"Way better. To be fair, Shutt didn't give me a firm date, and you weren't here, so I took advantage of the opportunity. Where are these people I'm supposed to take?"

"Not coming."

"And the equipment?"

"Not coming, either."

"I see." Bal examined the deserted water. The river that ran by the factory debouched into the shallow bay. The mouth of the bay was several miles away, and at least two miles wide at the outlet. As the tide turned, waters funneled out. The boat creaked as it settled farther into the brown ooze. Dirt banks covered with pine trees lined the bay, and the human habitation of the factory was invisible upriver.

"Welcoming place. Love what you've done with it. Which is nothing."

"It's our humble home. What do you think?"

"I think low tide is in a few hours, next high tide is in the middle of the night, and much as I want to go back to see Shutt and tell her that she owes me money for not picking up things, I'm not sailing out in the dark, so you have till tomorrow's high tide to get things loaded up. I'm only paid for the one trip, so whatever or whoever you haven't got on board by noon tomorrow, is staying."

"Fine by me." Russell dug in his pocket. "I don't suppose you have any cigarettes?"

Bal pulled two out of an inner pocket and handed them to Russell.

"Only two?"

"For now."

"What do I need to give to get more?"

"An explanation as to why there's nothing here."

"We're staying."

"Because you like the rustic life?"

"I'm partial to it now. Me and SPD."

"Who's SPD?"

"My mule. We've all got one."

"I see." Bal yelled some nautical speak onto the boat and got an answer. Something about fenders and slack lines. "You and your mule are staying?"

"All of us."

"How you going to feed yourself?"

"Food, we've got. We need a few other things. We will be sending one passenger back. Chaudhari. He'll be looking for some things."

"Will he? Fascinating."

"You still talk to all of your . . . friends . . . back in Landing? The ones who can get things that somebody needs."

"Talk sure. But I don't do that now. Not anymore. I work for the council. Major Shutt. Official approved government contracts only."

Russell lit one single cigarette and took a huge drag. "Ahhhh. That's good. Want to stay for dinner?"

"Do I have a choice?"

"Not if I understand those tide things, no. Come up to this factory, have some dinner, have a chat."

127

"What's for dinner?"

"Opportunity." Russell took another big drag. "Opportunity is on the menu."

CHAPTER 14

Jose raced to the door and took Dashi's arm. "Sir, you shouldn't be out of bed."

"Why not?"

"It's dangerous here."

"Rogue Militia blew up my shuttle with me in it. Galactic Growers tried to crash into my station, every time I walk around Landing random people take potshots at me, I need a guard to get on the train, and half this moon is scheming with the other half to reduce my authority and take over my powers when I'm not at these meetings. I'm in danger wherever I am. Hello Major Shutt, Hello Ms. Marianne."

"You're sick, sir. Coming here will make it worse."

"I can barely walk. The doctors are worried about complications from the removal of my spleen. I had issues with getting enough food during the recent emergency, and my younger exposure to orbital radiation is catching up with me. How will sitting in a dusty room make it worse?"

"I—"

"Don't make me sicker by delaying things." Dashi held Jose's arm till he arrived at the council table. "Ms. Marianne, or Legate Marianne I should say, you have questions about the Senate's elections?"

"Why the hurry?"

"Why not?"

"We need more time to campaign, or introduce ourselves."

"This is a tiny moon, with a tiny population, which we've made an excellent start of wiping out in a war, famine, and death. The only one of the four horsemen we're missing is the plague, and that may have started earlier—I'm waiting to hear back from Mr. Stewart on that. In any event, our reduced population knows exactly who you are and what you do and have done—and did." Dashi handed Jose his cane and dropped into a chair. "Are you planning on running for senator?"

"I, well, the Free Traders do need a representative—"

"Which is a yes. Major Shutt? I believe the admiral has announced he will run."

"Yes. As will I."

Dashi placed both hands on the table. "Not expected, but not unexpected, either. Who do you think will vote for you?"

"The Militia, of course. Many corporate people. Many unaligned folks. And not all the Free Traders are enamored of Ms. Marianne's suggestions."

"Hah!" Marianne snorted. "Not a single Free Trader will vote for the likes of you."

"I think, Legate, since we will soon be senatorial colleagues, you should get used to treating me with more respect. And you bother some of your first families with your Imperial snootiness. Some of them would be more comfortable with a mere Major, a junior officer representing them. I'm not as arrogant as some."

"You speak nonsense," Marianne said. But her face flickered in thought.

"And everyone loves Mr. Jose, of course." Shutt grinned. "He is a shoo-in with your support behind him, Emperor Dashi. As he should be, as your deputy. In fact, he's such a shoo-in, that I have mentioned to many of his supporters that perhaps it is not necessary to support him directly, their vote would be wasted, as it were. Perhaps they could consider who else is running and vote strategically. After all, they don't want some random Free Trader to get in."

Jose raised his eyebrows. "You're telling people not to

vote for me?"

"I'm telling them there is no need to."

"That's an unrealistic interpretation."

"Is it?" Shutt grinned. "I'm the officer who saved Landing from the fires for the admiral. You're the one who helped keep Dashi alive. What's her campaign going to be? 'Vote for me,' I sleep with Dashi's assistant."

The snarling went on for a few more minutes till Dashi coughed. All three shut up. Dashi poured a glass of water, raised it to his mouth, then sniffed. "Aha. Even the water smells foul to me. Are you three finished?"

"How do you feel, sir?"

"Horrible, if you must know. The doctors are treating me as a science experiment." He set the glass down. "I am moving the elections for Senate up. They will take place in two weeks. The nominations will close in six days, then seven days for campaigning, then the election. The votes will be at large, the thirty-two people who get the most votes will become senators and offer me, as the Emperor, such advice as they see fit. In all ways, they will function as the Imperial Senate did. They may propose legislation to me by majority vote. I may either approve or deny it. They have some other functions—If my heir has not reached their majority when I die, they will form a regency until such time as they are. They have some other ceremonial functions as well."

"And some other real ones," Marianne said. "If you really follow the Imperial Constitution. Senators can command armies and be invested by the Emperor as governors, acting in the Emperor's name and with his powers until relieved."

"Indeed," Dashi said. "You have been reading up on this?"

"Jose had given me many books to read, your Imperial Majesty."

Dashi laughed. "Just call me Dashi, in private. That is interesting."

Shutt's mouth dropped open. "Jose. Sorry, Tribune Jose. You've been teaching her how to seize power? Are you completely insane?"

Dashi laughed again. "I am going to watch the video of the first session of the new Senate with glee. Especially the part where you choose the Speaker of the Senate, the one who handles issues of decorum."

"We're not animals that you prod to fight for your amusement, Dashi," Shutt said.

"No prodding seems to be required," Dashi said. "The fighting resembles an ingrown attribute, like bison locking horns. But consider this, Major. Jose appears to be advising Ms. Marianne on the best way to achieve her senatorial ambitions."

"It's stupid."

"There is that old saying, keep your friends close."

"So?"

"The second part is to keep your enemies closer."

Jose laughed this time. "I don't think Ms. Marianne and I are enemies, sir, far from it."

"For now. And as they also say, something about being inside a tent pissing out, rather than outside a tent pissing in. In any event, let me 'complete my briefing,' as you military people say." Dashi finished describing the remainder of the items surrounding the election. The details, while necessary to advertise, were not contentious. Given the "recent unpleasantness," voting was to be in person. Landing was the preferred site, but polling was to be available in three other major monorail stops and a good dozen orbital stations. Questions from Dashi revealed that Marianne had already started staging remote ships into stations for polling day. Shutt had plans to allow serving Militia time off from duties to vote. Jose had fleets of ships and ground cars standing by to shuttle voters in.

"As I expected, all of you tried to bend these rules to your advantage, and in so bending each of your efforts has nullified the others' efforts. Two wrongs do make a right.

Or three in this case. I remind you that you cannot pay people to vote for you."

"Remind them who does pay them for their regular job," Shutt said.

"Indeed. Such jobs, including being in the Militia." Dashi steepled his hands.

"Or promising promotions if they vote for you."

"Listen, you—"

Dashi held up his hand. "Children, please. There are always issues like this in an election. In any event, I will enforce all the strictures of a regular Imperial election, including reporting expenses, public statements, incitements to violence, and so on. The only one I am ignoring is proof of Imperial Citizenship and residency. We've all been stuck here since the abandonment, so it's irrelevant. At least for now, or until Mr. Stewart returns from his mission of discovery to the other systems."

"Any word back yet, sir?"

"None. But none was expected. We'll have to wait and see what the rest of the Empire holds for us. Either way, whatever we discover, I plan to meet it with a unified Senate and Emperor. Are there any other procedural questions?"

Each had a few minor issues, but nothing of substance. At the end, Dashi hoisted himself up by leaning on the table. Jose dashed to assist. With Jose's assistance, a cane-wielding Dashi shuffled back to his quarters.

Marianne and Shutt stood as Dashi left, then sat and recovered comms and notes before leaving. Shutt stood. "That's one of the smartest men I've ever met. Will ever meet."

Marianne nodded. "On that, at least, I can agree."

"His comparisons—that one he said—keep your friends close, but your enemies closer. Hey Free Trader girl?"

"What?"

"Wonder which you are?"

***

Chaudhari stood next to Bal as their ship sailed into Landing. Since they could make no headway without a rising tide, one could say they swept into Landing, along with a cloud of other sailboats.

"I'm not afraid of Sergeant Russell," Chaudhari told Balthazar. "Not exactly."

"Doesn't seem that way." Balthazar swung the ship's wheel to keep the bow pointed forward. "Seems like you are afraid of him."

"I'm not afraid."

"No?" Balthazar swung the wheel. "There's more boats here than a year ago. Look at that beauty. That schooner."

Chaudhari looked at the schooner, a sleek two-masted sailboat riding by. "Looks nice. Is it bigger than us?"

"Longer, but narrower. Fast and seaworthy, but we carry more cargo."

"'Cause we're boxier?"

"If by boxy you mean built like a bathtub, and as maneuverable as one, yes. But that's merchant ships for you. So, you're not scared of Russell?"

"Not scared, no. Terrified. He can be one ruthless SOB when he puts his mind to it."

"He doesn't seem that smart."

"He plays dumb all the time. But it's an act. He got us off those stations without getting us killed during the fighting. We were following orders from the old officer's council. When they lost, we should have been shot or spaced beside them. Instead, he figured out a way to have us hooked up to Shutt and the admiral's side. Work for the winners."

"Didn't they try to hang you?"

"Shutt talked them out of it. She's the admiral's number two, and Russell does what she says, and she keeps an eye out for us."

"For now. What if she changes her mind?"

"He's got a plan for that, too." Chaudhari hefted his backpack. "I've got a few things to show her. She'll like them."

"What type of things?"

"Things that go boom."

"Looks like it works for everyone. Uh oh."

"Is that a whirlpool?" Chaudhari pointed at a spinning circle of water ahead.

"Yep. Tide current meets river current at an angle. Tide will win, eventually."

"How do we avoid it?"

"We don't. Hang on."

"You don't mean we're—Emperor's ankles." Chaudhari gripped a metal pole next to the wheel. The boat dove right into the spinning vortex, pivoting sideways, then backward, then sideways, then forward again, then sideways and backward again. It raced out the far side of the maelstrom stern first but kept sweeping up the river.

Balthazar looked back over his shoulder as he spun the wheel. "Current is what is driving us now. We'll swing right up to the docks at Landing."

"We will, will we? And if you can't steer us backward?"

"I can."

"That was insane."

"Just a whirlpool."

"What if we got sucked into that hole in the bottom of it? Would we disappear into the depths?"

"Depth is like thirty feet here. Nowhere to disappear to."

"Oh." Chaudhari wiped his brow. "Good."

"We'd just smash into the bottom of the river and the pieces would swarm around the center. Even if you got over, you'd be sucked down and drowned."

"Shouldn't we have put on our life jackets?"

"They'll keep you afloat. Won't keep you from being bashed head first into the rocks on the bottom. And besides"—Balthazar pointed at the life jackets on the rack behind him—"red isn't my color."

"Bloodred?"

"Not that. What the heck is that?" Balthazar pointed at the dock ahead.

"You laid on a party for me. Thanks, Bal, that was sweet."

"Not for you but for somebody. Can you read that banner?"

The arrival pier was packed with people. A band stood on shore belting out songs, and people were clapping to the music. Female dancers in bright blue and sober gray colored costumes were doing tumbles along the deck. One woman in tights and a pleated dress was tossed in the air, swung her legs out into the splits, then pulled them back in.

"That's quite an impressive set of acrobatics," Balthazar said.

"And the jumping was pretty neat too," Chaudhari said.

Balthazar blinked. "What do you—never mind? What's all this in aid of."

Chaudhari dug in his backpack and produced a pair of binoculars. Draping his arms on the hull in front of the wheel, he peered forward. "There's a banner. I'm trying to read it."

Balthazar yelled out preparations for docking and had his brother's stage ropes—which he called "lines"—on hooks—which he called "cleats"—and gave orders for tying up. Once he was happy, he turned to Chaudhari. "Well?"

"It's an election rally. The campaigning for Senate has begun."

"Who's running?"

Chaudhari handed over the binoculars. "See for yourself."

"Pletcher for Progress," Balthazar read. "Support Vincent Pletcher for Senator. Progress! Jobs! Sponsored by

Owl Ship sales!"

"What do you think?"

"I think he's a low-down lying, profiteering, two-faced merchant who'll try to swindle the system for his own benefit."

Chaudhari took the binoculars back. "I agree. He'll make a great senator." He adjusted the screen a bit. "Think he'd introduce me to one of those cheerleaders?"

CHAPTER 15

"Offer a path to stability after the recent unpleasantness." Jose extended his arms above the crowd and pointed at the agricultural building. "There. There, the new Imperial Council house, where the current council sits. We will continue our good work, stabilizing the colony. We've been successfully handling various crises up till now, the food distribution, the items with the power grid . . ."

Jose, Marianne, Shutt, and a group of three committee organizers sat on the stage in the classroom. A satellite campus, down the street from the monorail station, was being used for the debate. The political science department in the university—the department chair, the assistant department head, and the associate professor, the only one who did any teaching—had arranged for a question-and-answer session for the upcoming election and invited the three leading candidates. The admiral had declined, saying it was beneath his dignity as a serving officer. He'd assumed Shutt would decline, but she had a higher threshold for her dignity being insulted, being on the dais next to the others.

The room was packed. With students. Who had been told it was a mandatory part of their course and that attendance was being taken.

". . . further refining the availability of the produced items." Jose finished the first part of his talk and glanced at his comm. "I see that I still have some of my allotted time. Perhaps I could briefly discuss our challenges in the transportation sector if any of you have any questions. Yes, the young gentleman in the back."

One of the students in the back row stood. He was skinny enough to disappear if he turned sideways, and his budget didn't run to frequent haircuts.

"Tribune, we all have the same question about the transportation infrastructure."

"Yes?"

"Will it be on the test?" The crowd burst out laughing.

Jose grimaced. "I don't understand. What do you mean?"

The crowd swiveled their eyes to the junior professor, seated to Marianne's right. He looked up from his comm, bit his lip and nodded once, then returned to his comm. The crowd sighed, and the young man in the back cursed quietly. "Please tell us about your transportation issues, Tribune."

Jose looked around, but the crowd peered up at him, nodding, and took out their comms to take notes. He launched into an impassioned discussion on the repurposing of monorail flat cars to carry bulk goods.

Shutt whispered to Marianne. "They can't possibly be interested in how the cars are welded together."

"They can if it's on their exam."

"Are they all students?"

"Every single one. Except for us."

"What a colossal waste of time."

Marianne shrugged. "I agree. Dashi should have just appointed Jose and I as senators and been done with it."

"And me."

"And me what?"

"Appoint me as a senator."

Marianne laughed. "Not a chance. Dashi doesn't like you."

"I don't think that figures into it, and this is exactly why I'm running for Senate against you superior cretins."

"Support the common man, will you?"

"Yep. Common man. And woman. Laboring for a better Empire."

"I'd puke except—what's that?"

Blue lights flickered through the windows facing the street. Someone outside swiveled a spotlight back and forth along the windows. A low rumble made Jose hard to hear. Jose raised his voice, but the chant got louder.

"There's supposed to be some rallies tonight," Shutt said.

"Pretty loud rally."

One of the students in the back peered out the window. "There's a parade out there. People, floats, and a band."

The crowd stirred, but refocused on Jose as he raised his voice.

The lights flickered again.

"Pletcher for Progress. Pletcher for Progress!" rang through the windows.

"What in the Emperor's name?" Shutt whispered.

"Vince Pletcher, that ship sales guy, that . . . . Merchant fellow."

The band finished with a flourish of trumpets, followed by the rattle of a snare drum. A man started a lengthy introduction in the silence.

"Sounds like a party."

"He has no platform. Only stupid slogans and lots of music."

Jose paused and checked his notes.

"They're giving away beer! And wine!" the student in the back yelled.

The audience stirred and exchanged glances, and a few on the aisle seats stood and strode to the exit.

The senior professor spoke. "I remind all of you, beer or no beer, this is on the exam, and there will be detailed questions, especially detailed on Tribune Jose's transportation plan."

The muttering subsided, and the standing students returned to their seats.

Jose turned and bowed with a flourish. "Thank you,

professor. As I was saying—"

"Empresses vagina," the student in the back yelled. "They're giving away food. Free food. They have a BBQ. Buffalo burgers! With mustard!" He sprinted to the side door, just beating the wave of others who stood and dashed out. The rest of the crowd pushed their way out of the seats, knocking the rows down. In seconds, the crowd had emptied the hall, shoving their way out the doors and down the stairs to the passing parade.

Jose stared at the empty classroom, then stepped down from the dais and confronted the university professors. "Free beer—and you can keep them here, but a few buffalo burgers, and you let them go."

The professor shrugged. "Their stipends are pretty low. Beer they can find, but food—good food. They really want that."

"You're saying only poor students come to the school?"

"What? Of course not. Some are wealthy. But we restrict their income and where they live and make them eat on campus. The food's expensive and lousy."

"You make your students eat horrible overpriced food?"

"Of course. We all do." the professor looked at his colleagues, who nodded. "Why not? They're just grad students, after all. Little better than animals." He and his colleagues collected their comms and climbed down from the stage.

"Where in the Emperor's name are you going?" Jose asked.

The prof yelled over his shoulder, "We're done here." He grinned at the other university people. "And it's been a while since I had a buffalo burger."

***

Chaudhari met two cheerleaders after the docking. Treea and Wendra. Treea claimed to be able to do the splits and touch her toes. At the same time.

"I don't believe it," Chaudhari said.

She bent at the waist and touched her forehead to her ankles, then dropped to a full split and touched each foot.

"Amazing." Chaudhari said.

"It's easier when I lay down, then I can put my ankles behind my ears," Treea said.

Chaudhari gulped. "Outstanding." He looked at Wendra. "Can you do that?"

"Nope. Not as flexible. I can do this, though."

From a standing start, she balanced on one leg and lifted the other and put it on Chaudhari's shoulder. "I've got better balance."

"Bless the Emperor, so you do."

A figure pushed through the crowd behind the women, who cheered, clapped, and hugged him, then had their picture taken.

"Corporal Chaudhari," Vincent Pletcher said. "Welcome to my election rally. Can I count on your vote in the upcoming Senate elections?"

"Absolutely. Me, my friends, and all my squad."

The two women bouncing on a nearby stage performed a set of acrobatic dancing, spelling out "P-L-E-T-C-H-E-R."

The women ended in splits. "The male members of the squad, anyway."

"Just the men? You sure?"

Two over muscled male cheerleaders mounted the stage. They picked the women up and tossed them high overhead, letting them spin and roll. They caught them and did it again. The men were working hard, sweating, their bare chests covered with body paint in Vince's blue and gray.

Chaudhari laughed. "Men and women both. The whole squad. And the mules, too."

"And how are my mules?"

"Your mules? Why are they your mules?"

"I sold them to the Militia, well, actually, I leased them at a daily rate with an option to buy but a guaranteed first right of refusal for a buyback, at ten percent of original sale cost, minus wear and tear, assuming they were not utilized properly by the military authorities, calculated by me, with a daily rate charged for providing animal maintenance services."

Chaudhari worked that one through. "You made the Militia pay you for buying the mules, pay you for maintaining the mules, and guarantee they would sell them back to you, for a price that you set. A low price that you set."

"Very good. Most Militia can't figure that out."

"Most Militia don't assume you're trying to rip them off."

"They ask me to price certain products and services and I do. It's not my fault if they don't read the fine print in the contracts."

"Most Militia won't read contracts, agreed."

"Most Militia can't read contracts. Not sure if they can read anything."

"Those are your mules?"

"Yes. Can I have them back?"

"Nope. We like them."

"I'll pay well."

"The squad has become attached to them."

"You could order them to give them up."

"Kim One named hers. She calls her Sweet Pea and talks to her all day."

"Kim One. Isn't she the quiet, unassuming, vicious one?"

"That's her."

"I guess I'll have to make do without mules."

Chaudhari spread his hands out. "This is all very impressive. Think you can make it into the Senate?"

"I won't be at the top of the leader board. But I'll get in. There are thirty-two spots, after all."

"You'll be thirty-two out of thirty-two? Not majorly impressive."

"Do you know what you call the thirty-second senator elected?"

"Nope."

"Senator. Exactly the same as the first one."

Chaudhari laughed again. "Good point. Maybe I should run for senator."

"Why not? You're here, you're in the Militia, your name is not unfamiliar. Sergeant Russell is well known, and you're known as his friend. I'll bet you would do well if you ran."

"Maybe I'll go downtown and sign myself up then. Why are you talking to me, Mr. Soon-to-be Senator number thirty-two."

"I was expecting to see your boss, and I'm curious as to why he's not here."

"We were supposed to get this factory sorted out, but it didn't work the way we wanted. There's some issues with the machines, so Sergeant Russell stayed to try to get them working."

"What does he know about machines other than how to blow them up?"

"Some of the locals stayed. He put them in charge."

"Why didn't he come back here to see Shutt?"

"He put me in charge of that."

"Delegation, very interesting."

"Why's that?"

"Learning how to delegate is an executive skill, an officer's skill. Not a sergeant's skill."

"He's still a sergeant."

"For now. Where are you going next?"

"I have to report to Shutt. I'd better get going."

"Too bad. The rest of the cheerleaders are doing the next exhibition in ten minutes."

"The rest of them?"

"Thirty on the squad."

Chaudhari looked at the crowd. "Shutt's probably busy. I can see her tomorrow."

CHAPTER 16

"Opportunistic weasel," Jose said. He stormed around the council room. "Jumping in to take advantage of others' hard work. Claiming credit for things others have done. Stealing their work." He and Marianne had retreated to their offices in the Department of Agriculture building after Vince's rally had disrupted their speeches.

"Are you angry or jealous?"

Jose ran his finger along the tabletop. "Dust and more dust. Where is all this dust coming from?"

"Sounds like jealousy to me."

Jose rubbed the dust off his fingers. "Both. Angry at myself for not seeing this coming, jealous that he's claimed credit for all our hard work. We need better cleaners."

"We have bigger problems than dusty tables."

"I'm still ahead of him in the election. I'll be a senator. So will you."

"And so will Shutt—and probably Pletcher. Do you know how many votes he'll get?"

"I've got people checking. The results so far indicate he'll make it in. My stacking isn't working."

"Stacking?"

"I've got sixteen people from a dozen corporations running under my . . . suggestions? Allied corps, TGI employees, prominent executives. People who are well liked and not incredibly stupid. They'll fill up the top spots and give me close enough to a majority that all I need is to pull a few people along to control the council."

"You found smart ones?"

"No. Stupid."

"But you said—"

"Not incredibly stupid. Just regular stupid. But popular, and they'll take direction from me."

"Does that include me? How many Free Traders in that group?"

"You, a couple of the prominent captains, and two Legionnaires who were especially brave. They won't take direction from me."

"But I will?"

Jose dusted his chair before sitting. "Where is all this dust coming from? Surely, it wasn't here before?"

"There was a permanent cleaning staff who did the chamber every day."

"Where did they go?"

"Killed in a riot. You skipped the question. Are you expecting me to take direction from you."

"We'll need to find others to do the cleaning."

"Emperor's earlobes to the cleaning. I'm not your proxy. I don't work for you."

"No," Jose said. "You don't. But you're amenable to reason. And you're smart enough to go along with people when their interests align with yours."

"Glad you understand that."

"Yes."

"Aren't you the least bit curious what will happen when my interests don't align with yours?"

"Nope." Jose smiled. "I've got a plan."

***

Vince had four rallies planned before election day. Jose couldn't match that, but he got his first running two days later.

"These animals are not going to listen to you talk about repurposing flat cars." Marianne surveyed the rowdy crowd.

Jose had blocked off part of a road in front of two restaurants, shoving food and booze out at the gathering crowd.

"They're not, no."

"How are you going to win them over? This is bad. Pletcher has raised the ante. He's got everyone excited about this election. They expect great things."

"We don't have great things to give to them. We're just trying to put things together here."

"They won't want to listen to you talk."

"Why not?"

"Jose, Cheri, you are competent, professional, detailed . . ."

"Are you going to say I've got a great personality? Or make my own clothes? Something like that?"

"You make your own clothes?"

"Of course not, it's an expression, means that you're boring."

"You are, kind of. You're Mr.—what's the word—Mr. Inside. You're Dashi's minion. You help execute things, planned things. Necessary things. But not things that, well, stir the soul."

"We've had too much soul stirring so far, Marianne."

"People need that. They want that. This crowd wants hope for the future. You need to talk about that, not about modifying rail cars."

"I disagree."

"Cheri, please tell me you're not speaking on rail-gauge interchanges, or whatever you mentioned before."

"I've got a different speech tonight. Watch." Jose marched through the crowded room and hopped up on the stage.

"Who needs more beer?" The crowd cheered him, and he waved the servers to fill up the raised glasses. "Food's coming, too! Let me introduce some people!"

He spent the next two minutes pointing out the clients, as he had taken to calling them—other candidates for senator, a favored local entertainer, some popular corporate executives, a few well-known workers. They were his people and he made sure the crowd knew it and that the candidates did as well.

"And me, of course, I'm Emperor Dashi's minion!" The crowd laughed. "And I'm proud to be Dashi's minion. You know why?"

"Tell us," a random voice yelled from the crowd."

"Because Dashi. Gets. Things. Done. He doesn't talk about honor, or glory, or things that are going to get you killed while he watches from behind. He doesn't talk about profit, or loss, or how you're going to make money for him out on a ship while he stays in an office somewhere. He talks about simple things. Practical things. Keep the monorails going. Keep the shuttles flying. The heat stays on. The lights stay on. The food keeps coming! Everybody likes food, right?"

The crowd cheered.

"Now the important thing to remember about me is this—" Jose paused.

"What? What is it?"

"Me. I'm boring."

The crowd laughed.

"Boring. Boring. Boring. Very boring. Extremely boring. I talk about converting tractors to cars. Different types of electrical conductivity for the monorail. Boring. Boring. Boring. I'll bet you're bored right now, aren't you."

Cries of "yes" and "of course" collided with each other.

"And I'm going to keep being boring. You know why?"

"Tell us! Tell us!"

"Because boring means things are working the way they're supposed to. The power flows. You get food. Remember, a few months ago, we ran out of food?"

Nods from the crowd.

"Wasn't that exciting? Exiting, action, adventure. Famine."

The crowd was quiet now.

"Famine is exciting. Shortages of equipment. Exciting. Power off and you're freezing. Civil war? Very, very exciting. Super exciting. Want more of that. Who wants another civil war? Raise your hand."

One drunken idiot in the back raised his hand. His friends smacked him.

"No takers on the civil war, huh? No more shootings, explosions, power cuts, injuries, deaths. No more excitement. Just boredom. You know what I want you to do?"

"What?"

"I want you to vote for me." The crowd clapped. "Why? Because I'm boring. Tell your friends that. When they ask who to vote for, tell them you're voting for Jose because he's boring. I'm boring. My friends are boring. All my friends over here—" Jose named all the others on his voting slate. "They're boring, too. Very boring. Oh, not as boring as me."

The crowd laughed.

"I'm the most boring of them all. Boring. Boring means the lights work. Boring means the heat comes on. Boring means you can take the monorail to your job because it's running. Boring means you can hop a shuttle to visit your friends in orbit because the stations have food and fuel. Boring means you don't have to hide while some drunken gangs shoot off their stolen weapons. Vote for me, or my friends, vote for us. Because we're boring. Boring keeps you safe. Boring gets things done. Boring. Boring. Boring . . ."

The crowd chanted along with Jose, then he gestured more beer from the servers.

"Remember," he yelled over the tumult. "You voted for Jose. Why? Because he's—"

"Boring. Boring. Boring."

CHAPTER 17

"Where is Russell?" Shutt grabbed a piece of wood from a pile in front of her and snapped it in half.

"Ma'am, I can explain," Chaudhari said.

Shutt snapped another piece. "Get started."

Chaudhari swung his pack off his back and set it on the floor. He'd been early at Shutt's office at Militia HQ, hoping to catch Shutt before her day started, only to find she wasn't there. After two comm calls and a high-speed march across town to the main supply depot, he found her in a back room snapping wooden stakes in half.

"Sergeant Russell sent his report, ma'am."

"He's an experienced senior sergeant. He can write ten thousand words in military-speak and say nothing. His report says that one, he's not here, and two because of 'operational necessity' he can't come back, and three, said necessity is a secret too difficult to go into in a nonsecure communication."

"I guess that's why he sent me, ma'am, to explain."

Shutt handed him a piece of wood. "Try to snap these in half. Gentle pressure, don't push hard."

"Ma'am. Sergeant Russell is not here."

"You said that already, cretin. Why is he not here?"

"Ma'am, he couldn't come."

"Why not?"

"The press of duties."

"Try again. I assign him his duties, and they're not that pressing. The plan was to take over that factory and keep it working, but after he got lost in the woods, the factory workers all came back here. And now, we need to ship them back again to get things working."

151

"We didn't exactly get lost. Things were different than we were told. It's all in the report. He stayed back at the factory . . ."

CRACK. Shutt made a particularly vicious split, then looked at the wood in Chaudhari's hands.

Chaudhari snapped his wood in half and grabbed another. "He thinks he can make the factory work."

"His report, the parts that weren't gobbledygook, said ninety percent of the crews had left and that there were random rebels hiding in the hills stealing things and that critical items were missing."

"Not quite, ma'am. He didn't say exactly that."

"I read the report, Corporal. Are you going to break that or not? Is it too strong for you?"

Chaudhari bent the stick between his hands. It didn't snap right away. "Should I try harder?"

Shutt pointed. "Toss it over there. Toss any others you can't snap easily over there. What did my minimal reading skills miss then?"

"Some portable machinery is missing. The first crew out on Bal's boat must have taken it. But most of the stuff there is too big to move. Some missing machinery is critical for producing some obscure food related items. But the big stuff is there. Power is the issue, apparently. We're cut off from the monorail and the big power supplies there, but there're local backups and solar things. Most of the stuff is automated, and the workers showed us how to get it restarted."

"The rebels, you mean."

"Workers, ma'am." Chaudhari snapped two sticks in quick succession and threw them on the broken pile. "They didn't rebel. More like a strike than a revolt. The management of the factory, former management, were tied into one corp. These folks were another, or their cousin was a Free Trader, or whatever. They were afraid something was going to happen to them, and the last factory manager refused to feed them, so they snuck into the woods and raided for food."

"No violence?"

"Some. There were two or three that had beaten somebody up and attacked some other workers. Sergeant Russell took care of that. They won't be a problem again."

"He used sweet reason to convince them of the error of their ways?"

"Shot them and buried them in the woods."

Shutt laughed. "That is a Sergeant Russell way of solving things."

"He gave me a thorough briefing and a complete set of reports that explained why he was staying. The workers in the woods, the desertions, the lack of most items, the difficulty of trading for food, the climate, the river traffic, the simple docks, the look-outs—"

Shutt held up her hand. "Stop. To summarize. The workers mostly hated working there and took the first opportunity to run away into the woods, or the first boat out, with the monorail damaged, trading is almost impossible except for small quantities that we can run in by sailing ship, but it's defensible, and he can feed and maintain his squad indefinitely there."

"That about explains it, ma'am."

"Which you should have started with. Why didn't he come back?"

"He says he can still make some of the things you wanted, but has to do it differently."

"He does, does he. Did he mention to you that if he encountered problems like that, his orders were to come back?"

"I never saw his orders, ma'am."

"Not coming back is mutiny."

Chaudhari shrugged.

Shutt leaned forward. "That's it, a shrug? I say mutiny, and all you do is shrug, Corporal."

Chaudhari braced to attention. "Major. Ma'am. I went there, as ordered. I'm here, as ordered. I don't see any mutiny. You want to send me back, I'll go. You want me to stay, I'll stay."

"What about Russell?"

"What about him? You're the boss, Major. You want him to come back, tell him."

"I might put you back on that boat and tell you to go back and get him. Bring him back."

Chaudhari held out his hand.

"What's that for?"

"Written orders, ma'am. I'll need them to show him, or anyone else."

"Verbal ones will be sufficient."

Chaudhari's hand stayed out. Shutt tried to stare him down, but all Chaudhari did was raise an eyebrow.

Shutt laughed. "Put your hand down. You're not going back with any orders. Interesting things about orders, Corporal."

"Ma'am?"

"If you get orders and disobey them, that's mutiny. But if you never got them, well, whatever you do, that's just initiative. What does Russell really want?"

"There's a list in there. Brass cartridges to make reloads for revolvers. He thinks that he can make primer and powder, he has some of the materials there. But he needs lead to make the bullets, too. I don't understand it completely, but it's all in the reports."

"Seems like a lot of work. Is he up for it?"

"He's not stupid, ma'am. He pretends. He's tired of being chased around and having to deal with so many idiots."

"Like me?"

Chaudhari shrugged. "How do you rate yourself against those Empire Rising idiot officers who started all this mess."

"I rate myself alive, and them dead. Good point. Can he do it?"

"Sure. Our squad likes him. I like him. He looks after

us. I think he can do it. Besides . . ."

"Besides what?"

"He likes guns. He'll love running an ammunition factory."

Shutt nodded. "Tell me. Is this the right thing to do?"

"I don't presume to question—"

"Shut up and tell the truth. You've been on his squad for years. You know what's what. Is he going to be able to do this?"

"Yeah. The people he shot out there were idiots and the other workers all hated them. Things were hard after the riots. Their corp abandoned them. The manager was a useless tool—one of those third sons of corporate stockholder types. Now they're gone, and Scott, I mean the sergeant. He listens to the remaining workers. One was a master machinist. He's getting the production lines up and running. Sergeant Russell convinced them all to join the Militia as auxiliary workers."

"I saw that in the report." Shutt grunted and flexed another stick. This one didn't break so she tossed it on the smaller pile of unsnapped sticks. "Loyal to the Empire, are they?"

"Ma'am."

"Or loyal to team Russell. I wonder which." She pointed at Chaudhari's hands. "Nobody said stop snapping. And don't snap them so clean. Make lots of splinters."

"Ma'am." Chaudhari grabbed another stick and snapped it, taking care to leave the splintered parts free, then continued working through others. "Are we expecting a vampire infestation?"

"Vampires?"

"Driving sticks through their hearts, that type of thing?"

"These are tent poles."

"Wooden tent poles? Aren't our tent poles made of metal?"

"Price has quadrupled."

"For metal poles? We're awash in metal."

"But not awash in metal extrusion machines, metal cutting machines, and bending machines that can handle metal. Those are being repurposed for pipes. There's a pipe shortage."

"A pipe shortage? That's a thing?"

"Everything uses pipes. Waters systems. Sewage. We have conduits carry wires. Conduit is a fancy name for a pipe. Want to spend a week on a cutter without a water system?"

"Can't, we'd die."

"Precisely. Plenty of pipes up in orbit, but I don't want to waste shuttle space having them dropped to us. We're experimenting with replacing any metal equipment that we can with wooden substitutes. Thus, wooden tent poles. If I told you to go back to that factory and carry direct orders for Russell to come back, would he?"

"Won't work."

"That's treason."

"No, ma'am. I meant no, this one won't break. Only three so far haven't broken."

"Completely crappy tent poles. No quality control. Mutiny then."

"Only if he takes up arms and convinces others to attack their officers. If he sits there and refuses to leave, that's a bit muddy. It's more like a military strike."

"Sounds like you looked this up." She snapped another pole.

"He did."

"What if I send you back with a squad to bring him back?"

"Please don't do that, ma'am. There's other ways."

"Which means I'll probably end up with you and the squad joining him there. What's the other way."

Chaudhari snapped another stick, then walked to the table and rummaged in his backpack. He produced a bullet and handed it to her.

Shutt held the bullet up to her eyes and examined it closely. "Looks like a revolver bullet."

"It does. It is."

She rolled the bullet between her fingers, weighed it, then unsnapped her holster. Juggling the bullet and revolver, she extracted a single round from the cylinder, then replaced it with the new one. "Feels fine, fits. Will it fire?"

"You're the major, Major."

"Come with me." Shutt walked through the depot, past piles of boxes and racks of random items, and pushed the back door open. The back alley behind the warehouse was dirt.

"Cover your ears."

"You're going to shoot it right here? In the middle of the city?"

"Not the first gunfire we've heard in the city. Not even the first this week."

Chaudhari covered his ears. Shutt aimed at the dirt twenty feet away and fired three shots into the ground. The first one sounded different from the next two. Puffs of dirt snapped up after each shot. She marched forward and stooped to where the ground was disturbed. Three holes patterned the ground. "He did it? He made these?"

"Took three people a day to make like a dozen. But that machinist guy says he can automate a lot of this. Stopping power's not as good—the powder he makes isn't as powerful. For this to work he needs a lot of strange things—empty cartridges, copper, lead. I've got a list."

"How many can he make?"

"Not sure—and not a lot. Maybe a thousand a day?"

"That's not much."

"He said you'd say that and to quote him, 'Tell her that's a thousand a day she doesn't have right now.'"

"Classic Russell." Shutt holstered her revolver. "You've got a list of what he needs?"

"We didn't put it in the report because—"

"I know. Others read those reports. Get what he needs, and I'll arrange to pay for it."

"That Pletcher guy has—"

"Of course he does." Shutt walked back to the door and entered the factory, Chaudhari chasing behind. "What else?"

"I've got personal messages for twenty friends and friends of friends. The workers who are left, the squad, they all know people. We've got space for people and food and work, so they're recruiting their friends."

"What's your biggest problem?"

"Raw materials for production, and transport to move things back and forth."

"Talk to that Bal guy and get a quote."

"The sergeant suggests giving him a piece of the action."

"Meaning he's already offered it. Carry on, Chaudhari. When you've got what you need here, go back and tell Sergeant Russell he can have his little independent command if he gives me 50,000 rounds a week, starting in a month. But that's just for the start, they'll be other things I need."

"Ma'am, he can't produce that right now."

"If he wants to be in charge, he's in charge. He can figure out a way."

"I'm not sure he can make that."

"I'm not sure he can make a salad. But gun stuff? He's our resident expert. How much room do you have in that backpack?"

Chaudhari looked at the table. "Plenty. Why?"

"Load up with as many of those splintered sticks as you can and come with me."

"Where are we going?"

"First, I have to register for an election."

"The Senate?"

"That's the one. Then second, I have a meeting with

the suppliers who provided those tent poles. They also provide a whole lot of other wooden items. I had a question about the strength of wood vs metal, and they guaranteed me that the wood could perform just as well."

Chaudhari started shoveling broken sticks into his backpack. "Doesn't seem that way exactly."

"It's not. But they swore up and down it would work, so I told them if anything failed quality control, I'd bring it back and put it somewhere they wouldn't like."

"That's why we were breaking the sticks? You wanted examples?"

"I have tons of examples. We were breaking the sticks because I wanted splinters. Lots of splinters. Coming?"

"Absolutely, Major." Chaudhari looked at the pile of splintered wood. "Outstanding."

CHAPTER 18

Admiral Edmunds got up from his desk and looked out his window. "I'm unhappy."

"Sir?" Shutt asked, standing at attention in front of the desk.

"Very unhappy with you, Major."

"What have I done now, sir?"

"Don't get snippy with me, Major. Remember, I'm your boss."

"Sir." Shutt took a breath. "Yes, sir. Could I have more details?" They were in the admiral's office. His decor ran to dark wood and elaborate rugs. Pictures of him shaking hands with important people lined the wall behind his desk.

Edmunds walked to his desk and pointed at his screen. "I've been reading your report on the factory out east."

"Yes, sir?"

"Bit of a fiasco, don't you think, Major?"

"You told us to try to diversify our supply sources, sir. We acquired a factory that produced food, some items that we could trade, and had some minimal repair facilities. We couldn't make major starship parts, but we could make small items, metals, basic electronics, hardware. Pipes."

"Pipes?"

"We have a shortage of spare pipes and conduits on the Militia ships, sir. This way, we'll be able to get more standard parts up to the ships."

Edmunds walked back to the window. "Glad we have pipes, but at what cost? That was an expensive purchase, and now, you're saying we don't have the people we need to operate it."

"We have people, sir, but the most experienced ones left before we took control. I'm trying to get them back, but I'm not hopeful."

Edmunds turned back to Shutt. "A fiasco."

"We're recruiting others from the city, sir."

"An even bigger fiasco."

Shutt turned her head. "I've never run a factory before, sir, nor handled technical specialists like these. I'm still learning."

"Learn faster."

"I welcome the admiral's input on how to run a production facility, from his extensive experience in that area."

Edmunds crossed his arms. "There's that snippiness. And do you think that is the proper way to stand at attention?"

Shutt dropped her attention pose entirely. "I'll stand at attention, which is a military posture, when we're talking about something military. Right now, we're trying to figure out how to restart a farm. Anything in the manual of arms or the infantryman's handbook covering that? Because, if there is, I'll read it. Otherwise, I'm doing my best."

"By the Emperor, don't talk to me like that. I'm the admiral of the Delta Militia."

"And I'm a major in the Militia, so why am I suddenly a second-rate factory manager? I'll tell you why, Admiral because I'm the only one willing to take on new things. I'm the only one who can adapt to our changing circumstances. Those Empire Rising Dorks were pining for the old-Empire times—pining for something that never may have existed as far as I can tell. The other officers were too stupid to even notice. You brought us back to the status quo—and that's not enough. We have to go forward—not backward like the Empire Rising people want, and we certainly can't stay still."

Edmunds walked back to his desk and leaned on it. "You're insubordinate."

"When necessary. If I hadn't been insubordinate during the riots, you would still be locked in a cell, or dead when the jail burned. I'm the one who went in and got you, remember."

"That was an illegal incarceration. You did your duty in releasing me, as required."

Shutt waved. "So do yours. Help us fix this mess. The Militia started the rebellion, the others finished it. We need to get the economy moving, focused on different things. We're losing capacity daily, and one day soon, we'll have an accident that we can't recover from. We need to be flexible in solving things."

"My job is not to fix this moon. My job is to keep the Militia running properly."

"If the Militia isn't part of fixing this moon, then we're going to crash along with the moon. Where will we, the Militia, be then?"

"We need to respect traditions. Not blindly, I get that. And we need less involvement in these things, not more." Edmunds sat. "But I do appreciate your point—I wouldn't have gotten out of that prison without your help. And you did good service in the civil war. But I'm not convinced getting more involved in the economy and politics is better."

"Admiral, we don't have a choice in getting involved." Shutt rubbed her forehead. "Look. We've got all sorts of supply and funding issues. Companies that used to deal with us before the rebellion—yes, I'll call it that, not a civil war—companies that sold us necessary things either won't do it anymore, or can't do it, or we can't afford the prices they're charging. Those items are going to private owners, or our enemies like the Free Traders. That Empire-damned legion is getting more than its fair share of small arms and equipment, and Jose's Department of Corporate Security is supposed to be security guards, not a light infantry brigade."

"It will never be a brigade."

"Both the Free Traders and Jose now have enough small arms to equip thousands. They're short of anything heavier than small arms, but they have communications and transport items we can't afford."

"We can take 'em."

"In space, sure. We have the ships and, more importantly, the people. But even our own people would be reluctant to operate against any sort of important infrastructure, no matter who controls it. They've learned that lesson—blowing things up means hard times for them. That's why this factory thing is important."

"You told me we were going to acquire some minor food-producing plants, minimal expense. You spent ten times the budget we agreed on setting this up."

Shutt opened her hands. "Sir, we need this factory. Sergeant Russell has a plan to use the facilities to produce ammunition and small arm parts—"

"And another thing, why did you put that reprobate out there? He's not fit for independent command."

"We can trust him, sir."

"He turned traitor with the Empire Rising people."

"Which means now that everybody has seen what happened to them, he can't sway anyone else. He'll be loyal to us."

"You mean loyal to the Militia."

"Same thing, sir."

"Didn't sound like it."

"Sir." Shutt drew herself up to attention. "If you don't have confidence in my handling of this project, remove me from it."

"Maybe I'll remove you from more than that. There are other majors."

Shutt smiled. "There are. Are you releasing me from my duties, sir?"

Edmunds glared at her. "You're not upset enough. Why not?"

"Maybe it's time for a change, sir. Something different

in my life."

"Such as?"

"I'm thinking of running for Senate."

"I heard the rumors. I forbid it."

"You can't do that, sir. It's in the constitution."

"We don't have a constitution."

"Dashi says we do. Wrote it himself. Anybody can run for Senate, as long as they pay the registration fee and are of legal age."

"I'll kick you out of the Militia if you do that. You've been a loyal officer, and I'll miss you, but I can't have that type of insubordination made public."

Shutt laughed. "Insubordination? Yeah, try that out if you want to. What are you going to tell people? That I'm a coward? Too many saw me during the fighting for that to stick. That I stole money? I'm not rich enough, and too many others who did steal things didn't get caught. They will not appreciate somebody looking into finances. I fought against the Empire Rising people, right there on the front lines. I voted to hang the ones we caught. I've done dangerous missions for the Emperor. I was one of the first to side with Dashi. I've been your right hand in everything that's happened since I got you out of that cell, and people know it. You could claim I was sleeping with the enemies of the Empire, except that's that other woman, and everybody knows that, too. The only thing that would happen if you kicked me out is I'd have more time to campaign, less BS work to do, and a lot of voters would wonder what's wrong with that old admiral guy that he just fired his most effective, most competent, and most loyal subordinate."

Shutt walked to his desk, picked up Edmunds's personal bottle of brandy, and poured herself a big glass.

"Sante," she said and gulped it down. "That's what those Francais Free Traders say. Health."

"You'll never win this Senate race without my backing."

"We'll see. I signed up this morning. Already registered, I'll be on the ballot. You can support me or not. Here's the thing. I believe in the Militia, in the Empire. In Dashi for that matter—he's been a great Emperor. But I'm not sure you have the vision to go along with all of this. I'm going to keep doing what I've been doing. In public, I'm the loyal Militia officer, which is easy to be because I am. When—not if, when—I win my Senate seat, I'll be right next to you as part of the Militia group. You're a shoo-in because of your leadership in the revolt and your visibility, but I can make it as well. We'll be part of the group that supports the Militia in everything they need, and together we'll deal with those lying TGI people and those cheating Traders. In private, I'll still be your aide and keep doing the work I'm doing because it's important work, and it needs to be done. But as far as safeguarding the Militia, if I see something needs being done, I'll do it, and you can follow along or not."

Shutt put the glass down. "Any questions?"

"I could have you shot for speaking to me like this."

Shutt dropped her hand to her belt. "Better not try. I carry a gun, same as you. And speaking of guns, where's yours?"

Edmund's holster was draped over the back of a chair.

"Shame on you for being out of uniform, Admiral. May I be excused? I have a long to-do list from you. Even if I only do the things I agree with, there's still a lot to be done."

Edmunds scratched his head. "I'd never have expected this from you. I don't understand. Where did this come from? How did this come about?"

Shutt shrugged. "You came to power by consistently disregarding the wishes of your superiors and doing what you thought was right. I'm doing the same. Honestly, though, it was Sergeant Russell who gave me the idea."

"Sergeant Russell?"

"Yep. He showed me that sometimes, no matter how

much you want to, you can't fire a subordinate if they're doing critical work. And I'm doing critical work." Shutt braced to attention and gave a full, historical, cross-chest salute. "Glory to the Empire."

CHAPTER 19

Jose ducked as one of the arriving revelers threw beer into the crowd. "Next election, we ban giving away beer on voting day."

"Can we ban traveling as well?" Rajput asked.

"Not unless we set up more voting stations."

"And if we ban giving away beer, then that means we—"

"Sun, hold the sign higher please."

Rajput's deputy, Sundarampili, held a sign up over his head. "Boring Boring Boring." The sign read.

Rajput pointed at the sign. "Aren't you embarrassed by that?"

Jose ducked another beer toss. His campaign group had cleared a space on one side of the square in front of the monorail station. Three- and four-story Empire-era buildings fronted the square, with shops and restaurants on the ground floors. Government, city, and university offices occupied the upper floors, guaranteeing constant pedestrian traffic. Hungry, thirsty, pedestrian traffic.

"It's necessary to win the election. For me and the others." Jose gestured at the line of people to his left. He'd dictated sober dress—skin suits or executive wear, no wrist or ankle ruffles, no neck cravats. The only items showing allegiance were sun hats in a dark green and white, Jose's preferred colors.

"Nobody knows their names," Rajput said.

"Nobody has to. They just have to vote for them. Are the cards ready?"

Rajput bent and pulled a package of palm-sized cards out of the box containing thousands at his feet. "All set."

"And the other . . . items?"

"All set, too." Rajput gestured to the far left. The line of candidates ended next to trestle tables. Paid campaign workers waited next to piles of unmarked boxes.

"Our first group should be coming off the train shortly."

"There they are." A group with green-and-white straw hats boiled out the station entrance and milled around. One of them pointed at Jose, and they regrouped and traipsed across the square.

Rajput waved at the band leader. A brass band in green-and-white outfits banged out a jaunty trumpet and saxophone tune. The campaign workers clapped along.

The green-and-white hats formed a line to meet Jose.

"Toma Capsell," the leading man extended his hand. "West of here. Point 55, or the double nickel as we call it."

"Thanks for coming." Jose clasped his hand. "I didn't know you did mining out there."

"We don't."

"But the nickel?"

"Some old-Empire word for five. No idea. Just a name."

"Thanks for coming. You and your friends both."

"We're glad to be here supporting the Emperor."

"I haven't been officially endorsed—"

"We know. That's fine. We know who's on Dashi's side and who isn't."

"Thanks for your support. How many are you?"

"Sixty-eight."

Rajput spoke. "You promised eighty."

Toma grinned. "Sorry. Only sixty-eight made it."

"Well, we—"

Jose cut him off. "Are grateful that you brought that many. I'm sure you'll take time to show everyone the city and make sure that they all know where the voting booths are."

Toma winked. "And who to vote for."

"I wouldn't dream of telling them," Jose said. "But I do hope they see their way clear to supporting me. And my friends."

"Of course, Tribune, soon-to-be Senator."

Rajput handed Toma a card with the names of candidates, including Jose on it. "Here's a list of Jose's friends. Remember that you're not allowed to bring it into the polling station."

Toma read it, then put it in his pocket. "Got it."

Rajput handed him a credit chip. "This is for your transport and food expenses. For eighty people."

"I'll buy them a better lunch."

"Whatever."

"There was talk of—"

"At the tables," Rajput said. "To your left."

Toma waved. "See you at the victory party, Tribune."

Jose shook the next man's hand and exchanged a few words, then the others after that. A group of younger women came next and hugged him. Jose smiled and returned the hugs with gusto.

Rajput handed each of them a card and admonished each to not have it in the polling booth.

The next man reeked of booze and slurred his words. He tried to hug Jose, who pushed him off to Rajput. Then he tried to hug Rajput.

"Take this card," Rajput said.

"Card?"

"It's the names of our friends."

"Have enough friends. Why would I want more?"

"Our political friends."

"Don't follow politics."

"You're at a political rally. And this is election day."

"Election day?" the drunk looked around the square. "What election? Whose election? Am I getting elected?"

"The Senate election."

"Senate? All crooks, the lot of them. Why we put up with those thieving, tabbo loving—"

A woman pushed through the line and grabbed the man. "Jik, I told you to wait for me."

"Tass, this here general," the drunk pointed at Rajput, "This general said I'm running for Senate. Think I'll make a good senator?"

"The best, Jik. The best senator. Want to have a drink and talk about it?"

"A drink. Yes! Where?"

Tass took a firm grip on Jik's shoulder. "Where indeed. Nice to meet you, Mr. Jose. Mr. Rajput. Where do we . . ."

"End of the line, take a box."

Jik staggered. "A box? I don't want a box."

"Come with me, Jik."

Jose turned back to greeting newcomers. Rajput watched the two stumble past the other candidates. Jik clapped their shoulders and grabbed their hands. Tass steered him to the tables at the end. The workers handed Tass two boxes. One was a mini tray, already heated to serving temperature, the other clanked when she shoved it over. Tass collected both and pulled Jik off into the crowd.

"There'll be trouble if we get more like them," Rajput said.

"There's plenty more like them, and there will be trouble regardless." Jose thanked the next two women in line, part of a group of older women carrying a banner labeled 'Grannies for Jose.' They all mobbed him while a bystander took a dozen pictures, then left, giggling like schoolgirls. But they took their boxes, including the bottles. "Do we have enough booze?"

"Enough for everybody who's coming with our groups on the trains. Not much for the locals."

"Prioritize any western trains, even if it's not one of our groups. They're more likely to be TGI and more likely to go our way."

"Might not have enough booze for that."

"Give it all out. No sense in ending the day with extra."

"Even if it starts a riot?"

"We'll blame the others."

"Sir?"

"Welcome to politics."

***

The group of eight Free Trader crew members crowded the two Militia next to the polling station. "Not supposed to wear uniforms at the polling station," the head Free Trader Legionnaire said. "Not allowed to vote."

"You're in uniform, you Imperial Turd," the senior Militia private said.

"This isn't a uniform. It's a ship coverall."

"With all those flags and unit designations on it, that's a uniform."

"Not an official government uniform."

"First all you tabbo-chasing Legion people want to be a real military unit, then the second it's inconvenient, you back off, take off your caps, and hide."

The Free Trader Legionnaire scowled. "We're not hiding. We only wear caps when we're on duty."

The Militia private grinned. "So, you're hiding. Afraid the big bad Militia uniforms will scare your people off?"

The Legionnaire placed his hands on his hips. "Can't pass in uniform."

"Fine." The Militia private took off his uniform cap and held it in his hand. His companion did the same. "Now we're out of uniform, same as you. Now are you tabbo lovers going to let us go vote?"

A Legionnaire stepped up next to the leader and pushed past. "Tabbo lovers? First, I'm going to break your arm, then I'll—"

The leader slammed his hand into the rogue Legionnaire's chest and held him back. "Then you'll apologize because we don't threaten people."

"But boss—"

The Free Trader leader shoved him back into the arms of the Traders behind him. "Shut up. Shut up. And shut up. No violence, no threats. In fact, no talking. You keep quiet, and you do nothing except stand here and look mean. Understand."

"But boss, Ms. Marianne said—"

"Not to stop people going to vote, not to start anything, not to cause any problems. All we can do is ask questions and stand in the way. Make things a little difficult. No direct action. Understood? Because if you don't understand, the others will take you out back and beat the understanding into you." The leader held his thumb and forefinger two inches apart. "We're this close to getting representation on the Senate and getting the authority we need to finally fix some of the problems those stupid Militia guys made. If this election gets canceled because the Free Traders were starting fights and intimidating people, we're in trouble. I'm in trouble, and that means you're in trouble. Big trouble. Got it?"

The mouthy Legionnaire nodded.

The Free Trader leader turned back to the two glowering Militia. "Well, I guess no caps counts as out of uniform. Why don't you head to the polling station and see if they agree? Let them through, troops."

The Legionnaires parted, and the Militia shoved their way through.

"Spread out," the leader ordered. "Talk to people, ask who they're voting for. Stand between them and the station. Mention the rules about uniforms, buttons, any sort of paraphernalia. Tell them they'll be arrested if they try to vote with them."

"Will they?" a voice called from the back.

"Of course not. They'll have to take them off, but they don't know that. Fear, uncertainty, and doubt. Make them worry. Tell them they need official Imperial ID to vote."

"I thought they were using fingerprints—"

"Shut up Thomas. Just tell them. No questions? Good. Scatter. Except you, big mouth." the leader pointed at the mouthy Legionnaire." "You stay with me."

The group scattered, and accosted voters on their way to the polls.

"Can I ask a question, sir?" Big mouth asked.

"As long as the question isn't—can I go talk to people because, no, you can't. You're too stupid."

Big mouth closed his mouth. That had been his question. He raised his hand.

"What?"

"Why are we here, sir?"

"I'm not here to help you with your existential doubt, Legionnaire. Ask your priest for the meaning of life."

"I meant why here." Big mouth pointed down. "This part of town. Why are we talking to people here and not next to the docks or headquarters or somewhere like that?"

Boulevards fanned out from the square, heading from the fusion plant to the shuttle port, the Department of Agriculture—aka the current Imperial Council chambers—the harbor piers, and residential neighborhoods. The far side of the fusion plant was light industry that faded out to food processing fields.

"Oh, why here here? First because Marianne said this was where we're supposed to be. But you mean why did she pick it."

"She's smart, that one, but what are we doing?"

"Intimidation. This is a Militia neighborhood. Lots of the people here work for the Militia, and we're here to gum up the works."

"Gum up the works?"

"Make people go home and change their uniforms. Lose their hats. Find a different ID. Some of them won't have the time, or they won't remember where they left their ID, or they don't have time before their shift starts, so they'll end up not voting."

"But we don't know who they'll be voting for."

"We can guess if we have good statistics. And if Ms. Marianne doesn't have them, her friend Tribune Jose surely does. The fewer people from this neighborhood vote, the better it will be for Ms. Marianne, and that's all that counts."

"But is this legal?"

"We're not stopping anybody from voting. We're not hitting people. We're just asking them questions and giving our opinions. Besides."

"Besides what, sir?"

"This is a Senate election. What does legality have to do with it?"

***

"Name, citizen?" The election clerk poised his hands over the desk comm.

"Corporal Weeklar," the freckled woman said.

"Corporal isn't a name."

"J.S. Weeklar."

"What does the J. S. stand for?"

The woman blushed and handed over a Militia ID chip. "Here's my ID."

Lines of potential voters snaked all across the docking bay of Transfer-13. The transfer stations had been co-opted as central voting points for the space-based population. Collectively, they had hundreds of docking ports for incoming ships and dozens of passenger ships dropping every day. Their orbits were optimized to make possible least-fuel intercepts for anybody flying in. Combined with plenty of facilities for transients, they were host to shiploads of orbital residents who would fuel up, pick up and drop off mail, and vote.

"Thank you for your ID, citizen." The clerk inserted it into the desk comm. "But you have to tell us your full name."

"Yeah, what does the J. S. stand for, Corporal?" the uniformed Militia behind Weeklar asked.

"Inquiring minds want to know," another Militia said.

Weeklar turned to the company lined up behind her

and put her hand on her hips. "I'm sorry, what did you say Smitty? Did I hear, 'Please, Corporal, I'd love to clean all the heads on the cutter because they're so busy with all the extra crew'? Is that what I heard."

"No, Corporal."

"All right then. Must have been Gudalar—you wanted extra duty. Is that what I heard you say? Do you want extra duty Gudalar?"

"No, Corporal. Sorry, Corporal."

"Don't be sorry, just shut up." Weeklar turned to the clerk. "Well?"

"Sorry, Citizen. Need your full name."

"It's printed on the ID."

"You have to say it out loud, rules."

"I can whisper it to you."

"We all have to hear it." The clerk pointed to a row of scrutineers lining the counter. Each candidate was allowed a monitor at each polling station. The clerk checked everyone's ID and made sure they were on the list. The scrutineers watched the clerk and made sure he followed the rules. "Everybody checks it against the master list."

"I can whisper it to everyone, then."

"No." The third scrutineer from the end shook her head. She had on station coveralls with bright company patches. "She might give a different name to each of us to confuse things."

Weeklar glared at her. "I don't recognize your corporate logo."

"Hey—" the clerk said. "No talking to them. And she's right. You have to give us all the name."

Gudalar muttered from behind Weeklar. "That's a TGI subsidiary, Corporal."

"TGI doesn't tell the Militia what to do."

The scrutineer raised her eyebrows and smiled.

"TGI doesn't, but I do," the clerk said. "State your full name, publicly, and you can vote. Otherwise, Citizen, move on, you're holding up the line."

Weeklar took a breath. "Justice Serenity."

The line behind Weeklar gasped.

"Justine?" The clerked typed.

"Not Justine, no. Justice. J-U-S-T-I-C-E."

Someone behind Weeklar sniggered. Weeklar spun, looking down a sea of blank faces. She glared at each one. When she turned away, they all grinned and poked at each other.

"And . . . Selena?"

"Serenity?"

"Ser . . ."

"S-E-R-E-N-I-T-Y."

"Your full name is Justice Serenity?"

Giggling broke out behind Weeklar. Her ears reddened. "Justice Serenity Weeklar. And I'd like to vote."

The clerk's comm bonged. "Confirmed, Justice Serenity Weeklar. Here's your ballot, Citizen. Go to the booth."

The TGI scrutineer giggled. "That's a stupid name. Who named you that?"

Weeklar grimaced. "Blame my parents."

"You should blame them. Giving you a dumb name like that."

Weeklar's ears burned more, and she stalked to the voting booth.

The TGI woman laughed again. "Serenity. Such a dumb name. Dumb name for dumb people."

Smitty marched up to the table and stopped in front of the TGI rep. "That's my mother's name. Are you making fun of my mother?"

Gudalar moved up beside him. "My father's name is Justice. Maybe you're making fun of my father."

"I'm not making fun of anybody."

"Probably are." Gudalar turned to the lineup. The grins were gone. "Was she making fun of my father?"

"Probably not, Gun," one said. "She's just jealous 'cause she doesn't know who her father was. Or her mother."

"Must not have wanted her around when she was a kid. That's why she works at her company. They don't require you to have Mothers or Fathers."

"Enough of this," the clerk said. "No talking to the scrutineers."

"I'm not talking to them. I'm just talking."

"If I shut this down, none of you will vote, understand, citizen?"

"Got it, Mr. Clerk, sir. William Alphonso Smith. Here's my ID."

The clerk found his record, then gave him a ballot. After that, the line of Militia stepped up and provided names and IDs, and marched to the voting booth. Every one glared at the TGI woman. After voting, the line of Militia collected in the hallway.

"Anybody have any questions for me?" Weeklar asked.

"No, Corporal!" they all chorused.

"No questions about my name? Anybody want to comment on it?"

"No, Corporal!"

"Good, good. Wouldn't want to overtax your little minds. Smitty?"

"Ma'am?"

"Thank you for talking to that TGI woman."

"It's no problem, ma'am. I felt like . . ."

"Felt like what?"

"Felt like—well, ma'am, I felt like justice was served."

Weeklar gritted her teeth as smothered giggles sounded behind her.

CHAPTER 20

"Polls are closed now," Dashi said. "The counting is beginning. I'll wait here for the results. Don't expect anything definitive for at least two hours, but as soon as I have results, I'll announce them here and via radio broadcast. Long live the Empire!"

The crowd cheered him as he shut the window and shuffled deeper into the building. Dashi, his entire council, various dignitaries and hangers-on crowded the Imperial Agricultural building for election night festivities. Dashi had appeared at the second-floor window overlooking the street and spoken to the thousands in the boisterous crowd.

Jose, Marianne, the Admiral, Shutt and a few others crowded behind him. Dashi took his cane from Jose and limped down the hallway. A small conference room had been outfitted as Dashi's command center. Once inside, he grasped the table and lowered himself into the chair at the head, then wiped his nose. "What a day to have a cold. I can't smell a thing. And so hot." Dashi sipped from a water glass on the table. "And I can't even taste the water. I hope the crowd doesn't get restless in the heat."

"They sound happy, sir," Jose said.

The admiral flopped down on another chair. "They sound drunk, and no wonder, you've been giving away free booze all day."

Jose sat next to Dashi. "Many people have had to travel into the town from isolated stations. Giving them something to eat and drink was the least we could do."

"The least you could do was nothing," Shutt said, closing the hall door. "Which is what you should have done."

"We're just helping people enjoy the first election in nearly a hundred years," Jose said. "People who have traveled into town on their own time and own resources, unlike hundreds of Militia troopers who were ferried in during duty hours and fed and watered at government expense."

"Militia troopers are citizens as well. It wouldn't be fair to them if their duties kept them from voting. Providing them with transport to a station was the least we could do, to use your phrase."

Marianne poured a glass of water. "One of my scrutineers reported that your Militia was menacing them at one of the Transport stations. Water, sir?"

Dashi sneezed. "Thank you." He drank from the glass Marianne had poured and rubbed his nose. "I fear I can't tell water from orange juice right now."

Shutt snorted. "Anybody who was walking near the docks district or by the fusion plant was menaced by groups of Free Trader Legionnaires in uniform."

"Not in uniform. None of my people were in uniform."

"Taking your hat off does not qualify as not being in uniform."

"In the Militia it does," the admiral said. "Dashi, have any more of that water?"

Shutt glared at the admiral. He glared back.

Marianne shoved the tray of water and glasses across the table. "Here you go."

"Thank you for your support, sir," Shutt said.

"Of course, Major. Good luck. Should you be elected, I look forward with dealing with you as a colleague." He poured himself a quarter glass, then upended the jug. "All gone."

Jose hid a grin and walked to the door. "I'll get us more." He opened the door, leaned out and spoke to somebody in the hall, and returned. "Kitchen people will send somebody up."

"That is an important point," Marianne said. "Soon we will all be colleagues."

"Pretty sure of yourself, aren't you?" the admiral asked.

"As sure as you are, Admiral. There will be some surprises at the bottom of the lists, but I feel confident that everyone in this room will become an Imperial senator tonight."

"I do as well," Dashi said. All eyes turned to him. "Time to stop this bickering. We all must work together to ensure the prosperity of Delta."

"I'm all for the prosperity of Delta," the admiral said. "I live here, after all. But the Militia must be an integral part of any solution."

Marianne pulled the tray back and took a glass. "As opposed to being part of the problem, by harassing innocent Free Traders who are going about their lawful business?"

Shutt transferred her glare from the admiral to Marianne. "Many Free Traders have been avoiding tariffs and smuggling goods and profiteering off goods that are in short supply by avoiding council requirements."

"The council and government exists to serve the people, not the people the government," Jose said. "Corporate citizens haven't got an easy ride out of the thing, either."

"Corporate citizens blew up several stations and attacked government offices," Shutt said. "And killed hundreds of Militia."

"Would that be your rogue Militia who started all this mess? You mean rebels, don't you?"

The admiral banged the table. "The rebels are dead. And I remind you that I was imprisoned by said same rebels. Suggesting that they are my rebels is insulting."

"We know that admiral. I released you, remember." Shutt shook her glass. "Where's that water."

"I know you released me, Major," the admiral said.

"But I'm trying to point out that those rebels have been punished or executed and that a new day has dawned."

Marianne made a rude gesture. "This to your new day. I represent the Free Traders, and we will see what the future brings."

Jose shook his head. "No, Marianne. The admiral is correct. A new day has dawned. The corporations, the Free Traders, and the Militia must work together. Otherwise, we're all in it."

Dashi laughed. "I am so looking forward to the first senatorial meeting. But to current matters. Once the elections results are in, I will certify the senatorial list, and I plan to schedule the first meeting of the Senate for tomorrow. The sooner we get everyone used to the Senate running some things the better."

"Some things? Which things?" Admiral Edmunds asked.

"We can discuss that tomorrow," Dashi said. "Tonight is for the elections results and for celebrations. I have ordered special drinks. In my personal items, I have held a number of bottles of old Earth champagne. I will be opening them tonight. To celebrate."

"To celebrate what?" Edmunds asked.

"The rebirth of the Empire, Admiral. What we do tonight is the first step in reestablishing Imperial authority throughout the former Empire." Dashi sneezed, then hacked and coughed. "I just hope I live to see it."

***

It was almost three hours before the results had stabilized enough for a pattern to emerge. Dashi had retired for a nap, leaving instructions that he was to be awakened when the outcome was clear. The four waiting there led handily and were guaranteed election. All of them, with the exception of the admiral, were part of some sort of slate, and each was now the leader of a group of senators. There were some surprises at the bottom of the lists, so the exact composition was in doubt, but each of the three led approximately a quarter of the Senate, with other votes spread around different factions.

"All of your 'friends' appear to have made it, Tribune Jose." Shutt said. "Giving away free booze seems to work for you. What are you going to give them next to keep them in line? Free foot rubs?"

"Inspired leadership and a path forward to prosperity," Jose said. "And you might start calling me Senator."

"You're not a senator until you take the oath during the meeting tomorrow."

"Nor are you, Major."

"Fine. I think Senator-elect would be appropriate for me."

"That's not a title."

"Call me major, then, for the next twelve hours or so. It's your last chance." Shutt's comm beeped. "Excuse me."

She stepped to a corner and spoke into her comm. Jose couldn't make out what she was saying. He walked to the admiral, seated on a couch. "Admiral?"

"Mr. Jose? Tribune. Senator-elect? What do I call you young man?"

"Colleague. I am planning on proposing you as the Speaker of the Senate."

"Why?"

"It's a great honor."

"Is it?"

"Leader of the Senate, first to speak to the Emperor. That's the post that maintains order and decorum."

"You want me to enforce decorum? In this group? Do I get a club?"

Shutt returned to the table. "He wants you as speaker because the speaker only votes when there's a tie. He's neutralizing your vote."

"It's a great honor."

"It's a political maneuver."

The admiral scowled. "I'll think about it."

"If not you, then who?"

"Ms. Marianne," Shutt said. "I hear she's big on decorum."

Marianne looked up from her comm. "Two more stations have reported, we're nearly done."

"Well?" Jose rubbed his head. "It's late. Don't keep us waiting."

"Mr. Pletcher tops the list of unaligned senators."

"Guess it is possible to buy your way into the Senate."

"Like you did?" Shutt said.

Marianne ignored her. "All your friends have won, Jose."

Shutt looked at her comm. "And all the Free Traders who ran, Senator-elect Marianne. Except for this one captain Jimi fellow. He did outstandingly bad."

"I told him not to stand," Marianne said. "He drinks, and everybody knows."

"So does that Pletcher fellow. And he did well."

"Jimi is cheap. He feeds his crew bad wine." Marianne shrugged. "Can't pin that on Pletcher. His wine is good. Best I've ever had."

Jose wrinkled his brow. "When did you have wine with him?"

"I drink with who I want. And he had some interesting ideas, ideas that would benefit the smaller corporations."

Shutt grinned. "Remember those corporations, Jose? You know those corporations? The ones that TGI keeps running roughshod over? They don't like you very much."

Jose held out his hands. "Perhaps I'll suggest him for speaker."

"If you do, I'll suggest you, Senator-elect Jose, and I'm sure I can find somebody who will suggest Ms. Marianne, and we'll let you explain why you've turned down this oh-so-honorable office and want others to take it. Then it can be your vote that's neutered."

The admiral fiddled with his cup. "That's an outstanding idea. Major, you're good at this."

"Thank you, sir. Or, thank you, colleague."

"You call an admiral sir."

"This is Senate business we're discussing."

"You still work for me."

"The people say otherwise."

The door opened and Dashi limped in. "People say otherwise about what?" He grasped the table and lowered himself into his chair.

Jose helped him get settled. "Nothing, sir. Just discussing who we will nominate as speaker."

"Well, then." Dashi reversed himself and pulled himself back up. "That is Senate business, and the Emperor should not be involved."

"We'd love to hear your suggestion, sir."

"No, we would not," Shutt said.

"No, we would not," Admiral Edmunds said. "She's right. If this is going to work, then this is Senate business."

Jose looked to Marianne. She pursed her lips and shook her head. Jose nodded. "Perhaps, colleagues, we can defer this till later. It's late, and the Emperor would probably like to go to bed."

"After I announce the results and drink a celebratory toast, I will retire. This is not my night. It belongs to you. Are the results conclusive?"

"Near enough." Shutt tapped her comm. "Second last station has reported in, and the number of votes on the last one can't change the results now."

Dashi examined his comm. "Very few surprises. Well done, Mr. Jose. Well organized, a complete victory for the green hats. And Ms. Marianne, I don't know what you were thinking. Jimi is an ass."

"His friends said he should be given his chance."

"Which he was, and apparently didn't have as many friends as he thought. Pletcher made it. He's a man to watch, an enigma. Most of your friends except for two, Senator-elect Shutt."

"It's my first election, sir." Shutt smiled. "I'll do better the next one."

"I'm sure you will. That is a surprise." Dashi pointed to the name at the bottom of the list. "He's not one of yours, is he, Admiral?"

"I didn't endorse anybody."

"This time," Shutt said.

"Ever."

"This time." Shutt repeated. The door buzzed, and she answered it. A courier delivered some bottles, which she took to the sideboard, and turned her back to the room.

Dashi steepled his hands. "Has anyone informed him? No? Perhaps one of you could contact him when you have a moment. Regardless, this seems decisive and comprehensive. A glorious day for Delta, and the Empire Returned."

"The Empire returned, sir?" Jose asked.

"That is what we will call it. The abandonment is over. The Return has begun. Please help me to the window and start the video feed."

With Jose on one side and the admiral on the other, Dashi shuffled to the window overlooking the crowd and waited for the video technicians to confirm he was broadcasting before addressing the crowds.

"The Abandonment is over. The Empire Returned is here. For the first time in over eighty years, we have an Emperor, an Imperial Senate, and a new Empire." The crowd's cheering interrupted him several times. Dashi spoke of the new Empire, the challenges ahead, and the need for optimism in the face of future events. Near the end, the crowd started clapping and continued for several minutes, uninterrupted.

Dashi let it continue, then called for the results. He read the names to the crowd to even more cheers, stopping repeatedly to allow the yelling to die down, before continuing.

At the conclusion of the names, he handed his comm back to Jose, and gripped the window frame with both hands. "As the Emperor, I designate these results as official. The Senate will meet here, tomorrow, in this building. Senators cannot take up their duties until they are sworn in. I have at my side, four of the senators-elect. To begin anew, I call upon them to stand with me, take the oath, and be sworn in."

The noise of the crowd overwhelmed his words, but he organized them by hand signals. Putting his back to the crowds, he placed the four facing him, and the crowd behind the window.

"Raise your right hands. Repeat after me. I do swear that I will be faithful and bear true allegiance to His Imperial Majesty, Dashi, and his heirs and successors . . ."

A single spectator slow clapped. Others joined. Soon a low volume bass clap punctuated each word.

". . . against all enemies, so help me God."

The four repeated the phrases. The clapping intensified. Dashi turned, waved, and gestured for his cane. Jose took one look at his white face and grabbed one arm. The admiral grabbed the other, and they hauled him down the hall to the conference room. Once inside, they dropped him in his seat.

Jose poured him a glass of water. "Sir, are you okay?"

Dashi sneezed. "I am well, Jose. I mean, I am, well, Senator. Just tired. And this heat affects me. I would like to sit for a while."

"Sir."

"Congratulations, all of you." Dashi coughed. "Where is the champagne I had sent up. I would like to toast your respective victories."

"Here it is." Admiral Edmunds picked up the bottle from the sideboard. "One's open."

"Some rascal has stolen a drink before us. No matter. Admiral, if you would do the honors?"

Edmunds poured five glasses, one for Dashi and four for the soon-to-be senators.

Dashi raised his glass. "I salute all of you. You are the

Empire's future. Together, you will decide the path to the future."

"Along with you, sir."

"The Emperor leads, Senator Jose. But you cannot lead people where they do not want to go. I will point the way, but it will be up to you four to convince people the way is correct."

Dashi sneezed, then held up the glass. "The Empire!"

The others raised their glasses. Dashi brought the glass to his mouth and gulped it down.

Jose brought the glass to his mouth, then stopped and sniffed. "I'm not that familiar with champagne—"

Shutt sniffed. "Is champagne supposed to smell like this?"

Marianne grimaced and pushed the glass away. "It's spoiled. Something is wrong."

Admiral Edmunds took a taste. "Tastes different."

"I noticed nothing," Dashi said. "Of course, my cold, my, my. Oh my gods." His eyes rolled up in his head, and his mouth frothed. He gasped, pushed himself up, gasped again. Foam rolled out of his mouth, and he crashed to the floor.

CHAPTER 21

"I can't find his pulse," Jose said. The council had piled around Dashi. His face was white, and his mouth was foaming. Jose took Dashi's head in his arms. "Can you hear me, sir?"

Shutt yanked on the door and yelled down the hall. "Medic. Find me a medic. Right now. The Emperor's had a heart attack."

"What's wrong, sir? Talk to me."

"Sit him down," Marianne said. "On the floor."

Jose and Marianne pulled Dashi from the chair. Shutt came in to help.

A Militia trooper with a red cross on their arm and a medical kit in their hand pushed in. "Clear out. Everybody back. Everybody, move."

"Sir, I." Jose slipped back.

The medic pulled out a stethoscope. "Keep talking to him. Hearing is the last thing to go."

"Sir. It's Jose. We're here. We'll get you a doctor."

The medic dropped his stethoscope. "Very weak, very rapid pulse. Shallow breathing. Flushed. Temperature is very high."

Jose wiped his brow. "Heart attack?"

"Heart attacks don't make you foam at the mouth." The medic bent over Dashi's face. "Strange smell. Did he eat anything weird?"

"The champagne. Old Earth Champagne. It smelled funny."

"Anybody else eat drink it?"

"No, we all thought it was strange smelling, so we put it down."

Shutt stood. "Admiral? Admiral, sir?"

The admiral wasn't visible.

"Anyone see him, I'll—"

"Here he is," one of the waiters said, pointing behind a chair. "He's foaming as well."

The medic pushed past and kneeled next to the admiral. "Same symptoms. They've been poisoned."

Jose paled. "We must get them to the hospital at the university."

Shutt stepped through to the door and called for the ready squad to find two stretchers, form up, and carry Dashi and the admiral to a ground car. She stepped back into the room, looked at the sideboard, then stepped out and called the guards in."

"Ma'am?"

Shutt pointed. "Secure that bottle. Nobody to touch it until I return."

Jose stood. "Rajput. Get a security detail up here. Watch that bottle. Make sure the Militia don't take it."

"Why would we take the bottle?" Shutt said. "We didn't do it."

"I just want to make sure it doesn't disappear," Jose said.

"Why would we—to the gods' death with it." She pointed to the guards. "Watch that bottle. Nobody touches it. Nobody takes it. Shoot them if they try."

Rajput looked at Jose's face, then gestured two TGI security to stand across from the Militia.

The ready squad pushed into the room. The medic supervised the loading of Dashi and Edmunds onto the stretchers and hustled out of the room with them. Jose and Shutt followed, both having quiet words with the guards left behind.

Marianne waited till both groups had left, then waved one of her assistants in from the hall. She had a low voice conversation, then raced to catch up with the medical crew, leaving her assistant standing in the room, watching the bottle, along with two Militia troopers and two TGI security men.

Later, nobody could recount the trip to the hospital. Darkness, city lights, celebrating crowds, sirens, a rush into the emergency room. The hospital was moderately busy with the type of injuries a party, alcohol, and boisterous groups that didn't get along would produce. The atmosphere was cheerful, and the waiting room was almost cheerful.

The attending nurse took one look at the two men on the stretchers, registered the waxy white faces and foam-covered lips, and ran to her desk. She didn't even wait for the Militia medic to finish reporting before hitting a button.

"Code thirty-seven" rang out from the overhead intercom. White-coated people streamed into the emergency room, transferred Dashi and the admiral onto gurneys, and pushed them away. One was already pushing a tube down the admiral's throat. Another attached electrodes of a defibrillator to Dashi's chest.

The crowd made to follow, but a white-coated man stepped in front of the door. "Nobody past here except medical personnel."

"I'm an Imperial senator," Jose said.

"That some type of doctor?"

"No."

"Then, stay here."

Jose gestured at the crowd—the armed Militia, TGI security, two Free Traders in Legionnaire gear. "We can make you let us in."

The man folded his hands. "You could. How is that going to help your friend?"

"It's not." Jose located a seat on the far side of the room. He stumbled over and slumped into a chair. "It's not at all."

The different groups stared at each other across the room. Shutt, Jose, and Marianne stepped into different corners and talked on their comms. Assistants stood by. Corporate security, Militia, and Legionnaires fingered weapons and unstrapped holsters, but mostly everyone stood around. A half hour in, a disheveled man in Militia pants and a T-shirt jounced through the door and stopped to talk to the nurse.

"Dr. Rodish?" Shutt came out of her corner. "What's the update on the Emperor?"

"I just got here. I don't know."

"You're out of uniform," Shutt said.

"Because I was asleep, and some idiot on the comm said get here as fast as possible."

"That was me."

"I'm here as fast as I can. I mean, I got here. To the Imperial Hells with it. Which room?" He got directions from the charge nurse and headed for the swinging doors.

Shutt intercepted him and grabbed his arm. "Dr. Rodish, we need an update on the Emperor's condition, and—"

"Which I will give you, after I've seen him. Thank you very much."

Shutt leaned in close and lowered her voice. "There's a possibility of deliberate action, and we're concerned about the other medical professionals present."

"It's probably accidental. Poisonings are almost always accidental."

"If it's not them, then the other medical people, we suspect—"

"Suspect what?"

"Well, are they competent?"

"You tell me. Das graduated from the same medical school as me. We only have one on the planet, remember?"

"Well, I'm concerned, that he might try to obscure the cause of this. The admiral's sickness."

"You are, are you? So, you want me to keep an eye on Das, make sure he does his job?"

"Yes."

"He's an emergency room doctor, not a pathologist. Same as me. We're not trained for that type of thing."

"Is there someone else you could bring in?"

"The best pathologist in the city is only minutes away from here. Want me to wake her up and call her in?"

"Please."

Rodish pulled up his comm and typed a number. The screen flashed and a sleepy voice answered.

"Hi, sweetie. That crazy major who woke me up wants you to come in as well and make sure that these guys were really poisoned. Merta can take care of the kids. Can you come to emergency and check this guy out? Thanks." Rodish hung up before she answered. "She'll come in. She curses a lot when she first wakes up, though. Better not to go through that."

"The pathologist is your wife?"

"Yep. And used to be Das's girlfriend in medical school. I scooped her out from under him."

Marianne walked over. "I've arranged for the senior Free Trader doctor—"

"How is old Franco-Caluga? I haven't seen her in years."

"Because of the political implications, we need a second opinion."

"So, you called in a specialist in hard radiation burns and decompression sickness. Which are great things to know if you work orbital. Good call. I'm sure she'll be extremely helpful with poisoning and internal medicine. Now, if there's nothing else, I've got a stomach to pump."

Rodish marched off.

Jose and Marianne retreated to their corners.

Thirty minutes later, Doctors Rodish and Das came through the swinging doors. Das led. Rodish had found a white coat and stethoscope and now looked like all the other medical people in the room.

Jose stood. "How are they?"

"We need the families, please," Das said. "To discuss treatment."

"Admiral's family is off planet," Shutt said. "He's on active duty, so I'll stand for them, and arrange to get them a message."

Jose stepped forward. "Dashi has no family. But he's like a father to me. I'll come."

Marianne tagged along. "I'm with him."

The doctors led the group to a conference room. They all crowded inside.

Das shut the door. "Admiral Edmunds is very ill. He ingested a poison. It's suppressed his respiratory functions. We have him on a ventilator. He's stable, but his condition is critical. We've pumped his stomach and are trying various counter drugs."

"Will he be okay?"

"If we can restart his breathing, possibly. If not, he'll have to stay on the ventilator. If he doesn't come off the ventilator, his prognosis is poor. Even if he comes off it, his prognosis is poor."

Jose wrung his hands. "What about Dashi?"

"Emperor Dashi was in much worse shape when he arrived. Both his respiratory and circulatory functions had failed."

Rodish fiddled with his stethoscope. "What my learned friend means is when he got here he wasn't breathing, and his heart had stopped."

"We were unable to reestablish either. We've been working on him for nearly an hour, and neither system has restarted."

Rodish put the stethoscope in his pocket. "I have some knowledge of Dashi's previous health conditions. You probably know he was seriously injured in an explosion some time ago. He took a lot of internal damage then, and his health has been precarious for some time. That was a complicating factor."

"What do you mean?" Jose said. "Spell it out?"

"The systemic reaction was too strong. We were unable to revive him. We've had no brain activity for an hour now." Rodish squared his shoulders. "Emperor Dashi is dead."

CHAPTER 22

"Do we have to leave in the middle of the night?" Chaudhari untied the rope from the dock. "And I can't see in the dark. Why do we have to load in the dark."

"Tides," Balthazar said.

"I don't even know who won the election."

"We can't wait to find out. With the river current being so strong, and the tides being so difficult, timing of when we drop out and run down the river is critical. Tides against us, we can't get anywhere." Chaudhari and the crew had finished loading goods for the factory onto their new ship and were preparing to get underway.

"I call BS. The tide is against us now. It's still going up river."

"With this wind, we can sail against it. The problem is, we're so far away from the river mouth, if we wait for slack water or the tide to run out, we won't make it to the ocean this tide cycle. We'll be at the headlands when the tide turns, and we'll get washed back upriver. We'll have to anchor, if our anchor holds, or end up back at a dock a few miles from here. Unless you want this to take four days, or hope that the wind is in the right direction."

"You sure this isn't you ocean people making fun of us land people?"

"Ocean people? We all live one monorail stop over. In houses. Don't untie that one from the dock. Untie it from the ship."

Chaudhari stood and fumbled for the black rope at his feet. "Why not?"

"It's a dock line, not a spring line, or a bow line."

"More ocean people making fun. Do we have to do

this in the dark?"

"Helps with our night vision."

"And keeps people from seeing you. Like police, or customs."

The ship was located at the end of an L-shaped pier. If you wanted to access the ship, you parked next to a stone wall facing the water, turned right, walked fifty meters along the shore, through another gate, left onto a bare concrete pier, then down a ramp to a floating dock, turned left, and walked another fifty to where the ship was moored. A long walk, all in view and weapons range of the people on the ship.

"You want to drive the boat? Last time we put a Militia person, like your Sergeant Russell, in charge of a boat it didn't end so well did it?" Sergeant Russell had opened a hatch in the bottom of the boat he was on and sunk it. He had saved the TGI lifting body from being shot down with important colony-saving cargo, but the boat was a total loss.

"Fair point. You don't live on this boat?"

"It's a boat. You don't live on it, not for more than a week. Not big enough. Take this from me." Bal unwrapped a rope from a deck cleat and passed it down to Chaudhari. "Try to coil it up, make it look neat."

Chaudhari wrapped the rope into a coil and walked to the stern. "But you sail for days and days . . ."

"Don't untie that rope yet. And we sail days and days to get somewhere, then come back."

"Why can't I untie this rope?"

"That's the stern line. It comes off last."

"The order matters?"

"Very much. Helps us pivot off the dock, end up with our bow pointing downstream. We use the spring lines to control the rate of—"

"Sorry I asked. Which one do I do next?"

"Disconnect those power and com lines. And bring them on board."

Chaudhari dutifully unplugged electric and communication cables and helped roll them up onto the boat. Headlights flashed over the pier. A ground truck pulled into the parking lot.

"Company," Chaudhari said. "You expecting more cargo?"

"We're full."

"Passengers?"

"Nope."

"Illegal, unsanctioned, illicit, or stolen goods?"

"We loaded them earlier, when you weren't here." Balthazar shaded his eyes at the glare. "Is that a car or a truck?"

"Funny."

"Not funny. Truth. That's a truck. Who has ground trucks?"

"The Militia. You have illegal cargo?"

"We're smugglers for Emperor's sake. We're full of illegal stuff. Most of it for your buddy, Sergeant Russell."

"What do we do?"

"Play it cool."

BOOM.

"Was that a shotgun?"

"Pretty quiet for a shotgun."

"Some other explosion?"

BOOM.

Balthazar leaned down into the cabin and spoke to his brothers. Dark figures scurried onto the deck. The engine whirred to life. "Chaudhari, untie all those lines now and jump aboard."

"But the order—"

"We need to get off this dock. Start at the stern. Move."

Chaudhari ran along the dock, pulling ropes off. The ship's lights went off. The shadows cast by the boat hid the black ropes. He stumbled over one, cursed, and went to his knees and tried to unwrap it by feeling. "Why am I running? I haven't done anything?"

"Why are they shooting? Does that matter?"

"I'm in the Militia. These people should be my friends, sort of. Are we sure it was a shotgun?"

"You know what they're capable of. Sounded like a shotgun to me. Want to stop and chat with your new Militia friends on a dark pier in the middle of the night, when nobody knows you're here?"

"How bad can it get?"

Flashlights lit the gate at the far end of the pier, and dark figures clustered behind it. The gate rattled. A voice called out. "Corporal Chaudhari, we're from TGI security. We'd like to have a word with you."

Chaudhari and his squad had briefly occupied TGI main. They had no love for him. "I don't want to talk to you."

"You must."

"I work for the Militia, not TGI."

"My instructions come direct from Senator Jose, of the Imperial Senate."

Balthazar threw the boat's motor into reverse. The motor reversed, the boat didn't. "Imperial Senate? Isn't this Jose guy the one who—"

"Wanted to have myself and the squad hung after the fight. Yes." Chaudhari tugged at the rope. "This rope is too tight. I can't untie it."

"Steph—" Balthazar called quick instructions into the cabin. The engine note changed, and the ship swung sideways.

"Stop it. That's making it worse," Chaudhari said. "Take the pressure off this line."

"Can't. Tide has us now. We need to get off this dock. I can drive the bow in. Climb onboard."

The boat pivoted on its remaining two lines and spun stern on to the dock.

"Too far."

"Stand on the line."

Chaudhari stepped up onto the bollard, then onto the rigid line. His weight, and the leverage, pushed the rope down, bringing the boat closer.

"Can't do this forever."

"Your weight will pull us closer. Grab the side and climb up."

The rope slackened under Chaudhari's feet. He slipped forward, cursed, but managed to get both hands over the side of the boat.

At the head of the dock, the fence gate snapped open. They'd brought up bolt cutters. Dark figures carrying flashlights rolled down the dock. "Mr. Chaudhari, please wait, we need to speak with you. There's been a development."

Chaudhari got his elbows over the side of the boat and pulled. He managed to get his right shoulder up, but stuck there. The boat pivoted more. He kicked sideways and got a foot up. Now he was firmly on board the boat, but one of the poles holding the metal wires that made up the safety barriers—what Balthazar would have called the stanchion holding up the lifelines—blocked his hips so he couldn't roll up. He pushed and scrabbled crabwise until his torso was on board and wormed his way up.

Balthazar loomed up. Searchlights from the shore lit his face up. "Stop rolling around. Get that line loose." He disappeared to the stern. "Cut it if you have to."

"Help me."

"Can't. Have to pull the loose lines in before we foul our propeller."

Chaudhari cursed again and pulled out a jackknife. He opened it one-handed in the dark, choosing the serrated blade, then crawled to the stern, dropped behind the bulwark, and sawed at the remaining line.

"Mr. Chaudhari, please stop. We just need to speak to you." A voice called from the dock. Uniformed figures reached the ramp that led from the pier to the floating dock.

"Why do you need shotguns? To talk?" Chaudhari sawed through the last part of the rope. It parted with a hum as the last strands broke. The ship pivoted stern first and spun in a circle. Bal yelled orders, the engines whined, and the spin continued.

The stern swung out to the river. The lights of Landing and the pier disappeared from view, and the mouth of the river appeared. Lights shone from the pier, and the boat continued swinging.

"Um, Bal, we're going to—"

CRUNCH. The bow of the boat knifed into the dock. The boat kept pivoting, the bow prying pieces of the dock loose.

"Sails," Bal yelled. Dark figures scurried across the deck. A white sail ghosted down above Chaudhari's head, then filled with a crack. The wind pushed the boat clear of the dock, backing it into the river. The foresail filled with its own crack, and the boat pivoted even more, then stabilized in the middle of the river.

Chaudhari crawled across the boat to the side near the dock and pushed his head up. Two searchlights stabbed out from the dock and figures called out. "Bal, they're not shooting. Why aren't they shooting?"

"How should I know? Bear away, tighten the foresail, and bear away!"

"Maybe they want to talk and not hurt us."

"Or the plan is to kill you, slowly, and they've been told to take you alive so you don't miss even a minute of the exciting torture they have planned."

"Why aren't they shooting?"

"On course, hold steady." Bal's shadowed head lengthened as he looked up the mast at the sails. "That's it. We're making way."

They were. The dock slid behind and past them. Chaudhari figured they were aimed downstream and at the far shore. "We should go back."

"Can't. We're in the tide now, we're committed. I

couldn't make that pier if I wanted to. Which I don't."

"Can we anchor it or something?"

"Not here, bottoms too foul. Give me two hours, and we'll be somewhere that we can anchor. And you're welcome."

"I'm welcome?"

"For us keeping you out of jail."

"How did you know they were going to take me to jail?"

"Middle of the night, Militias, shooting. Where else would they take you? To a roller derby?"

One of Bal's brothers yelled out that he liked roller derby. Bal told him where he could put his roller skates.

Chaudhari climbed up to stand next to Bal. "I can't see anything."

"Keep the lights off, and you can see enough."

"Do you use satellites to navigate?"

"If they're overhead, yes. But they're not right now. When Delta was founded, we had a full constellation of navigation and communication satellites, I've been told. Now we have to make do with what's left."

Chaudhari's eyes adjusted. The river was a darker black between shades of lighter black that was the shore. "I see the shore."

"We just need to keep midway between the two, where the deep water is. Follow this till morning, then we can anchor if need be. Do you want to drive?"

"I think—" Chaudhari's comm bonged. "Priority message. Wonder who from?"

"The council asking you to surrender yourself for a scheduled torture session. Who is it?"

"The council."

"Really?" Balthazar's head turned in the glow. "Called that one right. Take it to the stern. You'll ruin my night vision."

Chaudhari retired to the rear of the boat to read his comm. He read it twice, then started laughing.

The sails flapped and Bal slid the boat sideways till they filled. "What's so funny?"

"You guys are in that funny religion—Christians, right?"

"Yes."

"Isn't one of your brothers a priest?"

"A Deacon. Why?"

"Let me check if he'll do—can he marry people? Issue a marriage license?"

"He has in the past. Only to others of our religion."

"But he can sign the license, right?"

"Sure."

"Well, wake him up, get him up, whatever. Tell him to bring his prayer book, and a camera."

"Why?"

"I need him to bless something." Chaudhari laughed again. "God does play jokes on people."

CHAPTER 23

"There's a message from Chaudhari," Kim One said. "Came in last night."

"What's it say?" Russell walked in and sat at his desk. He hated desks, but running a factory was like running a squad, you had to be where people could find you. "And where's that kid, whasshername—did she show up for extra duty today?"

"Haven't seen her. Chaudhari's message seems to be in some sort of code."

"No, it's not. We don't have a code. We have encryption."

"No, we don't."

"We do. It's on my comm."

Kim One pointed at the long-range radio against the wall. "Comms don't reach the city. He came through on that radio."

"Right, the comms need a network, or line of sight. Something like that. What's the radio message say?"

"It's on your comm."

"You just said the comms don't work."

Kim One sighed. "Sergeant, the comms work fine here, around the factory and to talk to each other because there's a network here. It's getting through to the city that's the problem."

"Right. Got it. Guess this technology is just too complicated for an old dog like me."

"Sweet Pea told me you'd say that."

"Sweet Pea?" Sergeant Russell sat his comm down. "Kim, mules can't talk."

"We have a cosmic understanding, Sergeant."

"Cosmic understanding?"

"A sort of unconscious connection. I know what she means. She knows what I mean."

Russell nodded once, then picked up his comm. "I forgot. Boy, you are one freaky mule-talking woman, Kim."

"Thank you, Sergeant."

"Glad you're on my side. What is this gibberish?" Russell waved his comm around. "Last one is called same as the first one. We need cheerleaders."

"I told you it was a code. We had problems making that out. He had to send it three times."

"Last what? And cheerleaders?"

"Trust Chaudhari to get involved with cheerleaders."

"I'm in favor of that. My ex-wife was a cheerleader."

"She was?"

"Well, she had the outfit, and she wore it and cheered when I asked."

"I'm amazed."

"That she would cheer?"

"That a woman would marry you, Sergeant. Sweet Pea is amazed, too."

"Tell Sweet Pea I was married twice." Russell looked at the message again. "Last one is called same as the first one. Any idea what that means?"

"None. I kept asking for a repeat, but we couldn't get through again. Sweet Pea thinks it's something to do with the election."

"Why does Sweet Pea think that?"

"Just a hunch."

"I see." Russell put down his comm. "Am I having a conversation with your mule?"

"She's not my mule, Sergeant. She's her own mule. But she's happy to help."

"Thank her, I guess." Russell looked around the office. "I'm thanking a mule. I've gone completely nuts. Does that bother you, Kim?"

"Is your being nuts going to affect how you manage the squad, Sergeant?"

"Me taking advice from a mule doesn't bother you?"

"Most of what you've done over the last year has been kind of crazy and nearly got us all exiled or killed. Did you take advice for that?"

"Lots. Not good advice."

"Maybe Sweet Pea will give you better advice."

Russell stood. "I've heard worse suggestions. Before you get off shift, go find that extra duty girl and beat her up for not reporting. I need to figure out what Chaudhari meant. Any messages at all direct from the city?"

"No, Sergeant. Satellites are out of position. We could ask somebody to hike down to the end of the monorail line and try to plug in there."

"Never mind. I'm sure nothing important can have happened."

***

The conference room containing the wine bottle had become the most heavily secured place on Delta. By the time every interested group had been informed of what was happening, it was almost dawn. The parties had ended peacefully long ago, leaving only the night Militia patrol and bored sanitation workers on the streets.

At Shutt's direction, the Militia had sent the ready reaction squad to the Imperial headquarters.

Marianne had called in more Legionnaires.

The TGI security force hadn't been able to get Jose to respond to his comm, so the lead agent, on his own initiative, had tracked down more agents, and also managed to get a full stop issued on all surface-to-orbit traffic, and all corporate orbital traffic as well. Their agents outnumbered the Militia, who called for reinforcements, causing the Free Traders to activate a good portion of their on-planet cohort. As the madness spread, hundreds of people roamed the corridors.

"The Free Traders will not obey random stop orders," Marianne said, pushing the door to the main floor of the Imperial agriculture building open. She and Shutt had collected the three doctors and brought them back from the hospital to inspect the bottle. "We expect the council to honor the constitution, and allow free passage of ships, persons, and goods."

"Blah blah Free Traders Blah Blah Constitution Blah Blah, that's what I heard," Shutt said, striding up the stairs to the second floor. "We need to find out who did this, and we can't take the chance of them getting away."

"I will protest strongly at the council meeting."

"Trader girl, you haven't figured it out yet, have you? There is no council. No Emperor. Dashi's dead, the Empire dies with him."

"The Empire is not dead, nor the Emperor. There is a Senate. Senators. Us. We can make laws. You swore to uphold Imperial laws."

"One of which is when the Emperor dies without an heir, the Senate chooses."

"We don't need an heir to make laws. We can function in the absence of the Emperor. We need to vote on them."

"We also need a quorum and a speaker and a few other things. What are all these people doing here?" The upper hallway was crowded with uniforms. Shutt pointed at a random woman. "Who are you?"

"TGI security, Major."

"That's senator. And get out of here, you're not needed."

"Disagree. Besides, I don't take direction from the Militia. I'll leave when Tribune Jose tells me to."

"Where is Tribune Jose?"

The woman hesitated and looked around' at her colleagues. Some shrugged, others looked grim. "He's not answering his comm. Hasn't for a while. Major— Senator—is it true that the Emperor is dead?"

"We'll update you later. We need to get these people

out of here so the doctors can get in. Marianne, can you get Jose on the comm?"

"Why me?"

"Because he's your boyfriend. Where are those doctors?"

Three white-coated figures pushed up the stairs. "Down here. Let us through."

Marianne played with her comm. "Jose's not answering."

"Outstanding. Absolutely outstanding." Shutt yelled down the hallway. "Junior Militia person, identify yourself. Raise your hand."

A few hands went up down the hallway, deep in the crowd. They called back and forth until one waved at Shutt. "Here, ma'am."

"Right, private? Private. Tap one of those Legio Sigma Draconis folks, one same rank or close. Then find a young looking TGI security person. Tap them. Then the three of you clear out and wait outside. One from each group, understand? Rest of the Militia, do the same. TGI, Legionnaires, report to your bosses outside. We need this corridor cleared, and there's a lot of mistrust going on, so this way everything is equal. Marianne?"

Marianne rose up on her toes. "Legionnaires, do as she says. One for one with the Militia and TGI people. I want a dozen of you out of the door as soon as possible."

"TGI head person," Shutt yelled. "If you can get Tribune Jose on the comm to ask permission, tell him his fellow senators need to talk to him. If you can't get him on the comm, use some common sense. There're too many nervous people with guns here, and we need to get into that room."

Marianne stepped to one side and flattened herself against the wall. A stream of trios pushed past them and climbed down the stairs. As they shoved to the doors, the idea spread. A few yells of Marianne's and the Legionnaires on the ground did the same. Within five minutes, the hallway was clear except for one guard from each group, and Shutt and Marianne and the doctors flowed into the conference room. One guard from each group remained in the room.

"Well?" Shutt said to the doctors.

"Well what?" Rodish said.

"Was he poisoned?"

"How would we know?"

"You did go to medical school, didn't you?"

"I surely did. I didn't go to poison detecting school, though."

"Why are you here, then?"

"You made us come. What do you want us to do?"

"You're doctors. Do a test or something. Don't you have labs?"

"Not poison labs. We can do some tests, but it will take forever."

Dr Das walked to the table with the open bottle, poured a glass, and sniffed it. He wrinkled his nose then passed it to the third doctor, who sniffed as well. She handed it to Rodish.

Rodish sniffed, then jerked his head away. "Don't need tests. Bitter almonds. You concur colleagues?"

The other two doctors nodded. Rodish handed the glass to Shutt. "Sniff. What's it smell like?"

"Almonds. Cyanide?"

"Sure smells like it. Symptoms were there, too. Might be mixed with something else, but cyanide will kill you by itself."

"Where do you get cyanide?"

"Anywhere with a chemistry lab. Even a small one. Kids in school can make it. Somebody makes it industrially on planet for industry. It's used in metal refining."

"Third Moon Chemicals makes cyanide," Marianne said. "I've carried shipments for them."

"That makes you a suspect, knowing where it comes from."

"Me and the other ten on the crew, plus the hundreds on the station, plus the thousands who work for mining, smelting and shipping companies."

"Still, suspicious that you knew."

"You knew the smell, we didn't. That's suspicious, too."

The doctor coughed. "It's pretty common stuff. But I'll tell you this much, you can't mix it in by accident. Somebody put it in that bottle."

"Can we check it for fingerprints or something?"

"How many people handled it already?"

"A dozen. Won't prove anything."

"There you go." The doctor yawned. "Time to go to sleep."

"How can you sleep at a time like this? The Emperor is dead."

The doctor yawned again. "We're doctors. People die on us all the time."

"But he was the Emperor."

"Everybody dies." Another yawn. "Even Emperors."

CHAPTER 24

". . . his heirs and successors, so help me god." The newly elected senators finished swearing their oaths and sat. The conference table had been removed, replaced by benches in an open C shape. At one end of the C was a dais with a chair on it—reserved for the Speaker of the Senate once they were elected. In the middle, a clerk stood, having administered the oath to the senators. The clerk pointed to Shutt, then sat.

Shutt stood. "Fellow Senators, our first order of business is to elect a speaker. We will need—"

Marianne had seated herself in the first row of the left side, with Free Trader senators to her right and behind her. Senator Vincent Pletcher sat cross-corner to her, in the front of the other row. Marianne scooted right and leaned close to him. "Want to be the speaker? Together, we have the votes."

Pletcher looked behind him. "I don't see Jose here. Where is he?"

"He's distraught over Dashi's death. He's not taking calls."

"You don't know where he is, do you?"

"I think you'd make a fine speaker."

"Are you sure he's alive? Was he assassinated as well?"

"Nobody was assassinated."

"Dashi and the admiral were poisoned. That's an assassination."

"It could have been an accident."

Vince grinned. "Sure. What does the speaker do?"

"Call the Senate to order. Decide who talks when, enforce decorum and rules of order."

"That doesn't sound all that hard. I don't see the admiral, either." Vince did a quick count. "In fact, I only see twenty-nine senators. Who's missing?"

"Jose, the admiral, and that random Militia guy. We can't find him. He disappeared from the city last night."

"Disappeared? As in beamed up by aliens?"

"As in, sailed away on a ship."

"Militia ship?"

"Don't know. Run by some guy called Balthazar."

Pletcher laughed. "I know where he is. Yes."

"Yes, you know where he is?"

"Yes, I'll be speaker. Propose me, and with your group and my friends, I'll be speaker."

"We have the votes to beat Shutt."

"Won't have to. I'm sure she'll be happy to have me as the speaker."

Shutt finished her speech and sat. She stared at Marianne and raised her eyebrows."

Marianne stood, but leaned over again. "You sure? I'll propose you right now?"

Vince gave a bad parody of the formal Militia cross-chest salute. "Glory to the Empire."

***

The random Militia guy, Chaudhari, threw a line to the dock. Russell himself grabbed it, and wound it onto one of the tie-down cleats, before knotting it tightly. Balthazar threw a second line. Kim One caught it. She wrapped it once around the bollard and waited.

Balthazar jumped off the boat, busied himself with the other lines. He pointed at Russell's knot. "What do you call this? Drunken half hitch? Idiot's bend?"

"What's a bend?"

"It's a type of knot."

"Not what?"

"A knot. In a rope. It's called a bend."

"Ropes don't bend. They're not metal."

211

"It's a nautical term."

"Here's some other nautical terms. Kiss my—" Russell threw in a combination of curses and denigrations. "Don't hassle me about your stupid knots. Have you got stuff for me?"

Balthazar retied the knot. "Talk to your friend. Make sure you use his title."

Chaudhari hopped off the boat. "We've got stuff. Lots of stuff."

"Corporal Chaudhari, how glad to see you."

"And you as well, Sergeant Russell."

"What was that stupid message?"

"Stupid message? Oh, the last first thing."

"We have no idea what it meant."

Kim One stepped up. "We even asked Sweet Pea. She didn't know, either."

Chaudhari furrowed his brows. "Isn't Sweet Pea your . . . ."

"Mule, yes."

"She talks now?"

Russell coughed. "Kim One has a cosmic connection with Sweet Pea. Their connection allows them to exchange thoughts directly without talking."

"I see."

"I've been consulting with her and Sweet Pea since you've left."

"I see." Chaudhari looked up at the shore end of the dock, where the mules grazed. "Has she been giving you good advice?"

"Outstanding advice." Russell fished in his pocket for a cigarette, but didn't find one. "I'm thinking of promoting her to corporal."

"Corporal?"

"Yes, she'd make a good corporal. For example, she always arrives when she says she will, and she's about as reliable and understandable as some other corporals I know."

"She's a mule. All she can do is bray."

"Yes, and that's about as understandable as 'The last is called the same as the first.'"

"About that . . ." Chaudhari started talking. As his explanation stretched out, Russell's face got darker and darker, so he talked even faster to get the facts out.

"So, it was a bit of a lark, but I figured why not. Have some beer, meet some cheerleaders, talk a bit. It seemed like a fun thing to do . . ."

"Let me get this straight," Russell said. "You were supposed to see Shutt and get more supplies and some orders regarding what we were to do here."

"You know as well as I do, Sergeant Russell, that it wasn't as simple as asking for orders."

"Well, talk to her, get some idea of what direction things were going. Instead, you joined Vince Pletcher's election party."

"Yes."

"Registered yourself to stand for the Senate."

"Yes."

"Campaigned with him."

Chaudhari stepped up close to Russell. "Those cheerleaders were amazing. We'd go to parties, and they'd do this toss thing, and all I had to do was give a little speech."

"What did you speechify about?"

"The Empire. The Militia. The Emperor."

"What did you say about them?"

"That I was in favor of them."

"Anything else you were in favor of?"

"Well, free beer."

"And?"

"And what?"

"Anything else?"

"I may have said that Senator Pletcher was a good guy and that he had the support of the Militia in a lot of ways."

"And did you say this was an official Militia policy?"

"I may have been in uniform when I gave this speech."

"Does Shutt know about this."

"Not before I left. Now, probably."

Russell fished in his pocket again. "Emperor's testicles. Who has cigarettes?" All the sailors and everyone on the dock shook their heads. "When Shutt finds out you were talking smack, she's going to drag you face down behind a mule for fifty miles. Probably my mule."

"I don't think the other senators will allow her."

"Other senators? Why would they care?"

"Because, well, because I won."

"One? One what?"

"The election. I won. I came in at the bottom of the list, but above the cut-off. I won the election. I'm a senator now."

Russell's mouth dropped open. "You're what?"

"Senator Chaudhari. I'm an Imperial senator now." Chaudhari thumped a hand on his breast. "Glory to the Empire."

The crowd gaped. Then Sweet Pea brayed.

"Thanks for your support, Sweet Pea." Chaudhari grinned. "She is a smart mule, isn't she?"

CHAPTER 25

"What do you mean, you can't find Senator Jose?" Marianne thumped the table. "He needs to be in the Senate meeting this afternoon. We're deciding what to do about Dashi's murder. And planning his funeral."

"He was broken up by it, ma'am." TGI security VP Rajput said. "Dashi was like a father to him."

"You must have some idea where he is?"

"He's in orbit. He launched the lifting body from our western base. It delivered him to TGI main, but we lost track of him after he left the dock."

"The Militia shut down all shuttle flights."

"TGI doesn't take orders from the Militia."

"What's he doing up there?"

"I don't know, and even if I did, I don't have to tell you. I work for Mr.—I mean Senator Jose. Not you."

"Of course. Of course. You're right. I'm distraught. Dashi was like a father to me as well. I feel . . . stunned." Marianne frowned. "We'll all miss him."

Rajput nodded. "I will. He was a good boss. I worked for him directly in the past, best job I ever had."

"Better even than Senator Jose?"

"Emperor Dashi was always the guiding influence. Jose executed his plans. They can be confusing. But, with Dashi, you always felt that he knew what he was doing and that it was for the best."

"If you speak with Senator Jose, will you tell him I've been trying to reach him."

"Of course."

Marianne stood. "I need to get ready for the Senate meeting. Will you excuse me?"

"Ma'am." Rajput stood, and Marianne walked out of the conference room and down the hall. On her way to the lobby of the Imperial agriculture building she passed dozens of staffers for the new senators. Several accosted her, and she told them all the same thing. Now that the new Senate was constituted and had elected a speaker, it would meet after lunch. The agenda included Dashi's funeral, a period of mourning, a temporary executive council, and how to choose an heir for Dashi. She told everyone she planned to propose a committee to meet and suggest heirs for Dashi and a method of choosing it. She smiled at everyone, looked grave, shook hands, and hugged more than one tearful figure.

She excused herself to sneak into a bathroom. After entering, she made sure she was alone and dove into a stall, activated her comm. Two transfers later, she was talking to Captain Mathieu, the only ship within comm range right now.

"How many ships can you have ready within the hour?"

"Define ready."

"Fueled and provisioned, crewed, moving, and with armed parties on board. Big armed parties.—two dozen or so per ship."

"That's a tall order, Cheri."

"Well, put down your wine and find out."

"What happened to Dashi?"

"Poisoned. The admiral, too."

"Who did it?"

"I don't know."

"It wasn't you, was it?"

"Of course not."

"You'd tell me if it were you, wouldn't you?"

"Of course not to that as well. Gather the ships. Jose is missing. He's planning something. I'm going to send you a list of key orbital stations. I need to get them under Free Trader control right away."

"We can do that. Maybe. What about the surface?"

"Too many other factions here. The Militia was activated for the election. I have enough support that they can't arrest me. But I can't accomplish anything here, either."

"What if you join with the TGI people?"

"What if they join with the Militia? And I have to talk to Jose for that. He's not answering his comm."

"He doesn't want to talk to you?"

"He doesn't want to talk to anybody. Get the ships together. I'll send you a list. Start right away. We need our people in charge for as much of this as possible."

"And if there's fighting?"

"Back off and leave them. We can't afford to lose any more stations. I need intact resources, not glorious battles."

"But glorious battles are such fun."

"How much have you been drinking today, Uncle?"

"Not enough, Cheri. Not enough to storm defended stations, that's for sure."

"No storming. Just quiet occupation."

"I'll get started. What will you be doing?"

"I'm going to make sure I don't get put on the committee to choose Dashi's successor."

"You don't want to be on that committee? I thought you always wanted to be in the room when decisions are made."

"Not this decision."

"Why not?"

"Because if I'm not part of deciding how Dashi's successor is chosen, then I don't have to support it. I can complain, delay, keep the talk going."

"And, meanwhile, your crazy uncle keeps occupying stations."

"D'accord."

"Huh. Who do you want as Emperor?"

"Wrong word."

"What?"

"I don't want an Emperor. I want an Empress. Me." Marianne laughed. "Empress Marianne the first has a nice sound to it, don't you think?"

***

"Look at it this way, Scott," Chaudhari said. "Now you've got your very own senator in the Senate."

"I didn't want my own representative in the Senate. I wanted boxes of empty cartridges, gunpowder, and all that other stuff on my list."

"You got most of it. I thought it was a good idea."

"You thought? If the Militia paid you to think, they'd be paying you half as much as you make now."

"Luckily, the Senate has an honorarium."

"What's that?"

"It's like an official bribe."

"Who's bribing you?"

"Right now, Pletcher and Balthazar."

"Both of them?"

"They each paid me to convince you to buy solely from them."

Russell held out his hand. "Gimme."

"What?"

"The bribe should come to me, not you."

"But you don't take bribes."

"Sergeant Russell doesn't take bribes for Militia business. Merchant Prince Russell needs the money to pay for stuff. I need copper. Clothes. Belts. Do you know how much belts cost?"

"I can't give you my bribes."

"Sure you can. Go back and ask for more. Tell them I took money from both of them, and I'm still not convinced. I need more money."

"No way I can . . ." Chaudhari tilted his head. "Actually, I can do that, can't I?"

"They probably expect it." Russell scanned the list of

cargo. "I need more primers and some more steel. Sheet steel to stamp the revolvers."

"Pletcher has the primers. He knows a factory that can make them, on the quiet. Balthazar has the steel. He has a friend in an orbital. They can land it from orbit if you'll pay. They're holding out for higher prices, and they both know that you need them. I don't know what to do next."

Russell ran down his list. "There's two or three times of what I ordered here—the quantities. Some cases, five times."

"Balthazar grabbed what he could, and Pletcher did, too. They figure your credit's good, so they gave you what you need. And did I tell you that Shutt wants five to ten times as much as you said I can produce? They want to get paid."

Russell ran his fingers down the list. "I can increase production, probably not that much."

"She was most insistent."

"Scared you?"

"I helped her make splintered wooden sticks."

"What was she going to do with those?"

Chaudhari explained to Russell about Shutt, the tent poles, and her suggested use.

"I approve of that," Russell said. "Gotta find me a mallet and send it to her. Tell her to hammer them in extra deep."

"Scott, we can make this work, but I'm stuck with Balthazar and Pletcher. They both want exclusivity . . ."

Russell spun his comm in his hands. "They don't expect to get it, it's just negotiating. We need to out-negotiate them. And I see you've stopped calling me Sergeant."

"I'm a senator now, after all."

"Last in line."

"Still Senator. How do we out-negotiate them?"

"Find somebody they're more scared of."

Both men traded glances. "Shutt!"

Russell snapped his fingers. "Head back with Balthazar. Go see Shutt. Tell her she needs to 'arbitrate' between these two for supplies. She threatened the bejesus out of them, and they'll sell me the rest of what I need."

"Why doesn't she build this stuff, this ammunition, back in Landing?"

"Wants it far away from any of the unpleasantness, as we call it now. Here, it will be under my control, which means her control. To her."

"You could sell to those other groups."

"I hate those other groups. I hope they all get tortured to death."

"Harsh."

"She's the only one who hasn't tried to kill me. She treats me even reasonably fair, and I've only got one customer for all this ammunition—her. And she knows it."

"And I go back and tell her that?"

"I've got a list of other stuff I need already. The engineer or whoever was here before knows his stuff. He gives great advice."

"Why'd they toss him?"

"Some religious thing. And he drinks a lot."

"How much?"

"Enough he couldn't do his job a lot of mornings. But he doesn't drink anymore."

"How'd you get him to stop drinking?"

"I didn't. I told him any morning that he wasn't at work, or missed his deadlines, he'd answer to me."

Chaudhari thought about this. "He still alive?"

"Alive? Yes. Able to walk? Not right now. No permanent damage. I think. Probably no permanent damage." Russell shrugged. "All right, ten times as much ammunition. I won't get all of it right away. Need more people. More people mean more food, which I have, but also . . ." Russell made a list, thinking out loud for a minute. Chaudhari waited. "Kim!" Russell bellowed.

Kim's head poked around the open door. "You want

me, Sergeant?"

"Were you eavesdropping?" Chaudhari asked.

"Of course. This was obviously an important meeting. Sweet Pea expects representation, so I've been listening for her."

"Kim," Chaudhari said, "you can't listen for a mule."

"She and I have a—"

"Cosmic connection. I got it."

Russell started typing on his comm. "Kim, take Sweet Pea and a dozen troopers and head east. We need more recruits. Talk to everybody at those cut-off stations, convince some of them to come here, or to start shipping stuff to us. We need more supplies."

Kim saluted. "Who should I take, Sergeant? Which troopers?"

Russell pursed his lips. "Let Sweet Pea decide. And check in with my SPD as well."

"Understood, Sergeant."

"Whoa, hold on." Chaudhari raised his hands. "Scott, you're putting a mule in charge of an expedition."

"Don't be silly," Kim said. "Sweet Pea can't command the squad."

"Glad to hear it."

"She doesn't have enough seniority. The sergeant is in command. But if he dies, Sweet Pea is next."

Chaudhari gibbered while Russell and Kim exchanged details. Kim saluted and moved out. Chaudhari regained control of himself. "You don't buy this talking mule stuff, do you?"

"Why not?"

"It's crazy."

"Maybe. But Kim's advice is sound."

"She says it comes from a talking mule."

"Wherever she gets it, no talking mule has ever convinced me I could jump between two warehouses in Landing 'with absolutely no problem,' unlike some."

"Right." Chaudhari nodded. "I admit that wasn't one

of my better ideas. And how is your leg? Any problems?"

Russell tapped his lower calf. "The wonders of titanium. They'll head out tomorrow, get us more workers. You have to leave in the middle of the night—those stupid tides again. Talk to Shutt. I'll give her as much ammo as I can, but I need those supplies. She needs to settle Bal and Pletcher."

"Right. Hey, if I leave tonight, why isn't Kim's group going out as well."

"Sweet Pea."

"What about her."

"It's dark out. She doesn't like the dark." Russell shrugged. "She's more of a morning mule, really."

CHAPTER 26

The red lights flickered on Jose's comm station. The locked wooden padded door he'd installed in imitation of Dashi blocked most sounds except the hand thumping and slamming on the exterior metal. He ignored both the lights, and the noise.

Jose rolled the pen Dashi had gifted him between his fingers. The inlaid pattern on the aluminum case was worn smooth. The top bent to the side—Dashi had told Jose he used it to pry a drawer open once, years ago. There was nothing special about the pen—it was of a common design, but old preabandonment. Dashi had used it for years for formal signings. But passed it on to Jose when he ran for election. "Senators need to sign things," Dashi had said.

The door noises changed. Rather than a low thump, it was now a large clang. They'd switched from hands, to using metal bars, or perhaps pipes.

"Pipes," Jose said. "I promised Dashi a report on pipes. Production and storage. I said I'd have it tomorrow."

Dashi was gone now. Jose dropped the pen on his desk and used his comm to display a list of calls that needed to be returned. There were hundreds. Marianne had called a dozen times, so had Shutt. Another call flashed as he watched. He erased the list, then manipulated the comm controls to activate the large screen to his left. On screen were a dozen to-do lists, construction plans, a program tracking critical—critical to him, at least—commodities, their location, also prices, education, and training programs. He typed a few words, and the display changed. It showcased a chart of materials needed to make pipes and production facilities, along with production timelines.

Need more manufacturing capability, Jose thought. Of course, that was always the answer—more places to build more things. Everyday items were wearing out and had to be replaced by equipment that was never designed to replace them. Then that equipment itself had to be replaced.

"Things fall apart; the center cannot hold." They were running out of everything, and the ability to repair everything. With Dashi he had been slowing the decay, trusting in Dashi's plan.

Now Dashi was gone. What of his plan? Or what of his planners?

The door screeched as metal ground on metal. It shook, then the handle and assembly rotated a quarter turn. Another screech, another quarter turn.

Jose ignored the screeches and brought his to-do list up. There were 139 items on it. He scanned them, then sorted it in reverse order of importance. What had he considered important enough to be on his list, but trivial enough to leave it at the end? Find a company that can manufacture musical instruments. Appoint a commission to review teacher qualifications. Buy new shoes.

Jose stuck his feet out to the side of his desk. Since he spent most of his time on stations, he wore his custom skin suit with executive garb on top. But he clad his feet with proper shoes, not station slippers or mag boots. The colors matched his skin suit. But they were scuffed and worn.

The handle screeched and turned a half turn this time. It clicked, then unwound till it dropped into the office with a crash. The door opened.

Rajput marched in. "Sir? Are you all right?"

Jose stuck his feet out. "Do you think I need new shoes, Rajput? Or can I polish these up a bit?"

Rajput's eyes dropped to the shoes, then up to Jose's face. "Polish? Like clean them?"

"Polish them. It's like paint. Paint for shoes. Take something old and paint them up a shiny new color. Make like they're new. What do you think?"

Rajput looked down again. "They look fine to me, sir. But I don't know much about shoes. I wear slippers."

"But what about the people who do wear shoes?"

"Sir, we need you."

"It's only fair. If they want to wear shoes, they should have them. But we don't have the capability to manufacture shoes."

"We have problems, sir. A great deal of unrest. Ms. Marianne called me repeatedly. She wants to speak with you. She threatened to do things to me if I couldn't get you on the phone. Very bad things."

"Nor do we have polish, either. I wouldn't know where to get it. I'd have to start another project. A shoe polish project." Jose tapped his comm. "What should I call it?"

"Free Traders are occupying stations, and Free Trader forces are in the streets in Landing. Senator Shutt wants to speak to you as well."

"Fighting? In Landing, again?"

Rajput shook his head. "Not in Landing, no. No fighting. They couldn't win. We have security people there, and Ms.—I mean Senator—Shutt has been particularly aggressive in showing her troops to the citizens."

"Have Senator Shutt's troops been fighting with the Traders?"

"No, sir. She's issued some strict rules to her people. No shooting if at all possible. No more damage to infrastructure. But there's been a lot of posturing. What should we do?"

"About what? The shoe polish?" Jose changed his screen display and brought up a blank Gantt chart. He labeled it: Project #237. Shoes and polish.

"The unrest. The Senate. Ms. Marianne. The Militia."

"You're the head of security. Secure things."

"I don't know what to do in this situation. Please call

them. Senator Shutt promised to jam splintered wooden tent poles—"

"Think."

"Sir"—Rajput brought himself into something like attention—"that's not my job. I apply rules other people give me. Sometimes good, sometimes bad, but I make the rules stick. It's up to you to tell me what rules, and when."

"Do it yourself."

"I can't."

"You mean you're too lazy."

"No, I mean I don't know how. Dashi knew how. You do, too."

"Dashi's dead."

"Yes. But you're not."

"I quit."

"You can't."

"I can and I will. The Senate, TGI, Dashi's assistant. Tribune. All of it."

"No, you can't. If you try, I'll do a Jose on you."

Jose turned from the screen. "What is that? What's a Jose?"

"It's a term people use. When somebody uses obscure rules and strange administration changes and odd bureaucratic things to force somebody to do what they want."

"That's what they call it?"

"Yes, sir. That's what they call it. Doing a Jose."

"Fine, what's your Jose?"

"You can't quit."

"You already said that."

"No, I don't mean shouldn't, but you shouldn't, or don't want to. I mean you can't. There's no mechanism. When you set up this Legate thing, you didn't plan a way to quit. Same with the Senate. You can get fired, or voted out, or impeached. But there's no way to resign."

"I won't go to the debates, then."

"Okay. But still your responsibility. If you don't go,

you'll be shirking your responsibilities."

"I don't want them."

"Doesn't matter, though. You still have decisions to make. As Dashi's assistant, Tribune, whatever. Still your responsibility."

"I'm going to resign those posts."

"You can't. Well, you could, except, who are you going to give your resignations to?"

"Dashi—Oh. He's dead. He can't accept a resignation."

"Nope. You're in charge of a whole lot of stuff until the Senate appoints a new heir. People are going to take your orders."

"I don't want to."

"That never stopped Dashi. That never stopped you from listening to Dashi."

"Dashi knew what he was doing. He had a plan."

"I'm sure he told you."

"Not all of it."

"Do what he told you and fix the rest later."

Rajput turned off Jose's screen. "Sir, we really, really need you."

"Not me specifically. Anyone in my position would do. There's nothing special about me."

"No. But you're what we've got right now. What would Dashi do?"

Jose removed the pen from his drawer and drew it out. "What would Dashi do? Good question." He rolled the pen from side to side. "Secure the succession. Enforce peace. Maintain stability and prevent disorder."

"The Free Traders are boarding orbital stations and taking them over in the name of the council."

"Has there been any resistance?"

"Not yet. People think the council authorized it."

"An aggressive move."

"She's an aggressive lady."

"I prefer the term proactive." Jose stood. "Very well. Rajput, prep a shuttle. Or the lifting body. I'll be down on the surface within the hour, and at Landing this morning."

"Yes, sir. Might I ask where you'll be going?"

"I'll arrange that right now. I'll need some privacy."

"Sir," Rajput said. He walked to the door, stepped outside, and pulled it shut. The door bounced back open. Rajput reentered, picked the discarded door handle from the floor, and slotted it back on. "Five minutes to reattach this, sir." He moved outside, and Jose waited while he coordinated the workers. Two minutes and a high-pitched drill later, the door swung shut, and the lock clicked.

Jose sat, rubbed his hands, and steepled them as Dashi would have. He sat in silence for sixty seconds, finally dropping them and flexing his fingers. "Godspeed Dashi, Emperor, first of his name." Jose opened a drawer at the bottom of his desk and pulled out a comm. It was bigger than his regular comm, more rugged. It took two long codes and a thumbprint to start up. Another code engaged the communication system. Unlike most calls, this one didn't have the option for a video, only voice.

The far side rang for over fifty rings before it was picked up.

"Yes?" The comm modified the voices. A listener could tell it was female, but that's all.

"It's me. It took a long time to pick up this call. Are you sure you want to talk to me?"

"Who is this? I don't recognize this number."

"Who would know this number, your secret number, and be able to call you from a number you can't trace?"

The other voice sputtered, then got control of herself. "Everybody, and I mean everybody wants to talk to you right now."

"You're my first call since he was killed."

"I am?"

"Yes."

"That's interesting. I mean. Oh, sorry. I'm sorry about all this. I know he was like a father to you."

"He was. I'll destroy the person who did this."

"Was it her?"

"It could have been. That's part of the reason you're my first call. I have some strong suspicions. But I won't move without proof. I don't like making mistakes. Dashi didn't, and neither did I. But that's not why I called."

"Why did you call me first? For that matter, why call me at all right now?"

"I'll be on planet within the hour. I need to meet you alone. Without aides or guards. I'll be at a monorail station—" Jose named a station two stops outside of Landing. "You can get there easily, get away and be back before anyone sees you. I'll be there one hour before dawn. I need to talk to you in person."

"Why? Want to shoot me?"

"Generally speaking, yes, I do. But I won't. Not today. Who knows what the future holds."

"Why not come into Landing?"

"At least for the start, it's best if nobody knows I'm there, or talking to you. I'll expect you to be there."

"What if I don't come?"

"Then, you don't. I have many other contingencies available to me."

"Good ol' Jose. Always a plan."

"Yes. Have you heard the phrase 'doing a Jose.'"

"Of course. Drowning people in administrative data."

"It's news to me."

"Well, it would be, wouldn't it."

"Yes. I'll see you an hour before dawn."

"And I you. I'm looking forward to seeing you, Mr. Jose. Senator Jose."

"And I you, Senator Shutt. I you."

CHAPTER 27

"Take this trash down the hall to the dish bin at the end of the car and dispose of it." Jose shoved a pile of dirty plates and cups into his guard's hands. The TGI security man balanced them in both hands and used his elbow to clasp a wayward plate into his side. He waddled down the corridor the five meters to the catering cart, ensuring red sauce from the main tray didn't slop onto his clothes. He positioned his arms over the dirty plate bin, opened his elbow to drop the loose plate, and slid the pile on top of the other dishes.

"Will that be all—" Jose's door slammed shut. The guard raised his eyebrows. The tribune was renowned for always being polite. But some people change when they get important. The guard resumed his post with his back to the door to Jose's private compartment.

Rajput had insisted on two guards. Jose then asked for four, and then organized them into four-hour shifts, telling the others to get a rest while they could. After coming down from orbit, all five had boarded the monorail for the trip to Landing. The ocean slid by on the right, the mountains on the left as they sped east. The rising Dragon in the east replaced the setting primary in the west. It was spring, so the Dragon shone brightly, its reflected light almost replacing that of the primary. Jose insisted on eating alone.

Jose had waited till the guard turned to dump the dishes, then dashed to the front of the compartment to hide next to the doors. His compartment door slammed shut by itself—the watching guard assumed he was inside. When they arrived at the next station, the computerized attendant opened the outer doors automatically. Jose stepped clear of the train, stepped one pace left and hid in the shadows. The platform was deserted, and dashing across it would make him visible to anyone watching from the train windows.

The doors hissed shut. The train accelerated in the direction of Landing, and Jose stepped clear. No matter if his guard saw him now or not, they'd have to break into his compartment to ensure they weren't wrong. It would be hours before they could get the train turned around. He'd be on his own.

Given who he was meeting, he wondered if that's a good thing?

Jose dropped onto the rail bed and stepped over the rails. The magnets were electrified when a train was passing, not after, but it paid to be careful. He boosted himself onto the cargo platform, getting a foot onto the rollers hanging down. He dusted his hands and used the side of a waiting container to lever himself up.

Long time since you've gotten your hands dirty, in more than one way, isn't it?

He counted six containers waiting for the next cargo train. The next arriving cargo train would line up a flatcar with the cargo loaders. The rollers would spin and push the container onto the train. The train would move forward to present the next empty flatcar, and the rollers would load again. It was all automatic.

All automatic, as long as they had electricity, spare parts, and time to do maintenance.

An entire train of two dozen could be loaded and unloaded in minutes. Most stations moved only a half dozen containers at a time, so a train could serve dozens of stations. The passenger station was likewise small.

Dozens of stations, but not dozens of trains.

Jose climbed down from the platform and entered the central square. Company offices occupied two sides of the square. One, Pawter Minerals, was an actual preabandonment building. The other local companies made do with repurposed containers that housed modular offices and habitations. One side contained a Militia container—administrative office, storage room, and jail. The lights in the square were out—either power failure or deliberate sabotage. And if it were a power failure, people hadn't been irritated enough to complain to central. It would show on Jose's comm.

Or they were too scared to complain, worried about what Dashi or his people would do to them. Which wasn't good.

"Stop there. That's far enough," a woman's voice said.

"No, it's not." Jose kept walking. "We need to go inside. I need a comm, a display unit, and a bathroom. Not necessarily in that order."

"Any farther and we'll shoot."

"Of course you won't do that. And you were supposed to be alone." Jose counted in the gloom. "I see three people. That's good. Major—sorry, Senator Shutt, send them out for some food so we can talk in private. Something to drink, too. Perhaps some wine."

"You're in no condition to make demands, Senator Jose," Shutt said.

"Of course I am. And it's not like I'm requesting good wine—any wine would do. Get rid of your hangers-on. We need to make plans, and we don't have much time."

"I should shoot you just for that. Gree, search him for weapons."

"You won't shoot me. And I don't have any weapons. One thing I learned from Dashi is that, if you think you need a weapon, you're not as smart as you think you are, and you should plan better."

"I always carry a weapon."

"Quod erat demonstrandum."

"What in the Emperor's name does that mean, you pompous freak?"

"Whatever happened to 'sorry about your father figure

dying.'"

"Are you making fun of me?"

"You know I am. It means, roughly. Thus it is demonstrated. Or if you prefer, Q.E.D.—quite easily done."

"I should shoot you for being pompous, jerk."

"If I got shot every time people were interested in shooting pompous jerks, I'd be dead years ago."

"I still could."

"But you won't." Jose raised his arms. "Search quickly and be done with it."

Rough hands checked him, pronounced him clean, and melted into the dark. A light bloomed ahead as Shutt opened the door of a metal shed. Jose followed her through into the light. "What is this place?"

The floor was concrete, stained with green and yellow fluids. A narrow pit deep enough for a man to stand opened in the floor ahead of him, one meter by eight. A chain hoist ran above it, on a rail system, that led off into the dark.

"Vegetable harvester repair shop. It's a garage for the workers to swap tires, engines, that sort of thing."

"Nowhere to sit."

"I wasn't planning on sitting much." Shutt waved her two guards out the front door. "Talk."

"Next time, if I say you come alone, come alone."

"What if I don't?"

"Then, I won't be there, and that would be bad for you."

"You're talking in riddles."

"My plan, my entire plan, has always been to follow Dashi in all things." Jose sauntered to a bench by the wall and pulled up a U-shaped piece of metal. "What is this?"

"It's a part for a harvester. Something to do with the shocks. Dashi's dead. What do we do now?"

"I will continue his plans, in his memory."

"Good to know."

"And I will destroy whoever has killed him."

"Kill them?"

"Eventually. Sometime. But first I will destroy them. Their works, their companies, their supporters. I will take what is theirs. What I cannot take, I will devastate. Their friends and allies will become mine. They will be left alone, bereft, and with nowhere to go. Ideally, they will take their own life, thus underlying their ultimate failure."

"Wow. I'm impressed. Very poetic. Can you say it again and make it rhyme this time?"

"Thank you. After I've done that, I will resume work on Dashi's plans."

"Which are?"

"Private for now, to be revealed at the proper time. I expect you to join me in this endeavor."

Shutt laughed. "Oh, you do, do you? And why would I do that?"

"Because there will be great advantage for you. Even if in destroying my enemies I weaken myself, that will take time. In the meantime, it's not practical for me to take over all their operations. There will be some that are inconvenient to target, or challenging, or are not an efficient use of resources. Those could be taken over by somebody else. It only makes sense to share my plans with you and let you take advantage of the opportunities."

"Are you sure she killed Dashi? Marianne, I mean?"

"She gains great advantage by killing him. With him gone, there's an opportunity for her to take control of this new Senate. Convince the naysayers. Proclaim herself Empress. Without Dashi she would be able to convince the waverers that she was the right person for the job."

"Waverers?"

"That would be you, and your allies. If you don't join me, you must join her. And you will join me."

"Whyever would I do that?"

"Because you hate her a touch more than you hate me."

"Isn't she your girlfriend."

"We were dating, yes. She has great taste in wine. I appreciate that."

"And other things, no doubt."

Jose shrugged. "Not relevant to this discussion."

"I have reports that she is taking over some nonaligned stations and even has her eye on Militia stations that are poorly defended. And perhaps some TGI assets."

"I have those same reports."

"So, we'll stop her."

"Absolutely not. We'll help her."

CHAPTER 28

Balthazar dropped Chaudhari at the Pier two hours before planetary or moonetary dawn. Balthazar checked his tide table. "I can stay either twelve hours or thirty-six—your choice. Either way, I expect a full accounting of the money owed me."

"I'll bring it up with Shutt. Senator Shutt."

"You do that."

"She might not agree with all these charges."

"If she knows what's good for her, she will."

"Should I tell her you said that? I can."

"Never mind."

"Didn't think so. I'll be back in a few hours with an update." Chaudhari climbed down off the boat and walked down the dock. The primary was up, shadowing the edges of the dock. A hole gaped where the fenced door had been—it had been cut off and set neatly aside. The lights of the city shone ahead. Fifteen minutes down the road past the steam plant, and he'd be in the city proper and could beg a ride.

It wasn't fifteen minutes of walking to beg a ride. It was five, and he didn't have to beg. A searchlight pinned him in the middle of the road, and a revolver cocked in the distance.

"Halt."

"Halting," Chaudhari said, raising his hands. "Corporal Chaudhari of the Militia."

"Corporal Chaudhari? Any relation to Senator Chaudhari? On the Militia council."

"I'm the senator, yeah. What's this about the Militia council."

"If you're the senator, wouldn't you know?"

Chaudhari screwed his eyes up to release the glare. He could make out figures, but that's all. "Senators, well. I've got lots of responsibilities. Things happen. Maybe they talked to my staff."

"Your staff? Who on your staff?"

Chaudhari lowered his hands. "I don't have a staff. It's just me. And some mules."

Another two guns cocked. "Nobody said put your hands down."

"Sorry." He put his hands back up. "But this is no way to treat a senator. Or his mules."

"You have mules with you?"

"It's an expression. A senator and his mules."

"That's a stupid expression."

"I agree."

A voice yelled from the dark. "Captain—the major says Corporal Chaudhari and Senator Chaudhari are the same person, and to quote 'get his stupid Imperial behind to headquarters ASAP.'"

The light blanked off. "Sorry, Senator. Would you like a ride to Militia headquarters?"

"Sure would."

"Follow us. Uh, you can put your hands down, sir."

"I will. But first . . ."

"Yessir?"

"First, can you all uncock your revolvers and put them in your holsters? Accidents happen, and I don't want to be one of them."

***

Chaudhari had to wait an hour till Shutt arrived at the building. It wasn't unpleasant—he was in a waiting room with chairs, a bathroom, and a private brought him drinks. But the door locked when the waiter left.

Shutt stormed through the door. "Chaudhari, you great ox. Why in the Emperor's name did you run for Senate?"

"It seemed like fun at the time."

"Fun?"

"There were cheerleaders. I like cheerleaders."

"Cheerleaders? Are you—oh, Pletcher's campaign. I'll give you that. He knows how to run a party."

"He does. Why's everybody so wound up? Guns? Locked rooms."

"The assassination."

"What assassination?"

Shutt filled him in on Dashi and the admiral. "As of now, the Senate is the supreme governmental body on this moon. We had a meeting that extended all government decrees and rules for seven days while we're in mourning for Dashi, and we figure out what the heck goes on."

"What do you mean what goes on? Find out who killed Dashi and kill them."

"And then?"

"What?"

"And then what. Let's say we do that, which we will. After we kill this unnamed person or persons, Dashi is still dead. We still don't have an Emperor, an heir, or a council."

"Appoint a new one."

"Can't. Only the Emperor does that. Or his heir as a 'counselor of state' or something like that. Emperor in waiting."

"Who's the heir?"

"Beats me. Your friend Jose is going for it."

"He's not my friend, Major."

"Call me senator."

"Yes, Senator, I will—wait. I'm a senator now, too. We're both senators. What do I call you?"

"Major still works. And you're not sworn in yet. Before you leave, I'd see the padre and get that sorted out."

"Doesn't seem really . . . something. Should I call you colleague? The Free Trader Lady says that."

"Is she another friend of yours, too? All that leveling

stuff. She wants to be Empress. Think she should be Dashi's heir?"

"I don't think she'd make a good heir."

"The smart money says she's the one who poisoned Dashi and Edmunds."

"Edmunds?"

"The admiral. He has a name you know."

"I never used it. He was always just the admiral to me. Do you want me to get a squad together, go after Senator Marianne?"

"Nope. Not part of the plan. Besides, she's got that legion around her. You'd need way more than a squad. We might not be able to do it with all the troops we have in Landing."

"Ask Jose for help."

"We're not starting another war."

"Why not?"

"Because, according to Jose, we won't win."

"What do we do?"

"He has an interesting plan."

"What's that?"

"Lose."

***

Chaudhari got breakfast from the Militia caf while he waited for Shutt to deal with some issues. Being a senator-elect didn't get him a better place in line, or any extra food. It did get him an extra cup of coffee when one of the cooks recognized him.

"You'll need to be awake when you talk to Senator Shutt again."

"And when will I be doing that?"

"Any minute now, her guest just arrived. They'll want you in there."

"How do you know all of this?"

"She's smart. She's partnered with that Mr. Senator Jose. The two of them will crush the Free Traders."

"Why are we crushing them?"

"They're our enemies."

"Why?"

The cook shrugged. "Don't know. But Jose and Shutt know what they're doing, and I'm on their side."

"It's that simple? They're on our side, so you believe them?"

"That's my system. It works for me. You want more coffee?"

Chaudhari stuck his cup out.

A half hour later, an unimpressed private brought 'Senator Corporal' into Shutt's office. Senator Pletcher sat in a chair in front of the desk.

"Senator Chaudhari. You know Senator Pletcher of course."

Pletcher stood and shook hands. "Call me Vince. Since we're colleagues now."

"Call me Chad."

"That's your name?"

"Nickname."

Shutt grimaced. "Why don't we stick with Senator?"

"Because it's impolite," Pletcher said. "We're equals."

"Imperial Vagina," Shutt said. "Fine. Clarisse."

"Your name is Clarisse?" Chaudhari said. "I thought the Sergeant was kidding when he said that."

"Haw-haw," Shutt said. "Here's the deal. Pletcher here—" She pointed.

"Vince."

"Pletcher here gets a pile of money. He likes money."

"I do."

"He gives you a complete boatload of copper, primers, things for gunpowder, all that stuff on Scott's list. Way more than he needs."

Chaudhari nodded. "Okay."

"You"—Shutt pointed at Chaudhari—"take that boatload to Russell—and that's not an expression. I want the gunnels awash when that boat sails out east."

"What's a gunnel? And why do you want it washed?"

"It's an expression. It means heavily loaded, the boat sinks down till the water almost goes over the side."

"I don't know much about boats, but I know the water coming over the side is bad."

"Almost over the side. Balthazar takes all that east. Stay seven days. Only seven. Vince has a tide table. We'll tell you exactly when we want him back. You make as many bullets as you can in those seven days with all your machines and suchlike. They, you, Russell, as much of your squad as you can take away and all his bullets come back here."

"And then?" Chaudhari asked.

"Then, we'll have a shuttle standing by, and he's going orbital. Him, his squad, more squads, and weapons. All the weapons he can bring back."

"And what will you be doing while this is happening?"

"Losing."

***

Marianne led the six Legionnaires from her crew out of the lock. Docking at transit twelve had been the same as normal, but two corporate passenger ships had dropped as she arrived.

"I've never seen two corporate ships scheduled to leave at the same time," Sikar, her assistant said.

"Me neither." Marianne surveyed the Traders' section.

"Over there, Senator." Sikar pointed. The main air lock at the end of the truss was closed, but with red lights showing. The lock was operational, and was aired, but not in use. "Never seen a working lock on a station blocked."

"No people." Marianne pointed to her Legionnaires. "You six wait here while we find out what's going on."

Her Legionnaires slouched against the walls and put their hands in their pockets.

Marianne walked past three empty docking bays before she found the single occupied one. "Good morning,

Shipmaster."

"Morning." A short, dark-haired man stood with arms crossed in front of a ship hatch. His uniform was a pale blue coverall over a skin suit. The coverall had creases down the sides of the pants, and he wore a starched collared shirt underneath. A bright yellow ship patch was sewn on his shoulder, and he had a name tape with matching yellow letters on his breast. But the coveralls clashed with the heavy mag boots, practical tool belt, and hard helmet clipped there. "You're Senator Marianne. I've seen your picture."

"That's true. Where are you off to today, Shipmaster?"

"Off station."

"Where off station?"

"Just off. You've heard the Emperor is dead?"

"I have. I was there."

"More problems." The shipmaster frowned. "We heard that late last night. First thing this morning, the night watch stander woke me. The corporate ships were loading up their people and pulling out."

"The corporate ships are leaving?"

The shipmaster nodded. "Left. All gone. I'm waiting for two parts I ordered. My first officer is leaning against the door of the shop. They open start of next shift. We hope. Soon as he has parts in hand and back here, we're dropping."

"What about the Militia ships?"

"They were the first to go. I'll bet there isn't a Militia person left on the station."

Marianne and Sikar exchanged glances. "Why would they do that? What's the threat?"

The shipmaster shrugged. "No idea. Shouldn't you senators know what's going on? All I know is that everybody is leaving."

"Everybody?"

"Well"—the shipmaster put his hands on his hips— "the two Militia ships left first. They were gone by the time

I got up. Then the corporate ships started dropping. All the TGI ships left in a rush together, then the other ones dropped one at a time after that."

"What about the Free Traders, like us?"

"Nobody knows anything. Dashi's dead. There's something going on in the city, maybe. Maybe something here. Whatever it is, I don't want to be part of it. One of my cousins had a ship, we talked with the other shipmasters. No idea what's going on, but this makes us nervous. We have a cargo. We don't need to be here. We're dropping. The others did the same."

"All of you?"

"I doubt there's a half dozen ships left, including me. And there will be one less in five minutes. Allez, Michelle!" He waved at a woman in a matching uniform to him, jogging down the truss. "We go now."

"I think—"

"Your pardon." The shipmaster hit the intercom and gave orders to his bridge crew. Chains clanked against the station as they unhooked and changed to magnets. The woman dashed by and vanished into the ship. The shipmaster finished his conversation, then grasped the station hatch. "We are going now, Senator. Free Trades."

"But where are you going? And why?"

"I am going away from here."

"But you don't know what's happening."

"Nothing good."

"How do you know that?"

The shipmaster paused and pointed a finger at Marianne. "You are here. That means there will be some sort of fight. When the great fight, the little get crushed. We nearly starved a few months ago. We're not getting in trouble again. Good luck."

"Whose side are you on?" Marianne asked.

"Whose side are you on?"

"The Free Traders."

"Maybe the council, not the rest of us." The shipmaster

pulled the lock behind him, but stuck his head around the edge before it closed. "Senator?"

"Yes?"

"Try not to break this station, not like the others." The head disappeared as the hatch snicked shut. Before it shut, he spoke again. "We do not have so many stations that we can afford to waste one."

CHAPTER 29

"That's correct. Collect all your people, cargo, and retreat to the core stations." Jose steepled his hands in an unconscious echo of Dashi. "I know, I know. Your routes will be messed up, but we want you back at the bigger stations. It will be safer there."

Jose waited while the other voice continued its complaints. He rolled Dashi's pen between his fingers as he spoke. "Of course you can continue trading, but we want you to keep to the inner stations, and the larger ones. No, no shortages. As much food and supplies as you want, the shuttles are still running. We're declaring some stations more dangerous than others, is all. It's for your safety, you understand. Good. Well, when will you be here? I'll be happy to see you, captain. Make an appointment, and I'll be happy to discuss your concerns. Of course. Yes. Long live the Empire, to you, too."

Jose hung up. His intercom buzzed. "Come in Rajput."

Rajput entered, and Jose gestured him to sit.

"We're doing as you ordered, sir."

"Good. Any issues?"

"Surprisingly, almost none. As soon as we say 'threats of violence and damage,' everybody falls into line right away."

"A year ago, we would have had to prove it. Now, everybody knows that people can get shot, stations can blow up, and they might be in the crossfire. They want us to be as far away as possible from any problems, real or imagined."

"But you're not saying that there will be issues."

"I'm not saying that there won't be, either. How do the

stations look?"

Rajput pulled out his comm and projected it on Jose's display screen. "I've got a list."

"Of course you do. Let me see it."

Lists of stations, names of ships, and tables of arrival and departure times showed up on the screen. Jose crossed his arms. "No, no, not right. We need a different display."

"Sir, that's the—"

"Wait." Jose manipulated the lists, then moved them aside. He brought up diagrams of the largest stations, and the innermost ones. He tapped a setting, and the docking ports lit up. They were either red, green, or yellow. "Red is halted. Green is open. Yellow is somebody is coming or going."

"Not a lot of green," Rajput said.

"We don't want a lot of green. We want as much red as possible. I want those ships docked. I want all those ports full. Look here."

"It's red," Rajput said. "That's good."

"Yes, but you've assigned other inbound ships to this bay, and it's already occupied."

"I need to fix that."

"Yes, yes, you do." Jose sighed. Working with Rajput made him understand why Dashi had valued him and others like Jake Stewart so much. It was one thing to give detailed orders, it was another to find people who could follow the intent of an order. "Get it sorted and report back."

Rajput stood and headed for the door.

"Rajput?"

"Yes, Senator?"

"Don't mess this up. We'll only get one chance. And even one missing ship could be a problem."

***

"You've kidnapped us and want to kill us?" the Legionnaire corporal asked.

"Do we look like we're killing you?" Shutt gestured. "You're in our headquarters, and talking to us. Killing involves lots of blood and shouting."

"You're shouting now."

"More shouting. Louder shouting. Killing is very loud. If we wanted to kill you, we would, but instead we're standing talking. You can keep talking."

"Can we have our guns back?"

"No." Shutt had sent a patrol out to find an isolated group of Free Trader Legionnaires. They collected a group of twelve and dragged them back. "We keep your guns, for now. That way, you can't do anything stupid."

"Kidnapping us was kind of stupid."

"You're not kidnapped. You can leave any time."

"How about right now?"

"Sure. Make room." Shutt waved her troops out of the way. "You can collect your guns on the way out. I'll detail a squad to give them to you when you're in the street. And go back and be sure to tell Senator Marianne that you were in Militia headquarters, in the armory no less, and you decided to leave. See what she says to that."

The group of Legionnaires exchanged glances. A tall brown-haired one said, "Explain this again. We stay and count weapons."

"Heavy weapons, yes. Look, things are too fragile right now to blow stuff up. We need our factories and warehouses and power plants and, well, restaurants and light poles, even. We need everything, no more blowing things up. We'll take two of you into the main armory. You can count the grenades, and the mortars—we only have like four anyway. The broken missiles from that last fiasco out east with the ships."

"You're disarming?"

"You wish. We've decided to limit the weapons we use."

"Which ones are you not using?"

"The heavy stuff. All my troops have personal

247

weapons. Revolvers. Shotguns. Shock sticks. There's probably a rifle or two somewhere, but not many. The rest is here. You count it, leave somebody to watch it, then report back to your boss that we're not going to do anything stupid and blow up important stuff. We—I—I'm trusting her to understand. No more destruction. No more explosions. No more shuttles being broken. No more stations exploding. But you want a street fight? Sticks and stones? Then bring it on."

The disarmed Legionnaires talked softly for a few moments, exchanging low-voiced comments in Francais. Brown hair spoke up. "How do we know these are all your big guns?"

"You don't. But once you count 'em, you'll know what is here, and if we move 'em somewhere else or take them out, you'll know."

"How will we know if you move 'em?"

"Two of you stay here, keep an eye on things. You can rotate which two and use your comm. But no weapons. That way we keep you from doing anything stupid. And we have a lot of troops here, at headquarters, and they're well armed. Also, to keep you from doing something stupid."

"How can we tell if these are real?" Brown hair asked. "I don't know what those missile things look like."

"Do I have to do all the work for you? Find somebody who does."

A thin woman stepped up to Brown Hair, muttered quietly, the group chattered again, and then they shoved her forward. "I will go count," she said. "I was in the Militia many years ago. Purchasing. But I remember the codes, and I know how to scan them for descriptions. With one other. Once we're sure what we're counting, I go back to see the senator."

"Good luck seeing her. She's not on planet," Shutt said. "But go somewhere you can talk to her in private. Pick three others. One to go with you, and two to stay after, so they can keep track of what you counted. The rest go now."

"Agreed," Brown Hair said. "I will go count as well. What happens then?"

"You stay, or you go," Shutt said. "I suggest at least two of you stay, with a comm, and the others can check in from time to time. You can swap them out anytime you want, or have them leave."

"We cannot make any promises for the senator," brown hair said. "She isn't promising not to do anything, or to do anything. She will have to speak with you about that."

"Fine with me." The rest of the Legionnaires left. Two of those remaining followed a double squad inside into the armory. Two waited in the anteroom. Most of the Militia followed the disarmed squad out the front door—two Militia sergeants carried bags of revolvers and shock sticks to be returned.

The two remaining Legionnaires stared at Shutt. Shutt stared back until they dropped their eyes and retreated to the corner. Fifteen minutes later, the two others returned.

Brown eyes pointed at one of the remainder. "Sallee will return and explain things to the senator. You—" he pointed to the other. "Will stay with me, and we will watch these guns." He spoke in Standard, slowly, so everybody present could understand.

"Good deal," Shutt said. She waved two Militia over. "See them out."

The two left. Brown hair fiddled with his comm. "May I make a call?"

"Not only may you, but you must. We require you to talk to your boss. Explain what's going on."

He typed on his comm. "I do not understand this."

"Everything that I, or the admiral, or the Militia does is for Delta," Shutt said. "We're trying to preserve civilization here. We can have political differences, but I'd rather lose than destroy what we have here."

"A noble suggestion. Will it hold if Senator Marianne takes advantage of it."

"I guess that's up to you," Shutt said.

"What do you mean? Why is it up to me?"

"Because if she asks you to do something stupid, like blow something up, or use heavy weapons or explosives, then you'll have to ask yourself which side you're on. The side preserving Delta, or the side destroying it."

Sikar and Marianne moved into the control room of the station with their six troops. "We'll have two of you on each shift, keep an eye on things."

"Meaning what?"

"Don't allow the Militia to manufacture anything they could use in a fight—no weapons, no ammunition, nothing like that."

One of the Legionnaires raised their hand. Marianne pointed. "Yes?"

"Do they make weapons here?"

"I have no idea. Ask them. We're leaving you now. We have other stations to visit. The Empire!"

"The Empire!" The others chorused back.

Marianne and Sikar left the operation room and headed for the stairs to the stations rim.

"Which spoke?" Sikar asked. "Ladder or stairs?" Two of the spokes had stairs, two had ladders.

"Doesn't matter. Let's take the ladder." Marianne and Sikar walked antispinward to the Bravo Spoke and climbed onto the ladder and descended foot first. The station's spin made out to the rim the same as down.

The lights went out midway between the inner and middle spokes. Marianne halted and cursed when Sikar stepped on her head. "Wait, I can't see where we're going."

"I can see lights in the mid-ring."

"We'll get off there." Moving half as fast as before, Marianne dropped down till the mid-ring lights shone in.

She swung off the ladder and into the corridor. Sikar followed suit, and they walked the ring.

Three-quarters of the lights went out, the remainder dimmed to half brightness.

"What in the Emperor's name?" Sikar said.

A shadowy figure stepped out of a doorway ahead and flicked a light down the hall into their faces.

Marianne held up her hand against the light. "Who are you? What's going on? Why are the lights out?"

"Didn't you get the message?" A skinny woman materialized from the gloom. "All the commercial sections are going into caretaker mode. Main power is shut down to everything except habitat and critical operations sections. The station is powering down."

"What?"

"Read your email. That's what I tell every one. At least read the urgent notices. They're important. But does anybody? No, of course not. Sorry, Cee, we missed that one. Sorry, Cee, I didn't know that my office was going to be de-aired to kill vermin. Sorry, Cee, couldn't you have sent another message. I already sent four and a group message and posted on the bulletin board. Some people's children."

"Could you stop shining that light in my eyes?"

The woman dropped the light. "And that's another thing. We tell everyone to bring their own lights, but do they? Did you? You're wandering around. Have any portable battery lights? You don't, do you?"

"Who has left?"

"The email—"

"Just tell us."

"Most of the residents are gone. Last ship left ten minutes ago."

"Our ship is still here. It hasn't left."

"You're those Free Trader people, aren't you? I heard one of your ships were coming."

"What if we are?"

"All the corps got notice to shut down the end of last shift. Emergency evacuation. And after what happened last year, with the explosions on GG main, we're not taking any chances. I loaded my husband and the kids up on the passenger ship. They left hours ago."

"Your whole family?"

"The corp even made an exception and let us take our dog. That was nice. They don't normally do that. Took clothes and a bunch of the kids' toys. School's out this week regardless. The corps promised food in the cafs on the other stations. Kids think it's a vacation."

"Why are you still here?"

The woman puffed up and struck a dramatic pose. "You're talking to the senior heating engineer on the station for my sins. I have to keep basic life support up, keep everything from freezing over. Shouldn't be too hard. We had a systems test nine months ago, and everything passed. I need to inspect and check each section, like I'm doing here. And since the corp people are gone, I don't even have to knock."

"But why evacuate the residents?"

"I told you." She spoke slowly, like to a child. "All the production facilities are shut down. What will the workers do?"

"Everything else?"

"All the offices and stores are closed. The foundry is running in maintenance mode. Last set of ingots came off the line two hours ago, and that's it till they start up again. Glad I'm not working for Third Moon Chemicals. Their startup procedure is a bear. Takes four days to get going again."

"Who gave the order?"

"No idea. I work for the station, not the corps. You'd have to ask them."

"But surely, you have an idea . . ."

"Surely, I don't. Not part of heat engineering, not my problem, that's what I say."

"You're not curious as to what happened?"

"All I know, I have to visually inspect the interior of every compartment on this ring before shift end and make sure none have any heating problems, and then next shift, 'cause I'm on a double, I have to start on the outer ring. That will take me two full shifts to sort out, provided nothing is broken, which it surely will be. Is your ship docked on the outer ring?"

"It is."

"Here's my comm code." She passed a number to their comms. "Call me if it gets cold, means the heating lines are screwed up. And don't complain when you get back and our lights are out. That's supposed to happen." The woman crossed the hall, consulted a list on her comm, then typed a code into the door lock. The door clicked open. "More to see. Oh, and try not to get more of us killed."

"Killed? What do you mean?"

"Whatever you're doing. When you Trader types and corporate types argue, something gets blown up or people get shot. I'd rather avoid that. What is it you two say?"

"Say?"

"Free Trades!"

CHAPTER 30

"I understand, Senator," Jose said to his comm. "But it's a necessary precaution. Things are unsettled right now. Once we've got all the ships onto the core stations, we'll be able to identify which ones could be causing problems."

The voice buzzed in his ear. Jose shook his head. "No, nothing is going to happen, not like last time. No stations getting blown up. No shuttles being seized. We're Deescalating before we start. Defense? Absolutely. But we're not going to be aggressive. We're in the process of pulling our forces back to protect critical infrastructure. Once that's secured, we'll discuss any outstanding issues with all parties, whoever they may be."

Jose twiddled his pen as the voice continued for another minute. He closed his eyes and shook his head. "Of course, of course. We'll let you know as soon as we can. Thank you for calling, Senator."

Jose hung up his comm and rubbed his brow again, then punched another code into his comm.

"Senator?" Rajput's voice came on.

"Are the trading companies complaining about not being able to run their trade routes yet?"

"They're more complaining that they can't get docking on the main stations."

"I told you to fix that—never mind. I'm sending you a list of stations right now. They can have trade routes to these stations, and these stations only. But they have to file their trade route with the Senate, and wait for approval. Otherwise they leave their ships open to confiscation."

"We're going to confiscate ships?"

"Absolutely not. Once some of them get moving, dock

those other ships. And as of right now, new rule. Once docked, all ships must remain docked for seventy-two hours, to give competent authorities time to inspect them."

"What competent authorities? What inspections? We don't have any inspectors except the custom people, and there's only a few of those."

"Doesn't matter. Tell them they have to wait either for inspection, or for seventy-two hours after docking. Once inspected, they can leave, or if the timer runs out, they can leave."

"But we're not inspecting anything. Or anyone. How do I set that up?"

"You don't."

"But that will mean these big corporate ships will be crowding the docks for seventy-two hours. We'll create a backup of ships waiting for slips."

"Yes."

"Okaayyyy." Rajput's breathing filled the channel.

"Are you at the gym?"

"I've been talking to corporate ships. They demand to see somebody from security."

"Make them come to you. Make them line up and wait."

"That will make them mad."

"That's the point. Remind them that once the current emergency is over, they can go back to regular trading."

"They'll want to ask when it's over."

"Tell them that's up to the Free Traders."

"Yes, sir." Rajput's side of the conversation bonged. "Your list is here. At least they'll be able to set up some trade routes. Sir, you sent me the wrong list."

"I didn't."

"Yes, sir, I think you did. This only has, like, only a fifth of our stations on it."

"The biggest fifth. Twenty-two point three percent, to be exact. But it accounts for over eighty percent of our orbital trade and population. I want them to limit

255

themselves to those stations only."

"They'll complain."

"Not when they pay attention. We've cut out the competition. The Free Traders are out of business, as far as the core is concerned."

"The Free Traders can trade to the smaller stations."

"If they get cargo to trade. Or fuel."

"You're going to stop selling them fuel and cargo?"

"They can buy whatever fuel they want. But they have to wait in line for a slot like everybody else. Speaking of . . ." Jose flicked his display up on the all screen. He paged through a series of screens, displaying station docking slips. Without exception, all the docking slips showed red, occupied, and a line of ships was shown waiting for access. He found one display, which had mostly greens. "What's wrong with Transfer-2?"

"Hardly anybody wanted to go there, or was near it."

"Divert some traffic there. Anybody you can. I want that station full up with a waiting list."

"Why do we want a waiting list?"

"Because I'm the senator, that's why. I want all those slots full, on all our biggest stations. No exceptions."

"You're the senator. I'll take care of it."

"Good." Jose covered a few more housekeeping issues, then signed off. He folded his hands, then unrolled his fingers and steepled them like Dashi used to. "The important thing, the most important thing," he said to himself, "Is to keep your nerve."

***

"You're a senator, Dashi's dead, we have more supplies than we need, and Shutt wants me to make a bunch of ammunition for her and bring it to town in a week. Have I got it right?"

"Sounds good to me." Chaudhari sniffed his drink. "This is good. What is it?"

"The troops have started distilling booze. They were

trying to hide it. I got them to do it out in public, gave them the supplies they needed, and we're going to sell it. I'll take a cut of the profit and the space in the factory and charge taxes when they sell it."

"Taking things over here, aren't you? Think the owners are going to stand for it?"

"That corporation abandoned this place. I occupied something that wasn't in use."

"Still, laws, and all that."

"Possession is nine-tenths of the law. And besides, I know a senator."

Chaudhari drank his wine down. "You know two senators. Three if you count Mr. Pletcher. Four, if you count Mr. Jose."

"I don't think Mr. Jose likes me."

"He did try to have you shot for mutiny. That's a strong indicator of dislike."

"I don't take it personally. I'd have done the same."

"You're not a big fan of mutiny."

"And I like shooting people. Let's get this on the road. Kim!" Russell yelled.

Kim One came into the office. "You want me to get the supplies loaded into the factory and ramp up production, Sergeant?"

"Yes, please."

"I've already started. At the dock, we're pulling the most important first and restarting production."

"We?" Chaudhari asked. "Who's we? Who's at the dock."

"Sweet Pea is advising me, and when I'm not there, she just shows the crews which box to take next."

"Kim, there is no way that a mule can do that."

"Sweet Pea told me you'd say that, and she says she forgives you for doubting her. And she anticipates that you'll show her more confidence and support once she helps get the factory up to speed."

Russell took a sip of his wine. Chaudhari blinked at

Kim, then looked back at Russell. Russell shrugged. "Thanks, Kim. And thank Sweet Pea for me."

"Will do, Sergeant." Kim headed out the door.

Chaudhari turned to Russell. "Her mule is running things?"

"Sweet Pea is an effective administrator."

"In the Emperor's name. You've got to be kidding me."

Russell stood and walked to a window and levered an outer shutter open. "Look here." He pointed. "She's got Sweet Pea with her. That mule likes her, or she thinks she's a mule, or something. Sweet Pea follows Kim around. They'll go down to the dock, Kim will think about things, give the crew orders, and make sure they get the right boxes to the right places. If the crew has questions, she'll talk about it, ask Sweet Pea some questions, nod like she's getting answers, then give them orders. The orders work."

"You can't believe that she's normal? Don't you think she's a nut?"

Russell levered the shutter closed. "That sounds like a medical problem, and I'm not a doctor. Ask one of them."

"They'll say she's tabbo excrement crazy."

"Probably. But, in the meantime, she's effective, organized, and gets the job done. If she pretends it's the mule doing it and not her, I'm not going to get in her way."

"I can't believe that you're taking suggestions from a mule."

"I can't believe that you're a senator. An Imperial senator at that. And I can't believe Shutt's one, the Emperor's dead, I'm running a factory, and frankly, I was more than a little surprised that I'm still alive after that abortive rebellion, fighting with the Empire Rising people, sinking that sailboat, and generally trying to stay alive while the world goes nuts around me. After all that, an intelligent mule isn't that hard to deal with."

Chaudhari slumped. "The world has gone mad."

"Madness stalks the land, as the writers would say. You want more wine?"

Chaudhari held out his glass. "Fill me up. What should we drink to?"

Russell filled both glasses. "How about Kim One? She's crazy, but she's our crazy."

***

"I'm telling you that we don't have any of those. We don't carry steel plates." Marianne shook her head. "We're a Free Trader, not a bulk delivery ship."

"Well, why did you chase them away then, if you're not going to deliver what we need? It's not like we don't have anything to trade for it." The station cargo master crossed his arms and pointed overhead. Windows showed a long truss heading straight down to a kilometer wide asteroid. Sharp-edged cliffs popped up, with digging machines grinding ore. The sharp cliffs meant this wasn't some millions'-year-old collections of orbiting rocks, but the internal hunk of some larger body that had been smashed open. "Finest titanium ore in the rings. Highest assay grade. But we need plates for the ore barges. We'll take reinforced containers and take 'em apart if that's all you have, but we won't pay as well."

"We don't have any steel plates or spare containers."

"Then why come here? And why did you prohibit the corporate lines from trading with us?"

"We didn't prohibit anything?"

"That's not what they said on the radio. Said the council that took over after the Emperor's death. And god bless Emperor Dashi. That was sad. But regardless, they've jiggered the trade routes. We're going to be served by you Free Traders. And we need steel plates."

"Make your own. You've got titanium."

"First, Trader lady—"

"That's Senator."

"Fine, Senator lady, you don't make steel plates out of

titanium, you make them out of steel, which, incidentally, is why they are called"—he made air quotes with his hands—"steel plates, not titanium plates, and second, we don't have any iron ore with which to make said plates, and third, even if we did, we don't have a factory to make 'em with. We're a mine. We dig stuff out, grind it up, do some metal distillation, and trade that for what we need. Which are steel plates."

"We're not here to trade, we're telling you that the council has authorized—"

"Takeover. Yes, yes. Take things over. Congratulations, you're now the duly authorized manager of High-77. So, manage. And why do you all have hands on your guns?"

Marianne looked behind her and waved her crews hands away from their holsters. "In case you resist."

"We're not resisting. Why would we resist? The council sent you. We support the Emperor and the council. They said you would take care of things. That's what our shipper said when they called. National emergency, something like that. The Free Traders were taking over some stations. If they came by, do what they said. We're doing that. Get managing. Oh, and side topic. When do you want your passengers?"

"Passengers? We're not here to take passengers."

"We had five folks manifested on the Destiny of the Stars before they said you'd be replacing them."

"We're not an Empire-damned passenger line that takes people out for drinks and parties."

"One's a girl who won a scholarship to the university. Premed. We're paying—she'll be our doctor for five years if we pay for training. That's how we get staff out here. Three are workers training to be heavy equipment mechanics, replacing some older folks who want to retire before they die. They need to go dirtside to work with the simulators."

"We have no space for passengers."

"One's a grandmother, going to her granddaughter's

wedding. She couldn't really afford the trip, but we all kicked in some cash, so she could make the trip."

"We're not going to the core. You'll have to find some other solution."

The cargo master stomped to the intercom and slammed the button a few times. "Operations," a voice said.

"Our new corporate masters are here. Senator Marianne and the Free Traders."

"Cool. What are they like?"

"They hate education and medicine, don't like people being promoted, and expect us to work till we die in unspeakable agony caused by preventable infections."

"They say that?"

"All of it. And Clea can't go to Sashi's wedding. Wrong direction."

"I see. I see. Did they bring the plates?"

"Of course not."

"I see."

The cargomaster glared at Marianne. "So, we're not getting anything we want. What are your requirements, shipmaster?"

Marianne put her hands on her hips. "We need hydrogen."

The cargomaster punched the intercom. "They need hydrogen."

"Hydrogen?"

"Hydrogen."

"Well, I think we're all out of that. I'm pretty sure it leaked away. Big leak in the tanks."

Marianne stepped up to the intercom. "Don't be an Imperial ass. If your hydrogen was leaking, you'd have a crew down there right away to fix it."

Laughter rolled out of the intercom, and the cargo master released the button and grinned. "That's funny. Fix it."

"What's so funny?"

"Fixing it. If there was a leak, we would fix it. Except for one thing."

"What?"

"Steel plates, that's what we needed to fix it." He grinned again. "The steel plates you don't have."

CHAPTER 31

"That's a fine body of troops you have there," Pletcher said, watching yet another group of Militia march onto the shuttle.

"It would be a finer body if they could manage to keep in step." Shutt looked for the sergeant in charge. A raised eyebrow and the sergeant started bawling orders at the walkers, who transformed into marchers.

"How many more are you sending orbital?"

"That's it. No more. We need to keep the rest here to keep that Free Trader Legion in check."

"You don't think they'll do anything."

"No, I don't. Because we've shown them that we'll respond, and we've co-opted them by having their observers in the armory. They're feeling like we're all in this together."

"We are all in this together."

"That message didn't get through before. It seems to now. As long as we don't blow anything up, they won't blow anything up, at least not down here."

"They could still cause problems."

"Blowing things up is half the fun of a revolution," Shutt said. "Things don't shoot back and things that go bang don't hurt you, as long as you're far enough away. With all that fun gone, they'd have to fight actual troops with actual weapons, and they might get killed or crippled. We're equal strength down here. Since they don't have much of a chance of winning, and we don't have much of a chance of losing, everybody is sitting around."

"Great idea of yours."

"Gotta give Senator Jose credit, it was his idea. We've

got mixed Militia and TGI everywhere. Militia headquarters, TGI headquarters. All over."

"Shows that you're together on this."

"And makes it hard for the Free Traders to count exactly how many people we have under arms. TGI gave us lots of people in uniforms. Corporate uniforms. Are they trained fighters with weapons under their tunics, or are they corporate drones who only have a spare neck ruff and a bag of dehydrated super-potatoes? Can't tell. Makes us look bigger than we are."

"How many active troops do you have here?"

Shutt smiled at Pletcher. "More than enough, Senator. More than enough. Did you receive payment for your shipment? Were there any problems?"

"I did get payment, of a sort. But there's one problem."

"Which is?"

"Too much money."

"You have too much money?"

"You gave me too much. You paid nearly twice as much as I asked."

"You mean, after you horrendously inflated your prices and overcharged us for everything, we still gave you more money?"

"More than I expected."

"And that bothers you?"

"It makes me really, really nervous."

"That's a surprise. I thought you liked money."

"I do, I do. But—"

"But now you have so much, somebody might want to take it from you."

"Who would that be?"

"I'm sure you have enemies. People who wish you ill. People who would be interested to know how much cash you dispose of right now."

"I'd like to give it back. Some of it."

"Oh, we can't have that." Shutt grinned again. "You just need to consider it differently."

"Consider it as value for value received?"

"Consider it as a bribe. You're on team Militia now. Lots of powerful people will notice. You decide to change teams, better make sure you've got a powerful protector. One with troops."

"Like the Free Traders?"

"The Free Traders are far away. TGI and the Militia are here."

"Maybe I should get some troops of my own."

"Outstanding idea. Should I pass the word that you're hiring? Curious to see who you hire to guard your money. You'll need some, since if you do that you can't count on the Militia for protection."

"I didn't ask for this. I'm not involved in these things."

"Yes, you are. You should have picked a side earlier."

"And why should I have done that?"

"Because then we wouldn't have to pick one for you." Shutt slapped him on the back. "Come back to my office. I've got another list of things I want you to deliver."

***

Jose met the arriving shuttle, greeted the arriving troops on behalf of TGI, then escorted them to the quarters for food and equipment.

"Senator Shutt takes your comfort and security seriously," Jose said. "As do I, on her behalf. You'll be working closely with TGI in the future, so we want to make sure you get what you need. If something is amiss, or you experience any shortages, tell your sergeant"—Jose pointed at the scowling woman in the corner—"she'll meet with my VP of security daily, so we should get things taken care of. Does anybody have any questions?"

A voice in the back called out. "What in the Emperor's name are we doing here?"

"We've been ensuring that all of our core stations are protected from unrest. TGI security and the Militia have been patrolling the most critical stations—the largest ports, the biggest factory stations, the most critical transfer and drop points. We've been ensuring that there has been no unrest anywhere."

"Are we at war with the Free Traders?"

"Absolutely not. The Senate has decreed that we're to provide protection against unreliable elements, wherever they're found. We can't afford the sort of fighting that we had before—no attacks on infrastructure, no fires, nothing like that. Your job is only to deal with the riffraff."

"The Free Traders are the riffraff?"

"I'm sure some are. And if you've ever met any Free Traders, I'm sure you'll agree with that." Jose waited for the laughter to die down. "But some members of TGI aren't as disciplined as I'd like, and I'm sure that if I asked your sergeant, she'd give me a list of some of you she might like to be more attentive to your duties."

The crowd laughed and cheered. The sergeant stood and yelled them shut. "Want to be on that list? Then keep interrupting the Senator. Sorry, sir."

"No need to apologize." Jose smiled. "Just high spirits. I'm sure you've all been bored down on the surface—nothing to do except stand around and stare at people. No excitement. No fighting."

The crowd of soldiers murmured 'yes'.

"That's because I'm boring." The sergeant jumped up, but Jose waved her down. Once the volume dropped, he continued. "I'm boring. I'm an administrator. I'm big on numbers and keeping things going. But that's what we need right now. The last . . . unpleasantness . . . didn't go well for a lot of people. Even people who weren't involved suffered. Well, we're not putting up with that anymore. TGI, the Militia, and key other groups have come together in the Senate to ensure stability. Oh, we'll have our disagreements, but that's how we will handle things."

"My cousin's been on garrison duty up here. He says he's only dealing with TGI stations and Militia sites. How come?"

"Just a coincidence. It's taken us a while to get things organized, and the first places we could protect were TGI assets and the key Militia points. Most of that was the new inspections and trade routes that we've established. It's taken time to get the ships where they needed to be, and we've had some hiccups and bottlenecks. Now that we've gotten ourselves sorted out, as it were, we'll start to extend our patterns to the other stations. You folks will probably be involved in that, in a few days."

"Who poisoned the admiral? Who killed the Emperor?"

The crowd shut up like somebody had dumped a wet blanket on them. Jose's eyes ran with tears, and he stared at the floor till he could get control of himself. "He was a great man. I miss him dearly. His death will not go unavenged."

"Senator. Do you know who did it?"

"Nobody wants to punish them more than I." Jose squared his shoulders. "The investigation continues."

"Do you have any suspects?"

"Until I have firm proof, I will not speculate. Making wild, unsubstantiated accusations benefits nobody. I would shame myself in Dashi's memory if I did that. I will not speak until I am sure."

"What will happen to the people who did it."

Jose walked to a table in the middle of the hall and pointed at two Militia troopers. "Boost me up." They tossed him onto the table. Jose stared at the crowd, meeting each set of eyes as he glared. He scanned the back, then right, then back to the left. The crowd stood mute at the end of his sweep.

"What will happen to the people who did it." Jose smiled. "When I prove it to my satisfaction, I will arrest them. Then there will be a trial, to make sure justice is done. And then, then, I will kill them."

***

"Buy up a docking slot if you need to," Marianne said over the radio. "Pay for it. Somebody will sell."

"We already tried," Marianne's uncle, Lalond, said. "Offered double the rate, but they said we have to wait in line."

"You need to get refueled, Uncle. We need you out here. I have places for you to go. There are Legionnaires—I mean crew—waiting for you."

"Don't I know this, ma petite? You are teaching me to drive a ship? Me, who gave you your first piloting lessons?"

"I know this, Uncle, but we—"

"And gave you your first trading account, and your first time off station—"

"Uncle, the troops are waiting—"

"And took you to that gather at that rim station, where you met that boy. What about the things he taught you?"

"Uncle!" Marianne yelled. "We have other things to discuss. I appreciate that you helped me when I was younger, but things are different now."

"Henri, wasn't that his name?"

"Uncle, you are confused about who was teaching who, at the station. I was not the student."

"You were not? But I thought . . ."

"Henri was a nice boy, but I didn't learn anything off him."

"But you were only, eighteen?"

"I was nineteen, and I assure you, Henri benefited more from that encounter than I did."

"I had no idea—"

"To business, Uncle. We need you to get on that station. There are packages waiting for you. People. I was counting on you being on the way now."

"Ma petite." Lalond paused. His voice stiffened. "Senator. There're no docking slots, we are told at least ten days wait. Sixteen other ships are lined up ahead of us. All corporate or related. Four Militia cutters. We've been here three days and only one ship has moved. The others are everywhere—fuel dock, repair trusses, everything. There is so little space, we've been assigned a far orbit."

"Can you get on the station at all? Take a shuttle, or a cutter, or something."

"None available. They've grounded them for maintenance and critical operations, so they say. A single Militia boat goes from ship to ship. We have to book a day in advance, and they'll take two people and no cargo."

"Have you looked at breaking out a broomstick—and powering your way in? Can you do that?" A broomstick was a hydrogen-oxygen engine with one nozzle and six tiny thrusters. Two occupants could strap onto a bench seat on the engine. In the front, one could use the basic controls to zoom through space.

"It's within range of the personnel air locks, and we could move a few dozen kilos of cargo, but not cargo and a passenger at the same time too far."

"We should chance it."

"Ma petite, Senator. It's a long dash in, and we'd be under a dozen telescopes and whatever sensors they wanted the whole time. No matter what air lock we headed for, the Militia could meet us there . . . no way to hide anything."

Marianne cursed. "We need you."

"One other Free Trader ship is waiting here, also loitering in a far orbit. They are behind us in the line for a port. They have some fuel left. We have some fuel left. If I combined the two, one of us could make a run somewhere. Somewhere with fuel. I won't get what you need here, but I will be able to be back in the game."

"The other captain is willing to do this?"

"Ah, no. No, he is not. In fact, after dropping a few hints, I think he will resist this idea. Resist strongly."

"How strongly?"

"I'll need to bring all the crew with me when I suggest it. We'll need guns. And probably tie them up."

"Tie them up? You think that tabbo lover would tell our enemies?"

"Ma petite, when somebody comes on your ship and takes all your fuel and leaves you drifting in space, even if you are related to them, they will reconsider who is friends, and who is enemies."

"Could you, I mean . . ."

"I won't shoot him. He is a cousin, and he has done nothing to warrant such actions, other than being somewhere with something I want. And besides, my crew would not stand for any serious violence. If I shot somebody, I would not be the captain ten minutes later. To keep him from calling, we will need to restrain or threaten them while we transfer fuel."

"Which means that the second you leave, he'll be on the comm to his new best friend, Senator Shutt."

"I think Senator Jose, he liked Dashi very much, and Jose got him some special cargo discounts when he was Dashi's assistant."

"Can you take fuel from one of the corporate ships?"

"Do you want me to? Piracy is not something that anybody likes."

Marianne keyed the comm off, wiped her brow, and punched the button again. "Uncle, I need you here. Take the fuel. Soon as you can. Will you do this for me?"

"Ma petite, I will do this thing for you, if you ask. But it is much you ask."

"I'm getting desperate here, Uncle. We need to establish our position."

"You didn't expect your boyfriend to get friendly with Senator Shutt."

"Jose has behaved unexpectedly, yes."

"Perhaps you should have paid more attention to young Henri, all those years ago. Your lessons are not complete?"

"And up yours, Uncle. Perhaps I just like Mr. Jose? Did you ever think of that?"

"I did. I believe it to be true. But this is politics, liking has nothing to do with it."

"Thank you, Uncle. I will see you soon."

"D'accord. One other thing."

"Yes?"

"I will do this thing, take this fuel, but this is the last . . . nonstandard thing I will do for you. I have my own position to consider."

"You won't help me again?"

"I will, but only under one condition."

"What is that?"

"Victory," Lalond said. "Win, and all is forgiven."

CHAPTER 32

"Senator Shutt, welcome to TGI Main." Jose shook Shutt's hand. He and some of his staff, including Rajput, stood next to the shuttle's docking bay.

"Fancy, Jose, Fancy." Shutt walked away from the air lock into the main section, uniformed Militia trailing behind her. "You didn't need to come and meet me."

"It's always best to give people something to talk about. Otherwise, they invent things. Your troops are going to be taken care of. Shall we go to my office?"

Conversation buzzed from the corner. A group of workers were pointing cameras at the visitors and talking on their comms.

Shutt put her hands on her hips and surveyed the walls. "Things seem different here. Did you . . . clean?"

"Painted. With all the ships here, we have a lot of bored crewmen looking for temporary work."

"For a space station, it looks . . . appropriate."

Jose stopped and regarded a stylized rendering of the rings on the corridor wall. A shiny silver shuttle blasted off from an iron-red asteroid. Skin suited figures with tools clustered around it."

"It's hideous. Like something from a child's vid."

Shutt pointed at the central figure of the tableau. "A very unrealistic child's vid. Is that an ax?"

"It looks like one."

"What's the use of an ax in asteroid mining?"

"Chop down rock trees? I don't know."

A flunky in TGI colors opened the door to the truss air lock as they approached and slammed it behind them. Another on the far side yanked the second door open as soon as the notification lights flashed to green.

"What fancy people we are. Marching through the station with no delay."

"You're an important person. And you don't visit often."

"Flattery. Think that will work on me?"

"It's worth a try."

They walked the ring antispinward. TGI main was big enough to have multiple internal air locks between sections. Two more flunkies shoved doors open and closed as they walked.

Shutt gestured at them. "Why not just leave both doors open?"

"It's not safe."

"I know that, Jose. But this is all theater so why not?"

Jose reached the stairs and gestured her up. "It's important that you seem, well important. But not unsafe. This way we show that the leader of the Militia is important enough to get special treatment, but still has to follow the same safety rules as everyone else. People understand that, it makes them feel better."

"I'm not the leader of the Militia. That's the admiral."

"Acting leader, then."

"Cameras in the docking bays. Painting on the walls. Are you plotting something, Jose?"

"Clarisse, you've known me for a long time. When am I not plotting something?"

"Ambitious young man you are, Jose."

"And you're an ambitious young woman, Clarisse."

"You don't normally call me Clarisse."

"You've never visited me at the station before."

Shutt stopped and regarded another wall mural. This one was more abstract—rounded asteroids, with the bright edge of Sigma Draconis IV in the background. A single cutter crossed the terminator, black and yellow, with a blue hydrogen glow behind it. "I never have. I like this one better. What's it called?"

"The artist called this Dawn in the Rings. I like it better, too. More astral."

"Hidden depths. What's the one in the docking bay called?"

"Mediocre Talent meets too much funding, if I had my way."

Shutt laughed. "You can always paint it over."

"Scheduled for Tuesday, second shift."

Shutt continued climbing. "Our docking bay was occupied until a minute before we arrived—the ship there dropped as we were on final approach."

"We timed it that way."

"Three Free Trader Ships are loitering in a far parking orbit."

"Yes, once a slot opens up on the station, they can dock. All the slots are full now as you can tell."

"Except the one we needed."

The gravity lessened as they climbed coreward. Both Jose's feet floated as he rounded a corner, and he used his hands to stop his swing. "That was on the schedule."

"Seems like a scam—all these ships here."

"They can leave as soon as necessary inspections are completed."

"When will that be?"

"I'd have to check. We have a backlog, though. Days at least. Perhaps longer."

"Jose"—Shutt grabbed his arm—"you can't leave those Free Traders out there to starve."

"They won't starve. Not yet." Jose grabbed a bar and swung down a corridor. "My office is one-quarter along, and another level down."

"Did we take the long way?"

"Yes. I wanted everybody to see the new senators conferring." Jose pointed at the wall here, which was just a mixture of different stripes, going in different directions. "What do you think of this?"

"I like it better. Simple. Clean."

"Unlike life." Jose turned onto another set of stairs and pulled himself down. "Anything new on the admiral's condition?"

"Haven't your spies filled you in?"

"Yes. It's not encouraging. The medical consensus is that the poison caused severe damage to his system. He probably won't wake up, and if he does, he'll be so ill he won't last long."

"That is the consensus. Your spies are good."

"The best. They tell me that there's nothing new on who killed Dashi."

"It was Marianne or one of her people, of course."

"Can you prove that?"

"Do I need to?"

Jose arrived at his office door. "Not today. Join me."

Both dismissed the various flunkies, subordinates, and hangers on, and settled into Jose's inner office. Shutt exclaimed over the features, including all the wood.

"I stole the idea from Dashi," Jose said. "Simple, elegant, and very, very expensive."

"I see that."

"I didn't understand the effect before," Jose said. "Rajput explained it to me."

"Did he? He must be smarter than he looks."

"Many people are," Jose said.

Shutt got up and walked to the wall. She ran her hand along the wood paneling. "Very nice. Well, Senator Jose, your people have seen my arrival—there was lots more activity in the corridors than I expected—obviously you planned on many folks seeing 'the senators conferring.' So, what couldn't you say over a comm?"

Jose brought a display up on the screen. "We've secured all the main corporate stations, the main transfer stations, and any orbital Militia bases of interest to you."

"Uh-huh."

"On the surface, things are quiet. The on-planet Free Traders are keeping a low profile as long as we don't threaten them. In return, my security and your Militia are keeping a low profile as well."

"Uh-huh."

"Thank you for the Militia personnel and ships that you loaned me. With those four groups, we'll be able to occupy several key Free Trader outposts and secure our situation."

"Uh-huh." Shutt rubbed her hands along the wall. "This is your style. No fighting. Just trading and ceding the initiative to Marianne. She and her 'administrative groups' have occupied over a hundred stations."

"Minor ones."

"Not to them. They're pretty happy. But people on planet asked me why we aren't doing something to stop them."

"That's why we're not doing anything. Right now, we're senators enforcing Imperial regulations. We haven't started any fighting, we haven't done anything except protect ourselves, concentrate our forces, and stop the most egregious issues."

"We've been wimps."

"We have." Jose steepled his hands.

Shutt regarded him. "That hand thing. Didn't Dashi do that?"

"That was his habit."

"Any other habits of his you're taking up? Becoming Emperor say?"

Jose shrugged. "All I have done is rearrange some trading routes and integrate my security people with the Delta Militia, who, according to charter, are the official security force of system. Nothing untoward."

"Untoward? You're even starting to talk like him. Fine. You've kept fighting from breaking out on the surface, maintained the peace, secured the main stations with no violence. But the Free Traders have occupied dozens of stations without effort or response. People think that you've gone soft."

"Do you think I've gone soft?"

"You're up to something. But you always are. I'm curious what part my people will be playing."

Jose stepped up and walked to his screen, and tapped a few buttons. "All the stations in orbit around Delta." A swarm of yellow dots displayed. "Our stations, that we control, in green." A core group of stations, mostly in close or geosynchronous orbit lit. "Neutral at the start, blue, Free Trader at the start, red."

Shutt surveyed the screen. "Going to show me the movement since then?"

Jose played with the screen. Lines of blue dots shifted to red as he modeled Free Trader ships moving away from their stations. Then most blue dots had disappeared. "That is Marianne's maneuver."

"She's grabbed almost all of the outer stations."

"Yes. But none of the inner ones. We maintain the main stations and main trade routes."

"We can't let her keep occupying stations forever."

"We will not." Jose tapped the screen. "All these stations that they have taken over, those, those are the rope."

"The rope?"

"Yes. We gave them as much rope as they wanted."

"Fine. What happens now?"

"The hanging, of course."

CHAPTER 33

Sergeant Russell stepped off the boat's gangplank onto the dock at Landing. "Well, that was unpleasant."

"What are you talking about, Sergeant?" Balthazar asked. "That was the smoothest sailing trip we've had yet."

"I was talking about the company, not the mode of travel."

"And always glad to see the back of you, too, Sergeant." Balthazar grinned. "Should have brought your mules out with you. They would have been better sailors."

Russell watched his green-faced squad stumble down behind him. "Kim One wouldn't allow it. Neither would Sweet Pea."

"You're insane taking orders from a mule."

"Smarter than a lot of officers I've worked for. More coherent orders, too, come to think of it. Hello, Senator Vince."

Vince Pletcher stepped up from the ground truck he'd been lounging against. "Sergeant, how are you."

"Wonderful. And, no."

"No, what?"

"Not sure yet. Whatever you were going to ask us to do. My squad is here at Shutt's request and orders. We're going to assist in some operations orbitally."

"Of course you are. It's good to have you back."

Russell pursed his lips. "It's been made very clear to me that we don't work for you."

"Of course. Of course."

"We won't be getting involved in whatever schemes you're planning."

"I would never dream of involving you in any

schemes."

"You're not planning any schemes?"

"I didn't say that. I said no involvement."

"Why are you here?"

"Shutt sent me to help offload your ship. You have ammunition and some other supplies. I'm supposed to bring them to Militia headquarters."

"That's it?"

"That's it. And bring you to Militia headquarters."

"We've got a lot of equipment of our own to be transported."

"I'm sure you do. Good deal." Vince smiled a dazzling smile. "Well, best of luck with that. I've brought a few people to help offload the ammunition and suchlike."

Russell counted Vince's companions. "I see four people. You have four loaders?"

"Of course not." Vince shook his head. "Four!"

"My mistake."

"Two loaders. They'll unload the ammunition, put it in the truck. The other two are security. They'll keep an eye on the cargo."

"They look like they're playing games on their comms."

"I'm sure they'll help us out if necessary. If there's some sort of threat."

"Of course." The two workers sauntered onto the ship, collected a box each, and walked back to the truck. "Only loading one truck?"

"Not enough security for both. Best to be safe, don't you think."

"Sure." Russell dug in his pocket. "Have a cigarette?"

Pletcher produced a pack from his pocket and handed it over.

Russell pulled out a cigarette, fiddled a bit, then lit it. "Didn't know you smoked."

"I don't. I keep a pack for emergencies."

"Emergencies?"

"Other people's emergencies. Are you heading off to

Militia headquarters now?"

Russell drew heavily on his cigarette. "Not yet."

"Shutt's in a bit of a hurry, I understand. You should move along."

"Have any transport for us?"

"Just for the gear, sorry. You could walk."

"We could. Need to bring our supplies though—combat loads, and suchlike."

"Oh, yes? Where is that."

"On the ship."

"And you're not getting it because . . . ?"

"It's on the bottom of the hold. Under all Shutt's stuff."

"I'll have my guys and gals look out for it as we empty the hold."

"Of course you will." Russell finished his cigarette. "You're really good at this, you know."

"I practice a lot."

"Sure you do." Russell raised his voice. "Listen up. First two sections, form a security perimeter. Weapons free. Anybody comes near this gear, one warning shot, then clean 'em out. Second two sections—grab those boxes in the hold and start loading up these trucks. Chop Chop."

The squad members boiled around, and a minute later, there were two riflemen in the trees, two shotguns on the road, and four others with revolvers roaming the area. The other eight stacked their weapons and formed a human chain, taking everything off the boat. Even Bal joined in.

Russell handed the pack of cigarettes back to Pletcher.

"Keep it," Pletcher said. "You've earned it. Besides." He grinned again. "I've got more where that came from."

***

"You unloaded his boat for him?" Shutt asked.

"You know how he is, Clarisse. It was inevitable." Russell fingered his pocket.

"No smoking in here. Did he bribe you with cigarettes?"

"After he maneuvered us to unload the boat."

"Not before?"

"Maybe before." Russell pointed to the bare walls. "Why can't I smoke in here? The smoke won't hurt anything. Everything in here is metal."

"My desk is wood."

"Smoke doesn't hurt wood. The admiral's office is all carvings and fabrics and stuff like that."

"His family had money—not sure which corp, but they had cash. He wasn't worried where his next meal was coming from."

"Why don't you make your office nicer? You're a senator now."

Shutt stood, stretched, and tapped her wall. "Steel. I'm used to it. All that time on ships, doing customs checks, and living off trays. I guess I'm more at home there. I spent over half of my career on ships. The rest on stations."

"All ships or stations? No ground assignments?"

"Not till the end. No staff or administration assignments. Ninety percent of the time on active operations. I never even had a place on Landing until a year ago. This is my first office."

"Unusual for officers to be . . ."

"Working for a living?"

"Didn't say that."

"You meant it, though."

"How come, Clarisse?"

"Money. I didn't have any. On operational ships you get flight pay. I needed that—no family or corporation behind me. I took the money and banked it. Figured I'd need it someday."

Russell pointed at the blank wall behind her desk. "You don't even have an I love me wall. Put up your awards and letters and suchlike."

"Don't have many. Not the usual raft. Admiral's aides get awards, or the Colonel's pet. I wasn't."

Russell looked at her medal bar on her uniform. "That's a Militia cross I see there."

"Only award I got. That's for that shootout with the pirates I had years ago. That's where I got the purple heart."

"That was a big deal."

"I should have got a second and a third, but they never put in for it. In fact, your old friend Roi," Shutt said, referring to a disgraced Militia officer that Russell had worked for before, "He has more awards and medals than I do. His Empire Rising buddies took care of that."

"Yeah, but you have the 'still alive' medal, and they eventually got the 'court-martialed and shot' medal."

"When they didn't get the 'blown up in orbit' medal, yes."

"But during the . . . unpleasantness . . . you led that squad that charged those Growers. That was pretty ballsy, I heard."

Shutt shrugged. "Admiral didn't think so. Didn't put me in for anything."

"He should have."

"If he wakes up, I'll tell him."

"You mean when."

"I mean if. The doctors are not happy."

"Meantime, you're in charge."

"Meantime, I am. Pletcher's games aside, I need you up in orbit with your squad."

"Pletcher was being difficult."

"He's showing you that even though he ostensibly works for me, he's got a lot of leeway."

"I hate it when you use those big words. I have to look them up. Can you not do that?"

"He wants you to know that I don't have his balls completely in a vise. Better?"

"Yes, small words. I like that. Thanks. You want me to

go put his balls in a vise?"

"No, I need you up in orbit, with your squad. Jose, Senator Jose, will be assigning you some clearance missions."

"Which means?"

"He's a fashion-obsessed poser, but he's smart. He's got the Free Traders zipping through the outer system peaceably occupying stations, while he and I have seized all the critical ones in close orbit. Now he's going to squeeze the Traders and their stations. He figures that ninety percent of the stations the Free Traders have occupied, they're going to get starved out and beg to come back with either a corporation or the Militia."

"The Free Traders become part of TGI?"

"Nope. He has some weird deal where he's formed a new corporation, with one of his reps, me or some Militia reps, and a Free Trader captain. They're going to buy up, or annex, I don't know. Something. This new company will be called Freedom Trading—and he's going to use it to take over those stations. He says it's a collective, but he changed the voting structure. It's complicated."

"I'm not good with voting structures, Clarisse."

"No? How do you feel about breaking heads?"

"Can I smoke while I do it?"

"You won't be breaking any heads in my office, so why not?"

Russell pocketed the cigarette. "Tell me more."

***

Jose performed his by now routine meeting of the upcoming troops. This shuttle had sixteen Militia and four TGI in the passenger compartment. A familiar face came out at the end of the line. "Sergeant Russell. Welcome. I thought you wouldn't be here for a few more days."

"Tides. Ships from out east have to deal with currents. Or waves. Something shippy. Either now or wait till next week."

"Shutt said you were coming next week?"

"That's what we told her. But then Sweet Pea made a change in plans."

"Sweet Pea?"

"She's our command mule. Runs the factory."

Jose nodded. "Command mule. Of course. Well, I'm glad you're here. Did Shutt explain your duties?"

"The squad and I are supposed to break some heads."

"That's not entirely correct. We're conducting a series of pacification operations with the unaligned stations. We've established a mixed group of TGI and Militia who will be reintegrating some of the other stations, the ones formerly owned by the Free Traders, into a new corporate structure, Freedom Trading."

"Freedom Trading?"

"Yes. It's a joint venture between TGI, some allied corps, and selected Free Trader families who want to join our new trading network."

"So, you've found some turncoat Free Traders, and you're buying them off by giving them other Free Traders stuff."

"We like to think of it as reorganizing the existing ownership structure in a more efficient manner."

"Good for you." Russell put his hand in his pocket. "Anywhere I can smoke?"

"Nowhere on the station. You can smoke outside."

"Outside? In hard vacuum?"

"Yes."

"Won't that kill me?"

"Yes. But if you feel that strongly about smoking, you could get a few quick puffs in."

"And then die."

"I never said it was optimal."

Russell rubbed his chin. "When do we go see these other stations?"

"First groups of ships leave day after tomorrow."

"Groups? More than one?"

"Four groups. Two Militia ships with crew and administrative personnel per group. Plus, a freighter with necessary items for trading. They'll be following up behind some Free Trader ships that have been traveling out to the rim stations."

"In other words, you're going back to recapture the stations that the Free Traders had under control and bring them back into your little mini Empire."

"We prefer to think of it as reinstituting corporate and Militia control of assets that a secondary group of Free Traders feels should not be under main Free Trader administration."

"I see. And what if these folks don't want to be reinstituted?"

Jose smiled. "Then you break heads."

CHAPTER 34

"I don't trust those people," Marianne said to Sikar. The two of them had dropped off the six 'administrators' at their latest destination—the operations room of a tiny rim station. "Something bad is going to happen there."

"They were polite and respectful, and they said that they would follow the administrator's rules."

"That's what bothers me." She glided antispinward in the middle ring's spin gravity, then turned into the spoke and climbed down the stairs. "They were too polite."

"They're doing what you say, and that bothers you. Whoops, inertia." Sikar had been hopping two steps at a time with the lowered gravity, but she'd missed the grab rail at the bend in the stairs. She rotated midair to take the far wall with her feet, compressed, and pushed off to take the next flight midair.

"Not spinning as fast as they should be." Marianne abandoned walking down the steps and switched to pushing off the walls to move down the shaft.

Sikar turned on her suit light. "And dark. And cold. And not enough gravity. I feel like I should seal my helmet."

"They're up to something," Marianne said. "Everywhere else at least protested about being told what to do by the Traders' Council, but here they nodded, said of course, showed us some greasy quarters and gave us lousy tea."

"What are they up to normally?"

"Normally?"

"What do they do here?"

"It's a station, they . . ." Marianne wrinkled her brow.

"I don't know. They're spinning here. They're a corporate station."

"But what type? No forge, no mine, no water."

Marianne stopped and typed a query into her comm. "Type of corporation. Miscellaneous. And this corporation only owns this single station."

"Transfer?"

"They only have two air locks. Pretty hard to do any volume of transferring."

Sikar sniffed. "And this air can't get much staler than this and be breathable. In fact, I wonder if we should be breathing it."

"You've gotten spoiled being with me on those big corporate stations, with new air recyclers. This is how air normally tastes. Why back when I did my recruit cruise—"

"You lived in a box in a cargo container, worked three shifts every two, got up two hours before you went to bed and only ate once a week, and that was potato peelings. Thanks, Mom. I've heard it before."

"I pity your mother, having silly, ungrateful children like you. But never mind. We will proceed on our way. Even six loyal Traders will keep them occupied behind me."

"Behind you? We're going farther out?" She sneezed. "I'm going to access the station records for analysis of this air."

"We have another two dozen stations to visit and bring under council administration."

"They have radios. Are you sure they'll buy that?"

"They won't care too much who takes over."

"Shipmaster, I'm with you. But why are we going out to all these little stations. Wouldn't it be better to occupy the main ones?"

"We need to establish trade routes. Let everybody know who is in charge. This is the most effective course. Start near the core, and travel out."

"As you say shipmaster." Sikar's comm bonged at her.

"It found the air quality results." She turned the display to Marianne. It was half red and half yellow, not a single green. "I'll be happy to be elsewhere."

***

"Concentration of forces." Jose punched up a display on his office screen. "The Traders have . . . well, occupied isn't the word. There hasn't been any fighting. They've mostly transferred control to themselves."

Russell stretched in his chair. "How many stations have they so-called-transferred?"

"More than a hundred."

"Occupying a hundred stations. That's a lot of work, even for these six groups you've got here. How many stations have you occupied in response?"

"Changed ownership you mean? None. We've reinforced our biggest stations. TGI Main. The main transfer stations. Ones with Militia cutters stationed there."

"You've abandoned all those other places? That's it?"

"Yes."

"Surrendered the initiative? Allowed the enemy to run roughshod over you?"

"That's been the plan."

"Surrender everything. Wow, you're a military genius."

"Thank you," Jose said. "I've been working on this for a long time."

"I'm being sarcastic."

"I'm not. Your ship leaves in thirty minutes. Are you ready?"

"To go out surrendering? I guess so. It doesn't sound so hard."

"You'll be occupying other stations this time."

"Great! How many."

"One."

***

"I just think that now that I'm a senator," Chaudhari said. "That you should be more respectful, that's all." The entire squad was formed up in a line on the air lock truss. Their cutter had docked at a station—Russell hadn't bothered to remember the name—and was disgorging two dozen armed Militia troops and a dozen armed TGI security. They flowed through the air lock in groups of eight, then waited between the mostly empty ship locks.

Russell made a rude gesture. "This to your senator. While you're in the squad, in uniform, you're a corporal. And you do what I say."

"You wouldn't say that to Shutt."

"One, she's a major. Two, she's a major. Three, she's a major. And occasionally, she knows what she's doing."

"And she grabs you by the ear and shakes it when you mess up."

Russell called his squad over and handed his shotgun to Kim Two. "Hold that for a minute. Wait, you know what? Keep that. Use it if you need it."

Kim Two cradled the shotgun. "Thank you, Sergeant."

Russell faced Chaudhari and crossed his arms. "Go ahead. Grab my ear. See what happens."

Chaudhari swallowed. "Sorry, Sergeant. I'll just follow along in the back."

"Good plan," Russell said. The air lock at the end of the truss cycled, and four people in Free Trader Legionnaire uniforms came through. They were armed.

Russell pushed his way to the front. The TGI rep, whose name Russell had forgotten, was finishing speaking by the time he shoved in next to him.

". . . don't want to fight you," the TGI rep said.

"That's not a universal opinion." Russell glared at the Free Traders. "I could use a good fight."

"Who are you?"

"Russell, Sergeant, Delta Militia, representative of."

"Do you know who we are?"

"Completely don't care."

"And who we represent?"

"Even more completely don't care." Russell pointed to the TGI rep. "Smiley, here—wait, what is your name?"

The TGI man opened his mouth.

Russell held up a hand. "Know what, doesn't matter. You Trader people. He gave you some sort of deal. Come with us, or something. Be locked up for a while. I'm sure he doesn't want to kill you."

The TGI man nodded. "No violence, I was told."

Russell turned to the Traders. "See? No violence."

The Traders exchanged glances. "What about you?"

"I'm the yes violence option."

"We represent—"

"Still don't care. I've got four full squads, all armed, all with lots of reloads. We'll stomp this place. You four and whoever else you have hidden."

"They've got a total of six," the TGI man said. "I'm talking to the station management."

"Six, that's not much. You're running an entire station with six?"

"The station management are afraid of us."

"No, they're not. Otherwise, they wouldn't have told us everything. We knew where you were. I'll bet we know where your other two are." Russell turned to the TGI guy. "Do you have a location for the others?"

The TGI man nodded.

"There you go." Russell dropped his hand to his holster. "Follow instructions from Mr. We-don't-want-to-kill-you here, or deal with me. And I don't care if you live, die, or move to the outer rim."

"I've been to the outer rim," the Free Trader Legionnaire said. "I'd rather die. Can you give us some time to decide."

"Sure." Russell drew his revolver and pointed it at the Free Trader's face. "Five seconds sounds good. Four. Three. Two—"

"Okay. Relax. Relax." The Free Trader Legionnaire

raised his hands. "Sheesh. Give us time."

"What about the other two?" Chaudhari asked.

"Compartment 2-4-27," the TGI man said. "Don't hurt them."

"Chaudhari, take a full squad and grab those other two." Russell holstered his revolver. "Shoot them all if they so much as sneeze wrong. Or sneeze right. Any reason will do. None of us gets hurt. Them, I don't care."

The squad thundered through the air lock. The TGI security took custody of the Traders. The head TGI agent muttered into his comm. Russell muttered to himself and kicked the deck. The head TGI agent came over. "The old admin team is taking back over. We're not leaving anybody here."

"Don't care."

"The Free Traders are going into protective custody back at TGI main."

"Don't care."

"All the other groups have achieved their objectives."

"Yay for them."

Russell's comm bonged, and he checked it. Chaudhari had the others. "All secure. Looks like we're done here."

"Senator Jose said to wait here for our next assignment. He'll have something in two days."

"Tell Senator Jose that I don't work for him."

"He said you'd say that, and he said that Senator Shutt is aware of what's going on, and approves."

Russell muttered a curse. "So, we just sit here for the next few days?"

"Till we have another target."

"Outstanding." Russell glanced around the docking bay. "Think anybody here has a cigarette."

***

"You have the station?" Marianne sat in her quarters, talking to her uncle Lalond.

His head rolled on the vid as he looked past her. "It's

all pink. Everything is pink. Is there something wrong with your comm?"

"I'm in my cabin. You took your station?"

"Yes, yes. No problem. Is that a pink chair? How do you get a pink chair? I didn't know they came in pink."

"I like pink. Enough about my cabin. When will you reach the next station on your list."

"Pink clothes I understand, but pink furniture? It's so . . . Feminine."

"I'm a woman, Uncle."

"Yes, but I don't ever think of you that way. I think of you as a shipmaster."

"I don't invite the crew in here for meetings. Only friends. Close friends. Close male friends."

"And they enjoy pink?"

"Perhaps—but the point is not their color preference, but to stop them thinking of me as a shipmaster."

"Does it work?"

"Better than it does for you, If Tante Liz is correct."

"Your Tante Liz is a huge gossip."

"But apparently not a liar. When do you take the next station?"

"When I get more crew. Troops. Whatever. I've lost a bunch."

"What do you mean lost? Did you leave them in a dusty corner of your cargo hold?"

"I'd be happy if that was the case. A quick atmo purge, and they'd get what they deserve. And I'd have a clean cargo hold. No, they left."

"Some of your crew just left? As in deserted."

"They were told by their family to come back. They were not the main branch, you know. Mr. Jose, or one of his people, got to them."

"Senator Jose."

"He's not a real senator."

"If he's not a real senator, what am I?"

"You're . . . good point. But I'm short people. Mathieu

was supposed to meet with me to give me some people, but he's late. He says he's delayed. Fuel problems."

"Everybody has fuel problems."

"As do I, niece. As do I. I barely got here, and I've drained their tanks to fuel up. I can get to the next station on your list, but the margin is closer than I want."

"I understand."

"Can you get me some people to replace the ones I lost?"

"Not and get them to you out there. I will have to think." Marianne turned her head up and frowned.

"What is wrong, ma petite?"

"Nothing, Uncle."

"I've known you since you were born. Nothing escapes me. Something unexpected has happened. You have your surprised face on."

"You're not—yes you are. Two of the stations where we changed the administration are not answering comms."

"Destroyed?"

"No, no. Still there. Still sending comms. I should say, they are not answering my comms."

"They were captured, or something?"

"I had no reports of fighting, and what info we can get from long range, there is no evidence of anything. Just, not as much comm traffic. And they don't answer any of mine, or anybody I can get to send them."

Lalond frowned. "They've gone quiet? That's it?"

"D'accord."

"They're changing sides."

"I have . . . friends with Senator Jose's people, and Senator Shutt's people. They say that is not the case. The missing station is not approaching them."

"Not changed sides, waiting to see who wins and claiming to be on the winning side."

"Cowards."

"Yes. But smart ones. Marianne, you must make sure that this does not get out. If people find out they can sit this out, then there will be more. We cannot afford that right now."

"I'm not telling anyone. And it sounds like they aren't, either. But we need to do something."

"Of course. We must do something. I know exactly what."

"What?"

"Win."

CHAPTER 35

"As soon as we hit, go, go, go." Sergeant Russell pulled his revolver from his holster and checked the loads. "Don't wait. Go where we showed you."

"Ummm . . . we need to get clearance from the docking people." The Militia had assigned a spaceman basic to stand with them at the lock. Their Militia cutter, assigned only a number, was surging into an empty docking slot. "The procedure is that we engage the magnets, and then they come and attach the chain—"

"The procedure is, as soon as I hear those magnets engage, open the outer door and don't wait. Don't wait for pressure equalization, just go. First squad rushes through and heads for operations. Who's last in line?"

A Militia trooper raised her hand. "Here, Sergeant."

"You stay." Russell pointed at another squad member. "And you. She slams the door, and you watch the dock while first squad runs to operations. Second squad piles in after that, then out through the air lock and head for the reactor and the main caf."

"Why the main caf, Sergeant?" a daring voice from the back asked.

"Because it's just before shift change, so probably the next shift of Free Traders will be there getting something to eat. Get in there and catch them. Last out is the TGI people. Where are they?"

"Back behind me, Sergeant," the daring voice answered.

"HEY TGI!" Russell yelled. They were so far down the corridor he couldn't see them. "You know where the other Free Traders will be?"

"By the time we're docked, yes."

"Grab them. Don't take no for an answer."

"Got it."

Russell surveyed the groups and raised his voice. "Remember. Speed. Move fast. Hit hard. Anyone points a weapon, shoot them."

Chaudhari sidled up to Russell. "Helmets," he whispered.

"Anybody who comes charging out of an air lock without their helmets is too stupid to live."

Chaudhari rolled his eyes and gestured to the waiting troops. "Are we going to make a bet on how many make it, then?"

Russell shook his head. "All you people." He yelled. "Close your helmets once you're in the air lock and keep 'em closed till you're on the run into the station. I don't want anybody getting sucked out through their open faceplates."

"Scott," Chaudhari whispered. "That can't happen. A faceplate is too small."

Russell shrugged. "People too stupid to live probably don't know that."

The intercom flashed, and the Militia Spaceman slapped the button. "Air lock three?"

"Thirty seconds," a voice said. "We'll be hitting hard and holding with thrusters. We'll engage the magnets remotely."

"Inside." Russell slapped the shoulder of the trooper next to him and counted eight people into the lock. "Helmets down. I'm locking you in." He slammed the lock door shut and spun the wheel.

The intercom blasted. "Brace for impact."

WHAM.

Russell hit the wall. Half the squad slammed into his back. Fire lanced his wrist. The ship pivoted and banged again. The lights all went out, except the green air lock status light. He fell, knocking the lead squad member down.

"Imperial Anus."

SNAP. The ship held position. Voices squawked from the air lock intercom. Russell rolled off the squad member. "You okay?"

"Wheeeeeerrr," the man gasped.

"Catch your breath." Russell pushed up with his hand and cursed. His wrist hurt. Voices yelled in the dark. "SHUT UP. SHUT UP." He slapped the airlock intercom. "GO. GO. GO." Voices burbled back at him—the status lights flashed red as the outer lock opened.

"Count off," Russell yelled. Two members of the squad didn't answer—the wheezing form at his feet and one other. "Broken ribs here. Medic."

"Medics down. Knocked out," a voice from the back said.

"Outstanding."

CLANK.

Russell turned to the Militia sailor. The sailor's face glowed white from the internal intercom display. His ear was pressed to the speaker.

"Well?"

"First magnet's on."

The air lock light flashed to red. The first squad would be exiting the ship now.

CLICK.

"Tell me second magnet's on."

Russell caught the head shake in the near dark. "Bridge says it's not engaging."

CLICK. CLICK. CLICK.

"Get Ready." Russell bent and dragged the wheezing trooper half upright with his left hand. "What happened to you?"

"Can't catch my breath, Sergeant. Hurts when I breathe."

"Ribs. Not fatal. Get up if you can. Go out with the third wave and guard the lock. Don't run anywhere."

The trooper gasped, nodded, and put a hand on the wall.

Red light flooded the corridor.

CLICK. CLICK. CLICK.

Russell reached for the locking wheel and cursed as again his wrist wouldn't function. He slapped the next trooper with his left hand. "Open it. In and move."

The trooper spun the wheel, helped by the two remaining in the lock. Russell counted them into the lock, waving two more than should fit in.

"Sergeant!" The Militia sailor raised a hand. "Bridge says they can't lock the second magnet. They want to disconnect."

"No. Tell them we've got the air lock open. If they disconnect, they'll empty the ship and the station."

"But—"

"But I'll go up there and shoot them if they don't hold us here. You—" Russell pointed to a helmeted figure coming out of the gloom from down the corridor. "Help me shut the lock."

CLICK.

The helmeted figure used both hands to spin the lock shut, and a second later the green display flashed to red.

Russell looked down the corridor. Six sets of hard helmets and suits stared back. "Hard suits? To storm a station?"

"They're protection." The voice came from a speaker on hard-suited man's chest. "Like armor. They'll stop bullets."

"Bullets won't penetrate, but they'll still knock you down, and you'll be wallowing like a buffalo on a monorail car. Get ready."

CLICK.

Russell flexed his right hand. Feeling was coming back. It didn't hurt, but felt numb. He tried to make a fist and couldn't. "Outstanding."

CLICK.

"Sergeant, still no—"

"I heard." Russell bent down and grabbed a loose shotgun and thrust it into broken rib's hand. "Through the lock, into the docking bay. Stay there and guard."

"I'll lean against the wall if I have to."

"Good man." Russell slapped him on the shoulder. The man screamed. "Whoops. Sorry."

The light flashed green, and the hard-suited TGI man spun the wheel and he and his comrades charged in. Broken ribs followed.

Russell stepped through into the crowded air lock and yelled to the Militia sailor. "Lock us in. Then see to our medic. Watch the lights."

"Then tell the bridge to undock?"

"Medic first. If this ship isn't here when I come back, I'll—"

The Militia sailor slammed the door on Russell's answer. Russell's eyes had adapted to the dark and emergency lighting. The Helmeted TGI man had his hands on the outer locking bar and his face pointed at the lights. The interior door spun to lock—the outer door flashed green—the TGI man whirled the outer locking wheel, pulled in the door, and dashed through, his group following.

Russell used his left hand to help broken ribs forward and out. By the time they exited the TGI men had disappeared. "I'll give them this," he said to the two waiting squad members. "Those TGI guys look weird, but they're keen. Let's get some."

Broken Ribs and one other stayed at the lock. Russell hustled forward. He tried to hold his revolver, but his right hand still couldn't grasp. He changed it to his left and marched forward, picking up a half squad as escort. They crossed past an automatic pressure door. His escort stopped and peered out a view port. "Wow, Sergeant. Check this out."

Russell leaned in and stuck his nose on the view port.

He could see down the docking truss. The Militia ship loomed up—it was big—too big for the port. This truss was obviously for small merchant ships, not big cutters. Rather than fitting easily by the docking area, it extended way beyond the regular area. The bow overlapped the next docking port in and nearly touched the main ring. The stern stretched beyond the second personnel port and nearly touched the refueling truss behind it.

"That's some docking. No wonder they couldn't get the magnets to engage. Too wide, probably."

"I'm surprised they got one. They would have had to push in sideways and match rotation at the same time." Russell nodded. "That's good flying."

"You going to tell them that, Sergeant?"

"Tell them? Don't be stupid. Navy is arrogant enough as it is." He nodded again. "Do need to find out who the pilot is, though. Need to be on their ship in the future."

They continued up the spokes. Two runners met him minutes apart. The first from the squad in the caf said they had two Free Traders in custody. The second from ops said they had no problems, had three Free Traders of a total of six in custody, and that TGI knew where the others had cabins, and the other two ships were executing simpler dockings on the far side of the rings.

"Five of six taken then. Any update from the TGI helmet heads?"

Both runners shook their heads. Russell ordered the Free Traders escorted to the soon-to-be docked ships, released the caf squad back to the ship, sent the runners to allow the ship and the others at the initial air lock to disengage at their option."

"Anyone have painkillers?" One of the squads had some. Russell took four, over their objections, flexed his wrist, and headed to find the remaining TGI group.

A ten-minute walk brought him to a group of helmet heads, as he now called the TGI people, clustered outside a cargo lock, yelling at a person on the far side, near a cargo lock.

One of the helmet heads sat inside the lock, pulling futilely at his helmet, which was rolled a quarter turn clockwise.

"What's going on?"

The senior helmet head spoke through his open faceplate. "He's over the far side, next to the lock controls. Says he disengaged the interlocks and can pop both doors at once and decompress this whole section."

"Can he do that?"

"It's possible. Not likely. Need a good mechanic. Set of tools. Knowledge and time."

"Go in hard. There's six of you."

"Too risky. Protocol is to wait it out. He has to sleep or eat sometime. We wait."

"How long?"

"Probably two, three shifts."

"Emperor's anus. We can't wait that long." Russell pointed at the TGI man out in the middle of the lock. "What's wrong with him?"

"He, well, he . . ."

One of the others spoke up. "He screwed up his air system. He's not getting enough air. And he jammed his helmet so he can't get it off and get station air."

"He can't get his helmet off?"

"He's not used to hard suits."

"He'll suffocate."

"Pass out first."

Russell shook his head, then waved at the Militia with him. "Ready with that shotgun. I'll give you a distraction. When he's distracted, charge the lock and shoot him."

"We don't think—" the helmet head said.

"Shut up." Russell unbuckled his weapons belt, handed it to the nearest man, and walked out into the cargo lock.

"Stay back. I'll blow the lock." The Free Trader pushed his hands onto the lock controls.

Russell held his hands high. "Our guy is suffocating.

I'm going to get him out of his helmet and drag him back. I'm unarmed, see?" Russell spun in place, keeping his hands open.

"No tricks."

"I'm just going to get him out of here." Russell walked to the fumbling TGI man, leaned down, ran his hands around the outside of the helmet. "Idiot. You didn't disengage both locks." Russell clicked a tab into place, and the helmet released. Russell twisted the helmet another quarter turn, then lifted it clear and stepped back two steps. The blue-faced man wiped spit off his face and gasped in lungs of air. Russell stepped back one more step, gripped the helmet firmly, then hurled it right at the Free Trader.

The Trader dropped his hands from the controls and ducked, but the helmet still hit him dead in the face. He dropped. The Militia shotgun man rushed past, halted, set his feet.

BLAM. The Trader shook, then lay limp.

Russell strode to the prone form. He'd taken a slug to the chest.

"One down. More to go." Russell flexed his fingers. "Man, those are good drugs. I need more of those."

CHAPTER 36

"Uncle, I need you to help me," Marianne said. "I need to collect our people together."

"I would if I could, Ma petite, but I have absolutely no fuel. This station has been almost stripped." Marianne's Uncle Lalond said.

Marianne growled, then pushed her comm button. She was in her quarters, surrounded by pink items. "How can a station be stripped of fuel? They need it to run their reactors?"

"That Jose fellow bought it. He paid extra to have their tanks emptied. They shipped it out last week. They can make fuel from the water here, of course, but they don't have any reserves."

"How long till you get a full tank?"

"Four shifts. Perhaps a little longer or shorter."

"I will send you a course to travel." Marianne dug through a drawer, then slipped on vacuum tight station shoes. "I need you to collect the men you dropped off and bring them back to me." She named a station. "We need to concentrate here."

"Concentrate, but we have . . ."

"Jose has outsmarted me. He sat back and let us occupy station after station, and he didn't do anything. Once we were too far away, he's been following behind. He puts an entire shipload of troops against our six. They've all surrendered—and who wouldn't— outnumbered five or ten to one. He's behind us and catching up."

"But eventually, he'll run out of people, too."

Marianne swapped slippers for shoes. "No. He doesn't

leave any garrisons behind. But he does arrest our people, puts them in a jail. They converted a passenger ship to be a prison—a big one, it travels with them. He doesn't leave anybody behind, so his strength isn't dropping."

"But after he leaves, the stations can do as they please."

"They have been doing as they please. And they don't please to help us. Some have gone back to their corporations. Some declared independence, and nobody is stopping them."

"Have any applied to be Free Traders?"

"Two. Out of twenty."

"Only twenty? You still have many others left."

"It's worse than it sounds. Yes, they occupied only twenty stations. But they picked the ones with the most fuel, or the ones that had Trader ships. The other stations, our people, are stuck there."

"But they must protect their core stations, and their dirtside operations."

Marianne checked her cuffs and collar to make sure they would seal properly. "I didn't see it. Defeat in detail."

"What?"

"I looked it up. He's keeping his people concentrated, and he's moving against our groups, who are split into small pieces. We may have more people, but we don't keep them together. His keeping his people together is winning him his war."

A bong rang on Lalond's side. He muted his microphone and spoke to somebody off camera, waved, then returned. "What are your plans?"

"I am collecting all the people I can collect quickly and moving inward. You should do as well. I will send directions for a meeting. I will call the others as well. Mathieu."

"And LaFerme."

Marianne was silent.

"I said—"

"I know what you said. LaFerme has declined. He said

he would occupy seventeen stations for us. He did four, taking his time. Now he is not answering comms."

"Then we cannot count on him."

"No." She pulled gloves from a drawer and attached them to her belt.

"And Mathieu?"

"I am not sure of him, either." Marianne ran her hand through her hair. "He has been working with us. He has taken most of his stations. But he avoided five. He's had excuses. Plausible ones, but excuses all the same. He says he can meet us here."

"How many will we have? All together?"

"Perhaps a hundred, all total. The rest are split between other stations, or trapped on the planet."

"We could ask the planetary ones . . ."

"No. No fighting on the surface."

"But if it is to our benefit . . ."

"Uncle, believe it or not, I am doing this for the Empire. We formed the legion to keep the Militia, the Empire Rising people from taking over and destroying our way of life."

"We still fight the Militia."

"Not the same Militia as before. They are closer to what the people want. They have much support. On the planet, we are overmatched by the TGI and the Militia people. Activities there would be useless."

"They could still fight."

"For what? All we would do is get people killed and have things blown up. Things we need. While those troops are on the surface, TGI and the Militia must keep people there to watch them. It balances out, and nobody gets hurt."

Lalond exhaled. "Very well, niece. But what are you saying? What must we do?"

"The decision will be here. My spies tell me Jose and Shutt are coming up, to be with their units. I don't think they entirely trust each other. I will collect the Free

Traders that I can, and we will occupy one station, and they must remove us from it. We will stand there."

"Which station?"

"Transfer-66. You can meet us at Transfer-66. I will direct Mathieu to meet us there. He will bring who he can."

"Mathieu? Make sure you bring lots of wine."

***

Jose and Shutt arrived in separate ships. Russell was waiting outside the cargo lock when Shutt's ship clicked on. He saluted as Shutt marched off the ship, followed by a group of bedraggled Militia.

"Sergeant Russell. Good to see you again."

"Ma'am." He sniffed. "What's that smell?"

"The troops. Water rations. Why are we using a cargo lock?"

"Passenger lock got broken off the station, ma'am."

"Broken off, as in, the doors jammed?"

"No more doors, ma'am. The whole lock assembly broke free. We're lucky the inner bulkheads held, otherwise this part of the station would be in vacuum."

"How the heck did that happen? How do you break a lock off a station?""

"It was attached to a ship at the time. It's in my report."

Shutt swiveled her head. The troops were marching by. Their steps would cover any whispers. "You wrote another report. In the middle of a fight. Really?"

"Nope. I haven't written a report." Russell shrugged. "But it sounded like the type of thing to say. But you're here now. Want details?"

"Not at all. Which way to the caf?"

Russell gave directions, and the new troops hurried off in a cloud of body stink.

Shutt waved a hand in front of her nose. "I can still smell the stink. That was not fun. How many troops can you muster."

She and Russell talked numbers. By stripping guard squads from TGI main and one of the other stations, Russell had jammed forty into her Militia cutter. "We need two shifts to recuperate. We were packed so tight we couldn't eat or wash. We can miss the washing, but the troops have to eat."

"And check weapons."

"Yes, check the reloads at least. We'll feed them, let them wash, clean weapons, and sleep one shift. Second shift tomorrow we drop. Assuming Jose doesn't dawdle."

A lock clanked open farther down the truss. Skin suited figures sauntered off, milled around, regrouped, and walked toward Shutt and Russell.

"I guess he didn't dawdle. Looks like TGI is here, ma'am."

Twelve sleek looking TGI security, suit coats over skin suits walked up, Jose in the lead. They had green neck ruffs—Jose's election colors—and hard collars for helmets.

"Senator Shutt, Sergeant Russell. Uggh." Jose stepped back. "What is that stench?"

"Three days travel with no water."

"The water was out on your ship?"

"Too many troops packed too tight. Had to save it for drinking."

Russell saluted Jose. "Sir. How many troops did you bring."

"Twenty-four. Twelve in this ship, twelve in the other—docking shortly. And we can scrape up some of the crew in a pinch. Say, thirty?"

"You have thirty with two ships?" Shutt put her hands on her hips. "I had forty jammed in one."

"Which explains the smell," Russell said.

"Really?" Jose sniffed. "My experience is that the Militia always smells that way."

"Jose. Not now." Shutt waved one of her aides over.

"We'll redeploy some people to your ships."

"No." Jose shook his head. "There won't be room. I need both for the foreseeable future."

"There isn't room? On two ships?"

"I said won't be. I've got plans for both ships. I'll explain to you later. Have you got the next targets picked out?"

Shutt grimaced. "We drop two shifts from now. We hit two tiny stations as we pass by to refuel, then the only transfer station they occupy. I expect they'll fight for that one. Transfer-66"

"I expect they will. They've got all the ships and all the people from orbit they can scrape together heading there."

"How do you know that?"

"Friends of mine told me. Reliable friends."

"We could bring up more troops from the surface—"

Jose shook his head. "No. My friends also tell me the ground Legionnaires are staying put because of the parity of forces. If we change that dynamic, they might make a different decision. We don't want anything happening dirtside."

"Dirtside." Russell laughed. "Listen to you, Mr. Orbital Fleet guy."

Jose smiled at Russell. "Sergeant Russell. I've missed you. Congratulations on your success here. My TGI people said that you occupied the station without a shot being fired on your side."

"Wait," Shutt said, "I, heard one of the Free Traders, died."

"Killed by a thrown helmet, I was told. But thank you for that, Sergeant."

"Sir." Russell saluted. "And fairness requires me to admit that your people were right in the thick of things, went charging into the mix. They were brave."

"Thank you."

"Stupid, but brave. And they're not . . . aggressive enough."

"Really?"

"Yes. They didn't follow through. Could have got us all killed."

"I'll tell them that, Sergeant. Will you be involved in the next wave?"

"Wherever possible, sir."

"Leading from the front?"

"If possible, sir."

"Good, good." Jose smiled at Russell. "I'll make sure that the people I send with you next time are suitably aggressive. So aggressive. In fact, I'm sure even you won't be able to complain. I need to see to my crews, please excuse me for a moment?"

Jose drifted back to his people.

Russell watched him go. "That man is going to have me shot in the back. I wonder—"

Shutt shook her head. "No."

"No?"

"No. You may not shoot him first. That's what you were going to ask, right?"

"Yeah. How do I keep from dying?"

"You'll figure it out. You always have before. But no shooting Jose. We need him alive. Delta needs him alive."

"I'd appreciate a little help."

"You've got all the help you need. Your own squad, people who've been with you for a long time. They're more like your bodyguards than Militia troopers."

"They know good leadership when they see it."

"If by good leadership you mean they know Jose or Marianne or a bunch of other people want them shot for what they did during the recent unpleasantness, then yes."

"Why do we keep calling it an unpleasantness? It was a war."

"A civil war, and the Militia started it, which is embarrassing, so we'll stick with unpleasantness. In any event, you, and your people get ready to drop with us in a couple shifts. We're off to Transfer-66."

"Can we beat them there? Occupy it first?"

"Not unless they walk. I expect they'll be there with everybody they can scrape together."

"Will we win?"

Shutt fiddled with her comm, then stepped up close to Russell. "It's possible."

"I don't like possible, Clarisse. I like yes."

"Jose has been in contact with some Free Traders. Talking to them without me."

"You sure?"

"Friends told me."

"These friends tell you what they talked about?"

"They couldn't get that. Just proof that conversations—many conversations—have been taking place."

"With Marianne?"

"Not her, that's the odd part. Some of her people. Be very careful at Transfer-66. Don't let the TGI people wander off on their own."

"Wander off on their own? They're armed security, not stray dogs."

"Keep an eye on them. Mix your people with them. Don't let them concentrate anywhere. And stay close to Jose."

"He wants to shoot me."

"Probably."

"So, I'm staying close to him to give him a better chance at it? And where will you be?"

"That's not important—Yes, it is. I won't be there."

"Why not?"

"Don't spread this around. The admiral's awake."

"He's awake? What? Since when? Is he okay?"

"Since less than an hour ago. He's decidedly not okay, according to the doctors. But he's awake, and he can talk, and he's lucid if very weak. They say he might float along for months, or he could die at any minute. It's not been publicly announced yet, but it will leak shortly. I expect

Jose already knows, and he's waiting for me to comment."

"What are you going to do?"

"Go see him, of course. He's the admiral. He's in charge. He's a senator. And there are some things I need from him. Codes, access, things like that."

"Isn't there a whole continuity of command thing. Processes, handover codes, three-person access if the commander is disabled, that sort of thing."

"Things don't always work the way they're supposed to. Nor the way they were planned."

"You're leaving me in charge of this goat rope up here?"

"Scott," Shutt said. "Scott, with Dashi dead, we're at a crossroads here. He was the glue that held things together, more than we realized. That Empire Rising revolt was a disaster for this system. We're barely holding things together economically as it is. Now we've got three—at least three—different groups jockeying for political power. If we don't get our political issues sorted out, all the future holds is a slow decline to eventual loss of resources and breakdown. Or another brief war, then disaster."

"We've got tons of food."

"And you know as well as I do that everything else is in short supply and getting shorter. You're running a factory that is only staying open because I'm diverting resources to it. And I'm only doing that because I can trust you."

"Clarisse, I've always done my duty."

"Keep doing it. But we need one group in charge, but we can't afford more fighting. Jose and his TGI people seem reasonable enough. For now. At least he doesn't blow things up. The Free Traders have screwed up, and when they screw up, people die."

"Then why are we fighting now?"

"Because we have no choice. I have no choice. The Free Traders have guns, and they're using them. But there's a chance here to remove their leadership all at once."

"What about all those people down on the planet? Those Legionnaires?"

"Surprisingly, they're fine with it. They nearly worshiped Dashi, and Dashi said there would be a Senate, so if the Senate says something they believe it. They don't want Marianne and her company to lose, but if they don't, as long as things don't get too bloody, they'll go along with the status quo. Which is what we need."

"I'm just a simple soldier. You need to spell it out."

"Don't let Jose take over control of the Free Traders. Keep them from merging."

"You want me to shoot your boyfriend?"

"He's Marianne's boyfriend, not mine. Just keep the two factions from getting together, somehow."

"By shooting Jose? His guards will chew me up."

"Russell, I'm counting on you to do the right thing here, for Delta."

Russell sighed. "Don't let them merge. Got It. I'll get the job done, I always do."

***

Word of the admiral's awakening spread. Some Militia spoke in cautiously optimistic tones with each other. Those who could read a medical report were less sure. Jose arranged for a small courier to divert and pick up Shutt. Four hours later, he and Russell bid her goodbye at the dock.

"They'll have you to TGI main in less than a shift. I told them max burn, and they can refuel there. We'll hold our shuttle for you, and as soon as the orbits align, you'll drop. Two, three shifts at most till you see him."

"Good." Shutt adjusted the single bag she carried. "Thanks for all your help."

"Glad to be of service." Jose nodded to Sergeant Russell. "Russell and I will take care of these Free Traders, right Russell?"

"Absolutely. Throw them all out an air lock."

Shutt shouldered her bag. "Sergeant. Don't be an Imperial twit."

"Yes, ma'am. Bring them to justice, but only those who deserve it. No air lock-throwing unless authorized by the Senate."

"Better." The station shivered minutely, and the dock magnets clacked. Shutt put her hand on the air lock wheel and, once the light flicked green, spun it open. "I'm counting on you."

"We won't let you down, ma'am. Our troops, and TGI's, we'll take care of things. Shoot people."

"We're not going in shooting." Jose frowned. "We'll start with a negotiation first."

"Do what you need to do, Senator Jose. We need peace and security. All the people of Delta are behind you." Shutt saluted. "The Empire."

Russell returned the salute. "The Empire. And don't worry, ma'am. I'll be there next to the Senator the whole way."

Shutt stepped into the air lock and swung the door shut. Three seconds later the lights flashed red—she'd already opened the far side and was boarding the courier.

The lights flashed green again as she closed the far side, and the magnets clicked as they disengaged.

"That courier isn't wasting any time," Russell said.

"I told them maximum effort. The Senator said she needed important Militia information from the admiral, information that could only be given in person."

"Did she say what it was?"

"Private Militia information, I assumed. Didn't she tell you?"

"I'm a sergeant. She's a major. And a senator."

"She doesn't treat you exactly that way." Jose smiled. "What a marvelous day today will be."

"You're pretty happy."

"Why should I not be? Dashi was like a father to me. I miss that man. He was struck down by a cowardly assassin, and shortly, the person who ordered that will get justice. Yes." Jose smiled again. "Justice. Do you believe in justice, Sergeant?"

"I do, sir. I do."

"Justice is blind, they say."

"Which is why we have to help it out sometimes, sir."

"My thoughts exactly." Jose beamed at Russell. "You'll be with us when we board Transfer-66 of course."

"Right beside you, sir, all the way. In fact, I probably won't leave your side."

Jose's smile widened. "Right by my side? Oh, I'm counting on that, Sergeant. I'm counting on it."

CHAPTER 37

"How many troops do you have?" Marianne stepped out of the air lock onto Transfer-66. She'd parked next to Lalond and arranged to meet him there.

"And good to see you, too, Niece."

"Uncle, we don't have time. Where's Mathieu?"

"En route, he says. ETA is next shift."

"The Militia people will be here soon."

"Not soon. Their ETA is the next shift."

"Both at the same time?"

"Accident of stellar geometry. This is a transfer station. We're designed to move between orbital zones and have ships meet up to exchange passengers. They're meeting up."

"Convenient accident."

Lalond gestured behind him. Uniformed Traders waited behind him. "But to answer your question, I have all the Free Traders who I could find here."

"They look young."

"Younger cousins and such like."

"Are they armed?"

"Yes, but it's best if we don't count on them fighting well."

"Uncle. We have a legion. A fighting Legion."

"On the planet we do. All those who had experience stayed groundside. That's why they joined the legion. We kept all the space trained ones up here. They can fight, but perhaps not as well as they think they can."

Marianne counted. "Twenty-three?"

"And nine more after I strip my ship."

"Don't strip your ship completely."

"Why not? I have no fuel. I'm not going anywhere. We stand here, and we win, or not. I can't leave."

Marianne cursed. "I have eighteen with my crew and six here. That's . . . fifty-six."

"Fifty-six. With handguns and little experience in fighting. Niece, we are not in a good position here."

"Mathieu has a strong force. He says he has almost forty in his ship. We will have nearly a hundred . . . the Militia and TGI cannot have much more. And they must come to us."

"But for what? What are we fighting for?"

"For the future of Delta."

"Sounds like we are fighting for a certain lady to stay as a Senator. Or perhaps to become something else. Now that Dashi is gone . . ."

"Now that Dashi is gone, what?"

"Ma petite. I thought all of this was so that the Free Traders could take their rightful place in Delta, in the government. But do we need all of this?" He swept his hand, pointing at all the troops. "Before, when the Militia was attacking people, burning factories, fighting in the streets, destroying stations, that was something that had to be dealt with. But now—"

"Now they are still our enemies."

"They are not our friends, I will agree. But they are much more reasonable. This Admiral fellow punished his own rebels. Senator Shutt never was a rebel. Senator Jose helped everyone. Is this fight just your own ambition?"

"Are you standing with me or not?"

"Ma petite, my younger crew find your cause romantic, and fighting in a glorious revolution is much more fun than taking cargo handler exams and loading ships for the next ten years. They're here for the excitement. I'm here because I can't leave, and I said you could represent us to the council and the Senate and make decisions. I don't like everything you've done, but I promised to support you and nobody will ever say Jacques Lalond doesn't finish what he started. I am with you to the end." Lalond slapped her shoulders. "Your Mother would be proud of you. I am proud of you. We all are. You are the first Trader to stand up to the dirtsiders in forty years."

"Thank you, Uncle."

"You are smart, brave, and our leader, so I am here."

"Uncle, you are making me blush."

"You are all these things. But that does not mean that you are correct. This day may end in disaster."

***

"Transfer-66 in thirty minutes," the intercom announced.

Sergeant Russell drained his cup of basic and stood. "Pass the word. Everyone, take a last drink, hit the heads, and check weapons. Load revolvers and shotguns, but anybody who fires one better be shooting themselves in the head because that's what I'll do to them next. Make sure that you have gloves, shoes, or vacuum socks, at least—and a helmet. And get out of my way."

The crowd in the lounge backed up as Russell moved to the head. All the cabins and corridors were jammed with Militia. Transfer-66 was a big station, but they couldn't confirm how many locks were open for docking. Russell had insisted on taking the great majority of the troops in one ship. That way, if they could only dock one ship at one spot, he could get the most people in the fastest. A second cutter trailed them, only one-quarter full.

Departing the head, Russell shoved over to Chaudhari. "Well?"

"It will take forever to get all these people out, especially if we have to move them out one group at a time. If there's any sort of shooting as we come out of the lock, we're in trouble."

"That's why I told the pilots to find a lock far away from everything."

"They'll know that and block the locks."

"It's a transfer station. It has, like, a hundred locks. They can't block them all."

"I still think we should loiter off station and send some troops in to seize an open lock."

"Which troops? Our Secret platoon of highly trained space assault commandos?"

"We have those?"

Russell smacked Chaudhari's head. "Of course not. We have part-time losers who needed extra cash and a bunch of near criminal losers who decided to join the Militia a few steps ahead of getting arrested. And then some regular losers."

"Which one are you?"

"I joined for the dental plan. Now it's twenty years later."

Chaudhari rubbed his forehead. "And you should be nicer to me. You shouldn't hit Senators."

"Senators who believe in secret commandos should be smacked. It helps keep them focused on reality."

"Reality? You take suggestions from a mule who has a mystic connection with one of your squad members."

"Privilege of leadership."

"Scott, if those Traders are right at the lock in force, we'll get massacred."

"There won't be a massacre. There's too many of us. I'll stay back here and push those others through as fast as I can."

"We can only get eight through at a time. The Traders only have to deal with the first eight."

"One, they have to be there. Two, they have to be willing to shoot first. They're not used to starting fights—they're bullies. And three, you remember Kostasi? The kid from the fuel company?"

"Yeah, what about him?"

"He's got some tools with him. He says he can bypass the safety interlocks on the air locks and let us pop both sides open. Once we hit the station, we can all charge out.

We'll flood them. The Traders might be able to take down eight of us in a couple minutes, but not forty-eight."

"It's a big risk. If something happens, we'll dump the atmo from the ship and the crew will be in big trouble."

"Not my ship, Not my crew," Russell said. "But it is my squad. Look, it will all work out. It's a big station. They won't be able to block every docking bay, not even a good percentage of them. They have less people than we do, so if they have to split them up even a bit, we'll have local superiority. And we're tougher. All our squad has seen shooting. We'll keep going, and when they flood out of this cutter, the defenders will run. Once we've got a docking truss, we can move more people in, and they'll know they're in trouble. We'll be good."

"It's a big risk."

"The only risk I'm worried about is getting shot in the back while we're moving forward."

"Yeah, that would suck. Getting all the way there and getting shot by accident."

"You don't understand."

"Understand what?"

"It's not getting shot in the back by accident that bothers me, it's getting shot in the back, on purpose."

CHAPTER 38

"Here they come." Lalond pointed to the radar in the ops room. "They're moving into a parking orbit right now." He and Marianne were watching near space, and waiting for the arrival of friendly ships. They'd chased the locals out of the ops room and were using it as a headquarters.

"I wish we had lasers like those Militia cutters, or some of the big corporate ships. I'd show them what's what."

"Well, we don't have any, and you wouldn't want to use them anyway. We need those ships."

"Not all of them." Marianne narrowed her eyes. "Not all of them. I wish we had better sensors. What are they doing?"

"Circling, seeing which locks are open. Might send some suits out to check out a few locks."

"Mathieu is late. He should be here."

"His ETA is thirty minutes, he says."

"Thirty-five now. According to his last message."

Lalond checked his comm. "He said thirty before. Well, it will take these ground people time to figure out what to do. Especially with the blocking ships." The Traders had parked ships, cutters, tugs, and everything they could find at all the air locks on four of the eight docking trusses, blocking half of them. There were two armed Traders in each truss, to confirm arrivals. The remainder of the Traders were held one ring in, waiting at a laundry facility.

"Will they dock all four of their ships on one truss, or split them up?"

"If it were me, I'd put each ship on a different truss and make us respond to each of them. Make us split our forces."

"Yes, that way they don't get trapped on one truss. Will they do that?"

"We'll know—there they go." One of the cutters was moving to dock. "First one is closing. We'll know destination truss in a minute. Tell the central group to stop cleaning their underwear and get ready."

Marianne spoke into her comm. "One ship. How many to send?"

"Your friends say there're perhaps fifty Militia, so half of the Militia per ship and some have to stay behind. They'll probably send only a single squad, maybe a dozen. With those two ships there, send sixteen. That should hold things. We can keep the other groups for the next attack."

"D'accord." Marianne spoke into her comm then clicked it off. "On the way."

***

"First half of first squad, in the lock," Russell said. The first eight wormed past him and into the air lock. "Kostasi, do your thing."

A uniformed Militia private squirmed in, pulled a screwdriver out of a skin suit pocket, and popped a panel.

The Militia sailor at the intercom leaned back for a better view. "Hey, stop messing with that. Those are the safety interlocks."

"Understood," Russell said.

"If you change the wires, the lock can pop open on both sides."

"Got it."

"Leave it, leave it. Don't mess with that, or I'll—" the sailor shut up.

Kim Two had been lounging on the ground in front of him. Now she stood to her full height—still only up to his chin—and pushed a revolver in his face. "You'll what?" Kim two asked. "You'll shut up?"

The sailor raised his hands. "Easy. Easy. You don't

understand. The safety interlocks keep both doors from opening."

Russell tapped the door. "We want both of them open. That's why Kostasi is fixing them."

"But if something goes wrong with both doors open, we'll vent the ship. We could all be killed."

"If I send eight troopers out blind into whatever is out there, if they hit heavy resistance, they could all get killed before we can help. Seems only fair we all share the same risk."

The intercom bonged. "Bridge to all air lock five. Two minutes to docking. Air lock five, confirm readiness."

Kim pushed her revolver into the sailor's face.

"Air lock five. Confirm."

Russell folded his hands. "Well?"

Sweat beaded the sailor's forehead. "What do I do?"

"Confirm readiness, you Imperial nostril."

The sailor reached for the intercom button.

"Wait." Russell held up his hand. "Just one thing. This is an opposed boarding. I guarantee you somebody, somewhere, somehow, in the next ten minutes is going to get shot. No way around it, I can't control it. But the thing you can control, though, is whether you're first. Think about that when you talk to the bridge."

Kim pushed the revolver closer.

The sailor squared his shoulder and slapped the button. "Bridge, Air lock five."

"Go ahead."

"Understand docking imminent. All ready here."

"Godspeed and good luck." The bridge clicked off.

Green light flared in the corridor. "Gotcha." Kostasi pocketed his screwdriver. "All clear, sarge. They can open the outer door anytime, but they gotta pull against pressure."

"First squad, stand by. You, at the door. Soon as you hear a magnet engage, pop that door and go. Rush them like we planned. Try not to kill us by opening before we're locked. Second and third follow first. Fourth, detach two for the other direction and secure the other locks. The rest follow first and second."

The intercom squawked. "Thirty seconds. Be advised, we're hitting closest to the ring. Militia-2 will dock at the next north lock after another orbit in approximately ten minutes. TGI one and two will be stationed north of us on the truss as soon as they are able."

The sailor slammed the intercom button. "Understood."

Russell faced the doors. "Ammo is cheap, troopers are expensive. Anybody who gets shot today has to deal with me. God save the Empire!"

"The Empire!"

***

Chaudhari stood in the air lock, first of the second group of four. The station corridors were small, four abreast was the most that they could cram in, and they'd still be rubbing shoulders as they ran.

The ship crashed into the station, and the group swayed with the impact. Then the magnets clicked.

"GO. GO. GO. GO," Chaudhari yelled. The doorman spun the wheel and heaved the door open a crack. Air blew from behind him as the ship atmo pressurized the empty interlock space. Once the doorman felt the pressure equalize, he stepped to the right, shoving the other three of his section into the wall. Chaudhari and his section stepped left, grabbed the edges of the hatch, yanked it open and secured.

The first four troops jumped over the hatch coaming and ran down the tunnel to the combined cargo docking bay. The tunnel was two meters long and ended at another hatch. It wasn't a true air lock, only a single hatch. Like all station hatches, it was designed to open inwards against pressure—escaping air would tend to slam it shut rather than open—which meant it opened inwards into the station. The doorman spun the wheel. His companions racked shotguns, nodded at him, and he shoved it forward. They jumped inside, turned right, or south, facing the junction with the outer ring and pointed their shotguns. The doorman followed, pulling out a revolver.

The Militia trained for boardings, and Russell had put his most experienced troops in the front. Once clear of the hatch coamings, they faced down the corridor. Two Free Traders appeared in uniform forty meters away. All four Militia stopped and fired two aimed rounds in the direction of the Traders, then raced ahead.

Two rounds from a shotgun at forty meters had as much chance of hitting them as if they had fired into the ceiling. And the only way to hit someone with a revolver at forty meters is to throw it at them.

But the Traders were not trained soldiers. The noises, smoke, sparks, frangible bullets puffing up in smoke and general mayhem heading their way paralyzed them. They stood stupidly still as the Militia section raced at them.

The other sections were now pouring into the corridor behind the first. Two troops turned the opposite direction and raced to the far end of the truss where the TGI ships would dock, making sure their rear was clear. The others ran full tilt behind the first wave, weapons at the ready but not firing.

The first section ran four steps, stopped, fired two shots, then ran four more steps, stopped, fired two more shots. One of the Traders dropped. The Traders hadn't returned a single shot.

After the sixth shot, the first section hugged the wall, dropped to a crouch, and reloaded. They took their time because the second, third, and eventually fourth section raced past. The second section, now in front, repeated the shoot-shoot-step-step-step-step-shoot-shoot-step-step-step-step-shoot-shoot-reload pattern, then the third and forth.

From the Traders point of view, a continuous fusillade

roared every few seconds followed by a charging group of screaming banshees.

One Trader thrashed on the floor, the other turned, tripped, rolled, then jumped up and ran away, with the Militia pursuing.

The first reaction group of Legionnaires clattered down the stairs from the inner rings. Half of them had drawn their revolvers prematurely, half had not. Some of them in the back had slowed as they heard the firing. Coming down the stairs, they came under fire and saw a uniformed figure racing at them. Five of them emptied their revolvers into the unfortunate Trader, dropping him where he stood and filling the corridor with gun smoke and frangible dust.

They paused in confusion, then started jumping to the side as the next wave of Militia came out of the smoke, firing. Half the Traders took frangible rounds and dropped where they stood. Two others fumbled their revolvers out and fired wildly. One dropped his. The rest in the back turned and fled.

***

"They're all hitting the same truss!" Lalond said. "All four ships."

"We'll have them together, then. Good!" Marianne said. "We can crush them there. They can only move a few out of their air lock at a time. If we take out all the first group, they won't dare send more."

"What does our watcher in that truss say."

Marianne played with her comm. "No answer. Never mind. Send the rest."

"We should keep a reserve, ma petite."

"I am in charge, Uncle. Send them all. Our problem up to now has been doing things in small pieces. One big push now, like a hammer. Send them all."

"I—Wait." Lalond's comm lit up. "Oui? Oui. Yes, we need you. Truss 13, you see the other ships there—can you come in behind them? Good, do so."

"Who was that?"

"Mathieu. He's almost here. He can see all the Militia and TGI ships are docked together. He says he can dock at the end of that truss and come in behind them."

"Formidable. Excellent plan, Uncle. We will catch them between us. You stay here and handle communications. I will meet these Militia. We will win."

"Ma petite, I do not think you should go."

"Mon Uncle, I must be there. I am their leader." Marianne pointed at the two remaining Trader Legionnaires in the operations room. "Come with me. To victory!"

CHAPTER 39

"Clear both sides," Russell yelled. "Section three and section four. I want this entire ring cleared. Run spinward till you meet other Militia or come back here. Go."

Two sections raced off along the outer ring. Two troopers trailed behind, facing backward, in case Legionnaires popped out of side passages behind them.

"Chaudhari?"

"Here."

"Casualties?"

"Us? None."

"No way."

"They ran or they shot badly."

"What about the Traders?"

"We've got sixteen prisoners, most wounded or beat up. Two dead."

"Dead? We were firing frangibles. People don't die of that."

"They do if you shoot them . . . twenty-seven times."

Russell cracked his knuckles—"Which one of our idiot sections shot somebody twenty-seven times?"

"Not us, them. Friendly fire."

"Huh. Outstanding. The other the same?"

"Not a mark on him. Heart attack maybe? We'll find out later. What now?"

"Take two sections. Go antispinward till you meet the others that left. Once you meet up, take all four sections up to operations and tell them we're in charge now."

"You're kind of all alone here . . ."

"I've got one squad from our other cutter."

"The worse trained one."

"They'll be fine with me standing behind them. And the TGI ships are docked. They can hold a truss. If I'm here to help them."

"Don't let them get behind you."

"Given the way they shoot, I'll keep my back to the Traders. That's safer."

***

Marianne and her remaining troops climbed down the stairs from the core to the outer ring.

"Come with me, mes amis." She waved. "They are that way. One quick push back to their ships, and they are done. Follow me!"

The group trotted antispinward from the stairs, Marianne leading. She knew most of the men and women here, they had been with her for a long time, either as crew, part of the legion, or in the fighting before. She exchanged a few jokes and slapped a back. They moved past the next stair spoke when a figure in Free Trader colors raced toward them.

"Stop." Marianne stepped in front of the running figure. "Who are you? What is going on?"

The runner was young, eighteen. His holster was empty, but his eyes were wide, and he cradled his arm. "They're killing us. Killing us. All of us. There're hundreds of them. They shot my entire squad. I saw them all go down. All dead. Dead."

"Dead? They cannot be dead. Not all of them."

"I saw them all, I tell you, all of them. Shooting everyone dead. Bullets and shots. Armored bullets, that cut through suits and kill us all."

"Show me your arm."

The man screamed and pulled it back. "No, I was hit. They are killing us. Armored slugs."

"If they are killing you with armored slugs, why are you not dead?" Marianne pried his fingers from his suit. "Didn't even break the cloth of your suit. It must be frangibles. They are not dead, only wounded."

"They are right behind me."

"They cannot be right behind you. If they were, we would hear them."

"They are chasing me!"

"Everyone be still. Be quiet and don't move." Marianne listened. "See? All is qui—"

"Footsteps," one of her troopers said. "I hear footsteps."

"Me too," another said. "Marching."

Marianne shoved the runner behind her. "Ready your weapons."

Her group peered down the hallway. A group of four Militia came into view farther down the ring. The leader saw her, stopped, and opened fire.

***

"Mr. Jose, good to see you." Russell said, as Jose's TGI group milled around his ship.

"Really?" Jose smiled. "I don't think you're telling the truth."

"How about, I'm happy to see anybody who isn't shooting at me," Russell said. He explained the plan with his squads sweeping the outer ring. "I've got one squad waiting at the junction of the outer ring and this truss. If your security people can secure this truss and the two adjacent ones, we'll restrict their movements and protect our ships. Could we split your people into four groups and . . ."

Jose and Russell conferred for another minute, then Jose dispatched his security groups to secure this side of the station. Left unspoken was that, lacking experience in capturing a station, they wouldn't be good at charging into things, but they could surely hold things taken.

"That's an excellent plan, Sergeant Russell. Well done. Does this battle need your complete attention this second, or can we have a small private conference."

"We're awaiting developments right now, sir. Nice suit. Do you have a job interview planned?" Russell pointed at Jose's outfit. "Must be uncomfortable wearing shoes with a skin suit."

"Depends on the shoes. These are new. Come with me." Jose led Russell away from the docked Militia cutters, past the crews. All nonessential crew had been armed and were at the far end of the truss, awaiting orders to assist the main squads.

At the second cutter, one of the pilots spun a revolver in his hand. Russell marched up and grabbed the hand.

"Hey!"

Russell thrust the revolver into the pilot's holster, then grabbed his shoulders and rotated him ninety degrees till he faced down the truss. "Bad guys are that way. Face that way. Look for bad guys. You see people, look at clothes. Clothes same as yours—good guys. Different clothes— bad guys. You see bad guys, then take out a gun. No bad guys, no take out gun till bad guys there. Understand?"

The pilot cursed him for a full minute, but kept facing down the corridor and left his revolver holstered.

"I'll take that as a yes. Senator?" Russell continued down the truss. They passed the two TGI freighters, both unguarded, and Jose stopped at the last docking slot. "That pilot's pretty unhappy, Sergeant."

"So am I. But I don't want to get shot in the back by accident."

"What about on purpose?"

"Keep your friends close, and your enemies closer."

"Interesting. Which am I?"

"I swear, Senator, I don't know sometimes."

"I serve the Empire," Jose said. "I did under Dashi, and I do now that he's gone."

"I serve the Empire as well."

"Then, why are you worried?" Jose grinned.

"That's what sergeants do. They worry." Russell staggered as the floor shook. "What's that?"

"Reinforcements."

"Whose?"

The hatch light spun red—a ship had docked.

Jose grinned again. "That remains to be seen."

***

Dust crowded the corridor. Marianne's group had ducked as the Militia fired. Two of her group dropped. Then her entire group let loose, shooting down the ring. Frangible dust hung in the air, obscuring the view. Wild shots flew in both directions.

Marianne bent down to one of the injured. "How bad?"

"Hurts like an Imperial Tax assessment, but they were frangibles. I'll live."

"Right." Marianne stood and yelled. "Mathieu is here now. And only a few of them ahead of us. We'll rush them and smash them like ore in a crusher between us. Ready?"

The Traders yelled.

Marianne fired three times into the dust. "Follow me!" She ran.

***

Russell whipped his revolver out and pointed it at the air lock. His finger reached for the trigger. A cold piece of metal jabbed into his ear.

"Please don't do anything stupid, Sergeant. You don't understand what's going on. Not yet."

Russell cursed as the hatch pushed open, and a man in a Free Traders shipmaster uniform stepped out. His name tag read. "Mathieu."

"Bonjour, Senator. And Militia person. I know you." Mathieu rubbed his chin. "You are Sergeant Russell. Senator Marianne has spoken of you."

"Nothing good I hope."

"She admires you greatly. Says you are very

331

competent."

"I'd like to shoot her."

"She would like to do the same to you, I think."
Mathieu stepped out of the hatch, and a crew rushed
behind him, pointing weapons at the sergeant. Russell
tracked Mathieu with his revolver. "Are you going to shoot
me, Sergeant?"

"I'd really like to."

"Mr. Jose has a gun at your head. All of my crew are
armed. You'll die right away. Why shoot me?"

"If you're dead . . ."

"If I'm dead, whatever is going to happen will still
happen. You are too late to prevent it."

"I can yell, and the Militia squad will come running."

"No, Sergeant," Jose said. "They're too far away. The
only one who might hear is that pilot, but he's facing the
wrong way, and I think he's playing a game on his comm
so he won't notice."

Russell cursed again, loosened his grip, and let the
revolver dangle from his fingers. One of Mathieu's crew
took the revolver and unloaded it. Two others pointed
shotguns at him and made him raise his hands.

"I'll take that." Jose holstered his own revolver and
took Russell's.

"You're all traitors and liars," Russell said.

Mathieu raised his eyebrows. "We are?"

"Yes."

"I had heard that the Militia was . . . dumb, but this is
certainly a new species of things." Mathieu turned to Jose.
"It is as we agreed?"

Jose was reloading the revolver taken from Russell. "Of
course. How many men have you?"

"Forty total. I have twenty-four ready to go right
away."

"You'll need them. For sure. How long will this take?"

"Once we're moving, only ten minutes. Everything is in
readiness?"

"The Militia squads are off fighting Marianne. The reserve squads are on their way. All of the TGI security is securing the other trusses and the rings. We are alone here."

"Formidable. Let us begin then." Mathieu. "Crew, as we discussed. To your places."

The two with shotguns stepped to one side so they could continue covering Russell. He counted twenty-four crew streaming out of the Trader ship, with weapons, supplies, and baggage, all following Mathieu marching down the truss.

And turn onto the corridor to the first TGI ship—the big freighter. They moved inside in a disciplined group—groups of eight cycling three on the lock. Three groups entered, leaving a lone woman with a junior sailor's insignia waiting on the station. She put her hands in her pockets and waited. The intercom bonged. She punched the buttons, exchanged words, then stepped into the lock and closed the hatch behind her. The locking wheel spun, and the hatch lights flashed from green to red.

The two shotgun wielding Traders lowered their guns, exchanged cordial goodbyes with Jose, reentered their lock. The locking wheel spun, the lights flashed red and Jose and Russell were left standing there.

"You're going to need this." Jose shoved the revolver into Russell's holster.

"What just happened here?" Russell asked.

"Are you going to put your hands down?"

Russell dropped his hands. "Those were Trader Legionnaires."

"Yes."

"But . . ."

"Captain Mathieu wanted a new ship. I gave him one."

Russell checked his loads. The green colors banded them as frangibles, but shiny—newly manufactured. He grimaced. He'd have no time to check how reliable they are.

"You gave him a ship."

"Why not? I have ships. I gave him something he wanted. He gave me something I wanted."

"What?"

Jose waved. "This station. Come on, Sergeant. Let's go tell Senator Marianne that her reinforcements aren't coming."

CHAPTER 40

"They're running," Marianne said. "Come on, after them!" She fired down the smoky ring. The Militia ahead had retreated so fast that all she could see was their feet as the ring curved up ahead of her. She jogged steadily ahead, emerging from the smoke into a clear area. Her crew ran beside her.

"They're running," Sikar said. "Faster than we can chase them."

"Yes, they are." Marianne slowed. "Yes, they are. Why?"

"Don't know." Sikar fumbled more shells into her revolver as she ran. "But we're winning."

"Moving forward is not the same thing as winning." Marianne stopped. The corridor ahead curved up, and there were no Militia to be seen. "Who is hurt? Anyone? Where are the others? Give us names . . ."

The Traders yelled out their names, and where the others were. Three Traders were wounded, not seriously, and three others had stayed behind with them.

"Too many. You." Marianne pointed at a Legionnaire. "Go back and get them. We need them here. Get the station people to come and help."

"They won't come."

"Go and get them. Go now." The man ran off and Marianne looked at the wall. "Where are we? Has anyone seen a spoke number?"

"I saw one back there. We are between Spoke thirteen and fourteen."

"The Militia isn't standing and fighting."

"We outnumber them. That's why they're running."

Sikar pointed. "Let's chase them."

"Do we outnumber them?" Marianne looked down the ring corridor. The barren, empty, having absolutely no cover corridor. "Tabernac! They have retreated to where the spoke intersects the ring. They can hide around the corridor and shoot us as we approach, and we have nowhere to hide."

"We have more than them. We can chase them."

"Better to send somebody around behind to catch them from both sides."

Gunfire rang out in the distance. Behind them.

Marianne shook her head. "Somebody has already thought of that. Well, Mathieu will be behind them soon. Forward! We will catch them, then turn to deal with those behind us."

***

Russell spun his revolver's cylinder. It still didn't feel right, somehow, but he had no time to check his loads. He and Jose ran down the truss. Ahead, Militia appeared from the spinward ring, retreating. Four turned and crouched on each side of the ring corridor, bodies shielded behind the corner, pointing revolvers down. Another four dropped flat on the ground, revolvers drawn. Six more crouched behind them, on knees or elbows, cradling shotguns.

Russell jogged up and stopped behind the group. "Don't fire until you see the whites of their eyes."

Jose stayed in the side truss corridor, undercover. "Historical reference, Sergeant? I'd never have thought it of you."

"Historical reference? What historical reference?"

"Don't shoot till you see the whites of their eyes."

"What's that have to do with history?"

"It's from old Earth. Ancient battle call."

Russell rolled his eyes. "We're on the outer ring of a station. The ring is spinning, so out is down. Which means that as you march around the ring, it appears to curve up in front of you and behind you, like a ramp. So, the first thing we'll see is their feet coming down, then their legs, then torso, and finally, their head. We're lying flat, so they won't see us at first. This way, if we wait till we see their eyes, that's when they're the most exposed they'll ever be, and we'll have the best targets. Physics."

"I liked my explanation better. Sounds more exciting."

"Well, mine has the advantage of being true. And in terms of excitement, we'll have plenty of that in a moment."

"FEET!" one of the prone Militia yelled. "I see feet. Lots."

"Standby." Russell crouched low. "I fire first, then the rest of you let rip."

The squads waited. Then gunfire rang down the corridor.

"What's that?" Jose asked.

"Chaudhari," Russell said. "He's behind them. Praise the Emperor! He knows we'll defend the corridor crossing. They're stuck between us now—no cover, nowhere to go. They have to charge one way or another. We'll blast them down."

The lower bodies of the approaching Traders appeared.

"Stand by." Russell cocked his revolver and waited. True to his word, he didn't fire until he saw a head. He couldn't make out the eye color, but that doesn't matter when twenty Militia emptied their revolvers and shotguns down the corridor all at once. Then did it again.

After thirty seconds, he called for a cease fire and marched through the smoke. "Senator Jose, you coming? Or are you going to hide behind the wall again."

Jose materialized through the gloom. "I'm not afraid, Sergeant. But I'm also not armed, so what's the point of my standing in a firing line."

Russell looked down. It was true, Jose didn't have a holster. "What happened to your gun, sir."

"I gave it to one of your troops. No need for it. I have

your Militia here to protect me. And you."

Russell rolled his eyes. "Whatever. Everyone, listen up. Double-check you all have frangibles. Any wounded, help 'em out, drag 'em back to the truss and let the medics look at them. No shooting unless they reach for a weapon. Then twice in the shoulders or upper chest. That'll shut them down but not kill them. Understood?"

The Militia growled assent and Russell stalked through the dust, revolver pointing forward. They reached the Militia front line, or what had been it. A dozen Legionnaires lay on the ground, moaning with broken legs or arms, or trying to catch their breath. Those who could, held up hands in surrender.

Marianne grunted as she rolled to face Russell and Jose. She had fallen near the front of the charge, her leg bent in an odd way. One hand held her up, the other was hidden inside her coveralls. "Sergeant Russell. I should have shot you when I had the chance."

"Too late now. Do you surrender?"

"Mathieu will be here in a moment."

"No, he won't."

"He will."

"Hear any more shooting? He came and went. Mr. Jose saw to that."

Marianne looked up at Jose, and her eyes darkened. "He's not coming, is he?"

Jose nodded. "We made an arrangement, he and I. You're on your own. Which means you lost."

Marianne twitched her hand.

"Show me your hands," Russell said, pointing his revolver at her.

"Jose, you lied to me all the time."

"Not all the time. Some of it. And you were always lying to me. I knew that. I put up with your games. Until Dashi died."

"I didn't kill Dashi. I admit, I took advantage of circumstances. You would have done the same."

"Circumstances, yes. That's why I talked to Mathieu. I told him to make sure that you started your little rebellion. That way, I'd have an excuse to kill you."

"Start my little rebellion?"

"Yes, I've been behind this from the start. Mathieu, the others. I maneuvered you into this. I knew if you were given the chance you'd take it. You're so greedy."

"Greedy. Me? Greedy? I did what I did for the Empire."

"And yourself. Because you're such a greedy, conniving, Imperial anus."

Marianne hissed.

Russell pointed his revolver at Marianne's chest. "I really need to see your hands. Now."

The noises of the squads helping the wounded rang around them. Chaudhari could be heard down the corridor ordering other Traders to surrender. Weapons clattered to the floor.

"Go ahead." Jose thumped his chest. "Shoot me. At this range, even frangibles will kill me. You can do it. You know you want to."

Russell gaped. "Jose, what in the Emperor's name— show me your hands."

Marianne hissed again and pulled her revolver out of her coveralls. Russell fired twice. The corridor walls rattled, and two ricochets tinged down the hall.

Marianne jerked twice, blood poured out of her mouth, and she dropped bonelessly to the floor.

The troops yelled curses back at Russell as the two bullets pinged down the corridor. He lowered his gun and looked at Marianne. There was no dust from a frangible strike, but there were two small holes in her upper chest and blood pouring out of her mouth.

"That's armored slugs. These are green."

"Green?" Jose asked.

Russell broke open the revolver and popped the remaining shells. Green bands encircled the cartridge.

"Frangible bullets are green. Armor-piercing ones are supposed to be red. You gave me armor-piercing bullets."

"Did I?" Jose shrugged. "Oops."

***

Shutt had commandeered a ground car at the shuttle port to take her to Militia headquarters. Her comm bonged as she arrived at the front of the building—the message detailed the events on Transfer-66. Jose wasn't the only one with 'friends' in different places.

The stairs at the front were guarded by two Militia, and also a Trader.

Shutt returned a salute, then addressed the Trader. "What are you doing here, Legionnaire?"

"Boss sent me over, Senator. We're all working together now, supposedly—so they asked for volunteers to swap with Militia folks—one for one. I'm here. One of your people is at our headquarters."

"You like standing guard?"

"Nope, Senator, not me. But this headquarters is in the center of the city, and I can get decent food on my break, and I can be at the monorail in ten minutes—visit my family out west on weekends. My Militia replacement is guarding a food warehouse down past the shuttle docks. Way, way down past the shuttle docks. Took me an hour to get there. This is way softer duty."

"You're not upset to work with Militia people?"

The guard shrugged. "I got cousins in the Militia. My second-best friend from High School does runs on a cutter. We Free Traders formed the legion because we thought Dashi and Delta needed protection from the rebellion before. Rebellion's over, most of these weird Empire Rising people are dead. You killed some of them yourself, didn't you, Senator?"

Shutt nodded. "I did."

"This is a small moon, Senator. We need all our pieces here. Anybody tries to take over, they break things.

Breaking things is bad for all of us. My family didn't eat right for three months after the fighting. The dossiers say the Empire will return, but I haven't seen it. We're alone, and we need to work together." The guard nodded. "I'm glad you killed those Empire Rising people and exiled the rest. The war's over now."

"You know there have been some incidents in orbit? Traders and Militia and corps—TGI?"

"Senator, me, Jayce, and Sal here." He pointed at the nodding Militia guards. "We're down here, not up there. Figure those up there can take care of things."

"Some Traders might get hurt."

"We've got a Senate now, and I voted for my senator. Better for everyone if we act together, and talk about things rather than blow them up."

"All you Traders feel that way?"

"You'll have to ask all of them if you want to know. But some. Enough. We need to give this Senate thing a chance."

"We do. We do. Enjoy the rest of your shift."

"Major," one of the Militia said. "I hear the admiral is awake."

"Barely, I've been told. And very sick and in a lot of pain. He can't move, barely breathe. The doctor's say it's a matter of time. I rushed down from orbit to see him."

"Too bad. Stuck in bed with no hope. Might be best for him if . . . you know."

"I know that I wouldn't want to lie there like that."

"Me neither." The guard shivered, then saluted. "Major."

Shutt returned the salute and went inside. She climbed two flights of stairs. The admiral had private quarters on the third floor, and he'd been moved from the hospital at Shutt's orders because his room was more secure.

A comm courier came up the back stairs and waved her over. "Major?"

"Yes?"

"Encrypted message from orbital communications. It should be on your comm—you haven't responded, and they sent me to find you."

"I'm kind of busy right now."

"Yes, ma'am. They said you'd want to read it right away."

"What's it about?"

"The details are in the message."

Shutt glared at him, but he didn't move. "Fine. One moment." She went through the process of authenticating herself for higher security messages, requiring a thumbprint, retinal scan, and two different codes. She read the message, then again. "Our Jump ship has returned. Do you know any more about this?"

"We're not sure it's our jump ship, ma'am. I was helping process the images. It looks too big to be the one we sent out, but it's broadcasting Militia codes, and there're personal messages in there encrypted with obvious Militia patterns. Some are for you, but you'll have to decode them yourself. We're pretty sure it's friendly, from the comms we've gotten."

"Jake Stewart is back," Shutt said. "Interesting. Very interesting. Thank you. Tell the comm center you delivered the message and I'll respond shortly." The courier saluted. Shutt entered the admiral's quarters, spoke briefly with the orderlies there, and had them clear the room. One of the guards—the admiral's man—objected, but the others talked him around. She'd made sure that her people on guard outnumbered the admiral's people long before .

The admiral was in his bed, a hospital bed, with the back raised. He was thin, pale, and his skin had a yellow tinge.

Shutt regarded him. "You look horrible."

"I feel horrible," he croaked.

"The doctor's prognosis is—"

"Total Imperial anal leaking. I'm dying, and I know it."

Shutt nodded. "Nobody can figure out how you're still

alive."

"Sheer bloody mindedness. Dashi?"

"Dead. Poison killed him right away."

"My best enemy. I'll miss him."

"Look, we—"

"Why'd you kill him?"

"What? Admiral, how can you say—"

"You're the only one who handled that bottle. Must have been you."

"There's no way—"

"Of course there is. Pills crushed into drinks with your fingers, liquids squirted. Doesn't matter now. Who's the Senate designated as his heir?"

"We haven't met yet."

"Given who's on planet and the factions . . . it will be you, or Jose, or Marianne."

Shutt smiled.

"What did you do?" Admiral Edmunds strained, but he couldn't move. "Did you . . . which one did you kill."

"I didn't kill anybody."

"The staff said Marianne rebelled. Details are kind of thin, but between you and Jose that won't last long."

"A mixed force of Militia and TGI security is dealing with her on Transfer-66 as we speak."

"And one or both of them is going to be killed in the fighting. Good for you." Edmunds groaned. "Hurts. And you're not there, even better. Can't be blamed."

Shutt wandered around the room. "Dashi was too old school. The Empire will return. It will be a new Empire now. We need to look out for ourselves now."

"And you're just the one to be in charge. Over a pile of dead bodies. Dashi's—and could have been mine."

"I remind the admiral that he came to power by bloodily suppressing a rebellion."

"Touche. But will the Senate back you as heir designate?"

"They'll have no choice. Marianne is dead, I'm told.

The Traders are tired of fighting and will be quiet. The Militia is solidly behind me."

"Jose has his own power base. You can't just sweep him away."

"TGI is a corporation, and they do things differently. Jake Stewart is back. His ship just came into the Jump Limit. Jose will have to deal with him first—the returning hero, Dashi's favorite son. Jose will have his hands full—I won't have to do a thing about that."

"Seems like you've thought this all out."

"I have."

"Did you have to poison me?"

"You'd have been Dashi's heir."

"I still can be."

"I could read some of your codes. Did you know that?"

"I assumed. I read some of yours, as well."

"One was telephone communications you had with some of your people. There was one in question, where you always referred to me as 'that shitbird Shutt.' Do you remember those?"

"I do. So? You are a shitbird at times."

Shutt rattled the door handle to make sure it was locked. She stepped to the sideboard shelf and selected a giant pillow, then turned to the bed.

"We need strong leadership. Centralized leadership. Leaders with vision, who are dedicated to Delta as it is, not some theoretical Empire that left a hundred years ago."

"Clarisse, what are you doing?"

"What I'm doing—" Clarisse stepped over to the bed and held the pillow up. "What I'm doing is for the Empire, for the people of Delta, for the Senate, and for the future."

Edmunds struggled and called out, but nobody came.

"And also." Shutt smiled. "Also, you shouldn't have called me a shitbird."

She pushed the pillow down.

GET A FREE EBOOK

Thanks for reading. I hope you enjoyed it. Word-of-mouth reviews are critical to independent authors. Please consider leaving a review on Amazon or Goodreads or wherever you purchased this book.

If you'd like to be notified of future releases, please join my mailing list. I send a few updates a year, and if you subscribe you get a free ebook copy of Sigma Draconis IV, a short novella in the Jake Stewart universe. You can also follow me on Amazon, or follow me on BookBub.

Andrew Moriarty

ABOUT THE AUTHOR

Andrew Moriarty has been reading science fiction his whole life, and he always wondered about the stories he read. How did they ever pay the mortgage for that spaceship? Why doesn't it ever need to be refueled? What would happen if it broke, but the parts were backordered for weeks? And why doesn't anybody ever have to charge sales tax? Despairing on finding the answers to these questions, he decided to write a book about how spaceships would function in the real world. Ships need fuel, fuel costs money, and the accountants run everything.

He was born in Canada, and has lived in Toronto, Vancouver, Los Angeles, Germany, Park City, and Maastricht. Previously he worked as a telephone newspaper subscriptions salesman, a pizza delivery driver, a wedding disc jockey, and a technology trainer. Unfortunately, he also spent a great deal of time in the IT industry, designing networks and configuring routers and switches. Along the way, he picked up an ex-spy with a predilection for French Champagne, and a whippet with a murderous possessiveness for tennis balls. They live together in Brooklyn.

Please buy his books. Tennis balls are expensive.

BOOKS BY ANDREW MORIARTY

Adventures of a Jump Space Accountant

1. Trans Galactic Insurance

2. Orbital Claims Adjustor

3. Third Moon Chemicals

4. A Corporate Coup

5. The Jump Ship.

6. The Military Advisors

7. Revolt in the Palace

Decline and Fall of the Galactic Empire

1. Imperial Deserter

2. Imperial Smuggler

3. Imperial Mercenary

4. Imperial Hijacker

Made in United States
Orlando, FL
25 June 2024

48290377R10207